D1161850

JASSY

(Robinson)

Norah Lofts

Jassy

NEW YORK · ALFRED · A · KNOPF

19   45

PR6023
O33J3

Copyright 1945 by Alfred A. Knopf, Inc.

All rights reserved. No part of this book may be reproduced in any form without permission in writing from the publisher, except by a reviewer who may quote brief passages in a review to be printed in a magazine or newspaper. Manufactured in the United States of America. Published simultaneously in Canada by The Ryerson Press.

This book has been produced in full compliance with all government regulations for the conservation of paper, metal, and other essential materials.

CONTENTS

165025

JASSY

Book One
GENESIS IN EXILE

"She was a local girl, of rather peculiar parentage. . . ."
So this story is told by BARNEY HATTON, *who lived
next door and took an interest in his neighbours.*

I FIRST set eyes on Jassy Woodroffe on the Michaelmas Day before
my fourteenth birthday. I was supposed to be working in the
garden; but the scene of my labour was well out of sight from
the house, so as soon as I heard voices, and hoof-beats and wheels
on the road outside, I went to the place where our garden wall
had fallen in and watched our new neighbours take possession of
the last cottage at the end of the Green.

There was little to hope for of interest or excitement in the
arrival of mere cottage people; but I hated gardening and the
circumstances that made it necessary for me to do it, so, bored
and miserable, I was in a mood to welcome any interruption. I
scrambled to the top of the heap of fallen stones, and with the
afternoon sun warm on my back, stared across the narrow track
which divided the Green from the end of our garden.

The family and their furniture had come in a farm wagon,
driven by a surly-looking fellow with a dirty beard. There were
three of them, a tall, gaunt awkward-looking fellow, a woman,
brown-faced and very upright, and a little girl whom I took to
be about six years old. They climbed out of the wagon, and the
surly man got down too, without speaking, and began to throw
their furniture out of the vehicle with an air of haste rather than
helpfulness. As soon as the wagon was empty he turned it and

(1)

drove away. It was his manner as much as anything which aroused my interest. His haste and his silence made him seem like a man who was, with the least possible trouble, getting rid of something: I could imagine someone saying to him—take these people as far away as you can and throw them out as soon as possible. And as soon as my imagination set to work on this theme I became interested in the family and watched more closely to discover whether there was anything really peculiar about them.

I noticed several things. First of all I observed that their furniture was very different from that of the usual cottagers. Out there on the Green, huddled together in the rays of the afternoon sun, it looked, as all furniture does out of doors, slightly pathetic. But, piece by piece, it was good. There was a tall clock with a brass face surrounded by a wreath of enamelled flowers; there were several sturdy chairs with red cushions, a dower chest, black with age and curiously carved. There were articles of brass and copper whose high lustre caught the sun's rays; a good deal of china, and far more bedding than there was in any other cottage on the Green. As I took note of this I began to wonder whether these people, like ourselves, had come down in the world. For I was already, for various reasons, acutely aware of social differences, and the sight of this good farmhouse furniture going into a clod cottage reminded me of the incongruity of the tulip-wood escritoire in our own low-beamed parlour.

Thinking in this strain I watched the people who were moving the furniture more closely. I decided that the female was lazy. She went into the house and came out again, never carrying anything of any size, never moving with any decision of purpose. She seemed totally uninterested in what should have been her particular province. The man worked hard, but clumsily, heaving and pushing and pulling like an amiable but not very sensible giant confronted by a task that was only just within his scope. The ruling spirit, the brains of the movement, seemed to me to be the little girl who, alone of the trio, knew what she was about.

(2)

She issued orders—I was sure they were orders, because some activity always shaped itself upon her words—in a low queer voice of which I could catch the sound but not the sense. Occasionally she would attempt something beyond her strength, and the great man would say, rather helplessly, "No, no, Jassy, that is too heavy." Then he would call, "Sary, Sary," or the child, articulate for once, would shout "Mother," and the woman, moving lithely, but indolent, would emerge from the cottage and lend a dissociated but wiry strength to the business in hand.

I lost sense of time and place in watching them. I began to notice trivial things, the cunning patches in the shirt which the man revealed when he took off his jacket; the fact that his voice, though countrified and unaffected never uttered a sentence which the Reverend Saunders, my tutor, would have corrected; the difference in the child's manner when she spoke to her mother; and the oddity of the child herself. She was so tiny her head hardly reached the top of the chest of drawers which, with the man's aid, she attempted to shift; yet she behaved like a grown-up person. And she was ugly and beautiful at the same time. Her face, I thought, was queer and hideous. The brow was enormous and emphasized by the way her hair was dragged back and plaited behind. From this great brow her face sloped away to a sharp chin, yet her mouth was so large that it seemed to occupy the whole of the lower part of her face, and although the rest of her skin was the colour of meal, her mouth was so red that even to me, seated upon the broken wall, it shone like a hedge berry. And everything she did was beautiful. When she stood still, regaining her breath after an exertion, when she stooped, or pushed, or braced herself beneath a burden, when she handled anything or hurried from place to place, every movement was perfect. Finally, when every other source of interest was exhausted, I sat just watching her move. I remembered Sharples, Nick Helmar's groom, saying of a colt, "Bad bone and bad temper, but the movement makes up for all," and, except for her temper, of which I could judge but little, the verdict applied to this little girl.

Presently the woman came out of the cottage and, without a word to the others, walked away rapidly in the direction of Layer Woods. The child hunched her shoulders and spoke to the man and then went indoors. Very soon a plume of smoke rose from the one chimney of the cottage. The awkward gangling fellow, after a glance at the sky, where the sun was sinking behind those same woods, redoubled his efforts and with graceless haste gathered the rest of his household goods and hurried them under the new roof. In the dimming light I could see the window of the cottage glow golden. At the same moment I was aware that the sun was no longer warm upon me, the sudden chill of an autumn evening had fallen upon the earth. I rose from my seat and went slowly into the house.

It was nearly time for our evening meal. The fire glowed red in the kitchen, and from the brick oven by the side there came a savoury odour. Mingled with it was the acrid, unhappy scent of the smoky fire in the dining-room. Either mother or Meggie, our maid-of-all-work, had been trying to coax the damned thing to blaze.

I took a jug from the row that hung from hooks at the edge of a shelf and was tilting the kettle of boiling water into it when Mother, with an apron over her tidy blue dress, hurried into the kitchen.

"Have you seen your father?" she asked.

"No," I said. "I haven't been in the yard though. I came straight from the garden."

"Well, get along and wash them. Everybody's late to-night. I'm not going to wait any longer." She pushed back her sleeve and jerked a pan from the centre of the fire. Snatching off the lid she prodded the pan's contents with a fork. As she did so I heard the rattle of Dane's hoofs on the cobbles.

"Here he is now," I said.

(4)

"Get along then," she said impatiently. "And mind you clean your nails."

"Clean nails and gardening don't go together," I said, addressing the words less at mother than at the injustice which demanded that I should work like a farm-hand and yet look like a gentleman.

"What doesn't go has to be driven," said mother in a more amiable voice. "Hurry, Barney. This is no time to argue."

I dashed away up the back stairs, reached my room, washed myself, brushed my hair, and put on a clean neckcloth. When I reached the dining-room the food was already on the table, and my father was standing on the hearth, pretending to warm his back by the smoky fire. Mother was fussing about the table, tweaking a crease out of the cloth and altering the places of the cutlery. Never in a thousand years could Meggie have set a table to her liking.

Father said "Ha!" as I entered and moved, rubbing his hands to the head of the table. He lifted the silver dish cover, stared at the small joint thus revealed, and began to carve it. He managed one slice and then, with an air of defeat, looked down the table at mother and said, "My dear, mumble mumble mumble quite impossible."

The greater part of father's speech always consisted of quite unintelligible mutterings. I often thought that his method of talking was the logical outcome of his policy of leaving all exertion to other people. When he spoke, whoever heard him must set to work and guess at his meaning. And that was usually easy enough to do, for he never thought to convey an idea, and his system of mutterings, punctuated here and there by a few loud words, was quite adequate for the business of giving an order or making a complaint. It was not lack of filial respect upon my part to consider him stupid past the ordinary: he was known as the most stupid and most handsome man in the whole county. He was extraordinarily good-looking, with the leanness

(5)

and the muscular development and the narrow head of a good hound; and since he never bothered about anything or anybody under the sun there was even now, in the forty-ninth year of his age, no line of worry or frustration or ill-humour upon his clear chiselled, high-coloured face, nor was a grey hair visible in the profusion of dark brown curls which clustered about his elegant stupid skull. In looks as well as in behaviour he was like a cunningly-made model of a man, made so that it could acquire certain habits, learn a few phrases, and perform a trick or two. And, like a model man, he would go on and on, unchanging, until at last some cog or bolt within him gave way and failed. Then he would come to a standstill, and it would be very different from the act of dying which overtakes the normal, living human being.

Mother went round to his end of the table and, with her lips pressed together from concentration of effort, severed, efficiently but not skilfully, several slices of the inferior meat. As she laid them upon the plates I stretched out my arm and served the vegetables from her end of the table. She looked at me in a peculiar way she had, possessively grateful, and I wriggled with discomfort in my spirit; because I was not consciously trying to help her, I was not trying to take father's place: I was merely trying to hasten forward the moment when I should be able to start eating.

That half-conspiratorial gratitude of mother's was the final proof—if proof were needed—of her inability to deal with *people*. It was not that she was stupid. In fact, she was an extremely shrewd and intelligent woman. That we had a roof over our heads, a horse to ride, and meat, however tough, upon our table, was entirely due to mother's activities and schemes. She could deal with things well enough; but with people she failed. She never saw that by shouldering all the burdens she left father free to be himself. If, long years ago, she had seated herself on a sofa, and played pretty, and said I want this and I must have that, *things* might not have turned out differently, but *father*

(6)

would have been changed somehow. This very evening, for instance, if she had remained in her place long enough, sheer hunger would have made him hack the tough meat at last. But mother came from a family—the Symmons of Suffolk—who were bustling and ambitious and successful to a man, and I suppose managing and endurance and contrivance were in her blood, just as indolence and carelessness were in father's. So she had failed with him, and she was failing with me, because by her almost cajoling air to me, as though she were asking me to be a prop, to be different from father, to league with her in being bustling and ambitious, she made me obscurely ashamed. And many things that I might have done I did not do out of sheer perversity, because I hated to see myself conforming to the pattern of a son which she had in mind. An adolescent male is a tricky creature, he has many and strange desires, but to be a paragon is seldom amongst them.

We ate almost in silence, as was our custom. But presently, knowing that sooner or later my failure to dig the garden would be revealed and mourned over, I volunteered the information that I had spent the greater part of the afternoon watching the Woodroffe's arrival. We knew the name of the family, because Nick Helmar, to whom the cottage belonged, had mentioned it to father.

"What's the woman like?" asked mother, who was always on the look out for a miracle of cheap efficiency in dairy-work. "I've been thinking that if I could find a really *good* woman I'd try another couple of cows and let her have a stall in Bywater on market day. Did she look likely, Barney?"

"I don't think so," I said slowly. "She looked rather like a gypsy to me."

"Good gracious! Surely even Nick Helmar wouldn't wish a gypsy on me for a neighbour. What about my chickens? And the drying line at that end?"

"Gypsy," said father, "mumble mumble steal from next door. Mumble mumble, risky."

(7)

"Any family?" mother asked. "A teachable girl would do."

"Only one, very tiny. She looked about six," I said. "But she had the whole business of moving in hand. She and the man—her father I guess—did most of the moving, and she got the fire going. The woman just went off."

"How peculiar," said mother.

"Woodroffe's a mumble mumble carpenter. Mumble clever," said father, with a spark of interest. "I've got the idea, mumble mumble, old Nick, mumble, great alterations mumble at Mortiboys. Stucco mumble, up-to-date, mumble panelling, new floors, Woodroffe mumble useful. Wouldn't have mumble else. Troublesome fellow, preacher mumble, agitator mumble Nick's sort. Surprised when mumble let him the cottage. Mumble be sorry. Fennel turned him out."

I tried to fight, as one may try to fight a nightmare, the feeling that had begun to come over me when father mentioned alterations at Mortiboys. Making an effort, I said:

"I thought somehow they'd been turned out by the way the man who drove the wagon behaved."

Mother—of father I expected nothing—might have asked about the man's behaviour, and then I could have described it and perhaps lost myself in the description and escaped the moments of anguish which were laying in wait for me, just as one may escape a moment of danger or embarrassment. But mother, disappointed of her good woman or teachable girl, had lost interest in the Woodroffes. She rang her hand-bell, gathered the plates, and waited for Meggie to come in with the pudding.

It was a blackberry pie, the last of the season, and I could smell the rich dark fruity scent and see the crisp brown pastry. But I knew that I should be unable to swallow a morsel. I knew how inflexible mother was about table behaviour, and I knew also that if I stayed there and ate nothing she would be suggesting a dose. So I did the one thing left to me. I clapped my hand to my head and said:

"I must go. I've just remembered. I have a task set that will take me four hours, and I haven't looked at it. To-morrow's Friday."

Nick Helmar's going to alter Mortiboys now, said the demon in my mind.

"Will ten minutes make such a difference?" mother asked, but she asked it diffidently. The whole business of my schooling was to her mysterious and awesome.

"Indeed it will," I said.

And *now*, said my demon, Nick Helmar's going to alter Mortiboys.

"Very well," said mother, giving me a fond, doting glance. "Meggie shall keep the pie warm and bring you a piece in an hour's time. That will make a little break for you." And I knew, by the way in which she watched me out of the room, that she was thinking what a boy I was for my lessons, and how probably I should be ambitious and industrious and emulate my uncle, Edgar Symmons, who through sheer ability had worked his way up until he was Dean of Ely. What would she have thought could she have known that as I hastened out of the room I was hating her and loathing father. Father was responsible for the loss of Mortiboys; and mother, though blameless, was capable of hearing of Nick Helmar's sacrilegious plan and of proceeding to cut into a pie as though the news meant nothing.

I reached my room, rucked the mat in front of the keyless door, so that anyone entering would be halted and obliged to give me a moment to recover myself, opened a few books and flung them about, and then went to the window, where, curled on the low wide sill I stared out into the darkness and gave myself to the demon.

Four years ago I had chosen this room for my own because it had the only southward-looking window on the bedroom floor, and on a clear day in winter, when the trees were thin and leafless, it was possible to stare out across the tongue of Layer Wood which licked down into the marshes and see a wavery, ochre-pink line which was the roof of Mortiboys.

I had been born there, under its shelter, so had my father, and his, back and back in an unbroken line, save for one Christopher Hatton, who had been born in Paris during the Commonwealth, since the first Hatton of note, another Barnabas, who, having made a fortune out of leather and twice been Mayor of London, had bought the place in the middle of the sixteenth century when the old monasteries were dissolved.

But Mortiboys was old then, and my interest in it went back beyond the Hatton's possession of it. I even knew and cherished the story of how it was named, away back in the days of Norman William and the Saxons who defied him. The owner of the place at that time, called upon to be William's liege or to surrender the place, "refused with many oaths," and when the day of reckoning came, opposed, with his little force of house-carls, the mounted knights. At sunset he was surrounded in the only spot which remained to him—a woodsman's hut in the centre of the woods. There, with the last three of his men dead about him, he set fire to the hut and died within the flames. And the Normans were sufficiently impressed by his performance to name the place Morte de Bois, which name upon the tongues of the common Saxon people was eased down to Mortiboys. Legend had it that his lady, being just with child, visited the new Norman lord on some pretence, and so enthralled him with her sorrow and her beauty that he married her and reared the child as his. If this were a true legend—and there is often a grain of truth in the most far-fetched of them—then that Saxon's blood ran, with innumerable dilutions, in my own veins. For the Norman family stayed at Mortiboys until the sixteenth century. Their history and their property was inextricably linked with the great Benedictine monastery at Bury St. Edmund's. When that fell before Henry Tudor's commissioners, Mortiboys came into the market and was bought, as I have said, by Barnabas Hatton the leather merchant. But his son, the one who was responsible for the building of the house, had married the daughter of the original family. And although that other alliance, of the Saxon widow and the

Norman lord may have been merely a romantic story, I often toyed with the idea of its being true. For I could understand, with my blood and my bones and my most inward marrow, the man who refused to relinquish the place and then, beaten, chose to die on the last foot of his own land. I felt that I would have died rather than leave Mortiboys. But alas! I had been carried over the threshold as a mere baby of eighteen months old; for my father, the handsomest and stupidest man in Essex, had parted with Mortiboys, with Layer Wood and the greater part of the village of Minsham All Saints *to settle his gambling debts!*

The Hattons had descended (a word too lightly and often too truly used) from the sensible, substantial burgher who had made a fortune and from his son who had had the shrewd good sense to ally his common blood with the nobility, until they had reached, in my father, a silly, idle, senseless creature who had no thought for anything outside a blind game of chance . . . how would a pack of cards divide, how would a dice fall, which of a number of horses would most rapidly cover a given length of ground, which of two ruffians could hit the other harder. He was, in this respect, just as I was in another, a creature obsessed and without reason. Before he was of age he had run up gambling debts and debts to money-lenders which had well nigh ruined my grandfather. When he was almost thirty years old things had reached the pitch where he must marry an heiress or face ruin. The estate was hopelessly entangled, and the impetus given to agriculture by the French Wars found him too penurious to take advantage of it. So he had married my mother, who, though not his equal by birth, had from Grandfather Symmons, a shrewd man and mean, a pretty little fortune. To marry a Hatton of Mortiboys, even though he were almost ruined and incurably dissolute, had meant achievement to her, and I gathered that she jumped at a proposal from which any girl with money and a better established family would have jibbed. But within ten years or less the Symmons' money had followed the Hattons' into the abyss, and my mother was living a life, identical in its responsibilities and far inferior in its rewards, to that which she would have lived had she married a man of her own class and kind.

For when I was a baby father's affairs reached another crisis, and it was to save himself, literally, from gaol that he sold Mortiboys, house and estate, to his best friend and biggest creditor, Nick Helmar. And it was typical of father's utter lack of feeling that he should then proceed to settle down and make his home where he did, at the Green Farm, Minsham St. Mary, which was just within sight, and well within the orbit of the place which he had betrayed and abandoned. Father found the farm very convenient, because he could ride, in just under half an hour, to Mortiboys and there play cards and drink and dine and gossip with Nick Helmar!

In this move, as in everything else, he showed his utter senselessness and lack of perception. And he spoilt life for mother and for me. In another part of the country mother could have begun, without foolery or subterfuge, to model the Green Farm on the lines of those which had paid her father so well: and I should never have seen Mortiboys and so conceived an obsession which must last as long as I breathed. At Minsham St. Mary mother was like a badly-driven mare, lashed perpetually by penury and cruelly curbed by dignity. For she had friends who remained faithful, women who had known her in the early days of her marriage, and she could not, comfortably, appear before them as a farm-wife. Later on, dignity wore thin and she abandoned pretence, and I believe that the day when Lady Fennel actually found her at work in the dairy, was a day of release for her, poor soul. But as I grew older and more conscious of what I had lost, my case grew harder.

I first saw the house on a spring evening when the sky was a sea of colour, green and lilac and primrose, smudged with black clouds. Father, mother and I were driving home from Bywater in the gig, and I remember mother saying, after a glance overhead:

"You'll get a wet coat shooting to-morrow. This sky means rain."

Father replied with one of his unintelligible murmurs and bore on his rein so that instead of proceeding in a homeward direction we swung left into a narrow lane.

"Where are you going?" mother demanded sharply. "I'm making no calls at this time of night."

"Mumble mumble have to," said father. "Merely mumble the Lodge for a word mumble Harding. Mumble guns to-morrow."

The lane ended suddenly in a wide smooth sweep of green turf which was spread like a carpet before a big archway built of narrow pinkish yellow bricks. On either side of the arch, built of the same material and continuous with it, was a kind of house with little leaded windows and nail-studded doors. Father leaned down and hammered on one of them with the butt of his whip, and a small man with a face of wrinkled leather peered out. Then he emerged and gave father his respectful attention while father mumbled away in an emphatic lordly manner.

While he did so I stared, first at the archway, which intrigued me by its novelty—I had never seen any erection like it before —and then, by leaning forward and making myself lower, at the view framed within the arch. There was a short gravel drive bordered by ornamental shrubs and then the great red bulk of the house, a three-gabled Tudor building with great mullioned windows and a vast shadowy porch. I could, naturally, see little of it, but I loved all I saw. Abler pens than mine have described the sensation of falling in love at first sight; but it is always a person who is reported to have roused the emotion. In my case it was a house; an insensate mass of timber and bricks and mortar, but to me, instantly, the loveliest and most desirable thing on earth. I had no time to sort out my feelings then, I merely stared and stared, so lost that the swerve of the gig as father turned round on the green sward caught me unprepared and threw me against mother's arm. As I righted myself I said, "What a beautiful house. Who lives there?"

(13)

Father muttered, but in those days, before I had caught the trick of listening to him, nothing he said had much meaning for me. I looked at mother, who said in a queer constrained voice:

"A man called Nick Helmar, a *friend* of your father's."

"Have you ever been inside it?" I asked, turning back to father and deliberately requesting information of him, for, I think, the first time in my life.

"Certainly I have, mumble mumble, think so indeed."

"I'd like to go in," I said.

"Well, it's unlikely that you ever will," said mother sharply. I was only eight years old then, a timid child, easily snubbed. And I had already discovered that many of my questions which received only mutterings and snappings from my parents could be answered at length, in racy picturesque language, and with great willingness, by Meggie. So I fell silent, and as soon as supper was ended, went to the kitchen and there discovered, luckily or unluckily, a fellow devotee in Meggie.

"You was born there," said Meggie, applying a live coal to her little black pipe with the tongs. "And so for that matter was I. Me mother was cook, d'you see, and your grandma was giving a masterous grut dinner party to mark something or other. Wait a bit, I'll remember—yes, 'twas the battle of Queebec. So me mother stayed by her pans till 'twas too late to git home. Me mother had been your grandma's cook till she married Cobb, the keeper, you see, and she allust went up to the house when there was a party. But time I was born she dint git home agin, and so I was born at Mortiboys. And it so chanced that Doctor Burrage, he was bid to the dinner and heard about me mother and came out and did her up all nice and tidy. And your grandpa sent her out a bottle of port. She said she never had sich a time with all the nine of us. I was allust her favourite," said Meggie proudly, "all on account of that night."

"Why don't we live there now?" I demanded as soon as I could cut in upon Meggie's flow of reminiscence.

"As to that, you'd better ask your Pa," said Meggie, with

unusual caution. "Or p'raps not, on second thoughts. It's not a matter the poor gentleman might care to tell of."

"Why not?"

"Because," said Meggie, studying her pipe with dissatisfaction, "debts was concerned. Now that's all I know, Master Barney, and you'd do well not to say any more about the matter."

I sensed a mystery, and for the moment desisted from asking Meggie what exactly a debt might be. But I asked her whether she had ever—apart from her birthday—been in the house, and received in reply an account which lasted until long past my bedtime. Meggie knew Mortiboys from attics to cellars. She had gone to work in it when she was nine years old, and had left only when my parents moved to Green Farm. She knew every draught and uneven board.

"Stands to reason," she ended, "only a masterous rich man could live there. Think of the winders alone. Why, in your grandpa's time there was a man and a boy did nothing all day but clean the winders. So many little corners, you see. I daresay it's the same to-day. And fuel. There's a fireplace there, in what they call the Old Hall, and I tell you, Master Barney, that that do take in a day as much wood as this one do in a week. Right big trees they used to saw into three or four bits and cast on that there fire, and they'd look like little owd logs."

"What happened then, did we get poor?"

"Now I towd you, Master Barney, that your pa's business ain't for me to talk about. Thass time for your bed, too."

And to bed I went, with more to think about in the darkness than I had ever had in my life before. My last thought before I fell asleep was about birds. For the last two years I had watched the swallows that nested in spring under the eaves of the farm-house thatch, and I knew that on both years one, at least, of the birds had been the same. It had a curious white streak on its back. And that bird went away in the autumn to spend the winter in a warmer place, mother had told me; but it knew its old nest when it returned. I was, I decided, like that bird. I had known, as soon as I set eyes on Mortiboys, that it was my home. Sleep, when it came, closed my eyes on the vision of that arch, and the three gables, outlined against the green and lilac sky.

From that day onwards Mortiboys became the main interest in my life. Meggie, relentlessly attacked, gave way and told me all she knew about it, but her information was, naturally, confined in its scope. She could discuss what she remembered and a few trifles which she had heard from her parents; she could tell me, even to the very names, about the men-servants and the maid-servants who had filled the kitchens and attics in her mother's time, and how, gradually, with the fall of father's fortunes, their numbers fell. She even, one evening after a glass of new ale, ventured to give an opinion upon deeper matters.

" 'Twasn't from your grandpa that your pa got his wild ways with the money. 'Twas from your grandma. A Miss Strawson she was, and her pa, Sir Henry, had gone through three fortunes by the time he was in his middle years. And she was just such another, such a spender as never was. Not enough for her, Mortiboys weren't; no, she must have a house in London, too. If the moon'd been for sale she'd have wanted it, Master Barney, and your grandpa would have got it for her somehow. And how did it end? You can see that for yourself, my dear, here in this poky little place with your mother, bless her! working like a black, though she'd hate me to say it, and only old Meggie, getting masterous stiff in the joints, to do the dirty jobs for you all. So you look out, now, and see that you don't take after your grandpa nor your pa."

"A fine chance I have of that," I said bitterly. "What have I to spend?"

"There's truth in that," Meggie conceded. "All the same, I never known you to eat your fat."

"What's that got to do with it, pray?"

"That show," said Meggie ponderously, "a wasteful spirit. Fat is bought with money the same as lean, and will fill your belly as good or better. That is what it do show, and I'm sorry to see it."

"What I'm sorry about is to think that my grandmother and my father could waste money so that now I mustn't even waste fat."

"But that's the way it is. What do the good book say? The fathers have eaten sour grapes and the children's teeth is set on edge."

I pondered that, and for the first time in my life understood metaphorical language. It was like a window opening in a blank wall. I was quite stunned. I said, after a reflective pause:

"It was clever of you, Meggie, to say that. They"—I jerked my head towards the parlour—"may not think you're very bright, but *I* think you're very clever."

"They're dead right," Meggie said with a savage note in her voice. "I ain't bright, don't I shouldn't be here at my time of life. If I'd took advantage like I should I might be cook now, in a grut house, or even housekeeper, maybe. There ain't many that know more about cooking and preserving and bleaching and cleaning than what I do. And here I be, Jack of all work and too old to make a change. No, I ain't bright."

I saw that I had hurt her feelings and muttered unhappily.

"No matter," said Meggie, "fools and children, they speak the truth. So now I'll say summat to you, Master Barney, as probably only a fool ud say. You forget all about Mortiboys. I noticed you, the whole of this week past, harking on about it. And all you'll do by brooding over it is make yourself miseruble. Looking back never did nobody a haporth of good. You gotta look forrards and mind your book and fit yourself for some sort of job—or if that ain't to your fancy, you must take to the farm and make a living outa that! Do you see?"

I said I did. I knew, even then, that the advice was good. Later on I had a truer estimation of its virtue. But, of course, I minded it not at all. The poison was already in my system, and I did nothing to purge it.

(17)

I began to ferret out every fact about Mortiboys. I learned a great deal about its history from a musty volume called "A Survey of Essex," which told me that the house was built in 1560 upon an older foundation, of which only the Great Hall remained standing. The "Survey" also mentioned, rather lightly, as though the compiler doubted his own story, the legend of how it was named, and how its Norman history was linked to the Saxon. From Nick Helmar's groom, Sharples, whom I encountered upon one of my surreptitious visits to the house, I gained a great deal of information of a very different kind. Sharples was taking a sick horse for a walk in the lane in order to work off the effects of a pill, and he asked me, rudely enough, what I was there for and why I was staring at the house. I told him, for in those days I was frank and outspoken, except with my parents, and Sharples, after inspecting me closely, accepted my explanation and showed himself friendly. He told me about the horse pill, and I asked his advice about Joby, my cob, who had a swollen fetlock, so that I was afoot that day, and had been obliged to walk across the tricky marsh pathway to reach my objective. Sharples seemed to like giving advice, and presently when the sick horse had been walked sufficiently, he took me through the archway and round to the stables with him. My heart beat so hard from excitement that I could hardly breathe, and had to keep dropping behind and opening my mouth to gasp, rather like a landed fish. I was disappointed, and yet somehow relieved, to find that once through the arch we turned aside and did not go near the house. I had a fear that someone might appear and say, "What boy is this?" and a kind of snobbishness was already at work within me, so that I did not want to make my first appearance in the home of my fathers sponsored by a groom.

Nevertheless I liked Sharples, and he seemed to like me. He said that if I brought the cob along he'd look him over. And I did that, on the very next day, leading Joby over the marshes. So we became friendly, and it was from Sharples that I learned all about the money my father had owed Nick Helmar, and how the estate had changed hands.

"And a bloody bad bargain Master made, too," said Sharples. "The house is tumbling down, the grounds are nowt, and every cottage want something done to it. Why he wanted it God only know!"

"I know," I said softly.

"Why then?"

"Because it's so beautiful."

"Get away with you. Did you ever see Sir Evelyn Fennel's place—Ockley Manor? Or Baildon Lodge, what Mr. Hodge bought for about half what Master give for this."

"Yes," I lied stoutly. "I know them both. They're not a patch on Mortiboys."

"You're crazy," said Sharples. We were just outside the archway then, and he moved across to the house part which was his and put his hand to the side of the nail-studded door. He brought it away with a lump of wood, worm-eaten and soft as a rotten cheese, in it.

"Don't do that," I said in agonized sharpness.

"Rotten!" said Sharples. "The whole place is like that, too. Here, look through there. See that big window on the left of the porch?" I looked, and saw the great window, with its hundreds of little panes, some of them coloured, jutting out in a square bay. "When that blow, and God know that can blow bloody hard in these parts, that window flap like a sheet. I seen it. The whole place is rotten."

"But it's beautiful," I persisted. "It's the most beautiful place in the world."

"Ah, well! You're a Hatton," said Sharples tolerantly. "It's like me and my old woman. Plain as a pikestaff, she is. But time I look at her I think about what she was like as a maid, and how she did work on me when I had a mucky poisoned finger and

(19)

was like to lose my arm. And, I swear I do be blind then to the grey hairs and the wrinkles and the way her teeth do hang like a brukken fence. See?"

This statement afforded me a moment's relief, for it drew my mind away from Mortiboys and rested it upon my fellow men. Life was hard on our country women, most of whom had large families to rear on very little money, and many of whom worked seasonally in the fields as well. A girl who had been quite pretty would look like an old woman who had never been anything but plain by the time she had been married a few years. But, if Sharples was to be believed—and Mrs. Sharples was certainly a case to quote from—this was not the tragedy that it might at first seem, if to their husbands they remained beautiful.

I thought of that as I turned away and went down the lane; but when I turned back to have a last look at the gateway and the house, framed within the arch, I forgot everything except Mortiboys again. I had a feeling of exile and destitution; and mingled with it was an ache of longing to be able to go through the arch and walk up to the great porch and to go within, unchallenged, by right that no man could dispute. For the first time I found myself hating my father and my grandmother, who, between them, had robbed me of my birthright. Two extravagant simpletons in succession was too much for any place to bear. If only, if only I had been my father, able to succeed while there was still a fragment to be saved. How careful I would have been, how I would have worked and saved and starved if need be. Why, I would have repaired the place with my own hands, clumsy as they were.

I was eight then, and for the next five years my passion for Mortiboys grew with my limbs. I had, of course, other things to think about and worry over. Mother, much of Meggie's opinion, it seemed, set about training me for a future which would hold little room for idle dreaming. In case I turned out to be a scholar, I must go to the Reverend Saunders and be tutored on three days a week and set tasks to keep me busy for seven; and in case this failed and I must be a farmer, I was always being hustled about the yard and the fields to watch how things were done. And Stoner, the man whom mother employed as foreman, since it was beneath her dignity to deal with the outside work, regarded me as her spy, and hated me and often, with the cruel bucolic humour of his kind, arranged that horrible, ludicrous things should happen to me. Consequently my natural distaste for farm work developed into loathing. And school, for other reasons, was little better. My life within doors, though comfortable enough, was not particularly happy. Mother's designs upon me were very obvious, and made me self-conscious and perverse and conscience-stricken. Father I could hardly look at without being reminded of his folly. And socially, except for father's stubborn contact with Nick Helmar and mother's dwindling circle of faithful sympathetic women—in whom, I often suspected, a kind of gloating sadism was at work—we lived in the awful isolation of the genteel poor, suspended as it were between the comfortable poor who had no appearances to keep up, and the comfortably rich whose place was secure. So I was lonely. And my infatuation, having few counter influences, grew and grew until it was, I suppose, a kind of madness. Like other forms of lunacy, it had tides and moons; sometimes I was just sentimentally sad, sometimes violently resentful. I dreamed great bright dreams about making a fortune in some vague fashion and buying the place back. I had moods of depression when I knew that it was not in me to achieve anything, much less so colossal a thing. And I had moments when, beginning in a word, or a memory, the whole question of Mortiboys and me would swell like a painful abscess and I would go through from the beginning the whole dreary story, and finally cry a little, and then feel better and be able to give my mind to my lessons or to the farm for a while.

One of these moments came upon me when I heard father say, so carelessly, that Nick Helmar was planning to alter Mortiboys, and that was why he had let the man Woodroffe have a cottage. I was just at the point where I was going to shed futile tears over the matter when Meggie brought up my share of the pie. I had snatched up a book as the door jammed against the rucked mat, and I steadied my voice and thanked her. When she had gone, moving very quietly in an effort not to disturb my studies, I looked at the fruit and the pastry and had, I think for the first time in all my mourning for Mortiboys, a sensible thought. I thought—well, I can't have Mortiboys, but I can eat this pie. And I did so. Then I worked for a while and went to bed. Before I slept, however, I made an addition to my "Hate List." It was headed by father; the second person on it was my grandmother; then came Nick Helmar, who had, after all, wanted Mortiboys, and probably suggested its sale as a method for settling father's debts; and last, much lower, was Sharples, who, although he was friendly to me, said such scathing things about the place. Now I added the man Woodroffe to the list, because he was going to help forward Helmar's scheme for spoiling it. And I thought, as I remembered his awkwardness and ugliness, that he would be singularly easy to hate.

But in that I was wrong.

Probably no move in our district, since our own spectacular one from Mortiboys to Green Farm, had given rise to so much gossip as the Woodroffes' move into the cottage on the Green.

At first all the interest centred about Mrs. Woodroffe. Every other woman in the village seemed to hate her on sight, and to have more virulent feelings about her as they came to know her better. She was a gypsy slut, a poacher, a maker of spells and, finally, a witch. I believe that their chief grudge against her was her complete immunity from the toils and anxieties which made up their own daily round. On Monday, the traditional wash-day, when every other cottage was a resounding welter of steam and soap-suds and loud complaining voices, when the linen lines ran out their signals for the attack on dirt and thriftlessness,

Mrs. Woodroffe would leave her cottage and go off on one of her walks. But soon after she was gone the Woodroffe line would blossom out in colour and the small Jassy, probably with a peg or two in her ugly mouth, would step down from the backless chair which she mounted in order to hang out the clothes and resolutely heave the prop into position. A neighbour, prompted by dubious motives, ventured to express sympathy with the poor, overworked little thing.

"I'm eleven," the mite said fiercely. "Most people my age are out to work." It was a shrewd thrust, for the neighbour's own daughter of that age was working in the dairy at Maybrook.

"But what's your mother doing?" the woman persisted.

"Curing a cow at Ockley. Nobody else can do it. And anybody can wash clothes."

This conversation, as well as all the other gossip, we heard at Green Farm through Meggie, who had cronies amongst the village people. From the same source we learned that Mrs. Woodroffe was not a proper gypsy, but a Stannary, a member of a separate tribe stemming from Norfolk. Tom Woodroffe, said rumour, had found her under a hedge in a storm when he was returning from preaching at Hedstone, had fallen in love with her, married her, and never known a happy moment since. And it was true that she poached; but wise people did not interfere with her. For once, when the Woodroffes lived at Sible Havers, she had been caught by a gentleman and threatened with prosecution. And she had "whispered" his horses, so that next morning not a single horse would leave its stable until she was sent for and "unwhispered" them. Romantic as this story sounded, there were uncharitable people in Minsham who did not accept it, but hinted that Sari Woodroffe's immunity, on this occasion, was purchased with quite another coin. Her morals, indeed, were so much suspected that if she were seen, as she was, very occasionally, to be seen, carrying her bucket to the pond which supplied the Green folks with water, those women whose husbands pampered them and usually fetched the water, would turn out themselves, lest, at the common meeting place, some word of civility might pass and lead to other things.

Soon after Christmas, however, the novelty of Sari's doings and appearance waned, and the male Woodroffe became the centre of interest. For early in the New Year he converted Bob Wicks.

Bob Wicks was a rogue and ruffian. His evil temper and his violence were so well known that when he appeared at the little pot-house out on the marshes, known as "The Evening Star," cautious men would leave the tap-room, and that though the customers of "The Evening Star" consisted for the most part of smugglers and poachers, tough fellows enough. He had twice been in trouble for assaulting women, and there were innumerable other charges laid at his door, but he was still in Minsham and still at liberty, for the simple reason that he was the only smith of any consequence within a radius of six miles. The nearest other one, old Ransome at Ockley, was semi-blind and a victim of "smith's disease," that constant tremor of the hands and arms that is the result of the trade. So to sentence Bob Wicks to a spell of gaol would have meant that the Constable—who farmed thirty acres—and the Justices themselves, would have had to go as far afield as Bywater or Baildon to get a shoeing job decently done. Consequently Wicks went on his way unmolested. He lived in a hovel behind the forge, with a thin woebegone wretch who called herself Mrs. Wicks, and a swarm of miserable ragged children. He himself was built like a bull, massive and square, and his face was so red that the colour seemed to have seeped into the whites of his eyes, which were netted with red veins. I hated him myself, and had even taken Joby over to Ockley to be shod, but old Ransome was so slow and so shaky, and made such a poor job of it, that I decided against a second visit. Bob Wicks was the subject of one of my father's rare flashes of comprehension. He had met him one evening reeling home, and next day had said, "Wicks, mum mum, drunk mum lord. Bad colour mum stand it. Do a bad job mum day and mum to gaol mum ill-driven nail mum his other mum."

But that day was still a long way ahead when Wicks rolled home one evening and set about the poor wisp of a woman who called herself his wife. She screamed, just as though she had not been screaming unavailingly for years; and this time she was regarded. For Tom Woodroffe was on his way home from what was called a Revival Meeting at Bywater. He may or may not have known the smith's reputation; having no horse he would not have had occasion to visit the forge, and Wicks was so much a part of Minsham that people no longer mentioned him unless he had just attacked someone or run foul of a keeper. However, warned or not, Tom Woodroffe, hearing the screams and the blows, went straight into the hovel, expostulated with Wicks, and received a blow on the cheek from the buckle-end of the belt which the man was using on the woman. Then he knocked Wicks flat. Such a thing had not happened to the smith since he was big enough to stand up to his father, who had been, by all accounts, just such another. Tom then lifted him on to the wretched affair that served for a bed in that house, and, discovering that the Wicks' cupboard was literally bare, went to his own house and returned with everything that was in his own. Judging by what I later knew of the Woodroffe diet, I imagine that this would be only bread and cheese, with perhaps a scrap of fat bacon, but it seemed a feast to the starving family, and for years Mrs. Wicks would cry as she mentioned it.

Next day, round about noon, Tom presented himself at the forge. Sharples was there with a couple of carriage horses at the time, so there was a reliable witness. Tom shambled in and said:

"Last night, when you were in drink, I knocked you down because I had no choice. To-day, when you're sober, I've come to reason with you."

Wicks hesitated between desire for instant revenge and the wisdom of not neglecting a job for Nick Helmar.

"You needn't of come," he said, when he had decided to go on with the matter in hand. "I'd a bin to see you afore, ony I had a job on."

"I can wait," said Tom, and seated himself on the bench. Wicks finished the shoeing and then, dropping his hammer, advanced towards Tom, saying: "And now stand up, you bastard, and I'll reason with you." He shaped himself for battle. Tom got to his feet and said:

"But you've dropped your hammer."

"What d'you think. I fight fair."

"It's as fair to tackle me with a hammer as it is to set about that woman with your belt."

"That's a jannock saying," said Sharples, who, like everybody else, detested the blacksmith.

"You keep your bloody mug out of this," said Wicks, "and you stop bandying words. I'm waiting."

"Come on, then," said Tom, and knocked Wicks flat again.

"There, you see," he said, as the smith scrambled up bellowing threats and oaths. "I'm the warning. Go on as you are and you'll see the day when a child can floor you."

Wicks, mad beyond description, rushed in again, took Tom's fist on the point of his chin, spun round and fell down like an ox in the shambles. Then—gentle as woman, Sharples said—Tom lifted him and set him on the bench, and wetted his handkerchief and dribbled water on his face.

"Now," he said as soon as the blacksmith's eyelids twitched, "be off, my friend. Leave him with me and with God." So we never knew what shape that queer interview took. Did Tom preach hell fire? Or go on with the physical warning? Or did the fires of Pentecost sit on his tongue? We never knew. But Wicks was never drunk again, and Betty Noakes, of "The Evening Star," had to look elsewhere for her ribbons and laces, and Mrs. Wicks had no more bruises to show. By the time that Joby needed his next shoes the congested colour was fading a little from the smith's eyeballs.

At first nobody believed in the conversion. That Tom had fought and won, without even taking off his rusty old jacket, had to be believed, for there was Sharples to vouch for it. And as the days passed and the Forge children grew fat and Mrs. Wicks blossomed, people began to see that some strange and powerful influence was at work. It became a nine days' wonder. But very soon people were asking, "Why don't he convert his own wife?" And presently I was in a position to give an answer to that question. For to be converted—or corrupted—one must have a soul of some sort. Sari Woodroffe had none. She was exactly like an animal. Evil in her was not a vice, nor was goodness, virtue. Watching her, in the year when I was frequently in the Woodroffe cottage, I learned a good deal about good and evil and the human soul, just as one might learn a good deal about disease by watching a perfectly healthy creature. And I am convinced that Sari Woodroffe was not a woman. She was female, but not a female of our kind. Whenever I saw her I was reminded of the story of the Bywater man who married a mermaid.

After Bob Wicks' conversion I became interested in Tom Woodroffe. Stephen Fennel, who was a fellow pupil of mine, had been sneaking into Baildon to "The Fox," which was kept by an old prize-fighter, and had paid a guinea for some lessons. He had passed on to me—since he judged me about his equal in weight and therefore a likely person to practise on—some of the rudiments of the noble art of self-defence. So I was, although I loathed the practice, academically interested in the subject, and I could not understand how Tom had floored Bob Wicks when he was sober. He was so ungainly, such a collection of knobs and bumps and hollow places, he moved so clumsily and seemed so slow and ill-balanced, that it seemed to me as though a mere push could cause him to collapse. So, physically, he interested me, and gradually the interest became deeper. I was going on for fourteen and suffering all the pains of adolescence, amongst which is the quickening of a religious sense. Twice, during the early spring of that year, I listened to Tom Woodroffe preaching, and on each occasion, if willingness to be converted could have brought conversion, about converted I should have been. I longed to share his simple, sincere and lovely faith. But it was quite useless. Whatever response he wakened in me came from my head, not my heart. I remained quite unchanged. But I remained also greatly interested in the man himself, and I was cogitating how best to get to know him, even saving a few odd coins and planning to ask him to make me some small inexpensive thing, when Chance—that capricious goddess whom my father worshipped so wholeheartedly—threw us together.

Every Monday, Wednesday and Friday I rode over to the Rectory at Minsham All Saints for my lessons with the Reverend Mr. Saunders. Mr. Saunders was Rector of Minsham St. Mary, too, but he lived in All Saints because the house there was better, and nearer the good turnpike road. He was a studious old man, ascetic in his habits, and not very popular in a district where sporting parsons were fashionable. But popularity was the last thing he craved, and I think he would have been perfectly happy to be left alone with his books and his papers and the gentle routine of unavoidable duties. Unfortunately for him, when the two Minshams were enclosed under the Act of 1778, the Squire of St. Mary was engaged in a violent feud with the parson who was then the incumbent, and managed, by some trick or sleight of hand, to reduce the tithes on that village to practically nothing. It was the only case I ever heard of where the tithe holder suffered from the enclosures together with the common people. But it had happened, and the Reverend Saunders, succeeding to the livings, paid for his predecessor's quarrel with his lord. Moreover, there were three Misses Saunders, alive and unmarried, and they were all simple in the mind, as though all the brains in the family had been concentrated in the one son. He hated the sight and even the very mention of them, and maintained a separate establishment for them in Water Lane in Bywater, and to meet the cost of it he himself took pupils from amongst what he called the sons of gentry. He detested boys and he loathed teaching, and did his best to avoid resident pupils. But at the time when I suffered under his tuition there were four big boys and one small one lodged in the lofts above the coach-house, and heartily pitied by the rest of us fortunate fellows who could, at the end of each session, ride back to our homes. They repaid our sympathy by envy, and I was most envied of all, for I went to school only three days a week. This was due entirely to our poverty. Mother would have had me there every day if she had had her way, and I did once listen, sweating and apprehensive while she argued with father that the six guineas tax on the gig every year would purchase me another day a week of education. Fortunately father, though he kept agreeing with her and saying, "Mum, my dear, mum course. Mum mum yes, yes," went the next week and took out the gig licence and I was saved. Actually it made little difference whether I went to school three days a week or six, like Stephen Fennel or Lord Latchmore's half-wit, who was being shaped for Eton. The Reverend Saunders never *taught* us anything. He assumed, with little reason in some cases, that we could read English and could stumble through a Latin or Greek sentence. And his method was to select a book for reading, and a primer for working on, roughly within our scope, set us to read it, ask questions on the reading, and whack us soundly for wrong answers. For me the system did very well. I read my English book and, I can say without boasting, never failed to answer a question; Latin and Greek remained Latin and Greek to me, I recognized a word here and there, but that was all, and I was whacked twice a week as a matter of course. I became hardened to the amount of physical pain which a lazy old man with a cane can inflict upon the saddle-toughened buttocks of a healthy young boy, and since there was no shame, but even a little glory, connected with the beatings, I did not mind them much. Some fellows went through their schooling without ever having been beaten, and they lived in dread of it, exaggerating the pain in their imaginations. Stephen and I, who were whacked so often, were looked upon as little heroes. Stephen was beaten because, being a natural genius at mathematics, a subject upon which the Reverend John never touched at all, he was bored by other lessons and took no pains with them, spending his time in working out curious problems about angles and curves and weights and measures in the margins of his books.

On this particular Monday which sticks in my mind as the day when I first came into contact with Jassy Woodroffe and her father, I had been beaten, as usual, for my failure with my grammar. I had, as usual, eaten my noon piece, one of Meggie's veal pasties, in the company of Stephen Fennel, who had described to me his plan for making a water clock, and given my second pasty and two apples to the little resident boy who complained that he did not have enough to eat, and whose looks bore out the assertion. Then in the afternoon I had answered, without a fault, the questions put to me about the book which I was reading in English. It was a vast tome called "Captain Anderson's Own Account of His Various Voyages," and when I first set eyes on it I had been thrilled by the promise which the title seemed to hold. But it was the dullest book I had ever read. The good sea-captain had been to many interesting places and seen many extraordinary sights. He seemed to be a brave and resourceful sailor, but he ought not to have attempted to write a book. He never used a short word if he could find a long one, and he never used one word if four could possibly be squeezed in. And in the very middle of a piece of narrative, where the subject was so exciting that even his pomposity could not obscure it, he would digress into a kind of lecture about the wonders of Providence or the mystery of Nature as though he guessed that his pen was running away with him, and was determined to check it. However, I had imagination of a kind and could see, behind the dullness and prosiness, the scenes and the people and the adventures which the captain had attempted to describe, and would probably have said he *had* described. So I could answer and thus escape a beating, whereas Stephen, who was working neck by neck with me, and who had planned a water clock when he should have been afloat in the good ship *Steadfast*, was beaten for the second time that day.

It was March, and Lent had started, so we were let out of school at four o'clock, a relief instituted to enable the Rector to devote more time to the duties which the season was supposed to bring. Stephen and I and two other boys had a brief sharp game of *Nobbin* behind the coach-house, and I lost a shilling, my only one, destined to last as pocket money for an unspecified length of time. The usual loss for one round was only about fourpence, and I reflected bitterly as I watched Stephen shuffle the cards for a second round, that whereas I had never *won* more than eightpence I had been able to *lose* a shilling. I had to refuse to play again, and since four players were needed the game broke up then, not without acrimony. And then, when we went to the stables for our mounts, I found that Stephen, whose fourteenth birthday had fallen two days before, had a new mare —a sweet, dainty, spirited little thing with a coat which had the colour and gloss of a newly-shed chestnut, and lines which told of blood and breeding. She had been a present from his father, and his mother had given him the silver-mounted saddle and bridle. Even Joby's delighted whinny and nuzzle of welcome could not blind me to the fact that he was only a rough sturdy cob, meant for a farm boy to hack about on.

"Care to try her? You can take her over the fence at the bottom there and I'll meet you on the road," said Stephen generously.

"No," I said. "Thanks. But I'd better be off."

"It wouldn't stop you. I'll bet a shilling that you'll be waiting on the road by the time I've got there on your cob."

"I know." Without offering any explanation I got into my saddle and turned Joby's head towards the gate. "Good night, Stephen. I'll see you on Wednesday." Conscious of Stephen's puzzled stare upon my back I jogged out of the gate. I felt miserable and resentful. Poverty, I thought, gripped you everywhere.

I was frankly jealous of Stephen, who had likewise lost a shilling and had been able to shuffle the cards with the knowledge that even if the next round cost him as dearly he could pay up like a man; and who had been given such a splendid birthday present. I was fond of Joby, and had been wildly excited when he had been bought for me, but he was just a cob, a boy's mount, a farm boy's mount, and my saddle was shabby, and my stirrups at their longest were now too short. And as far as I could see, I should never be mounted any better.

I gloomed my way out of Minsham All Saints and reached the turnpike. There I hesitated. My mood prompted a visit to Mortiboys, whose rambling red roof showed about a quarter of a mile along the road. But by this time I had gained a certain amount of wisdom and no longer went out of my way to make myself wretched. So I crossed the turnpike and took the road to home.

This road, known as the Upper Road, hugged the edge of the higher land and was long, on account of its windings. The marsh road, called the Lower Road, was shorter, and in dry weather one could ride between Green Farm and Mortiboys in twenty minutes, whereas on the Upper Road the journey stretched out to thirty-five or forty. But in March, unless the winter before had been phenomenally dry, the Lower Road was a sheer lane of mud, covered in parts with water, and nobody chose it unless his errand was urgent. It was much used by smugglers bringing up contraband from Bywater inland. To-night, riding along the Upper Road in a surly mood which did not welcome the journey's end, I travelled slowly, and the long drawn out twilight of the spring evening was beginning when I came in sight of our village green. Just there the road left the higher land and sloped down into Minsham St. Mary, and at the head of the slope a man, particularly if he were mounted, had a clear, unimpeded view of the village. On this evening, as I looked ahead and saw the Green, dun coloured with the old grass through which the new year's verdure had not yet broken, and the great pond, and the ring of cottages, I heard, made thin by distance, a strange and oddly disturbing sound. It was a weird howling in which ferocity and sadness were oddly mingled. I have heard it since, but on that evening it was new to me, and I was halfway down the slope before I identified it as the mass voice of human beings. By that time, straining my eyes, I could see a knot of people gathered upon the side of the pond which was farthest from the road, and in another second, since distance would not account for their smallness, I could tell that they were children. Some new game, I thought, and wondered why they should, of choice, make so exceedingly dismal a noise about it. It was louder now that I was nearer, and it was remarkably disturbing, like the howling of angry and yet frightened animals.

Now I could recognize, by a few salient blobs of colour on the general drabness of the little crowd, certain individual children. There was the incongruous red patch which Jem Meekings had flaunted all winter on his old buff breeches, Nonny Fayres' grass-green knitted cap, little Fanny Moy's orange scarf, a present at Christmas from my mother, in whose dairy Mrs. Moy worked at times. These bright recognizable specks moved as the crowd milled and shifted, but the whole crowd hung together, like a bee-swarm, and it was this fact which, combined with the howling, convinced me that the children were not playing. I checked Joby and rode slowly for a moment or two. I was disinclined to interfere; my position in the village was already an awkward one, and I had no wish to lay myself open to the implied insult of the speechless, sullen stare with which yokels, even young ones, can accuse one of busy-bodying. Moreover, I was in a surly mood myself, and not disposed to be even a putative Galahad. But then I thought of a dog. I could well imagine that howling circle holding in its midst some rail-thin little stray, either paralysed by terror, or futilely ferocious. My imagination kindled easily in those days; and was, at that moment, capable of making me see the dog, its wild glance in search of a protector, the feeble, placating, unavailing wag of its tail. Nevertheless, it was still reluctantly that I looked about and weighed up the position. I was on the road, and the pond, roughly pear-shaped, lay between me and the children. If I rode—and the coward in me knew exactly what advantages belonged to a mounted person —I had to go along the whole of my side of the pond, round the wide part at the end, and so reach them. The narrow, the stem-end of the pear-shape was closed—to a horse, at least—because it joined on to Clem Barber's stackyard, and he had erected a fence to keep his property divided from the Green. But between the rails of this fence and the edge of the water there was a narrow crumbling bank along which an active person, not too heavy, could run. I decided that that was my quickest way. I slipped out of my saddle, said "Stand" to Joby, hopped over the fence and plunged forward. Once the bank gave under my feet and I fell into the water, splashing even my hat, but I held on to the fence and pulled myself out, angrier than ever and already re-solved that I would take a smack at Jem Meekings, a big lout who had annoyed me before. I was within six feet of the edge when the dancing jeering circle broke; little Fanny Moy fell flat on her back, borne down by some pressure from within, and through the gap thus made there dashed a wildly dishevelled crazy figure which I did not instantly recognize as the Woodroffe child. She ran like a hare, and her face, turned my way, was a white muddy mask of horror. The other children who had been facing inwards in a circle, turned about, collided with one an-other and stumbled over Fanny Moy, who lay where she had fallen and screamed like a pig-killing; but very soon they had sorted themselves and surged forward, a human pack in full cry. There were no words, just primitive sounds of hatred. Every mouth was open, and in every mouth the eye-teeth seemed sud-denly longer than usual, fang-like. They were the children of our village; they came to carry away skim milk from the dairy; at Christmas time they sang carols on our porch; after harvest they asked permission to go gleaning in the fields. But to-night they were changed and hideous. All reason had gone out of them; they had swung back across the centuries into the primeval abyss which

—according to Captain Anderson—lies behind even the most civilized races. They were so mad that if they had caught their quarry she would have been mauled and trampled before the sanest one amongst them could have realized what was happening.

But I was there. She ran straight at me, so blind with terror that she did not even see me at first. When she did, she thought I was one of the hunters, heading her off, and she screamed like a hare, and like a hare, swerved aside, almost into the arms of Jem Meekings, who was running on one of the horns of the crescent-shaped pack. I caught her by the shoulder, yelling, "Get along the bank and hold the fence." She obeyed me, and I backed after her and took up a stand at the edge of the bank, shouting and waving my little riding crop, conscious that it was nothing more than a toy, and longing for a proper horse-whip.

The pack, panting and thudding, checked itself.

"Get outa road, Master Barney," said Jem Meekings. "We doon't mean you no harm. Thass she we're arter."

"Not now," I said. "Anybody coming any nearer will feel the weight of my arm."

"Coo, Master Barney, doon't you go sticking up for the likes of she," said Essie Beam. "Rare little drab she be."

"Put a spell on you like as not," said a voice from the rear.

"That's witch's stuff in her hands this minnut," said another.

"Come on now, stand aside, Master Barney. We be ony gorn to duck her, see if she git the davil to howd her up." That was Jem Meekings, and he took a step forward, and a surge of something I had not felt before, a real lust for violence, rose in me. All right, I thought, and swung my arm. But the silly little crop whistled harmlessly through the air, meeting no resistance. He had thought better of it and stepped back. And the madness was already seeping away from the children. Their mouths were closing, one or two were beginning to stare at their feet and shuffle away to the edge of the crowd. The final, comic note was sounded from the nearest of the cottages. Jem Meekings' mother, a great strapping creature who worked in the fields like a man, from choice, came to the door and called, in a voice that might have been heard in three parishes:

"Jem! Jem! Where's that water? I'll warm your backside for you, my boy!" Jem turned and began to run back to the far end of the pond where the water was deepest and the bank had steps worn in its slope, and the scum and duckweed on the water was pushed away by the regular plunge of the buckets. Other children, reminded of similar duties, or glad of a leader in retreat, followed him. Fanny Moy was already a receding blob and a lessening howl over by the cottages, and in a minute or two Jassy and I were alone.

"You can come back now," I said, and reached out a hand to help her up the bank. Her thick black hair, usually strained back from her face and tightly plaited behind, had broken loose and streamed about her shoulders. There were several scratches on her face, and the blood was beading along them. Her poor neat clothes were torn and even muddier than mine. Altogether she was a pitiable little object. But she had recovered her self-possession, and although the hand she put in mine was icy cold, it was quite steady. So was her voice as she said, as soon as she stood beside me, "Indeed, I am most deeply grateful to you."

"That's all right," I said awkwardly. "Now I'll see you home. And we needn't walk, either." I looked towards the far side of the pond and putting two fingers in my mouth I blew a shrill whistle. Joby was trained to answer it, and I trusted his sense to bring him round the big end of the pond to meet me. But he was thinking of his supper, and chose to imagine that I was whistling him from the farmyard gate. Holding to the road, he set off for home at a rattling pace.

"Stupid clown," I said angrily. "He knows better than that. Now we shall have to walk."

"I'm glad really," she said. "I want to look for my hair-ribbon. I think I know just where it fell." Her voice was pleasant, low

(36)

and rather deep for such a small person, and with a smoky quality about it. We began walking. She fumbled about and produced a little handkerchief and began to dab at her scratched face. When most of the blood and mud had been transferred to the handkerchief she tucked it away and shook her hair backwards, raking it with her fingers and smoothing it with the palms of her hands. Her hands were small, with narrow palms and long delicate fingers. They were brown with exposure and rough from hard work, but their shape was delightful, and as I noticed them I realized that I had never noticed hands before. What were mother's like, I wondered.

Perhaps she was conscious of my staring, for she said:

"I must tidy myself before I go in. Father would have such a fright. He shan't even *know* if I can help it. He *abhors* violence."

"Rumour says differently."

"Oh, you're thinking of Bob Wicks. That wasn't *father*, that was *God*." She laughed, and I could see that the scratched side of her face was swelling. It resisted the pressure of her smile and made her look lop-sided and uglier than ever. Yet just at that moment she lifted both her arms and began to plait her hair behind her head, and when the plait was long enough she pulled it forward over one shoulder and worked on, weaving away with her lovely little hands until the plait ended, tapering below her waist. Just as it was finished she said, "How timely," and darted to one side, bent and picked up a scrap of yellow ribbon, and having tied it firmly to the end of her hair, tossed the plait back over her shoulder.

"Do I look *fairly* tidy now?"

"Fairly," I said, "but I think anybody would guess that you'd been in the wars a bit. Tell me, why did it happen? Why did they chase you?"

She hunched one shoulder and hesitated. "It's on account of my mother, I think. Well, I know really. It's been the same wherever we live. And father, too, a little, perhaps. But he doesn't annoy the *ignorant* people so much. He gets wrong with the gentry

(37)

and parsons. Would you believe that we've lived in six villages in seven years?"

"If you say so."

"We have. Mother likes that, naturally. She's a Stannary. I suppose you know. She shouldn't live in a house at all." She took out her handkerchief and pressed her cheek. "Your mother is very house-proud, isn't she?"

"How do you know?"

"Oh, I've watched. Your drying ground, you know. Your linen makes mine look very mucky. I've tried and tried since I've been here, but mine never looks so good."

"Well, you're not very big or strong," I said. "And actually mother doesn't do the washing in our house. Meggie, our maid, sees to it."

"Ah, but it's the good mistress who makes a good maid, you know."

We were near the cottages by this time, and we could see the door of the furthest one open. Against the firelit glow of the interior, Tom Woodroffe's ungainly figure outlined itself. Jassy gave a tiny sigh, half patient, half exasperated.

"He's coming to meet me," she said. "Do you think I could *possibly* say that I'd just had a fall? He'll be so upset. And he'll talk about turning the other cheek. It isn't true, you know, I did try that when they first set on me. Mother was nearer the mark. But I can't tell *him* that."

"What did she say?"

"Oh, once when I was chased at Ockley she said, 'Never run. Stand still and draw first blood.' And I did get away by knocking over that nasty little Moy girl. But then I ran. So I haven't pleased either of them."

"It must be rather difficult to please parents with such con-flicting ideas," I said feelingly.

She flashed me a glance, eloquent of appreciation and con-spiracy, but she said no more, for her father, after searching the Green, had seen us and was loping towards us.

(38)

"Jassy," he said, in an agitated way, "are you all right?"

"Perfectly," she said in a funny little prim voice. "Why?"

"The Moy child ran home a moment since with some horrible tale in which you were concerned." I heard the little sigh again. "Jassy, are you hurt?"

"I have a scratch on my face and my dress is torn. Master Hatton here will assure you that otherwise I am. . . . No, father, he must have his due. He did save me. I was in trouble and he did rescue me."

The big man made a gulping sound, and with his right hand—his left arm was clasping Jassy—reached for mine and gripped it. A torrent of incoherent thanks poured from his lips so that I was embarrassed and began to utter false disclaimers which belied my inmost feelings; for after all I had gone, alone, to the rescue of, as I supposed, a dog; and I had saved her, if from nothing worse than a trampling or a ducking. But my self-conscious murmurings went unheeded. Tom Woodroffe continued to thank me until, with disconcerting suddenness, he broke off and, snatching the little girl up into his arms, said almost tearfully, "Oh, Jassy, Jassy, why do you provoke them? I've told you before. You're all alone so often. You must be more cautious."

"But I was," said the little voice. "I didn't do anything. I was coming home with a few catkins for grandmother's blue jug. Father, you *know* why it is. How *I* behave doesn't make any difference at all."

"I must go," I said, for we were now on the edge of the Green. Tom Woodroffe began to thank me again. I cut him short, saying "Good night," and walking away. Then, over his shoulder, Jassy called, "I'm grateful too," to which I said "Good night" again and began to run.

When I reached home, in a better mood and very hungry, I found the place in an uproar. Mother had heard Joby and come out to meet me, and found him with an empty saddle. She had immediately concluded that I, who had been riding safely to and from the Rectory for a matter of three years and more, had

(39)

on this evening met with an accident. When I opened the yard gate Stoner and one of the labourers were just setting out, in thoroughly bad tempers, to inspect the Lower Road with a lantern, and mother was standing over father while he saddled Dane in preparation for a search of the Upper Road. At sight of me mother burst into fresh tears and hysterical expressions of reproach and affection. Father, who probably hadn't yet comprehended the situation, said "Ha!" and then, looking closely at the girth, "wants oiling."

"Leave it now," said mother sharply, "and come in." She put a hand on my shoulder and said, "Now, where have you been?"

I told her. And I think her marked distaste for the Woodroffes began with that story. Without knowing it she connected the name with her moments of fright. Or perhaps she resented my friendship with a cottager. In any case, my subsequent friendship with Tom and Jassy went forward in the face of a good deal of opposition.

My own reasons for allowing what, after all, was only an incident to lead to a friendship, were so mixed and so numerous that if half of them had not existed the other half would have been motive enough. I was interested in the personality of the man; I still hankered to share the religion which he professed; I had a more mundane fancy to see his workshop and play with his tools; I was curious about Sari Woodroffe; and I had found that Jassy was good company, if only for the reason that her odd manner of speaking and complete self-possession held constant elements of surprise. And I could not forget that she had, quite unwittingly, made me forget myself and my penury and my lost Mortiboys for a full thirty minutes. There was still another reason in which none of the Woodroffes was concerned. In a few weeks I should be fourteen, and I was suffering from the urge to self-assertion which is a common feature of that age; and a routine so dull and circumscribed as mine offered few opportunities for aggressiveness. Nor was mine the kind of mind which could readily invent occasions for mischief. But here was one ready-made. Being friendly with the Woodroffes, in the teeth of opposition, made me feel like a person with taste and choice and a will of his own. The last reason of all, and the least tangible, though perhaps the most powerful of them, was a certain kind of fatalism which had already found an anchorage in my forming mind. I could trace the links of the tenuous chain: I had watched the family's arrival because I was working in the garden and bored; I had been interested in Tom beating Wicks because I had just been introduced to the art of fisticuffs; I had attended two of his meetings because they coincided with the first prickings of my soul; and I had rescued Jassy because I liked dogs. And during the days after that rescue I awaited, half credulously, half scornfully, a further sign. For I could not, as things were, begin to haunt the cottage at the Green's end or show any extraordinary interest in the family. So I waited, and ten days after that Monday, sure enough, there was Jassy, looking over the yard gate when I went out to attend to the horses, and she said, trying to keep the excitement out of her voice, and succeeding, though it shone in her eyes:

"Do please come round to our house. Father wants to see you."

And in the shed at the back of the cottage which Tom had turned into a workshop, untidy and cluttered, he presented me with a little oak desk, admirably and imaginatively made, with more partitions than ordinary, and a little secret compartment, and a lock, and with my initials and the hooded jennet which is the Hatton badge carved into the lid. And from that moment Tom Woodroffe held a place in my heart second only to Mortiboys —and perhaps to mother, who held me to her with peculiar ties of conscience, genuine affection and sheer exasperation.

All told our friendship was brief enough. He gave me the desk at the end of March, and by the middle of October in the same year he was gone. And I cannot say that he influenced me much. He did not even save me from my infatuation with Mortiboys.

Once, during that summer, which was wet and disastrous, I had hopes that he might. For he was, in himself, a completely un-worldly person. He showed me how a man who has nothing except skill which he has no time to exploit, a man whose private life is strangely horrible, whose one earthly affection is fraught with fear and anxiety, whose very labour seems abortive, can yet be a happy man, because all his hope and confidence are centred about a supernatural belief. Tom Woodroffe was too busy to earn a living properly; his marriage was worse than a failure, his love for his daughter was a pain, his gratuitous toil on behalf of other men never bore fruit in his time; but he believed and he trusted in God Who had made all things, to Whom all things were plain, and Who would never fail a humble, earnest servant. And he was a happy man. I have never met another.

I had, as I have said, high hopes that I might, by sharing his beliefs, reach the point where to me, as to him, it did not matter where I lived, how I was clad, whether my pockets were full or empty, or whether men esteemed me or not. But destiny, or breed-ing, were too strong. Tom could not change me.

He taught me things. He had a powerful ally in my imagina-tion, and he made me squeamish about much which other men take for granted. Tailors, for example.

Soon after I had begun to visit the cottage Tom saw, in By-water, a youth of perhaps fifteen snatch a slice of bread from a child of about four. He spoke to the boy admonishingly, I imagine, and then, noticing that the apparent bully was avidly consuming the bread, was thin and pale, and had a badly bruised face, in a more sympathetic fashion. He learned that the boy was an apprentice at Calthorpe's, the best tailor in the place. He took him into a chop-house and treated him to a bowl of mutton broth and learned, in ten minutes, a great deal about Calthorpe's treat-ment of the boys who worked for him. Armed with this informa-tion—which he implied had been gained by observation and inference—he visited the shop and tried to reason with the tailor, who, perceiving that he was not dealing with even a potential customer, dropped his obsequious manner and roundly told Tom that the treatment meted out to his apprentices was well within the law. There was nothing in their articles to demand that the boys occupied his best bedroom, ate rump steak twice a day, or had leisure to indulge their pranks. He had undertaken to house and feed and teach them, and that he was doing. He defied any-one, even the Sheriff himself, to bring complaints on legal grounds. I can picture the man, so sure of his ground, gloating over the discomfiture of the great awkward ill-dressed busy-body, who merely said:

"Very well, Mr. Calthorpe, if you won't listen to the voice of humanity, and the law won't help me, I must try another means."

Oblivious apparently to the fact that the amelioration of the lot of three tailor's apprentices would put no penny in his pocket, and that obsequious attention to Nick Helmar's wishes would employ him profitably through the coming winter, Tom, with a list of abuses in his hand, set out to visit every gentleman and every farmer who, according to another list supplied by the original protégée, patronized the tailor. Before starting out he worked feverishly in the shed, finishing off commissioned articles, and I know for a fact that he had left with Sari and Jassy every penny he collected on them, trusting himself to the charity of the countryside.

In due course, working on a narrowing circle with our village as its centre, he came, on a June evening, to call upon my father, whose name was on Calthorpe's books, with, at that moment, the sum of fifteen pounds outstanding against it. I was in the parlour at the time when Meggie showed him in, and I noticed the signs of fatigue and hunger on his always cadaverous face. He had caught cold, too, and was almost voiceless, so that conversation between him and my mumbling parent was a test for one's hearing. He offered the paper which bore the evidence against Calthorpe to father, who never read anything if he could help it, and who pushed it away, saying in a puzzled fretful manner, "Read mum mum must!" Tom read it and it made sorry hearing. Then, in his husky shredding voice, he said:

"Now, Mr. Hatton, sir, I ask you, can you happily wear a suit of clothes that has been made in such circumstances."

"Mum never could mum any clothes Calthorpe mum," said father, still puzzled but emphatic. "Mum can't *cut* mum. Not that I blame mum apprentices. Mum at all. Mum should mum the scissors. Certainly. Apprentices mum." Then some idea, misleading, but an idea, dawned in that stupid, handsome head, and he straightened his back and lifted his chin and spoke out quite plainly for a second or two. "What is all this about? Is Calthorpe dunning me? Mum mum! You tell him from me, will you, that the things he made me last would disgrace a scarecrow and I don't intend to pay for them. Mum mum! Moreover," said father, thrusting his chin out and looking at Tom with accusatory eyes, "it's not a bit of use coming here and blaming the apprentices. If they don't work, damme, he should take a stick to them. Mum mum indeed."

I saw an expression of despair gather in Tom's sunken eyes. He had had, as I heard later, many and various receptions, but never, I am certain, had he been met by such complete lack of comprehension.

"But, sir, you misunderstand me," he said patiently. "I'm sorry, perhaps I didn't make my point clear. I came here to tell you how Calthorpe treats these wretched boys, and to ask you, in the name of God and common humanity, not to deal with him again until he acts more fairly to them."

"Mum," said father, who, with his head slightly on one side, had really been giving Tom his whole attention. "I see. Well, all I can say is mum. Never deal with him again. Never. Said so the instant I mum mum that last job. Don't care who knows."

"But you are withdrawing your custom on account of his bad workmanship, not on account of his treatment of his apprentices."

"Eh?" Father's face was deepening in colour. The demands made upon his attention were beginning to annoy.

"All this that I read you," said Tom, thrusting the paper forward again. "Weren't you disgusted, sir?"

"Utterly disgusted," said father, and moved to the bell for Meggie to show out this bewildering visitor. He never learned that Meggie, knowing herself indispensable, could ignore bells as easily as insults. I rose from my obscure seat and went over to Tom.

"There you are," I said. "That's one more. Now you come along home and get some food inside you and get to bed. I'll walk across with you."

Tom hesitated, but after another glance at father, bade him a respectful good evening and allowed himself to be drawn outside. As we crossed the little hallway which seemed too brilliantly lighted by the lamp we had brought from Mortiboys, I saw him shake his head, like a big puzzled dog.

"But I wanted your father to put his name to it. Several gentlemen have done that, and four or five even said that they'd write letters independently."

"I'll write for father," I said eagerly. "Our names are the same, and I write a far better hand."

"Would that be honest?"

"Well, you heard what he said. And that stands for me, too. I'll never patronize Calthorpe, or any other tailor that I know treats boys like that. When you were reading I felt quite sick; and very glad that mother gets old Sam Jolly to make my things, badly as he fits me."

"Ah yes," said Tom with a sigh. "But later on, when you're a young gentleman of fashion, Barney, my boy, will you bother then?"

"I just said, I'd never wear clothes made in such conditions. If I knew."

"There's the rub," he said. He stared straight out into the lovely evening without seeing anything. "If people *knew*. But they don't, and it's difficult to tell them. I wrote a letter to the *Bywater Gazette* about Calthorpe, but they didn't print it."

"For a very good reason," I said. "They carry his advertisement every week, summer and winter."

"I hadn't thought of that."

"And I've just remembered another thing. Don't carry that paper to Jonas Rigger at Marsh Place. He's some kind of relative to Calthorpe, brother-in-law, I believe. I remember his telling Stoner, our foreman in the yard, that he got his breeches made for nothing. He'd set the dogs on you as soon as spit."

"I had aimed to go there now. But it'd be a waste of labour. So I've finished, save for Mr. Helmar, and I can ask him to-morrow when I go along to start work. There're many things I'd sooner do, but I've got to think a bit about the winter's food, I'm afraid. By the look of things, the harvest won't be good this year."

A sharp pain, as though a hot rod had transfixed me, shot from my skull to my heels, as Tom mentioned going to work at Mortiboys.

"What is going to happen there?" I asked.

"Where? Around here? Scores of people will starve I'm afraid."

"Oh, no," I cried impatiently, "I didn't mean that. What are they going to do at Mortiboys?"

"Pull it down, I should say, from the sound of it. Well, hardly that, but great alterations are planned, I hear. There're going to be a dozen of us at work with a Mr. Sedley, a London architect, to tell us what to do. The whole gateway is coming down for one thing. I know that, because before I went off on this job," he patted the pocket where the papers now rested, "Mr. Helmar asked me my opinion of the wood, and I told him it was rotten as a pear."

"I don't think I can bear it if that archway comes down."

"Why, Barney?"

"I can't. And it's all nonsense. It's made of brick, isn't it? What's wood got to do with it? And for you to say that, Tom. I thought you were my friend."

"Wood has this to do with it," said Tom, ignoring my outburst. "Those brick and timber buildings that those old folks put up last as long as the timber and no longer. There're places in that arch, and in the little houses either side, where the beams have gone and the bricks are sagging. 'Tisn't safe any longer."

"It'd be safe enough for me," I said violently. "It's just that Nick Helmar shouldn't live there, with his stinking money and rotten ideas. Mortiboys should belong to somebody that loved it, and would rather cut off his hand than alter one bit of it."

"I'd go further and say that places like Mortiboys shouldn't have any money spent on them at all—not with wages at seven shillings a week and flour at a shilling a quartern. But that's by the way. Barney," he put his hand on my shoulder, "I thought you'd got the better of that weakness. Let Mortiboys go. Haven't we thrashed this out before and agreed that you weren't to ruin your life over a whim?"

"I know," I said wretchedly. "I did agree once. But I don't now. Just the mere mention of that gateway going shows me how much I care still. I tell you I'd stop at nothing if only I could have Mortiboys for my own."

"Barney, you mustn't say such things. Stop at nothing, indeed. Think what that means. Sometimes I fear for you, boy. I had a dread that that place'll twist you and give Satan a hold on your soul."

"Satan!" I said wildly. "If Satan would give me Mortiboys—as it is, mark you—he could have my soul and welcome."

"You're overwrought, Barney, and maybe this isn't the time for me to say much to you, but all the same . . ." and at that moment his voice, which had been growing weaker and hoarser, failed suddenly. He cleared his throat and then looked at me and laughed. "There," he said in a whisper, "God must have known that nothing I could say now would help. I'll get along. And would it be too much to ask you to think over that first talk we had ever about that place?"

My conscience smote me. I had seen how exhausted he was, and I had left my house in order to see him home. And here we were on the darkening Green with me bothering him about my personal problem.

"I'll think of it, Tom. Good night."

"Good night, boy. God bless you."

I walked back to our yard gate, and when I had closed it for the night, turned back and rested my arms on the top bar and my chin on my clasped hands. My mind was busy with Mortiboys, seeing the gateway as it now was, the arch of little bricks, the deceptively sturdy timber, the houses with their diamond-paned windows; and then seeing it dismantled, destroyed, gone for ever from the sight of man. I went through the whole story of the Hattons and their home, and although my face was steady and my body motionless, it was as though within me my heart was shedding tears of blood, and through the hollow of my marrowless bones great waves and surges of anger and impotence, of longing and hopelessness, were shaking me to destruction. I could feel my mind reaching out into the empty evening, into the universe, into the past, seeking, demanding strength from something, from somebody, from God, or the Devil, or those Hattons, long dead, who must have loved Mortiboys as I did. I couldn't be left here, one small tortured poor boy hanging on a gate. I must be more, more, more. And suddenly, when the tension had reached an untenable pitch and I was about to burst, something happened. I did, in actual fact, touch something with my mind, and it was like a steady cold hand being laid on my pounding heart. I straightened myself and lifted my face to the sky, where one great star hung unwinking. And I knew that out of the very essence of my soul I had saved Mortiboys. I was as sure that it was going to remain, fundamentally untouched, as I was sure that I was standing by the gate into our farmyard. I began to shake in every limb, even my head wagged, and there was a queer pain, the like of which I had never felt before, in the back of my skull.

I waited until I had some control of myself, and then went into the house, hoping to reach my room without being seen. But mother, who had been trying to get from father an account of the business which had brought Tom Woodroffe into her parlour, was watching for me, and after exclaiming at my pallor—which she attributed to standing in the night air with him—must hear it all again from me.

"It's a wonder he can find time to run round minding other people's business," she said acidly. "I thought he was a carpenter."

"So he is, mum mum," said father. "Mm told you when he came mm going to work for Nick mm Mortiboys. Taking down mm dangerous arch I hear."

Listening to that assertion, which he made as though Mortiboys were no more to him than an Indian wigwam, some of my inflation left me. How could I, just by standing in the dusk and willing something alter the schemes of a rich, powerful person like Nick Helmar? Reason told me that I was daft. But deep down, below reason and commonsense and fear, deeper even than thought or desire, there lay a little grain of certainty. Resting upon it, too exhausted to even think about the matter any more, I took myself to bed.

Six days later the whole countryside was shocked, or excited, or maliciously tickled to hear that Mrs. Helmar of Mortiboys had run away with the young architect from London. Apparently he had been her lover for some time, and it was in order to ensure his employment—and easy proximity—that she had worked upon her husband until he gave his consent to the alterations and improvements at the house. Sedley had been staying at Mortiboys for a fortnight, we were told, tapping and measuring and working on his plans; and then Nick Helmar, returning from a ride or a visit, caught the pair in circumstances which could have but one explanation. He had ordered Sedley out of the house, but had not, according to rumour, shown any great animosity to Mrs. Helmar, of whom he was dotingly fond. However, when Sedley went she went too. All the workmen were paid off and sent home, three of them, skilled workers in plaster and marble, all the way back to Italy. And the work stopped.

I was stunned by the news, and a little frightened; but I was not surprised. I remembered the cold, unshakable certainty which had laid hold of me on that evening six days before, and I hoped that Mrs. Helmar would be happy with her lover, for in losing Mortiboys she had saved it, and in some inexplicable fashion for which mere human language has no terms, I felt that she, and Sedley the architect, and Nick Helmar, the cuckold, had been puppets at the end of a string. A string which I had not pulled, but which I had indicated.

July and August passed, a wet cold summer. The prospects for the corn harvest were the worst for years. And in a two-handed fashion this fact brought Jassy Woodroffe to work in our dairy. Mother, seeing that the harvest would be poor, began to concentrate upon the dairy as a source of profit and was in a mind for more help; Jassy, knowing that bread would be dear, and that Tom would not be engaged in the promised regular work at Mortiboys, was determined to find a situation.

Mother engaged her, largely through my mediation, and dubiously enough. For a few days—until Jassy had caught the knack of the unfamiliar work—my life as well as hers was rendered miserable by constant criticism. But even mother could not long withstand the intelligence, the superhuman energy, the fury of concentration which Jassy could bring to bear upon any task, and within a fortnight mother said, "She's better than I expected." That was as far as she would go; but the criticism stopped, though I noticed with amusement that my visits to the dairy were now looked upon with as much disfavour as my visits to the cottage had been.

But there came, in the middle of August, four blazing hot days, memorable because they were the only taste of summer that the year brought us. On one of them—the third—mother went down to Bywater in the gig with father. As soon as they had gone Meggie put on her hat and announced her intention of taking the day off too, and hobbled away to visit her cronies.

At mid-day I went indoors and, taking a jug, walked into the dairy for some cider at which mother had tried her hand the previous autumn, with indifferent success. But though a sour and windy beverage, it seemed attractive in the unaccustomed heat. In the dairy I found Jassy, bowed over the handle of the churn and crying. She lifted her head as I entered, and I remember being struck by the contrast between her neat, child's figure in the faded lilac print bodice and skirt, her slim brown arms under the rolled-up sleeves, her slender little ankles and feet, and her face. There was a film of sweat on her bulging forehead, her eyes were swollen with tears, her cheeks, usually so pale, were duskily flushed and glazed from crying. Her expression was both miserable and furious.

"Why, Jassy," I said, "what's the matter?"

"I don't know. I've done everything I should. And it just won't come." She began to cry again.

"Wait a minute," I said. And I filled the jug, drank from it, and turned back to her. "I'll take a turn, shall I?"

She stood back and I took the handle and turned the churn over. Inside it the cream flopped with a flabby, unhopeful sound.

"It beats me," I said, "how you can turn the thing at all. Don't you find it heavy?"

She shook her head. She had almost stopped crying and stood looking at me with an expression which I often caught on her face. It had embarrassed me at first, and I had tried to think myself mistaken. Then, seeing it again, I put it down to the fact that I had gone to help her against the mob of children, and I thought it would wear off in time. But it lasted—a curious meditating look with an element of adoration in it. I had seen it when I said that I would speak to mother about giving her work, and once or twice since then when I had spoken to her about the place. And now here it was again. I turned away from it, uncomfortable, and swung the churn violently. After a few minutes she said, in her primmest voice:

"I'm rested now, thank you. I'll try again. I think you are a little rough with it."

I relinquished the handle and she began to turn it, smoothly and without obvious exertion, though I could see the sweat start out again on her face. Below her arms and in a patch between her shoulders, the faded lilac print was damp, darkening with moisture to its original hue. She turned for some minutes, and still the cream flopped, and at last she was drawing her breath in gasps that were quite as noisy and as frequent as the flops.

There was a backless chair under one of the dairy shelves, kept there so that mother could sit sometimes when she was supervising, not working. I dragged it out and told Jassy to sit down while I took another turn. Before I began I took another pull at the cider, and then handed her the jug. "It's quite awful to taste, but it is cool," I said.

I turned for ten minutes more and then gave up in disgust.

"Where's old woman Moy?" I demanded. "Let her do it!"

"She isn't coming to-day. It's the first time I've been alone with it. I did so want it to turn out well."

"Go and fetch her."

"No. I don't want to do that. I won't be beat. Don't you bother though. Leave it with me. I'll do it."

"I bet you fourpence you won't."

"I can't bet," she said primly, "because I can't afford to lose."

"I'll bet, all the same. If it comes I'll give you fourpence."

I sat down on the chair and she took the churn. She swung it steadily, almost persuasively, for another ten minutes. Then she stopped suddenly and all the colour left her face. It was as though she blushed white. Then she said, in rapid succession, three of the worst swear words I had heard, put both hands on the churn and gave it a push that was plainly intended to send the whole

(52)

thing flying. But the churn merely lurched, ran forward a little, hit the shelf and knocked down one of the wide, shallow pannikins in which the new milk was set for the cream to rise. I got to my feet and stared in helpless horror as the white pool widened about the floor. But even the crash had not sobered Jassy. Beside herself with temper, she jumped with both feet in the milk, snatched up the biggest bit of the broken crock and dashed it to the floor. Then, turning a wild white face to me she said:

"I'm going home now. And you can tell your mother that if she comes there with any idea of beating me I shall kill her!"

"You little devil," I cried, catching her as she dashed past me to the door. She kicked at my shins, and since that did not release her, dropped her head and bit me on the hand.

"Blast!" I said, and let her go, and stood looking at my bitten hand. The blood was gathering in the two punctures which her eye teeth had made, and I suddenly remembered the glittering fangs of the children who had chased her. And my mind was slipping away to Captain Anderson and his theories about the animal in civilized people, when Jassy, transformed again, seized my hand, kissing it and crying that she was sorry, that she didn't mean it, that she was mad and sorry, sorry, sorry.

"Come and let me bathe it, or you'll fester and die," she said.

"Shut up," I said impatiently. "It's nothing." I was indeed ashamed that for so small a hurt I had let her go. To restore myself I pointed to the floor and the broken crock and said sternly:

"It's that I'm worrying about. Mother will make you pay for it, you know."

The spirit of defiance which had been in her a minute since, and the passion of penitence which had succeeded it, gave way to meek sanity. Jassy moved her small hands in a gesture of resignation and said, deeply: "I know. I'll get another job and some money somehow. How much would it be worth, do you think?"

Immediately I was sorry for her, and thought of the whole pile of similar crocks stored in the cupboard under the back stairs. I fetched one out, and telling Jassy to remove all traces of the other, and the milk, took a pail out to the meadow and milked a cow at the untimely hour of one o'clock in the afternoon.

"You're sure it'll be all right. I wouldn't want you to be blamed," said Jassy anxiously, as I tipped the new milk into the new bowl.

"It'll be all right," I promised, and refrained from saying that mother's wrath would hardly visit me in the same fashion as it would have done Jassy. Then I put out my hand to pull the churn into place, and the body of it tilted, and within we heard the unmistakable thump of the butter.

"You did it," I almost shouted, "you did it after all." And being young and easily amused we rocked with laughter at the thought of the butter coming just at the moment when Jassy despaired of it. I took out my fourpenny piece and, when she tried with arguments to refuse it, I put it into her palm and closed her little fingers over it.

Our rather green friendship had ripened rapidly in that hour, and when, with the dairy tidy and the butter awaiting further attention on the cold slab, we went and ate our midday meal together at the kitchen table, we were on better terms than we had ever been before. We talked a great deal and, presently, were telling one another our dearest wishes. Jassy said, with point blank frankness, that she wanted a farm.

"I might have had one, too," she said. "My grandfather and grandmother Woodroffe have a nice little place. But Granny Woodroffe wanted my father to be a scholar and, do you know, she saved her egg and butter money for twelve years so that she could send him to the Grammar School at Bury St. Edmunds. And he was so clever and worked so hard that he went from there to Cambridge. That was where he got religion and got into trouble because he wanted to be a preacher, though he wasn't a parson. And that broke Granny's heart. Then he married mother, and his father wouldn't have him home any more. But when Granny died she left him all the things that really belonged to her, the clock and the other things we have in our house. He told me all about Granny and the furniture once, how she loved it and used to polish it. And since then I *have* tried to keep the house nice." She leaned a meditative face on her hand and added, "I'm afraid that's as much as I can do towards being *like* her— my granny, I mean."

"Do you want to be like her?"

"Father would like it. I could hear that in his voice when he told me about her. But then she hadn't a furious temper. Besides, if he thought granny was the best woman he ever knew it seems odd that he should—" She stopped, looking at me for a moment with clouding eyes, and said, "But you haven't said your dearest wish yet."

"Mine is mad and yours is so sensible. You could have yours. You've only to marry a farmer. Mine is impossible."

"Is it?" If her voice had held more avid curiosity and less sympathy I should have been warned and made up some trivial nonsense. As it was I said, "I'd like to own Mortiboys." Her ugly little face flashed interest and approval.

"Ah!" she said. "Back in June, when father worked there for a week, he forgot his dinner one day and I went over with it. I thought that it was pretty. I was sorry about the work stopping, for father's sake, but I was really quite glad to think that they hadn't pulled down that arch and the dear little houses."

"So was I," I said heartily. I was pleased, and a little excited, to discover in Jassy a fellow admirer of the gateway, but I was jealous, too. I wanted her to understand that her light and facile admiration of a "pretty" place was very different from the feelings which I entertained for it. And also, at the back of my mind was a faint, unworthy thought that it was a little presumptuous in her to apply an endearing diminutive to anything connected with Mortiboys. So, beginning with, "Ah, but you don't understand . . ." I went on to tell her more about my passion, and about Hatton history than I had ever told anyone, even her father. I might even, in my egregious folly, have hinted at how I had

(55)

saved the gateway from Nick Helmar's vandalism, but before I reached that point Jassy looked up at the clock on the kitchen wall and jumped to her feet.

"I've got that butter to salt and shape," she said, and went flitting across the kitchen. At the door of the dairy passage she halted and turned back.

"I never thanked you properly."

"What for?" I asked, still thinking of Mortiboys and forgetting all about the business of the broken pan.

"For saving me again. I am grateful, because I do like working here."

"Oh, go along!" I said. "And, Jassy, if you're going to marry a farmer you'll have to learn not to take your spite out on the milk crocks."

"Yes, I shall indeed," she said, quite seriously. But as she closed the door she looked round the edge of it, a roguish smile on her ugly little face, "Still, I brought the butter, didn't I?"

Mother never discovered that the pan was broken, and Jassy was still working in our dairy when the October troubles began.

By October the harvest was in and the price of corn fixed. In October, too, the summer wage rate ended, and the winter one, a shilling or two less on the week, came into force. There was often some slight dispute at this season between the farmers and landowners and the workpeople. Looking back, I think I cannot remember an autumn when there were not complaints and a little mild rioting. Mother, being a payer of wages, took her stand upon two tried arguments: one, that if the men could not support their families on their wages they should have fewer children; two, that if they could not afford to buy the best white bread they should make do with a cheaper kind mixed with rye or barley. Father never argued about the matter at all; he would mumble about the damned Radicals and the country going to the dogs. I, until this autumn, had never given the subject much thought except to agree, blindly, with mother. But this year there was Tom Woodroffe to shatter my complacency. He told me all about the evils of the recent enclosures; he drove into my unwilling mind many uncomfortable facts about the rise in prices lowering the value of money, so that now, with nine shillings a week a man was worse off than he had been years ago with seven. And he made me miserable without convincing me completely. Because, after all, we were farming and we were not rich, and I did not see how mother could afford to pay higher wages.

"A living wage to labourers would benefit everybody," said Tom, when I put this point to him. "If the men in this village, for example, had more money to spend in Bywater, there'd be more trade done in the town, and there'd be an increased demand for your mother's butter and eggs."

"Then prices would go up and things would be just as they are."

"Not necessarily," he said patiently. "Your farm, and every other farm, could produce as much stuff again without doubling the cost of production. Your place would support twice the number of hens without giving much more work, and to sell forty eggs at twopence would pay better than to sell twenty at threepence. Can you see that? And there'd be forty people with an egg instead of twenty. It's the same with everything. These men aren't asking for money to chuck in the pond, they're asking for money to spend. They're customers—or would be. That's what I'm trying to make people see."

How often I had heard him say those words in the few months I had known him. But that was the last time. The wage dispute in that autumn was Tom Woodroffe's last battlefield.

There had been rumours of rioting in Kent as early as September; but our own district remained quiet for a little while longer. Sir Edward Follesmark, of Sible Havers, who was known as the Mad Squire, had professed himself willing to raise the wages of his own men and to intercede with other employers in the district to do the same. This Sir Edward was the son of the Squire who had cheated the Reverend Saunders' predecessor out

(57)

of the tithe rights at the time of the Enclosures, and he, like his father, was anti-clerical, and, despite his many acres, Radical in his views. He had called a meeting of wage-payers which, since mother could not well appear in public as the owner of Green Farm, father attended. He understood very little of what had happened, but he did come home and mumble that everything was all right. And for once he had the gist of the matter, for from mother's point of view the meeting had been a success: the increased rate was overwhelmingly voted down.

A few days later Nick Helmar at Mortiboys and Jonas Rigger at Marsh End had stacks fired, secretly in the night, as though in warning; and within a week the genuine rioting had begun. Mother, like every other farmer in the neighbourhood, took precautions. Live stock was carefully stalled at night, the shutters of windows were bolted into place, gates were locked and reinforced with faggots and hurdles, and Stoner, his son Phineas, father and I guarded the stackyard in turn. Job Mash and Timothy Rudd, our two labourers, did not come to work during that week, and I wondered to myself in what guise I should next see them. Like everybody else, I had read stories of the French Revolution, and I could not imagine Job and Timothy, so meek and so slow, being part of a mob which with threats demanded bread or blood. In that I was right. For when the men visited Green Farm it was in the daylight, mid-afternoon of a golden October day, and they were as orderly and formal as a deputation from Parliament.

Mother, Meggie and I were alone in the house when the men, headed by Tom Woodroffe, stopped at our front gate. Father, in his usual light-hearted way, had accepted an invitation to shoot at Baildon Lodge. Tom came up the short flagged path alone and rang the bell. Mother went to the parlour window and asked in a stony civil fashion what he wanted. I stood at her elbow ready to close the shutter at the first sign of rowdiness. I was—and had been for weeks—in an invidious position. I did not pay wages, neither did I earn any. I was dependent upon mother, and knew that she had struggle enough to make ends meet with wages as they were. But I had also heard Tom's description of the men's case and found it reasonable. So, though I was prepared to defend the farm if it were actually attacked, emotionally I was neutral.

In answer to mother's question Tom flourished a paper and said:

"For myself, madam, nothing. On behalf of everybody here, five minutes of your attention."

"I am listening," mother said.

Tom read out, in plain clear phrases, the causes for the present dissatisfaction. He gave, from the paper, exact details of the cost of living and the decreasing value of money. Then, looking straight into mother's face, he launched into an impassioned appeal that the recent decision about wages might be reconsidered.

"We hold the view, ma'am, that Sir Edward's proposal failed to enlist sympathy not on account of ill-will, but of ignorance. We admit that it is difficult for people in a different station of life to rightly estimate the burden which the labouring man has to bear. You, Mrs. Hatton, ma'am, and the rest of the landowners are not hit, as we are, by the rising price of food. Therefore, in order that you may not again err through ignorance, I offer you these few facts and ask you to believe, from that evidence and from the solemn word of all those here assembled, that unless wages are increased many of us, with our wives and children, will starve miserably before the winter is out."

There was a bumbling sound from the knot of men at the gate. A general assenting sound, shot through by a few intelligible words, "We're starving now"; "Fix the wages on the price of bread"; "We must eat to work."

I looked at the little group and was struck, for the first time, by the miserable appearance they presented. Here and there a young man, as yet unburdened by domestic responsibility, not yet worn down by years of labour, was straight and healthy looking, but they were few. For the rest, although wind and weather had reddened and bronzed their faces, cheeks were hollow, shoulders bowed, knees bent, feet flattened. The common expression was one of anxiety; and after hearing Tom's analysis of their budgets I could understand it. And my sympathy was engaged by their meekness, their remarkable lack of venom. They were only asking, after all, for the right to live. They were not demanding comfort or privilege, but just enough food to enable them to keep up strength sufficient for the day's labour. My vacillating mind sided with them once again. Fidgeting with the shutter I whispered to mother, "Say that you will reconsider. That will satisfy them and they'll go away." Mother looked at me dubiously. Then she turned back to the window and said boldly:

"The rise in prices affects other things than food. That must be remembered, Woodroffe."

Tom inclined his head awkwardly, but with a curiously adequate deference.

"At least you are reasonable, ma'am." And one of the clear voices in the crowd said, "You can live without other things. Food must be got."

And then mother said, and as she said it I was amazed at the cunning of women, and saw why she had so happily seen father ride off leaving her to face whatever might happen that day.

"I have listened, and I have taken in what you have told me. But you must all understand that though I take an interest in this farm, mine is not the final word. However, this I will promise you. What you have said my husband shall hear, and I am certain that if Sir Edward and the other gentlemen and farmers decide to reconsider the matter, he will do likewise. Will that do?"

I realized that I had, for fourteen years, lived with, and for several of them underestimated, a very clever woman indeed. A voice in the crowd certainly said, "Just words, Mrs. Hatton, words," and another answered it with, "The master be shooting pheasants. Whass the price o' meat to the likes o' him?" But on the whole the crowd, which had never once been truculent, seemed placated. Tom replaced his battered old hat and the men began to shuffle into a pitiable imitation of marching order, and the visit to Green Farm would have been concluded uneventfully but for Meggie.

The room immediately above the parlour was hers, because it opened upon the back stairs, and she had evidently been listening from her window as Tom Woodroffe read his facts and figures and made his appeal. Now, to mother and me, from just above our heads, came Meggie's rough voice, thickened with tears.

"Wait, wait," it cried. "I got suthin for you. I know what thass like to be hungry, and you lot not working this week while you're fighting, I reckon you could do with a square meal. So wait, wait, all on you." There was a sound of scuffling overhead, and then, down on to our flagged front path and the road beyond the fence fell a shower of coins, vigorously thrown. And mingled with the rattling and little thuds of them came Meggie's hysterical cries. "Bin saving for my owd age, but that don't matter now. You get your rights and I'll work till I drop. Now you, Job Mash, don't go spending your share on ale; tek your missus and babies suthin home."

The coins she threw were mostly coppers, and I could imagine Meggie saving penny upon penny and never thinking of changing her hoard into more valuable and easily portable coinage. The shower seemed to last for several minutes. And it transformed a knot of men who had borne themselves with remarkable restraint, even with dignity, into a grotesque, grovelling mob. Tom had seen, with horror, a lout in his teens take bread from a four-year-old. We were witnesses of a more horrible sight, two full-grown men fighting one another for the possession of a penny from a servant maid's poor hoard. And yet Meggie, hysterical as she might be, had been visited by insight beyond the ordinary. These men, seeking their rights in a disciplined and dignified manner, were hungry. They were not working, so they were not earning, and there was not one in a hundred of them who had even enough to keep himself for a week in reserve. They fell upon the money madly, jumping into the ditch to retrieve a rolling coin, pushing and jostling, and looking up to Meggie's window and holding out their hands and caps and shouting, "To me! Throw to me! Bless you! Bless your kind heart!"

Meggie threw the last coins, cried, really sobbing again, "Bless you all!" and slammed her window shut. Her loud crying, harsh, as though her physical means for the expression of sorrow was rusty with lack of use—was audible to mother and me in the parlour. Mother had turned white with fury, and her expression boded no good for Meggie. But I could not mind that at the moment, for outside, on our garden fence, awkward Tom Woodroffe was giving another exhibition of incongruous agility. As the brown shower of coppers began to fall I had seen his expression change, become alert, anxious, a little wild. Then he had looked about for some object which he could mount. There was none. Our front garden, with its two flower beds, its flagged path and low box hedges, offered no rostrum. So he went to the fence, tested its strength, and then set first his hands and then his feet on the top rail, which was a mere spline perhaps three-quarters of an inch in thickness. He squatted on it for a second, released his hands and stood up, balanced on that narrow footing. His feet were across it, at right angles, too. He could not stand like a tight-rope walker because the pointed tops of the upright rails broke the surface at intervals of four inches or less. He just stood there, steady as though he were on a rock. And he shouted:

"You've got to give it back, every penny of it. I'm sorry. But you've got to give it all back. Why? I'll tell you why. If you carry away so much as a penny you're liable to be charged for demanding money with menaces. That's true. Down at Oslefield in Kent a farmer gave a man eighteenpence in similar circumstances, and the man was charged and convicted. *He was transported for seven years!* If you keep so much as a penny, you are liable to the same punishment. Come on now, into my hat! Into my hat, I say!" He flung his hat to the ground at his feet and stood there, balancing, waiting.

Reluctantly the great bony fists approached the hat, hung over it, opened, and dropped the coveted coin. And as they did so I had a moment's illumination about men and money. Money had enslaved men, and it had established a system of false values. Those men by the gate, every one of them down to the roughest, least likeable specimen of them all, were too good to be there grovelling for a charitable copper coin, scooping it up with avidity, and only letting it go—and then reluctantly, wistfully—in the face of a dire threat. And, similarly, there was mother beside me with her whole nature being slowly warped because she had not enough money. One could run one's eyes slowly up the social edifice, rung by rung, and find that lack of money, or the desire for it, was the motive behind almost every action. A few eccentrics, like my father, if indeed there were any others like him, seemed to be indifferent to it; but even he was in a better temper if he had won money at Faro than if he had lost it. And this rule of money was wrong. I had a flashing vision, tenuous, unrecapturable, but real while it lasted, of a world wherein the money value was not supreme. In such a world these men would be reckoned on their merits, good with the plough, careful with animals, clever with tools—yes, even the fact that they were faithful husbands and affectionate fathers would count. In such a world Mortiboys would be mine on account of the love I bore it; whether I could buy it in hard cash would be immaterial—the fact that I would gladly buy it with my blood would be the thing that counted. But I realized, even as the thought came, and went, that to measure what a man is, and what he loves, is impossible; therefore mankind, seeking always the easiest way, had fallen victim to the money value because money is easily reckoned, visible, tangible. So there were the men by the gate, threatened with starvation if they did not get an increase of two shillings a week, and there was mother by the parlour window thinking that to give Job and Timothy and young Phineas another two shillings —and Stoner a proportionate rise—would result in her ruin; and that made two shillings, which is a paltry round thing made of adulterated silver and stamped in a special fashion, of more worth than industry and strength, than charity and justice, than human flesh and blood.

Outside on the fence Tom, balanced in some phenomenal fashion, reached down, retrieved his hat, and held it in one hand while he counted the money. Then, turning his head, he shouted up to Meggie:

"My dear, how much did you have in your stocking?"

"Matter of fower pound ten. I don't want it back," said Meggie, her voice even more sodden than before.

"Can't you say exactly?"

"Fower pounds ten shillings and ninepence. But you let 'em keep it, Mr. Woodroffe, for the sake of the families. I bin hungry when I was a little 'un."

"That's what we're fighting against," Tom called back. "But if we take your money—and it lacks four shillings at the moment— we risk some poor family losing its man and being hungry for seven years. And spies are everywhere." He swept his gaze around, not excluding either the crowd of his own followers or Meggie herself, or mother and me at the window. Then he brought it to rest upon the men. "Come on now," he said, cajoling, "hand it over. Better a hungry week now than a visit to Botany Bay. There's four shillings missing. *And I think I know where they are.* Now then, shut your eyes every one of you, and those that are able say a prayer for the cause and meantime those with a shilling stuck to their palms, break them loose and chuck them in. Otherwise I give up and you can make your next visit without me."

I kept my eyes open and I saw the four shillings thrown into the hat. And one of them came from the hand of Kit Barber, Clem's ne'er-do-weel brother, who had no wife and no child and was, at the least, always sure of a meal in Clem's kitchen. He had been keeping the shilling, I was sure, to spend at "The Eve-

ning Star." And I thought that it was very difficult to make any
rules of conduct, or laws, which were to include on a dead level
men like him and, say, Bandy Fayres, who, according to Tom,
never ate anything but bread and potatoes in order that his wife
might have tea and his children bacon and milk.

Tom opened his eyes, dropped easily off the fence on the
garden side, counted the money into neat piles, and looked up
at Meggie's window again.

"We're just as grateful as if we'd taken it," he said. "Put it by
again for your old age, and may that be long deferred and easy
when it comes. Good day to you." He flourished his hat and replaced it. Then, scorning the gate, he vaulted the fence, and
crying, "Now for Marsh End, my lads," took his place at the
head of the crowd.

Mother flung back the parlour shutters. "That man," she said
thoughtfully, "is the most dangerous of them all, for all he is so
civil. He is *enjoying* this!"

I hope she was right. I hope those last days of his were happy.
For in less than a fortnight after that visit to us Tom Woodroffe
was dead. And he was the only man in our parts—labourer,
farmer, landowner or yeoman—to be hurt in any way.

Autumn that year had been as unfriendly as the summer. After
a wet September, October opened with a week or ten days of mild
blue and golden weather, with mornings and evenings full of
pearly mist, and languorous, warm afternoons.

But by the middle of the month the east wind, which is the
curse of our weather, was blowing hard from the sea, bringing
heavy clouds and fogs that might have suited the end of Novem-
ber. Bywater was reporting unusually high tides up the river,
and there was every sign of a long, hard winter ahead.

And still the wage disputes were not settled. Sir Edward's
second meeting had, after a more embittered, rancorous course,

reached the same conclusion as his first. And then the men were going round again, this time demanding, not a further consideration of their claims, but a point blank "Bread or Blood."

The landowners and the farmers had retaliated by sending for a troop of Yeomanry from Colchester, and three labourers had been arrested and convicted of breaches of the peace. Shortly afterwards all the men in our neighbourhood had returned to work, though they were still out at Summerfield, not far away. After a week it was thought unnecessary to preserve the state of near-siege which had been making life so uncomfortable, and life swung back into its old pattern.

On the last Saturday in October my parents were invited to Ockley Manor to a party given to celebrate the engagement of Mary, Stephen's sister, his elder by some years. Mother was almost tremulously delighted by her invitation, though outwardly she affected to be indifferent. But she said, "Naturally, Lady Fennel remembers the old days," in a voice which betrayed to me, at least, that she had not until the card was safely in her hand, had implicit faith in her ladyship's good memory.

However, the invitation had come, and the rioting had ended, so that the guests felt able to ride and drive abroad after dark, which was lucky, for if Mary Fennel had chosen to get herself engaged a few weeks earlier she would have had very few guests at her celebration. Mother, rigged out very grand, though complaining bitterly about the old-fashioned cut of her gown, had shrouded herself with pelisses and shawls and climbed into the gig beside father, who, very handsome and, in some incongruous way, apparently dressed in the latest style, had driven away as though it meant nothing to him that every other married couple would arrive at Ockley in a carriage with a pair of horses and a coachman. I envied him as much as I pitied mother.

So Meggie and I were left alone in the house, and we were spending the evening on the pattern laid down by happy ones in the days long since, when I was not considered to be fit company for my parents in the parlour. We had a great red fire in the kitchen which seemed to be the only apartment at Green Farm with a really serviceable chimney, and we had a prolonged supper which included all our favourite dishes. And now, as the weather grew rougher and I thought with relief that at least mother would be safely at Ockley, and that I had not to watch in the stackyard, Meggie and I settled down to make toffee. The sugar and butter were ready, and there were filberts which it was my job—and how pleasant it had once seemed—to crack and split for the embellishment of the top of the "stick-jaw." Meggie (who in deference to my age and the long time which had elapsed since mother had spent an evening from home, had lighted the fire and set my supper in the dining parlour when I came in from an afternoon with Stoner, wet and cold and in a mood for company) was quite pathetically delighted when I said that I would prefer to take supper with her and then sit by the kitchen fire.

"And make toffee, eh? Like old times?" she said, with a wide grin that showed the fewness of her teeth.

But I knew, almost before the evening had begun, that old times are gone for ever and can never be recaptured, and that to attempt to relive even one evening of a childhood which has been, or is rapidly being, outgrown is to invite an experience which brings pain more than pleasure. Now, as Meggie set the pan on the fire and the familiar toffee scent sweetened the warm air, I thought back with wistful nostalgia to the days when Meggie, in a good mood, could make heaven for me; when her tales were the most thrilling in the world, and her rustic jokes the funniest. In all material things this was an evening after the old pattern; but I had grown away from the simple little boy who knew nothing about money, or Mortiboys, or other people's troubles.

Still, for Meggie's sake I must pretend. And to pleasure her further I took off my wet boots and wore a pair of slippers which Meggie herself had given me for my birthday. They were made of felt from an old hat, I believe, and they were fearfully and wonderfully decorated with scrolls and twirls of woolwork and a wobbly B.H. on each toe.

The wind shrieked in the big chimney and we could hear the rain thrown violently against the window behind its cosy red curtain.

"I'm glad that we haven't to watch the stacks to-night, anyway," I said, dragging my chair nearer to the fire. Then I remembered that I ought not to gloat over that to Meggie. For she was on the side of the men, and they had been defeated.

"I'm glad you're not out this wild night, Master Barney," Meggie conceded. "But I'm sore at heart for the poor chaps. Still, we oo'nt talk about them sort of things and spoil our cosy evening." And this conciliating speech, kindly and well-meant as it was, chimed sadly with my recent thoughts about the inevitability of change. Once no question of parochial politics could possibly have come between Meggie and me; now, despite ourselves, we were on the opposite sides of a great gulf. She was on the wage-earning side of it, and I was growing up on the other. That was why we must not mention the matter.

"I think thass beginning to be heavy," said Meggie, lifting the spoon and letting a golden stream pour back slowly into the pan. "Oo'nt be long now."

Just then the gate of the yard slammed heavily against the wall.

"Damn that gate," I said crossly. "I left it on the snack and didn't fasten the chain, so that they could get in easily. But I can't let it bang, it'd be all to pieces in an hour."

"Don't you go out in them slippers," said Meggie. I said "Damn" again and reached for my boots, and had just inserted the toes of one foot when there came a small but urgent tapping on the kitchen door.

"Someone at the door," I said, and took my toes out again.

Meggie pulled the pan aside and said grumblingly, "Who on earth can that be at this time of night?"

She rose and moved stiffly to the door. As soon as she had

pulled aside the heavy curtain which hung there all the winter, the door opened and Jassy Woodroffe edged her way around it.

"May I come in, Meggie, please. I want to see Master Barney."

"I'm here, Jassy," I said. "What can I do for you?"

She ran across the space between the door and the hearth and flung herself on her knees, clutching at me with wet cold hands. The red shawl over her head and shoulders was dark with rain, and beneath it her thin cotton skirt hung limp and soaked.

"Please, please," she said, "take me to Summerfield. If you'll take me to Summerfield on your horse I'll serve you the rest of my days. If only you'll take me to Summerfield there's nothing I won't do for you, for ever and ever."

"Why, Jassy?" I said rather helplessly. "Why do you want to go there?"

"I'll tell you as we go. Please. Father's there and he's in danger. Deadly danger. I know. I'll tell you how I know on the way. I've got to get to Summerfield quickly. I did start to run and then I thought of you. You like father, don't you, and you have got a horse. Please, please do come."

"Where's your mother?" asked Meggie in the hard voice which she reserved for Jassy and other people of whom she disapproved. Speaking to Jassy about Sari, Meggie's voice sounded like a stone hitting a rock.

"She's at Horringer sheep fair. She won't be back till to-morrow. Oh, Barney, please take me! It's a matter of life and death and every minute counts."

"You're not to go," said Meggie, as I began to fumble with my boots. "Do you hear me. Your parents are away and you're under age and I'm in charge here, Master Barney. I'm not gorn to hev you out on such a night, running into danger, gorn God-know-where on behalf of a lot of rag-tag-and-bobtail like this'n!"

"Be quiet, Meggie," I said. If in my rushed, bewildered mind I had had the slightest doubt of the wisdom of such a journey, this crumb of opposition dispersed it.

"Be quiet I will not," said Meggie. "Summerfield is a mighty rough place. Allust hev bin. You ain't gorn to Summerfield, Master Barney, except that be over my dead body."

"Dead or alive, you can't stop me, Meggie," I mumbled, bending over my boots.

"Oh, thank you, bless you! I'll never forget it," cried Jassy, with a shudder that made her wooden shoes rattle on the stone floor.

"Shut your noise you daft little faggot," Meggie shouted. "It'd be a fine thing if the last of the Hattons went out and caught his death of cold, or got in with some rough doings all on account of you and your pa. Be off home with you and tend to your own business. Don't come here bleating and disturbing decent folk."

"Now, Meggie," I said, standing up and stamping my boots into comfort, "get me my greatcoat, if you're so mindful of my health. And remember that Tom Woodroffe is on the same side as you are. You ought to be concerned for him, too."

"I ain't concerned with nowt except keeping you here safe and sound," said Meggie, not moving. So I reached down my coat myself, and from the peg beside it took the thick old cloak, worn by Meggie and mother impartially when they went out in bad weather to feed the hens. I held it open towards Jassy. "You'd better have this," I said. Jassy ran towards me, her big mouth quivering in her white face; Meggie moved towards the door and took up a stand with her back to it. I laid the cloak on Jassy's small wet shoulders over the shawl and we both turned towards the door. Meggie, I thought to myself, would never actually engage in a physical struggle, and if she should I was, I knew, more than a match for her. But as we moved to the door I saw Jassy glance at the clock which wagged a deliberate pendulum against the whitewashed wall. She stopped. I looked at the clock, which showed that in three minutes it would strike eight o'clock.

"I didn't know the time," she said in a small voice. "Father had his watch and the grandfather stopped this morning. I didn't know the time. It's too late now, thank you. It's too late!" I had never heard any words spoken so tragically, so doomfully, in all my life.

"How do you know it's too late?" I asked, and my voice was small, too, hushed by my sense of being in the presence of something uncanny.

"I know," she said. With her eyes fixed on the clock's face she waited. Neither Meggie nor I made a sound or a movement, but the wind threw itself violently against the house and the rain rattled on the window. The clock gave the grating jerk which preceded the chime and then struck solemnly, eight times.

"He's dead now," said Jassy. "I heard the church clock chime just as it happened." She turned her white demented face to me and cried, "He's dead. They've killed him." She put both her hands to her head and, with her face hidden, drew two or three long sobbing breaths. The cloak which I had laid on her shoulders fell off and hit the floor with a soft thud. I found myself able to move again and ran forward, taking her by the elbow and leading her to the chair which I had recently occupied. It was like guiding a blind, paralysed person, for she kept her hands pressed to her face, and strong vibrations, part sobs, part shudders, shook her body so that she seemed incapable of movement. When she was in the chair I took off her soaked shawl, poked the fire to greater heat, and muttered stupid, unconvincing words of comfort. She went on shuddering and sobbing.

"Get the cordial," I said to Meggie. "You can see that I'm not going out, so don't stand there like a fool." For Meggie had made no move. I should hardly have believed that she—always so kind to us—could have maintained such detachment in the face of a child's sorrow, however mysterious its cause. She moved to the cupboard, unstoppered the cordial, a powerful restorative made by soaking ripe raspberries in cheap brandy, and poured some of it into a glass.

I took it and leant over Jassy. "Here, drink this," I said, "it'll make you feel better." But she might have been deaf. She stayed crouched in the chair, with her hands pressed over her face.

Sounds like the rending of calico came from her chest, and her shudders rattled the chair, the poker in the fender, and the things on the mantelshelf. I stood helpless, with the glass in my hand, and Meggie, moving to the far side of the hearth, stirred the toffee with that same air of detachment. I felt awkward and silly, and finally vented my feelings by saying, "Leave the blasted stuff alone!" Meggie looked at me like an unjustly-chidden dog, pulled the toffee pan clear of the fire and sat down in her own chair, vastly injured and offended.

After perhaps ten minutes, incredible stretched minutes which had nothing to do with that wagging pendulum, Jassy drew two great breaths, steadied herself, and dropped her hands in her lap.

"I shall always remember that you were *willing* to come," she said. She lifted her face to me, and I was irrelevantly aware that she was not ugly any more. That brow was no longer a bulging, disproportionate deformity, it was the seat of calm; and her mouth, resolutely controlled, seemed smaller. But it was her eyes, so blue-grey, so clear, as though washed by her tears—though I had seen none fall—which, fixed on mine in a look of indescribable gratitude, made me conscious of beauty. They also made me uncomfortable. I said again, "Drink this," and she took the glass, drank its contents as though it had held water, and then turned that clear, adoring gaze on me again.

"Now," I said in a brisk, sensible voice. "What is this all about, Jassy? Why should you think that something happened at eight o'clock? Did you have a dream? Or was Tom threatened? Or what?"

"No," she said, looking down at her hands, which she had clasped again after giving me back the glass. "I just *knew*. I saw it, you see."

"Saw it? I don't understand."

"No. Nobody would, except mother. She can't see herself, but she understands it. And I've never seen anything until this evening."

"Then you mean that you saw—or imagined—something happening at Summerfield. But, Jassy, that's all rubbish. Come along now. I'll guarantee Tom is home. He was just a little late, and you were worried and got into a state. Let's go. I'll come with you, and if he isn't back we can get the fire and his supper ready."

"I was doing that," said Jassy, "when I saw it. It's no use, Barney. I *know* he's dead. He was killed, just as the clock struck. A man hit him. I saw him do it."

"But, Jassy, you couldn't. You were here at eight o'clock. The only people you saw then were Meggie and me."

I spoke urgently. I was, in the heart of me, scared. I didn't want to believe that Tom Woodroffe was dead, and I just as passionately did not want to believe that Jassy, at some moment before eight o'clock in the evening, could be in a cottage at Minsham and see what would happen at that hour in Summerfield, a good six miles away. I had had my own experience with supernatural prescience, and, although I did my best to forget it, it had opened a crack in my mind. I knew how certainly and how dangerously that kind of thing could smite at the solid foundations of actuality.

"Yes," Jassy said, quite calmly, "I daresay it sounds mad. But it is true, all the same. I was putting wood on the fire. I had everything ready, the table set, and the pot on, and the kettle just about to boil. I didn't know the time. I knew I went from here at five, and I tried not to be ready too early in case the meal spoiled. I had a piece of wood in my hand when I began to see, and I had it in my hand still when I ran out of the house. I was just going to put it on the fire when I couldn't see the fireplace at all. Instead I saw an open space with a sort of broken stone thing in the middle. There were a lot of men, crowding round a man who stood on the stone thing, shouting. I couldn't hear anything, but I knew he was shouting, by his face and the way he moved his hands. And the men were getting very excited. Several of them had torches, and when the man in the middle

stopped and wiped his face, they waved the torches and looked
as though they were all going to move off somewhere else. But
then father jumped on to the stone and held his arms above his
head and started to talk. It looked as though he was trying to
calm them down. I saw two men drop their torches and stamp
on them, and the rest shuffled about as if they couldn't make up
their minds. Then some men on horseback came into the space
and the crowd broke up and began to run away. And one of
the men brought his horse close up behind father and hit him
on the head. I saw him fall, and I knew he was dead. I could *feel*
that he was. It was awful. Hit from behind, like that. He looked
so astonished. And then I heard the clock strike, and as soon as
I could *hear* I seemed to come to myself. And I thought that if
I could get to Summerfield before eight o'clock I could warn
him. So I ran along as far as Clem Barber's, and then I thought
that I might not get there in time. So I came to you. And you
were coming. You would have saved him if you could. I shall
remember that, always."

"I still think you were dreaming. You were tired and fell
asleep over the fire and had a dream. Don't you think that's
possible?"

"No. I wish it might be. But I know what dreams are. You
wake up and know that you have been dreaming. This was
different."

"Well," I said weakly, "if it is true, Jassy, I'm very sorry.
Very, very sorry."

She stood up slowly, but quite steadily, and reached down to
take her shawl from the floor. She held it in one hand and rested
the other on the back of the chair.

"Thank you," she said calmly. "Yes, you liked him. Many
people didn't. The rich men hated him because he tried to make
them see reason, and the poor men hated him because he tried
to make them see sense. And between them he's dead now. That's
what you get for being *good*." The faintest trace of wildness crept
into her eyes and her voice. She let go of the chair back. "For

being good," she repeated. "You'd better mark that, Barney. Because you could be good too. I can see it in you sometimes. But now you know. Don't let being good make a mess of your life, like he did." The little wild flash faded and her face went calm again. "I'll go home now. And thank you once more for being willing to help me. Good night."

I started forward with a hasty muddled protest against her going back to stay in the cottage alone. I made a whole series of suggestions. But she said quietly, "I don't mind at all. I'm often alone. Thank you." She had lifted the curtain and slipped through the doorway before I could speak again.

"Leave her go," said Meggie. "She's best by herself."

"D'you think it's true?" I asked, forgetting my annoyance with Meggie's behaviour in my desire to discuss the thing. "Or will Tom be home when she gets there?"

"She's right enough," said Meggie, quite carelessly, drawing the toffee pan towards her. "I allust knew there was something queer about her. And now me toffee is ruined."

Next day we heard all the story. In essentials it did not differ from Jassy's. The agitation in Summerfield had outlasted that in other places because, in the early days, a farmer had set his dogs on a peaceable crowd of men who had visited him with their request for a consideration. One dog had bitten a labourer, and he had turned and throttled it. The farmer took action, valuing the cur at thirty shillings, and the bitten man had been sent to gaol. His fellows had regarded this as legal discrimination against them, and been very bitter about it. Tom Woodroffe had gone over to Summerfield because, he said, knowing nothing of the law, the men were likely to land themselves in deeper trouble. On the evening in question the brother of the imprisoned man, a simpleton converted into a firebrand by circumstances, had mounted the ruined Market Cross in the centre of the place and urged the men to burn every stack in the district. Tom Woodroffe was advising caution and milder, legal measures when the mounted Yeomanry charged and dispersed the crowd. And it was Phil Rigger, son of Jonas, and nephew of the tailor Calthorpe, who from personal spite exceeded his duty and struck Tom down.

In our house, and at our table, this event shared attention with the account of Mary Fennel's dinner and ball. And whenever it was discussed I could only think of two things. One was Jassy's voice saying, "He looked so astonished." There was something in that plain statement which made Tom's death real to me. And the other was the memory, constantly recurring, of the man himself at work in his shed. I could only remember how, given an order for a plain wooden box, the cheapest of its kind, destined to carry a poor girl's few clothes to her first place of service, he had carefully asked her full name, and when the utilitarian job was completed he had carved, on the lid, her initials and surrounded them with a wreath of daisies, which somehow lifted the dull box into another sphere, making it an individual thing, a thing of beauty. Every time I thought about it I could feel the tears burning in my throat. I reached the state where I could not bear to look at the desk he had given me, and had to put it away, not because it reminded me of him so much as because it made me realize that, to him, a servant girl's wreath of daisies had been as important as my hooded Jennet; and in that fact was implicit the whole of the man.

So dead, he might have done for me what living he had not been able to do, wrest my mind out of its material groove and save my soul. But just then, about ten days after the tragedy, Nick Helmar himself stopped at our gate and bellowed an invitation for father to spend the following Thursday with him, and catching sight of me, he added, "Bring the boy along, too. He'll be company for Dilys, and he can guide you home!" He burst into a gust of laughter in which father joined; for not long before that father, returning home not too sober, had, ignoring Dane's protests, ridden straight into Clip End Bottom and almost drowned himself.

That invitation split our home in two, and half of me was on one side, half on the other. Partly I sided—though not for her reasons—with mother, who was determined that I should never come under the influence of Nick Helmar; and part of me supported father, who held, mumblingly emphatic, that it was time I learned something of polite society. I wanted to visit Mortiboys, yet I dreaded it. And between my own indecision and my parent's arguments, I had little time or interest to spare for other things. So I heard, as it were with the rim of my mind, that Sari Woodroffe was selling everything in the cottage and going back to her own people. Once, it is true, I did have a flash of feeling about that, and saw her, a strange wild creature, trapped by some momentary passion, bearing captivity badly, yet bearing it, and now at last set free. And I did ask what Jassy was going to do. Meggie, who seemed to know everything, said that Jassy had fallen out with her mother over the selling of the furniture and as stoutly refusing to go with her to the Stannaries. So then I asked mother if she would consider giving Jassy house-room and letting her continue to work in our dairy. And mother said "No. She and Meggie don't get on. It wouldn't do to have them under the same roof. If the child likes to live with another family she can go on working here." That answer set me against mother. It lacked generosity. There was no favour entailed in employing Jassy, who worked so hard and was so clean and clever. And a word from mother would have settled Meggie, I knew. But she was not willing, at heart, to saddle herself with an orphan. I saw that, and so my mind veered away from mother and was less willing to please her by staying at home on the momentous Thursday. So even there Jassy Woodroffe had an influence on my affairs.

And when, very late on the Thursday, father and I came home, he reeling with liquor and I equally drunk from experience, Meggie was waiting up for us. She gabbled, as she helped father out of his boots, of the gossip she had heard during her evening in the village. Amongst the things she mentioned was that the Woodroffes had gone—Sari to Billericay, where a fair was in progress, and Jassy to Baildon. Where? To a job, Meggie reckoned. She added, as an afterthought, that some time during the afternoon Jassy had called to say good-bye to me.

I was touched. But I was exhausted from a day of intense emotion. I had, in one short day, in one timeless, immeasurable day, added to my old love and found a new one. I was dazed, more drunk than father. Jassy, and everything connected with my past life, except my passion for Mortiboys, was very far away, completely unimportant. My ears heard of her going, but my heart was deaf.

Book Two
COMPLAINT FROM LESBIA

"She was a person of some education. . . ."

So this story is told by ELIZABETH TWYSDALE, *who ran, very successfully, A School for Young Ladies.*

JASSY WOODROFFE was brought to me by my old maid, Amy Partridge. I was taking my Senior embroidery class, and I remember, in the way one does remember incongruous trifles, that I was showing Hilda Besson how to mitre the corner of the new altar cloth for St. Giles', which was our special article of work that term, when the message that Mrs. Partridge was waiting to see me was brought in. I fastened the needle and told Hilda that she had better not attempt to go on until I had demonstrated a little more fully. Then I went into the hall, a little impatient at the disturbance, but determined to conceal my feelings, since I owed Amy a good deal. Also it was more than likely that she had brought me a present. Since her marriage and her prosperity she had taken a delight in making me little offerings—a cake made after an old Hampshire recipe; a bottle of wine; a fresh cheese or a jar of honey.

And I was right. For to-day Amy had brought Jassy Woodroffe.

They stood in the hall where, at that hour, the pale afternoon autumnal sun poured through the two windows and the transom. Amy, who was still in her rather ostentatious mourning, looked bigger and more imposing than ever standing there beside the tiny child who wore a print dress of a very familiar pattern.

It had been cut down from one of those which Amy had worn when she was in my service. It had been tucked and seamed until it fitted her perfectly, and it was stiff with starch. And I remember that my first thought was one of wonder as to what Amy was doing with a little girl in tow; and my second was the mental comment, "What a very neat little girl." It was, then, the most striking thing about the child, that meticulous neatness. Her hair was pulled back, plaited in a long tail and then turned back on itself and tied with a narrow, stiff little bow. Her white cotton stockings were spotless and taut; her thick new shoes highly polished. She stood neatly, too, with her back very straight and her head held well, and her feet at the right angle. A very neat, pleasing-looking little girl. Probably, I thought, a young relative of Amy's, sent from Hampshire to taste the charity of the aunt who had, by a late and surprising marriage, become the proprietress of the prosperous little "Red Dragon" inn.

But why bring her here? I thought, as I greeted Amy and began to move across the sunny hall towards my private sitting-room.

"Just a minute, Miss Beth," Amy said, hesitating before she followed me, "I want you to take a good look at this young person."

I did as she requested and surveyed again the small figure, from the top of its smooth black head to the toes of its shiny black shoes.

"That's right," said Amy, her eyes following mine. "There, now the lady's seen you, dearie, you just sit there and wait for me."

The child moved, almost soundlessly despite the thickness of her shoes, and sat on the hall chair, sitting, I noticed, as neatly and compactly as she stood, with straight spine, indrawn feet and hands folded in her smooth lap. Amy and I went into the sitting-room and, as soon as I closed the door—while, in fact, I had the knob still in my hand—she turned and said:

"Miss Beth, I've come to ask a favour of you."

I guessed what it was and was instantly wary. The child was

a relative, and Amy, flown with pride and heady with prosperity, had no better sense than to come seeking a place for her in my school for young ladies! How dreadfully awkward. How tactless of Amy. And how on earth, without hurting her feelings and alienating her affection, could I refuse such a request?

"Well, Amy, you've done me many in your time," I said with more amiability than I felt, "so tell me, what can I do for you?"

"I want you to take that little thing," she said, jerking her head with its feathered hat towards the hall.

"You mean . . . into the school?" I asked cautiously.

"Lor' no, Miss Beth! Would I ask that? I got a bit of sense in my head. In the kitchen, of course."

I tried to conceal my relief.

"Who is she, Amy? And how old? Has she ever been out before? Tell me about her," I said, sitting down and thinking how silly I had been to doubt even for a moment Amy's sense of propriety.

"She ain't nothing to me, in a manner of speaking," said Amy, easing herself into a chair and beginning to take off her tight black gloves. "And I must say that I don't know much about her. She come to my door late last Thursday night arsting if I could give her a job or tell of one. You get a lot of people arsting that at a public house, you know. I was going to shoo her off quick when something struck me. She look at you very straight you'll notice, and she spoke nice, and though she was dressed very poor she was tidy. So I arst her in and had another look at her. Then she told me her name and about her dad. Woodroffe he was, killed in the stack riots at Summerfield about a fortnight ago. P'raps you remember about it. A decent sort of chap, I heard, though he never come in my place. Not that sort." There was an odd note in Amy's voice, and I remembered, with amusement, that until Walter Partridge came wooing, Amy had always had a puritanical dislike for what she called strong liquor and everything connected with it. And it was still plain that, though she had, for two years, run the "Red Dragon" single-handed, and run it very well, she had, in her heart, more respect for those who were not her customers than for those who were.

"And her mother?"

"Not much," said Amy briefly with her old disapproving look. "One of them Stannaries, half gypsy like. Run off and left the poor little old thing. Notwithstanding," she added, with an obvious effort to be fair, "her, or somebody else, have brought the child up right well." She proceeded to give me a list of almost incredible length and scope of what the child, tiny and young as she appeared, was able to do.

"How old did you say she was?" I asked, conscious that I had put the question before, but uncertain whether Amy had answered it.

"She's twelve. Maybe you reckon, Miss Beth, that that's a bit young to be so handy, but I tried her out. Why, only yesterday she baked me as good a batch of bread as you'd find in a day's march. You'd find her wonderful useful."

And it was then, at that moment when some answer was obviously demanded of me, that I first had an inexplicable, but very definite, feeling that I did not want to employ Jassy Woodroffe.

It was completely without reason. Good girls for the kitchen were harder to come by every year. Each generation of working class youth seemed to be more ignorant, less teachable, harder to deal with than the one preceding it. I could, at almost any moment, find a place for a clean, neat, handy girl. And Amy, who had had full charge of my kitchen until her marriage, knew it. I have no doubt that she brought Jassy Woodroffe to me in exactly the same spirit as she would have brought me one of her little faithful presents. I knew perfectly well that I ought to be —and normally would have been—extremely grateful to Amy, who still had my good and comfort at heart.

Yet, knowing all this, I found myself, to my own surprise and Amy's manifest impatience, making foolish and inadequate excuses.

"Are you certain, Amy, that you wouldn't like to keep her

yourself? You could find her work, and she'd be company for you, too."

"Ah, that's true. And in a manner of speaking there's nothing I'd like better. But a house like mine, Miss Beth, ain't the place for a decent little girl. That's no good being mealy mouthed about it, you can't run a pub like a school. Betsy Flitch and Lottie Prout they do draw the men, and they're decent girls *in their way*, I see to that. But if she was there she'd be bound to come acrost them, and that wouldn't do her no good. I thought it over and said to myself, 'No. The school's the place for her.' That's why I brought her. Your girls get a good home and a quiet place, as I know."

"But it seems to me that her gifts are going to be wasted, Amy. You know what I want young girls for, scrubbing and scouring and to do the grates and shoes. If she can cook . . . and do the rest of the things you say she can, don't you think it's rather a pity that she shouldn't go to, well, some old lady like Miss Dimmock, who can only have one maid. She'd be a godsend there."

"I wouldn't let her go there," said Amy stubbornly. "All alone in that great old house, worked to the bone and near starved." She tilted her head and looked at me curiously. "I thought you'd be pleased, Miss Beth. You and me know the new fashioned girls, and I can tell you this is one of the old sort. Real good. Is it on account of her size you don't like her?"

What could I say? I had a queer feeling that Amy and I were on a very narrow path, and that Amy, on the inside, was resolutely, but gently, urging me off into the gutter. I was surprised and oddly weakened by my own indecision. Why didn't I want the child? I had a notion that there might have been something about her which I had not really noticed, but which had stayed in the back of my mind, influencing it. I had seen a very neat little girl—but did she squint or show some other deformity?

"Ask her to come in, will you?" I said.

Yet, when the child stood there before me I could see nothing. Her face was not pretty, but what could matter less in a maid? She had an extraordinary forehead, far too big for her face, and her mouth was too large. But I had, for eighteen years, been dealing with young females, and I knew as well as anyone living that a girl's looks can alter unbelievably between the ages of eleven and seventeen.

And her manner was impeccable, modest, frank, and, in an unusual way, self-confident. She was, in fact, the very girl I would have picked out of any dozen applicants for work.

But I didn't want her. I grew quite flustered with the confusion in my mind. It was so plain that a refusal to employ the child would puzzle Amy and offend her; and there wasn't even a shadow of a reason for such a refusal. I am not in the habit of giving way to my whims, and it was unthinkable that I should turn to Amy and say, "Take her away, she gives me a peculiar feeling. I don't think she's lucky." But, as I realized how unthinkable such a statement was, I knew that there was exactly what something within me wanted to say. I did feel, in that very first afternoon, that Jassy Woodroffe boded me no good. And that in itself was ridiculous. There we were, a twelve-year orphan, seeking menial work, and the middle-aged head mistress of a prosperous school, with that work in her gift. How could she hurt me? Mrs. Whiting, Amy's capable, short-tempered successor, would see that she did not even waste my food, or soap or floor polish.

I took another look at the child and decided that my reluctance to take her was probably due to her dress. It had been Amy's, and it reminded me of the days when Amy, growing old in my service, was apt to take advantage of her position, was growing sour and dictatorial. That was it. Nobody would ever realize how much relief I felt when Walter Partridge fell a victim to Amy's almost obliterated charms. And the print dress, fetched out, cut about, sewn and tucked and starched, reminded me of the time when Amy was a resident tyrant, not a visiting friend.

"She don't eat much," said Amy. "And being so young she wouldn't expect more than her keep and twenty shillings a year, would you, dearie? She could come and drink a cup of tea with me now and then. And it'd be a pleasure to see to her clothes myself."

What could I say except, "Very well, Amy"? That my farewells did not show quite the expected glow of gratitude was made clear to me by Amy turning and saying, "I reckon you'll be glad I brought her along, Miss Beth."

I remembered the days when Amy's loyalty and labour had saved me from the most degrading results of a penurious marriage, when but for her I should have had to scrub and scour; I remembered those days, too, when the school was starting, wobbly on its legs, and Amy had done the work of four women. I relented and said exactly what was expected of me.

I thanked her, quite fulsomely, for bringing Jassy Woodroffe into my house. And turning back to my Embroidery Class I thought how typical of Amy to begin by saying that she was asking a favour and to end by forcibly extracting thanks.

I went back to my class, and all thought of Jassy Woodroffe passed from my mind. During the next few days I certainly saw her, for although Mrs. Whiting was competent and, I think, honest, I am one of those women who believe in keeping an eye on everything. But now that the moment of deciding whether to employ the child or not was over, I had no further interest in her so long as she performed her duties. I should think that it was quite six weeks before I was called upon to give Jassy my full attention again.

It was cold weather and near the end of the term. I was spending the evening in Katharine's room, as I almost invariably did. It was not until long after that it went through my mind that there had been something significant in my regular climbing of the stairs, carrying my work and settling down by Katharine's fire, prepared to stay silent if she was working, or to talk as entertainingly as I could if she were in a mood for conversation.

When I did notice the significance I thought bitterly—yes, it is always the dog who is allowed into the parlour, never the master, who for a favour spends an hour in the kennel. But that is neither here nor there. At that time, the December after Jassy's coming, those evenings by Katharine's fire were the happiest part of my day.

Katharine was writing at her desk and I was putting the last finishing touches to the altar cloth. Suddenly Katharine hunched her shoulders and said, "It's cold, Beth. Put on another log, will you?"

I peered into the queer basket of African native workmanship which Katharine had bought at a missionary bazaar and insisted upon using for her logs, though it was ugly and took up a great deal of room, and saw that it was empty. I rang the bell, rather angrily. Katharine's comfort was my nearest and dearest concern, and I was annoyed to find that on this bitter December evening she had been left without fuel. Suppose, I thought, this had been an evening when I was playing whist at Mrs. Dulcimer's, or had visitors of my own: Katharine would merely have looked into the basket, seen it empty and gone back to her writing, too remote or indolent or careless to ring her bell, and she would have caught cold, perhaps even been ill.

A gentle tap interrupted my increasingly furious thoughts, and there was Jassy, saying quietly, "You rang, ma'am?" to Katharine.

"No," I said. "I did. I'm very much annoyed to see that Miss Hamilton's log basket has not been filled this evening."

"I'm sorry," the child said, and moved forward with that odd soundless grace which I had noticed before, and lifted the thing by its ugly out-sticking handles, which always reminded me of a yokel's ears.

"Saying you're sorry isn't enough," I said, and something—heaven knows what—made me add with unusual spitefulness, "Mrs. Partridge spoke so highly of your ability that I can only attribute such a lapse to carelessness. Don't let it occur again."

The mite changed colour and set the basket down. Something about that sudden pallor and the way the basket went down prepared me for insolence, and something else, in me this time, rose to meet it. I was prepared to make an issue of this moment. Why? But she said, with a gentle politeness behind which some other emotion lurked:

"This room isn't usually my concern, ma'am. Daisy is crying with toothache, so I answered the bell."

Then I was aware that Katharine had stopped writing and was staring at us.

"Very well, fill the basket," I said. "And make haste. The fire is very low."

She lifted the basket and went away. Katharine, with her pen still in her hand, twisted on her chair and said:

"What girl is that, Beth?"

"One of Amy Partridge's finds," I told her. Katharine and Amy had never got on well, and so I was impelled to add, "She is a very good little girl." But even as I said it I thought, why did she set the basket down in order to answer? There was something subtly truculent about that gesture, as though for two pins she would have refused to fill it at all.

"She came last week one evening," said Katharine, screwing her short-sighted eyes to look at me. "I find her extremely fascinating, Beth. Her movements. Have you noticed?"

"Yes. Girls are usually so clumsy. Even our girls—in school I mean."

"I wonder," Katharine said, "would it cause a lot of shifting and bother if I had her instead of Daisy to look after this room."

"Well," I said in the voice of slightly facetious indulgence which I often used towards her in order to cover more real emotion, "I daresay it could be arranged." And then, as soon as I had said it, I thought sharply—you agreed to that out of habit; it was a stupid thing to do. But why? Why shouldn't Katharine have the best? Why shouldn't she have the quietest, most capable little maid? Why? There was no answer. No answer at all. And within a moment Jassy was back, her slight figure braced against the weight of the heavy basket.

As she set it down I said, "Thank you." But Katharine, reaching out with her hand which held the pen, halted the child on her way back to the door.

"In future," she said, "you're going to look after me. What's your name?"

"Jassy Woodroffe, ma'am."

"What? What before Woodroffe?"

"Jassy."

"Jassy. Is that a name? What does it mean?"

"It is short for Jacinth, ma'am. I was named after a stone that is mentioned in the Bible. In the Book of the Revelation."

"Ah, yes. I remember," Katharine said. "A list like a poem. I knew it once. 'The first foundation was jasper; the second, sapphire; the third a chalcedony; the fourth an emerald.' Lovely names. Well, Jacinth—but I shall call you Jassy like everybody else—good night."

"Good night, Miss Hamilton. Good night, ma'am."

She closed the door softly and I began to set the logs endways on the dying fire. The flames leaped upwards. Katharine left her desk and came, rubbing her thin hands together, towards the glow and the warmth.

"You never told me," she said.

"Told you what, Katharine?"

"About her," she said, with an inclination of her head towards the door.

"About Jassy Woodroffe?" I asked in genuine astonishment. "But why should I? I never tell you about the kitchen staff or anything of that kind."

A curious, dreamy expression dawned upon Katharine's face.

"Kitchen staff, no. God spare me that! But a nymph, Beth. Surely you saw that. Why, even her voice is full of wood smoke. Wood smoke; Woodroffe. Marvellous. And Jacinth to crown all. Hyacinth. No. The extra letter spoils it. Jacinth stone. Her eyes should be blue. Are they?"

"How on earth should I know?" I asked, a trifle impatiently. "I don't engage girls for their eyes. Or their names."

"Perhaps you should. Perhaps that is the secret. That one I have now—Daisy Snell. What could one expect of Daisy Snell? I shall expect a good deal of my nymph, Beth."

"Well," I said, "don't go calling her a nymph to her face, Katharine; or asking her if her eyes are blue. You'll spoil her if you do, you know. Girls don't understand that kind of thing. They think you're soft and take advantage."

"Oh, of course," Katharine said more briskly, and with a certain air of closing the subject. "I know that. It was, just for the moment, the combination of those names and that peculiar grace. Don't grudge, Beth. Delight comes rarely."

She leaned forward, rubbed her hands in the flame light, and then went back to her desk. I put in the last stitch and folded my work. Then, leaning back in my chair, I looked across the room to the circle of lamplight in the centre of which Katharine was sitting.

The lamplight was cruel. It showed how the years had hollowed her cheeks and eye-sockets and dimmed the flaming russet of her hair until it looked as though a film of ashes rested on it. A lover—in the ordinary sense of the word—a lover would have been sad at that moment, staring through the lamplight at the wreck of the beauty which had once been hers. But I had never loved Katharine for her beauty; I had been the pretty one, always; and that made what had happened to me the stranger, the less easily explained. I could well imagine how some plain, lumbering woman might fall in love with another who had beauty and liveliness. Why should I . . . ? But there was no sense in going over again. I had, as a rosy, flaxen-haired, spoilt little girl of nine years old, incurred an infatuation for this pale, red-haired half-cousin of mine, who had been sent home from India because the climate was killing her; and I had never shaken myself free of it. To think about it now was foolish. Yet there seemed to me something that demanded thought, and I looked away from Katharine to the fire and tried to remember. Ah, yes. She had said, "You never told me," when she was speaking about Jassy Woodroffe; rather as though she had expected me to run to her with the news that I had engaged a new kitchen maid. And that set me wondering. Did Katharine feel, perhaps, that she was not consulted enough? But that was nonsense, too. She loathed all practical affairs, and it was my duty, as well as my delight, to shoulder all that side of the business of keeping school. When we first set out in partnership it was agreed that I should attend to all the housekeeping, interview parents, supervise the girls' food and clothing and general well-being; while Katharine taught what and how she pleased, and for the rest remained in her sitting-room, as private and comfortable as a gentleman in his study. That was the arrangement, and I had adhered to it. It had worked perfectly for eighteen years. But to-night she had said, "You never told me"; and she had leaned out towards that child and said, "In future you're going to look after me." She shouldn't have done that. It was for me to say. Suppose I had taken up one of her girl's exercises and marked it?

I pulled myself together, mentally and physically, sat up in my chair and resolutely banished such thoughts. It was near the end of the term and I was needing a holiday. That must be it. It was unlike me to be introspective and resentful of trifles. With Katharine, too!

I don't think that Jassy Woodroffe was mentioned again until the Easter term was within a week of its end. Spring was early that year and the weather was warm. Amy had brought me an armful of daffodils from her garden, and I had put half of them in a glass bowl and had carried them up to Katharine's room when I went on my usual visit. I remember standing by her table, gently moving back into place the heads which had massed together during the journey upstairs. Katharine, as usual, was busy amongst piles of papers, and as I stood back from arranging the flowers, she patted some loose sheets into place and looked up.

"Beth," she said, "I want to take Jassy Woodroffe into school after the holiday. As a pupil, you know."

"What?" I said. I could hardly believe my ears, and my frank incredulity certainly rang in my voice.

"You sound astonished. Is it such a fantastic suggestion?"

"Fantastic?" I said. "It's unthinkable."

"Why?" Her tone was mild and questioning; but I had the idea that it was adopted merely in order to mislead me, so that I might voice the obvious objections only to have them disposed of—like setting up skittles for another person to knock over.

"You don't need me to tell you why, Katharine. What would you say if anyone suggested introducing a kitchen maid into school?"

"That would depend upon the girl, surely."

"Not at all. You couldn't do it with *any* girl. As much for her sake as for anything else. What do you imagine the other girls would say and do about it?"

Katharine shrugged her thin shoulders; the expression of contempt which she often wore when talking of the pupils was strong on her face.

"I am indifferent to what they might say, and I am prepared to deal with anything they might do."

"Prepared to deal . . ." I repeated. And it flashed through my mind that she must be ill, demented, delirious. Prepared to deal . . . Why, she had never dealt with anything in her life.

"It wouldn't be fair to the child herself, Katharine. She's cleaned their shoes, handed their plates . . ."

"A social injustice that I propose to remedy, Beth. She understands all that. I've explained it. Actually, I think there'll be

(91)
165025

less difficulty than you imagine. The girls seem to like her very well."

"How can you know that?"

"I've seen them in conversation with her—laughing, you know the way they go on."

"You should have told me then. I dislike the girls and the maids being friendly. It always means that they're bringing in indigestible food, or carrying notes, or some such nonsense."

Katharine gave a loud, fierce sigh. Her thin red eyebrows ran together until they made one line, and she waited—a disconcerting trick she had at times—for an appreciable time before making a fresh start. Until someone of whom you are weakly fond has tried that trick on you you have no idea how discomforting it can be.

"Have you, Beth, any personal opinion upon this subject?"

"Yes," I said, "I have. We've always been very particular about the girls we accept. We agreed that Miss Gould made the mistake of taking anyone who could pay the fees, and so her school lost caste. We've built it up again. Why, only last term I refused to take the little Jepson girl, Jepson, the miller, you know."

"I don't know. I'm sure I never had anything to do with it. Could even a miller's daughter be more stupid than Mamie Pierce? Or more exasperating than Dilys Helmar?" She closed her eyes and put her hand to them, her thumb at the corner of one, her first finger at the corner of the other, in a gesture that conveyed a curious combination of arrogance and weariness.

"I'm sure I don't know what we're talking about," she said, when she had comforted her eyes for a moment. "I happen to have discovered that this child has a mind worth educating. I propose to try my hand at it. God knows I spend time and energy on dolts and fools. It'll be a pleasure to teach somebody worth teaching."

"What do you imagine the parents will say when the girls

(92)

tell them that one of the kitchen maids is now in the classroom?"

"I've no idea."

"Well, I have. I can imagine it very well. I shall have nothing but complaints and withdrawals. It's all very well for you, Katharine, to take this high-handed attitude about it. The school is our livelihood, after all; and the parents make the school possible."

I said that in a reasonable, if argumentative way. I did not intend to provoke her. But she was suddenly furiously angry and, in anger, the living image of the fiery, red-headed old Scotsman who was our mutual relative. "Send them along to me!" she shouted. "I'll tell any pie-faced piffling parent that this is my school, and if they don't want their drooling offspring in it they can take 'em away. God knows there're brats enough in the world. We'll get some new ones whose shoes Jassy hasn't cleaned. I could do with a clean sweep."

"Katharine . . . !" I began.

She put up one hand.

"Beth, please. Any more of this and I shall be angry. I think you might let me have my way for once. Just once."

"Have your way?" I gasped. "But, dear, you always have your way. Come, Katharine, you must admit that. Nobody ever crosses you."

"You do," she said, still angrily. "I make a simple, sensible suggestion regarding a matter that is important to me, and you instantly start to make a coil about it, dragging in the possible opinions of a lot of middle-class dunderheads, and talking about some miller I never heard of. It's intolerable."

I just gaped at her. I had known for almost a lifetime that she had the easily irritated temper of the constitutionally nervous person, but she was usually too indolent to display her anger. And then it occurred to me that she was, over this matter of taking a maid into the school, more actively and nearly concerned than she had been over anything for years. She was, in fact, so set upon it that even my mild reasoning was fiercely resented. And I had, after all, only ventured an opinion for which I was asked; and I was only pursuing a policy which had worked admirably for eighteen years. My feelings were deeply injured.

"I had no intention of crossing you," I said. "I should be the last person to deny that you had a right to bring anyone you liked into your school. For it is, we know, your school. I'm only sorry that you should find it necessary, after eighteen years, to remind me of the fact."

"Now you're angry," she said, suddenly retreating into her usual helpless, slightly puzzled manner. "I didn't mean anything by calling it my school. God knows it's the last thing I should ever be possessive about. I only wanted to make it clear that by taking Jassy as a pupil I am within my rights."

"Very well," I said, mustering my dignity. "You'd like me to arrange for her for next term?"

"Please, Beth. But not now, naturally." For I was going towards the door. I knew that in a few moments I should be in tears, and it annoyed Katharine to see me cry.

"I've remembered something that I must do," I said.

I went and sat in my own room. The words "This is my school," rang in my ears. Of course it was her school. It had been bought with her money. But it was Katharine herself who had suggested that I should assume the responsibilities and position of Head of it.

"How should I know when somebody needed a pill? Or how many rice puddings to order? Besides, the mothers will like to leave their precious darlings with a nice respectable widow with charming manners." She had said that herself. And for eighteen years I had worked and planned, cajoled, reproved, interviewed, soothed and supervised all on her behalf. Now, over the question of Jassy Woodroffe, Katharine could flash round and say, "This is my school." It was like laying bare a sharp and dangerous rock.

I wept with self-pity. And weeping, remembering how Katharine had spoken to me, remembering how my opinion had been swept aside, I began to hate the real culprit, Jassy Woodroffe.

Within the next few days I received evidence that Katharine, so remote and indolent, had been nearer the heart of the school than I, who seldom considered anything else. For two days after that momentous interview Dilys Helmar came, in the hour between lessons' end and supper, and knocked on my door.

I had, during all my years of acting as Head in Katharine's school, sedulously avoided having favourites amongst the girls, and although, being human, I was bound to have preferences, I had always concealed them. But Dilys Helmar was very dear to me. If I could have been given a miraculous power to re-arrange my life I should have Katharine for my husband and Dilys for my daughter. It was, I must admit, odd that I should be fond of two such extremely different people—Katharine so clever, bookish and eccentric; Dilys so lovely and silly. But there it was. If a fire had broken out in school I would have saved Katharine first and Dilys second.

Dilys had come to us about a fortnight after her mother had gone off with another man. She was a delicate, sensitive, rather precocious little girl, and the upheaval in her home life had affected her badly. During the last summer holidays she had been ill—and, I think, neglected—and had not been able to return to school until the middle of the term. During that absence I had often thought about her, left to the care of servants, I was sure. I had once seen her father, and he had impressed me most unfavourably. Since her return to school I had kept a very watchful eye on her.

She came, on this evening towards the end of the Easter term, into my sitting-room and stood, rather nervously, just inside the door. I said, "Come to the fire, my dear, and sit down." I pointed to a stool. She sat down and I looked at her, half appreciatively, half professionally. Yes, she looked a little less fragile, a little less nervous; and, having satisfied myself upon that score, I could take delight in the lovely shape of her face, the golden halo of her hair, the lustrous softness of her great golden-brown eyes. She was the loveliest little girl we had ever had in school.

"Well, Dilys," I said, "what have you come to see me about?"

"About Jassy Woodroffe, Mrs. Twy-Twysdale, please."

"Oh, what about her?" I asked, and I thought, so it's starting! The girls had heard the news and talked it over and sent Dilys —as the most important pupil in school, to make a protest. And, I thought angrily, I shan't attempt to deal with it. I shall turn it over to Katharine; she was the one who spoke so boldly about dealing with complaints.

"We d-d-d-didn't think she'd have any c-c-clothes."

She opened one of her clenched hands and held out to me a little netted purse, quite heavy by the look of it. "So p-p-please, we made a little c-c-collection, and will you g-g-get her some?"

"Well," I said, completely astonished, "it's very kind of you, Dilys, very kind of all of you. But I think that Miss Hamilton and I will be able to deal with her clothes. We hadn't really thought about them yet. Jassy must be quite a favourite with you for you to have thought about making a collection."

"Oh, yes. She's very am-m-musing," said Dilys, with one of her lovely smiles.

I was visited again by that same spitefulness which had made me snap at Jassy herself about the unfilled log basket.

"Isn't it a pity," I said, "that you can't master your stammer, Dilys? It doesn't matter much now, but later on, when you are a young lady, it will be a terrible handicap. I thought Miss Ogilvy was going to give you voice exercises."

The delicate wild-rose colour on her oval cheeks deepened painfully, and I felt a certain remorse at having vented my spite against Jassy, whom I hated, upon this child, of whom I was fond.

(96)

"She d-d-does, Mrs. Twysdale. I am better, indeed I am. It's only when I'm ex-excited."

"Am I to understand that you are excited about Jassy's entering school?"

"Yes," she said, speaking very slowly and carefully. "It is like a story, isn't it? It hasn't happened before. We thought she would look nice in a red dress."

She stood up as she spoke and, coming towards me, laid the little purse gently in my hand.

I suddenly thought that I understood. The girls had evidently adopted Jassy Woodroffe just as they might have adopted and pampered a stray kitten. That remark about a red dress was very significant. It reminded me that our girls had most of them outgrown their dolls, and the next objects of that kind of affection—their babies—were still far away in the future; but the instinct to be fond of something small, and to dress it, was active in them because they were female.

"We'll see about the dresses," I said, "though I can't promise that I shall use your money. And Dilys, here is something that I want you to remember, and to tell the other girls. Jassy will be happier and derive more benefit from school if you don't spoil her. The kindest thing you can do is to treat her exactly as though she were a new pupil you had never seen before. Do you understand that?"

"Y-yes, Mrs. Twysdale. I think so."

"And now, tell me, have you had any more headache lately?"

A guarded, almost secretive look came over the lovely little face like a shutter.

"I'm better now, thank you," she said. I saw her eyes look towards the door. A kind of anger seized me—oh, go along then, I thought; go back and talk over Jassy Woodroffe's dresses, and next time your head aches don't expect sympathy from me.

"I'm glad to hear that," I said. "Good night, Dilys."

But when she had gone, with a last smile of remarkable sweetness, I sat for some moments thinking about Jassy Woodroffe. It was an absurd thought, but it seemed to me that, without knowing, and certainly without intending it, that mite of a child had poisoned my relationships with three people. I should always feel some resentment towards Amy, who had forced me into employing her; I should never forget that the nearest thing to a quarrel between Katharine and me had been on her behalf; and now I was annoyed with Dilys.

I remembered my first foolish feeling that Jassy was not lucky to me. Suppose there was something in us more perceptive than our reason; older than thought; more direct than sense? Suppose I had been warned, but, relying upon reason and thought and sense, had disregarded the warning because it came from a quarter which I could not identify. What then?

I put the ridiculous thought from me.

Once, in the school's early days, we had an assistant named Alicia Copping—a youngish, capable, willing woman, but an insufferable colleague because she was such an unmitigated bore. I could never exactly point to the root of her capacity to bore until one day Katharine said, "That woman is a natural bore; she mentions *everything*." It was, like most of Katharine's sayings, pungent and shrewd; and after Miss Copping had gone from us we would jokingly refer to Coppingising. I should be guilty of it if I recalled or related every little thing about Jassy Woodroffe during the years she was in school.

But certain things stand out, painful and unforgettable.

She ended my evenings in Katharine's room.

I went up, as usual, one evening after supper, prepared to drink tea, and to talk if Katharine felt like it, or to work quietly if she were reading or writing, and saw, as soon as I opened the door, Jassy Woodroffe seated at the desk. She had some books spread out before her and another in her lap, supporting a sheet of paper upon which she was writing. Her heels were hooked into the rung of the chair, and her face, bent over the paper, was parallel with her lap.

Such a posture, since it must inevitably lead to rounded shoulders, a sagging neckline and a protruding chin, was forbidden in school, and almost automatically I paused by the desk, moved away a book, lifted her paper to the cleared space, and said, "Never sit like that to write, Jassy. And put your feet on the floor."

I had spoken quietly, but my voice, or my presence, had shattered something within the room. It was as palpable as though I dropped a glass on a brick floor. The child looked up with a glance so cold and hard that it was almost one of hatred, and Katharine, looking round her chair back and blinking towards me, looked like someone just wakened from sleep. Never in my life had I been so conscious of being an intruder.

"Oh, hullo, Beth," said Katharine, almost in a whisper. She motioned me towards a chair with a gesture too vague to be called a nod. I sat down, put my feet on a footstool, and took out my work. I had a feeling that I was unwelcome, but I ignored it. I had been spending my evenings here in this room before Jassy Woodroffe was born; I was not going to break a habit on her account.

It irked me even to preserve silence; after all, she had the whole day to study in. However, I worked silently until three-quarters of an hour had been measured on the face of Katharine's clock. Then I cleared my throat and said in a deliberate, normal voice:

"Miss Hamilton, there was a matter which I wished to discuss with you."

Katharine, turning her head and speaking as though to a sleep walker, said softly, "Jassy. Jassy. I think you'd better leave off now."

There was a distinct and audible sigh. Then the sound of papers being sorted and books closed and replaced. Then a deep voice said:

"Thank you very much for letting me work here. Good night, Miss Hamilton. Good night, ma'am."

We bade her good night, I briskly, Katharine with a kind of lingering fondness.

"Well, Beth," she said, as soon as the door was closed, "what was this urgent matter?"

"Urgent matter? Oh, nothing. I thought it was time she went away. I hadn't anything of importance to say, but I was tired of sitting mute. What was she doing?"

"Making up for lost time. You see, in some ways she's very backward. I told her she could come here and read a little in the evenings."

"But that's disturbing you. She could read in the Small Classroom. That's never used in the evenings."

"It isn't heated either."

"We could keep the fire in, if this extra study is essential."

"She doesn't disturb me," said Katharine, with—or did I imagine it?—the slightest possible emphasis upon the first pronoun. "I fancy concentration must be contagious. I've worked better myself to-night than for a long time."

"In fact, I disturbed you both."

Katharine looked at me with some embarrassment.

"Sewing isn't quite the same thing," she said evasily. "I always feel that you would rather talk, Beth. So even when we're quiet I have a kind of—well, almost guilty feeling."

"You should have told me that before," I said.

"One gets into habits . . ." It was said in a curiously inconclusive way, but it was more eloquent than most completed sentences. All my skin went hot. Years and years and years I had been going to Katharine's room in the evening, never thinking, but concluding that I was welcome. I had sat for hours resolutely restraining my chatter and she had been conscious of strain all the time.

"I'm sorry, Katharine," I said. "I'd no idea. As you say—habit. But that can be altered. What would be your suggestion?"

"Suppose you left the bookworms together until half-past nine, and keep tea back till then. Then we could drink it together and have our little talk. Would that suit you?"

"Perfectly. You should have suggested that before, Katharine. Surely you know that I only want to do what suits and pleases you."

She looked at me curiously. "Such knowledge often nips suggestions in the bud, Beth."

So after that I spent most of my evenings alone until half-past nine, except on the occasions when I invited Miss Ogilvy or Miss Smithers, whichever was not on duty, to sit with me, or went out to Mrs. Dulcimer's. And my life was that much duller and poorer, and my hatred of Jassy Woodroffe mounted steadily.

Still, for a little while, there were the holidays. I had always looked forward to them, for then I had Katharine absolutely to myself. And we could shake off our dignity and our responsibilities and get back, in a way, to those days of childhood in Hampshire when we should have laughed and stared incredulously at the idea of being school-marms, carefully calling one another Miss Hamilton and Mrs. Twysdale.

We had established a regular routine for holidays. At Christmas we stayed in Baildon, snug by the fire, mildly entertaining the few friends we had made in the town and being entertained by them. At Easter I was usually busy, for we did our spring-cleaning in the holiday, and there were visits from the sweep, and blanket washing, and a thousand things to see to. But often in the afternoon, if the weather were nice, we would hire a carriage from Storey's and take a drive. In the summer we took a real holiday at Brighton, where the family of one of our pupils who had fallen on evil days entertained summer visitors at reasonable rates.

For a year after Jassy's entry as a pupil this pleasant routine was maintained. And I must admit that, in my blindness, I had never even feared that the holidays were threatened. As each one

(101)

came round Jassy went off to stay with Amy Partridge, and I gave her no thought until school opened again.

But during the Easter holiday of the next year, I came one morning out of the parlour with a pile of curtains and covers which were to be washed in my arms and almost run into Jassy, who was standing in the hall. I was not even surprised to see her there, imagining that Amy had sent her with a message.

"Good morning, Jassy," I said. "What brings you back to school this morning?"

"I want to see Miss Hamilton."

Oh, do you? I thought.

"About lessons? About books?" I asked.

"In a way, yes."

"Look," I said, "Miss Hamilton works hard during the term, Jassy; she needs a holiday like everybody else. I can't have her bothered. You run along back to Mrs. Partridge and give your books a rest. If you've nothing else to do you can lend her a hand about the place."

She gave me the hard cold stare which I remembered. But she said, quite gently: "I have been working since six this morning. And I wouldn't bother Miss Hamilton. I've got a book to return and just a question to ask."

The pile of soft material in my arms was unsteady and annoyed me. So did the sight of Jassy Woodroffe, standing there looking stubborn; looking also almost unnaturally neat and fresh in a pink cotton dress and a wide hat tied with ribbon. I spoke sharply:

"Leave the book on the chair. I'll take it to her. And you must save your question for next term. I can't have girls running in and out during the holidays."

"Miss Hamilton told me I could . . ."

"Miss Hamilton is too kind. I won't have her imposed upon. I should have thought that you might have enough perception to realize that you already receive far more than your share of her time and attention. Run along now, there's a good girl."

(102)

She favoured me with another long stare, and incredible as it seemed, I could feel the strength ebbing from my legs; my heart began to pound, and one of the hot flushes which were the curse of my middle age rushed up, suffusing my face, my neck and my ears. We seemed to stand there for a long time, fighting one another with our eyes. Then Jassy turned abruptly, put the book down on the chair which I had indicated, and walked away without a word. The door closed gently behind her.

I went to the service door at the back of the stairs and, since my hands were full, thrust it open with my shoulder. I pushed too hard and, as soon as I was on the other side, it swung back sharply and hit me on the elbow. The pile of curtains and covers quivered and fell to the floor.

Crossly, I began to pick them up, and as I did so I thought I heard the front door open again. Kicking my feet free, I shot back into the hall, and was just in time to see a fold of pink dress whip round the bend of the stairs. A glance at the chair told me that the book had gone.

I went and sat down in the comfortless, stripped parlour. I felt weak and furious. The only thing which would have relieved me at that moment would have been to charge up the stairs, take the little hussy by the back of her neck and bundle her out of the house. I was surprised—even a trifle shocked—by the violence of my feelings. But I could not vent them without risking a scene with Katharine, who was obviously so infatuated with the girl that she had given her grounds to believe that she would be welcome at any time. There was the real trouble. Jealousy more than outraged dignity was causing me this pain.

However, within an hour I was rational again. In future, I thought, I should see that the front door was locked and that the servants had orders not to admit Jassy during the holidays. And, I reflected, this morning's visit could not be of long duration, since dinner was ordered for twelve o'clock. Katharine and I were taking a drive that afternoon, and the carriage was to come at one.

It would be the first drive of the holidays, and I wondered whether I could persuade Katharine to go to Colchester. The shops there were far more attractive, and better stocked than those in Baildon, and I enjoyed seeing them, and the bustle and stir of the people, and taking tea in the Blue Parlour Tea Rooms. Katharine preferred to drive the other way, into the— to my mind—gloomy country on the edge of the marshes. And perhaps to-day, after all, I would defer to her wishes, as a penance for the hard thoughts I had been indulging.

Just before dinner I went upstairs to my bedroom to wash my hands. When I reached the half-landing from which Katharine's sitting-room was reached the door opened, and there was Katharine, with Jassy close behind her. The girl was not in the least discomfited; she met my eyes with a look of supreme serenity.

"I was just coming to look for you, Beth," said Katharine, not even remembering that we always addressed one another formally before the pupils. "I thought it would be nice if Jassy stayed to dinner and took the drive with us. . . . My dear, you're quite out of breath. Have you been working too hard, or is it the stairs? Come and sit down a moment."

For the first time in my life I shrugged away from Katharine's outstretched hand.

"I'm all right," I said. The harshness of my voice frightened me. "Perhaps you'd ring your bell and tell Emily about setting another place. I'm just going to wash my hands. Dinner is ready."

My dressing-table faced the door, and as I entered my room I caught sight of myself. My face was quite white except for two burning red circles high on the cheek-bones; and my eyes were glassy, as though with fever. Small wonder, for I was consumed with a threefold fever of fury and frustration and jealousy. I crossed to the wash-stand, saying over and over again in a whisper, "I can't bear it, I can't bear it!" My hands were shaking so violently that in pouring water from my ewer I spilt it and soaked the front of my skirt. I dabbed at it frantically, and then, turning from the wash-stand, with my hands still un- washed I began to pace about the room, finding some small com- fort in movement. As I walked I framed scathing or pathetic sentences in my mind. I told Katharine exactly what I had done for her in the course of nearly twenty years, how I had served and protected her, pandered to her; how even this morning I had been working hard while she, serene and remote in her room, had been entertaining the girl who had defied me, and had been concocting a plan which was to rob me of the one small pleasure I had counted upon.

I walked round and round, ranting, denouncing and imploring in silence until there came a quiet tap on the door.

"Yes, Emily," I cried, for since Jassy's promotion there was only one person who tapped like that.

"Miss Hamilton said to tell you, ma'am, that dinner is on the table."

I opened the door, ready to voice a decision which was only framed as I laid my hand on the knob.

"Emily, will you please tell Miss Hamilton that I can't eat any dinner, nor can I drive this afternoon. My head had begun to ache suddenly. I shall lie down now. I don't want to see any- one."

"Shall you like a cuppa tea?"

"No, thank you, Emily?"

"Will I draw your curtains?"

"Yes, you might do that."

Left alone in the dim room I turned the key of the door and flung myself on my bed. I lay for a long time, still talking to Katharine in my mind. Then I fell asleep.

When I woke I felt no better, but my common-sense was at work again, and I saw that I should do myself no service by shutting myself away and sulking. I rose, washed, put on my nicest dress, and did my hair carefully. I had been downstairs a few minutes when the carriage arrived and Katharine was back . . . alone.

She inquired sympathetically about my headache and said what a pity it was that I had been unable to take the drive.

"But I ordered it again for to-morrow afternoon at the same time. I hope it's as nice a day. It was lovely to-day. We turned off the Bywater road and went to look at the house where Dilys Helmar lives. I had no idea it was so near the main road, or so interesting. Jassy knew such a lot about it. Apparently part of it dates back to pre-Norman times. I must look it up in Hopkins' 'Survey' and see how much of the entrancing story Jassy entertained me with has a basis in fact. Poor Jassy, I think she rather hoped to see Dilys, but there wasn't a sign of life about the place, and I didn't like to keep the carriage outside too long."

"Have you invited Jassy for to-morrow?"

"No. When we set her down I hadn't thought of ordering it again. A pity. The air would have done her good. Perhaps I could send round in the morning."

"No," I said. "No Katharine. Let us go together to-morrow, please. I've had so little of your company lately, you know. And . . . well, in front of a pupil we have to keep up a certain dignity. It spoils that holiday feeling."

"I'm afraid I forget dignity with Jassy. She's such good company. And full of country lore and sayings. I don't remember when I've enjoyed a drive more. Still, to-morrow shall be your day, Beth, dear. Shall we go to Colchester?"

"Please," I said. And I thought of the beggar in the Bible who supported life on the crumbs that fell from the rich man's table. Loving can be very ignominious.

Jassy was in and out of the house almost all the holiday, and I made no further effort to circumvent her. But there formed in the depths of my mind a hard little bud of a plan. Remembering the impudence with which she had defied and disobeyed me over the matter of that first visit, I concluded that she could not be so meek and law-abiding as she appeared. That action seemed to have within it the suggestion of practised duplicity. I decided to watch her closely; to keep my eyes and ears open and see if I could not seize upon something which, properly presented, would lessen Katharine's opinion of her, or even lead to her dismissal from school altogether. Meantime I must watch myself as well, taking care to make myself pleasant and indispensable to Katharine and endear myself to her, so that when I finally had a case to present against the intruder it could not be weakened by a charge of jealousy or peevishness.

But some months passed before I had a legitimate cause for complaint. It was a June evening, almost ten o'clock, and the long slow twilight was darkening when Miss Ogilvy, with her hair slightly ruffled and a harassed expression on her face, came into my room. Miss Ogilvy took turns with Miss Smithers, our other assistant, to be on duty in the evening, supervising the girls' study and recreation and preserving order.

On this evening she came quickly into my room, stared at me with a boldness very different from her usual meek manner and said:

"Mrs. Twysdale, you really will have to do something about that Jassy Woodroffe. I've just spent an hour with Cecily Drew, she's half crazy with hysteria."

"Sit down, Miss Ogilvy, and compose yourself. What connection is there between Cecily Drew and Jassy Woodroffe?"

"This afternoon, during the walk, Jassy and Dilys Helmar walked at the rear of the seniors, Cecily and Margie Phelps at the head of the juniors, which means, as you know, that Cecily was directly behind Jassy and Dilys. Jassy was telling Dilys about this being St. John's Eve . . . and a lot of silly rubbish about old country customs of looking into mirrors at midnight and seeing the man you would marry, and so on. Cecily, of course, overhead all this superstitious nonsense. Whether she was planning, as I believe some of the others are, to get up at midnight and study mirrors and bowls of water, I don't know. But I do know that she went to sleep and dreamed about it and woke screaming, and it's taken me a full hour to quiet her." Miss Ogilvy drew a hissing, much-needed breath and went straight on before I could speak. "I've often wanted to speak to you about this matter, Mrs. Twysdale, but it seemed none of my business. However, now the time has come and I shall say it. I wonder at your decision to make Jassy Woodroffe a pupil; I disapprove of it, and I say straight out that I think she has a bad influence on the girls. To-night is only one of a hundred little things."

I confess that Miss Ogilvy's attack startled me. It was like seeing a soft white rabbit with pink eyes suddenly behaving like a bull dog. Miss Ogilvy, who had been very fair and had drifted almost imperceptibly into white-headedness, was not unlike a rabbit. She had no chin to speak of, her teeth projected, and her pale blue eyes had reddish rims. I had never known her to criticize a rule, or to question an order; she was as unobtrusive, as reliable and as uninteresting as the chair in which she sat. But to-night she bristled with fury, and her manner was the quintessence of accusation.

"One thing at a time, Miss Ogilvy, if you please," I said, as calmly as I could. "First of all, this is not the first time that Cecily Drew has waked screaming. She is rather highly strung and has occasional nightmares. I don't think we can accuse Jassy Woodroffe of deliberately frightening her. Can we?"

"No. I didn't make that accusation. My complaint was that the Woodroffe child is conversant with, and talks about, many things which the average girl of thirteen, if she be gently reared, knows nothing about. She is old for her years. Her upbringing is questionable, and if my opinion had been asked, as it never is, I should have had a good deal to say about introducing her into a school for young ladies."

I said: "As a matter of fact, Miss Ogilvy, the idea of doing so was—"

"Miss Hamilton's. There's no need to tell me that, Mrs. Twysdale. I guessed it all along. And that brings me to another point.

I've been here long enough to make several observations, and I must say that it strikes me as singularly unfair that Miss Hamilton is the *only* assistant whose opinion is ever asked, or whose wishes are ever studied. I might tell you that that fact has been responsible for many upsets in the past. The rest of us aren't blind, you know. And I don't mind telling you that when Miss Copping had given in her notice she said to me, 'I'm going to teach in a school with only one Head in future.' That just shows you. I've borne it because I like you, Mrs. Twysdale, and I can see that Miss Hamilton is a very clever woman and I get on quite well with her. But when it comes to bringing up a girl from the kitchen just to please one teacher and to plague the rest, it does seem to be carrying favouritism a little far."

"Do you mind leaving that matter for a minute, Miss Ogilvy. Oh yes, I'll explain later. Look, I was just about to take tea. Perhaps you would join me." I rang my bell and ordered two cups to be placed on the tray, and then returned to Miss Ogilvy.

"Tell me, Miss Ogilvy. You say that Jassy Woodroffe has a bad influence on the girls, that she is a plague to you and Miss Smithers—and the visiting teachers too, I assume—and you say that Cecily Drew's fright is only one of a hundred things you hold against her. Can you, will you, explain as clearly as possible exactly what you mean? It would help me enormously if you could."

Miss Ogilvy's truculent expression faded and gave way to one of bewilderment.

"It's very difficult to put into words, Mrs. Twysdale. It is indeed. Like when you say that she didn't deliberately frighten Cecily. She probably didn't; but she had the *power* to frighten her, and she used it. She just is different, and probably for that reason she has a great attraction for the other girls. Therefore they notice what she says and does. And she is far more mature than they are for her age. So harm is done. For instance, do you remember when there was a lot of bother about the Senior table not eating their soup?"

(109)

"Yes, I do. They just refused it, and when I substituted bread and water as a punishment they accepted it with exaggerated delight. I thought it was some kind of fad about soup being fattening, as I believe it is held to be; and since those girls had their figures to consider, I discontinued serving it to that table."

"It wasn't a fad, Mrs. Twysdale. It was because Jassy Woodroffe would not eat soup. And she said, 'If you'd seen it made, as I have, you wouldn't eat it either.' She hinted that discarded pieces from the plates were always scraped into the stock-pot, and after that none of the seniors would touch soup. She may have been telling the truth . . . she may have been lying. But she spoilt the idea of soup for everyone who listened to her."

Miss Ogilvy's expression showed very plainly that she had been amongst the listeners. I felt impelled to say, in self defence:

"Every week four pounds of neck of mutton, or four pounds of beef shin, are ordered specially for the stockpot. I could show you the bills, Miss Ogilvy."

"They wouldn't prove that Mrs. Whiting didn't scrape the plates into what was originally a good mixture."

"No. I'll look into that, though perhaps it might not be such a *very* disgusting thing to do. It's all boiled again. However, I will give an order." I drew my writing tablet towards me and made a note. "Thank you for telling me, Miss Ogilvy. You should have done so sooner. You are so much more in personal touch with the girls. What else have you noticed about the Woodroffe child?"

"Nothing else so concrete, perhaps. In class she is attentive enough; in study hour she is inclined to whisper and make the girls laugh too much. And she tells fantastic stories about her past. One of them concerns herself, how she was going to be drowned by a mob of children and was saved at the last moment by a handsome young man who was the Squire's son. Harmless, perhaps, but palpably untrue, and I am, myself, opposed to encouraging girls to take a silly romantic view of life. You never know. Some of them are senseless enough to deliberately get into a scrape in the belief that a handsome young man will rescue them. There's that . . . and, oh, lots of stupid little things, like pretending to foretell the weather, and cast fortunes for the girls. Nothing bad enough to make a fuss about; but not what I have been accustomed to. And I must say, Mrs. Twysdale, I don't like it."

"No," I said slowly, "nor do I." But even as I spoke I knew that the core of Miss Ogilvy's complaint lay in those words, "Nothing bad enough to make a fuss about." There was—and to me this was the only point—nothing which I could carry to Katharine and prove that my foreboding had been justified. And that was what I wanted; that was what I had waited and hoped for. But it had eluded me. Miss Ogilvy had failed to give adequate grounds for her hatred of this child. For hatred, nothing milder, had transformed the white rabbit into a bull dog. And, as in my own case, it was hatred, not of the child's actions, but of her essence. A feeling of helpless frustration swept me. I knew precisely what Miss Ogilvy meant; I wanted to support her; and I thought ironically that had Jassy been a pay-feeing, ordinary pupil I could have banished her at once; I need not even have told Katharine why. As it was, I was powerless.

I looked at Miss Ogilvy, wondering what to say next, and I suppose my helplessness showed on my face. For suddenly, as if all my lost confidence had flowed across the room and entered into her, Miss Ogilvy stood up, looking more erect and purposeful than I had ever seen her.

"This puts you in an unpleasant position, Mrs. Twysdale. I can see that. In fact, I feel quite sorry for you; though I could have told you, before the end of my first term, that such a situation was bound to arise one day. Never once, in the twelve years I have been with you, have you crossed Miss Hamilton in any way. And naturally you find it difficult to disregard her wishes in this matter, after giving her her head for so long. But if you like I and Miss Smithers, who feels the same about this matter, will go and have a straight talk with Miss Hamilton. After all, we are in the majority, and though we may not be so clever, or so self-willed, surely we could, backed by you, make some impression. . . ."

She broke off as Emily brought in the tea tray and set it down. The moment while the girl was in the room gave me time to think—not clearly, but hurriedly and frightenedly.

"I don't think that that would have any effect at all, Miss Ogilvy. Until we can produce some more conclusive evidence of the girl's bad influence we could hardly hope to shake Miss Hamilton's infatuated determination to educate her. Moreover, unfortunately, I spoke very frankly when the idea was first proposed; so I'm afraid that complaints as indefinite as yours would merely be attributed to my spiteful influence. Miss Hamilton would think that I had conspired with you and Miss Smithers and then sent you to say what I daren't say myself."

I was too confused to realize the implication of my words, but I did so as soon as they were spoken. Miss Ogilvy's face enlightened me. She came a step towards me and then said in a curious voice:

"Did you say 'daren't,' Mrs. Twysdale? You must excuse me if I speak frankly. It's a matter that I've given a lot of thought to, and about which I feel very strongly. Earlier this evening I quoted to you Miss Copping's words about this school having two heads. Now why is it? Why must Miss Hamilton's word be law here? Why does she never take an evening duty; or escort the girls to church; or go with them on their walks; why does she have a sitting-room to herself while the rest of us share? And why, for heaven's sake, daren't you cross her, or even criticize her, about this preposterous notion of bringing a ragamuffin up from the kitchen to upset the whole school?"

It was like the eruption of a volcano, or the bursting of a boil. The words simply bubbled from Miss Ogilvy's meekly-formed mouth, and a blob of froth came with them. She looked mad. And it was suddenly clear to me that beneath her meek, uncritical exterior these questions had been rankling for a long time.

I lost the last inch of my head. Or is it that, faced by any attack, mental or physical, the instinct for self-defence overrides everything else? Either way, I spoke out, senselessly, disastrously. I said, "I think, Miss Ogilvy, I had better be frank with you and give you a truthful answer which will satisfy all your questions. This school belongs to Miss Hamilton. In order to spare herself from the bother of the practical side of it she allowed me to pose as its Head. Actually I have no more *power* in it than you and Miss Smithers. If she wished, she could instal any efficient woman in my place. So you see the position. So far as diet and staff and similar matters are concerned, my word is law. But when it comes to dictating to Miss Hamilton about personal affairs, I am as helpless as you are."

I said all this, looking straight into Miss Ogilvy's face. A series of remarkable changes were taking place there. First she looked like an old cow that had been pole-axed; then confusion and embarrassment replaced the stunned expression; and, finally, she looked at me with nothing less than vindictive loathing. When I had finished she clutched her hands together in front of her hollow waist, stuck out her receding chin, and glared at me.

"I see," she hissed. "I see. So that's how you've deceived me for twelve years. I've been saying 'Yes, Mrs. Twysdale; no, Mrs. Twysdale; certainly, Mrs. Twysdale,' and it meant nothing at all. And at the same time I've hardly let a day pass without making some stab or another at Miss Hamilton's privileges. Really, when I think of the times I've said 'Some people are lucky!' meaning her to overhear . . . well, really, I wonder she hasn't dismissed me right away! Naturally all these things we've resented so much are her *rights*. She was the one we ought to have respected and considered. It isn't fair. I don't know what to think or do. I can never apologize sufficiently. As for this other matter . . . of course, it's her school. She wants Jassy Woodroffe in it, who am I

(113)

to question that wish? Really, Mrs. Twysdale . . . when I think that in another minute I should have been attacking her on the subject. No, it isn't fair. It isn't fair at all."

Even in my wretchedness I could derive a sour amusement from the little turncoat's change of attitude. I could see why Katharine had so often said, "I wonder why Miss Ogilvy stays, she always sounds so discontented." Poor thing, she had shot her barbs at Katharine and always turned a meek face to me. And now everything she had ever said to Katharine or *at* her must stick like choke-pears in her throat. But under these superficial thoughts the main part of my mind was given over to fury and rancour. For almost twenty years I had been the figure-head of the Baildon Academy; now, with my own hand I had smitten down that imposing figure, revealed it as the myth it was. And who had forced me to do so? Jassy Woodroffe. In this one evening's work was the justification of that sly dread which I had felt when I first set eyes on her. My guardian angel had stood by, warning me, on that day when Amy Partridge brought her, and I had disregarded the warning. My punishment had begun.

I pulled myself together, resolute to save what remained.

"Sit down, Miss Ogilvy, and have a cup of tea. We can both do with one. There are two other things which I ought to make clear to you." I poured the tea quickly, and after a second's hesitation Miss Ogilvy seated herself again and accepted the cup I offered her. "Now," I said, "I was compelled to speak frankly to you and in a way I don't regret it. And I am willing to overlook a certain insolence in your immediate response to my information. But the first thing you must understand is that this matter is a secret. It was arranged between Miss Hamilton and me at the very beginning; it was for her convenience, and while she accepts me as Head of the school you must be willing to do so too, if you want to stay here. The second thing is this. It would be very unwise of you to make a display of your sudden transference of loyalty. Oh yes, Miss Ogilvy, this interview has been extremely illuminating. I know that after this you are prepared to treat me cavalierly and reserve your yeses and noes and certainlys for Miss Hamilton. She would resent that, not only on her own behalf, I can assure you of that. By all means curb your criticisms in her presence, though that advice is redundant; otherwise, you would show wisdom by going on exactly as before. Have I made that plain? You must remember that Miss Hamilton and I have been friends from childhood. Long years of loyal affection have bound us to one another."

I spoke confidently. I could see, by the shaking of Miss Ogilvy's hand as she held her cup that my words had found their mark and were having the effect I desired. Now that I had recovered from that momentary madness, brought on by the feeling of extreme helplessness, I was competent to deal with Miss Ogilvy. Katharine might rule me, exploit and defeat me, but that was her privilege, hers because I had given it to her with my love. But I was not having any nonsense from anyone else.

Yet, even as I spoke my brave words about loyalty and affection, even as Miss Ogilvy, in the last stages of confusion, spilt tea into her saucer and turned back into a white rabbit before my eyes, the shadow of Jassy Woodroffe rose before me, monstrous and menacing. A shadow which could threaten and frighten, but which could not be fought, because it was only a shadow.

Next morning at breakfast, which we all took together, I was conscious of Miss Smithers' eye looking at me furtively and with speculation. I knew instantly that Miss Ogilvy had told her something, at least, of the previous evening's interview. But, although I watched for it closely and was prepared to check the first sign, there was no lessening of respect either in her manner or Miss Ogilvy's.

I spent the morning, while I went about my duties, in pursuing the thoughts which had been with me during the hours of a sleepless night. And during the afternoon, acting upon considered judgments, I sent a request that Jassy Woodroffe, instead of going for the usual walk, might come to my room.

(115)

I was aware, directly I had sent the message, of a mounting and senseless nervousness. I had to force myself to sit still in my chair, not wander about the room fingering things. My digestion went wrong and my dinner lay like a lump of hot lead in my chest. And all the time I was arguing fiercely with myself. I had had a complaint about the girl and I had sent for her to talk to her, just as I should any girl in the circumstances. Wasn't that right and fair? What more could even the most devoted partisan wish? And yet . . . and yet . . . I wished I had let the matter slide. Some deeper wisdom in me knew that my only hope for success in this affair was to turn a completely blind eye, an utterly deaf ear upon Jassy Woodroffe and wait patiently for the day when she would tire Katharine, or bore her, or, failing that, simply grow up at last and be gone. That way I should survive her, both at the Academy, and in Katharine's esteem. Interference was dangerous. Yet, knowing this, I seemed to be driven to interfere.

Presently there was a gentle tap on my door and my enemy—for that was how I now regarded her—entered. I kept her standing, and I regarded her deliberately for a moment; it was a method of approach which I had often found useful. Even truculent girls will lose confidence if silently regarded. But to-day, perhaps because I was not completely sure of myself, or because this girl was not like others, it did not work. She did not drop her eyes, but stood still, regarding me; not defiantly, but with a calmness which was even more unnerving.

"I sent for you," I said at last, "because I have been receiving complaints about you."

"Yes?" It was a question, not an acceptance of a statement. That low voice of hers, which Katharine dotingly called full of wood-smoke, was extremely flexible. She could infuse a simple word with a great deal of meaning. That "Yes?" said, "Oh, have you indeed? And who has been complaining? And why?"

"Yes, indeed," I said. "For instance, what is all this nonsense

(116)

that you've been spreading about the way soup is prepared? I should hardly have imagined that you would have suffered from undue fastidiousness in that respect."

"The soup?" she said slowly. "Oh yes. I never ate mine. Having been in the kitchen I knew that Mrs. Whiting will put practically *anything* in the stock-pot. The other girls pestered me to know why I didn't eat it, and finally I told them. I thought it quite likely that they might mind too."

"Such extreme delicacy . . ." I began angrily, trying at one and the same time to snub the little upstart and to remember whether I had ever seen Mrs. Whiting at the stock-pot, and thus confusing myself and leaving the sentence uncompleted.

She interrupted me, answering what I had intended to say, her grey eyes very clear and pale in her biscuit-coloured face.

"I've often lived on very poor food, but I happen to be particular. At home I got it ready myself, and I wouldn't put turnips or carrots in soup without washing them. Nor would I spit in the frying pan to see if the grease was hot enough to fry in. Mrs. Whiting does that. I'd rather be hungry than eat her fried stuff."

My dinner, which had not digested, had included pancakes. My stomach heaved and my mouth stiffened with nausea.

"I didn't know that!" I said sharply.

She said nothing, but "Well, you know now" shone in her eyes.

I was angry with myself for that cry of disgust and weakness, and mingled with my anger was something else. I realized that this child had, in some curious, inexplicable fashion, the gift of making things bare. She had, on the first day I saw her, clarified the position between Amy and me and made me realize that I didn't really like Amy as much as I thought, as much as I wanted to. And it was through her that Katharine had, in a few words, made our relative positions plain. Now she was exposing horrors which had existed, all unsuspected, in what I had always thought my well-run, speckless kitchen.

I wanted to say, all at once, "Tell me more. What other filthy tricks have you seen out there?" and "How dare you mention such things? Even if they were true decent people wouldn't notice them."

I wished I had left the wretched soup till last, but I knew I had fastened upon it as the most concrete complaint I had to proffer.

"That wasn't all," I said, knowing that I was going from bathos to bathos. "Other complaints about you include frightening the young girls with foolish stories and pretending to tell fortunes for the elder ones. I know that your training has been defective, and you are perhaps to be pitied rather than blamed, but surely your own intelligence must have told you that the school is not the place for that kind of superstitious rubbish."

She appeared to be casting back in her mind.

"I don't think I ever frightened anybody," she said slowly.

"Cecily Drew was in hysterics last night over some nonsense about St. John's Eve."

"Not from anything *I* said. I don't think I've ever spoken to her at all. Certainly not yesterday."

"I'm not talking about that," I said, a little wildly. "Can't you realize that it's your general attitude that is at fault? You may not have spoken to the child, but you brought within her range of notice a lot of silly chatter which ordinarily would never come near her . . . the sort of thing that only old country cronies talk about. It mustn't happen again, do you understand that? If you are going to stay here and justify Miss Hamilton's very high hopes of you, you must try to forget your unfortunate past and settle down to be an ordinary young lady; not try to make yourself noticeable by silly stories and sillier pretensions."

For the first time during the interview her facial expression changed a little. Her eyes narrowed and her lips moved. It was as though the whole calm surface of her face shifted a little. She said, quite sharply:

"I never *pretended* anything. When there was nothing there I said so."

"What do you mean? Are you seriously claiming . . . ? Why,

that is even worse. I cannot have this kind of thing in school."

"But I haven't *done* anything," she said on a rising tone. "Dilys Helmar comes from my part of the country and told the girls about my mother being a Stannary. Then they started crazing me to tell their fortunes. Nine times out of ten there was nothing to tell...but now and again...there is! When Hilda Besson was sent for because her mother was supposed to be dying I helped her to pack, she was crying so hard she couldn't do it. And while I was kneeling by her valise I *saw* her mother walking with Hilda in a garden, walking very feebly with one arm in Hilda's and a stick in the other hand. And I told her. I only said: 'Hilda, they may say she's dying, but I'm certain she'll get better.' And she did. When Hilda came back she told the girls about it. That's all."

I stared at her in horror. But for a moment I could find nothing to say. The confident matter-of-fact way in which she spoke of the incident was as impressive as her actual words were shocking.

"It's all nonsense," I said. "You may have had an idea that Mrs. Besson would recover—but to claim that you foretold her recovery is rubbish and not far short of blasphemy. Only God can tell what the future holds." I paused for a second and then said, less violently, "Well now, I've tried to point out to you just where your behaviour, your general attitude falls short of what we require and expect of our pupils. I hope to have no more complaints about you. You have been singularly favoured in being taken into school at all, you know; you must endeavour to repay the kindness you have received by being worthy of it."

I usually ended interviews over discipline with some such homily, pointing out any natural advantage a girl might have—intelligence, a good home, kind parents, and so on—as the reason for good resolutions. And almost always the girl left me tearful or apologetic. But Jassy Woodroffe merely looked at me for a moment and then, with a little perfunctory bob, turned towards the door.

Instantly—and I only realized afterwards that it was as soon as her eyes were off me—I was aggressively angry. I thought of all the nice girls, well-born, gently-reared girls, whom I had reproved, and often for no greater crime than undue levity and high spirits, who had gone from that very door with words of apology on their trembling young lips. In justice to them, if not to myself, I could not let her go away like that. I said sharply:

"Jassy Woodroffe! Is that how you turn over a new leaf? Aren't you even going to say that you're sorry?"

She turned back and walked to my table.

"I'm sorry that I annoy you," she said. "But I do that just by being here, don't I? You never liked the idea of taking me into school. Miss Hamilton told me so. I try to annoy you as little as possible and to keep out of your way. But I can't help being myself, and it would be silly to apologize for that."

It was as though I had been reading, not hearing, the words, and as though "Miss Hamilton told me so" had been printed in thick black type, a shout on the page. I felt sick. Such disloyalty to me, such proof of intimacy with this creature. I looked at her, loathing her face with its pale tan and its great red mouth and horrible eyes, loathing that ridiculous mode of hairdressing, even the taut, conscious neatness of her body. What could Katharine see in the vulgar little wretch that she should prefer her to me, talk about me to her?

I should have liked to shout, to call her horrible names, to smack her on both cheeks of that insolent calm face.

"I have now lost all interest in you," I said, mastering my rage and speaking coldly in order to prove to myself that I could control my desire to scream at her. "I have tried to do my duty by you and to study your welfare. But you are a vulgar, coarse, unresponsive girl upon whom kindness is wasted. In future, whatever you do I shall regard with indifference, knowing that one cannot make a silk purse from a sow's ear."

For a moment I thought she was going to attack me. Her eyes

had a dangerous glitter. Then she swung round towards the door. The edge of my little table caught her thigh, and instead of re-coiling, or trying to save it with her hand, she pushed against it, with deliberate violence. It tilted and fell over. My little vase of flowers, my tea-caddy, and the miniature of my mother fell to the ground. Water and Su-Chong and flower petals mingled upon the carpet.

I knelt down, picking and sorting and mopping and tears fell upon the wreckage. My hands were too shaky to be safe to deal with the miniature's broken glass, and as I stared at them I thought that now was the time to go to Katharine, and then she could see to what a state her protégée had reduced me. I forgot that Katharine hated to see me cry, forgot that displays of emotion disgusted her. I just wanted to run to her and say, "Look what Jassy Woodroffe has done to me."

Surely, I thought, making for the door, even Katharine's doting patience with the little wretch would come to an end now. Even she must see that we could no longer harbour a girl who deliberately pushed furniture over.

I was a little mad, I think. I twisted my sodden handkerchief round the finger which had caught on a splinter of glass and ran upstairs, dashing into Katharine's room as though the devil were after me. She said, "Who's that?" very sharply as I opened the door. But I was inside the room before I realized that she was not alone. I might have known, I thought, halting myself clumsily and feeling that I must scream and scream and scream—for, kneeling on the hearth, with her head in Katharine's lap, was Jassy Woodroffe, crying as though her heart had broken. And Katharine, who had always seemed to possess a fastidious abhorrence of physical contact, was passing her hand over the girl's hair.

She looked towards me as I stood by the door and said in a smooth, quiet voice, "I'll be down in your room in five minutes."

Perhaps she found even Jassy's tears exasperating, for within five minutes she was in my room, staring at my overthrown table, which I had purposely forborne to right. But I had, in the five minutes' grace, mopped my face and tried to regain my composure. The sight of Jassy Woodroffe crying had staunched my tears.

Katharine came into the room quite briskly.

"Now," she said, rather as though she were addressing a refractory class, "perhaps *you* can tell me what all this is about, Beth. Upon my soul, I'm glad to see you alive and well. From the way Jassy is weeping and wailing I thought she'd committed mayhem at the least."

"Look at that!" I said, pointing to the mess.

"I expected worse," she said, stooping and setting the table on its legs. "And your finger? She didn't *bite* you, did she?"

"Would you have minded if she had, Katharine?" I asked bitterly for her callous levity cut me to the heart.

"Oh yes. I bar biting." She looked at me, trying, I knew, to coax me into smiling. But this was no smiling matter. So she changed her manner abruptly. "Beth, dear, don't look so tragic, *please*. I hear from her own lips that she behaved atrociously, and she shall apologize on her knees if you like. But please, please don't make a tragedy of it."

"I don't have to make it one, it is that already," I said. "I little thought that I should live to see myself insulted, all but attacked, by a pupil in this school, and then hear you you standing up for her."

"Oh, but I'm not doing that, Beth. There's been no time, and she wasn't in much of a state for me to give her a proper dressing-down. But I shall do so, I assure you. What I want to know is how it all started and what it's all about. She says she lost her temper when you abused her. Why did you abuse her, Beth?"

"I didn't. I tried to reason with her. Last evening Miss Ogilvy came to complain . . ." I began. I was halfway through my account of that visit when Katharine said suddenly:

"Can we have some tea? I know it's early, but I feel like tea. No doubt you do, too."

I rang the bell and gave the order and went on with my story, halting for a moment when the tea came and then proceeding. When I had finished Katharine set down her cup and said:

"And that's all?"

"Isn't it enough?"

"Enough? Yes." She walked over to the little elbow chair by the window and sat down. "Tell me, Beth, suppose it had been Dilys or Mamie or Hilda who had refused the soup and dabbled in fortune telling, as you call it, would you have taken it like this?"

"I would have reproved them, certainly. And they would have accepted the reproof. Not knocked over my table and spilt my little treasures."

"That's true. But, Beth, we must remember that Jassy isn't quite like them. I've talked to her a good deal, and her early life sounds most peculiar, a radical ranter on one side, a half-gypsy on the other. Then consider her mind, active and receptive, fed until lately upon nothing but the Bible and folk-lore; and then the kitchen, with nobody but ignorant and superstitious people for company. Don't you think that exonerates her a little? No, no, I'm not making excuses; I'm stating a case."

"Her case!"

"Well, she's the culprit; she needs counsel for the defence, doesn't she? Or did you provoke her; do you need defending, too?" She looked at me again with a twinkle, inviting me to smile.

"The worst thing about it is that she says you told her that I objected to taking her into school. That seems to me to be a real breach of loyalty, Katharine."

"Oh dear! None was intended, I assure you. I merely warned her that you were not predisposed in her favour and that she must behave impeccably. I had an idea that in some matters— table manners, for example—she might offend you. Beth, please, don't make all this of more importance than it is. I like the child, I enjoy teaching her, her company delights me; you find her irritating, rude and distasteful. But then you like Dilys Helmar, who to me is the essence of all that is detestable in the female sex —selfish, deceitful, coy and precocious; but if you told her I didn't like her I shouldn't make a coil about it or bring up the question of loyalty."

"There's a difference."

"Where?"

"Dilys doesn't live in my pocket for one thing."

"If she hadn't a home for the holidays, or a friend in the world except you, you might feel like offering her that amount of hospitality. Anyhow . . . I can assure you that Jassy is truly penitent, and if she apologizes and takes any punishment you care to name, will you forgive her?"

"I don't want to punish her, and I don't want her apologies. I want her to keep out of my way and to refrain from upsetting the school."

"I'll see to that then," said Katharine. The lightness had gone from her voice and manner. She sounded tired. I thought, she knows as well as I do that Jassy Woodroffe stands between us like a thick hedge; she seems not to care, but perhaps at heart she does. With Katharine one never knew.

I looked at her; her long thin hands lay along the arms of the little chair; her thin straight shoulders, long thin neck and beautifully moulded head were outlined against the light of the window; her skirt of grey silk shot with purple was spread sedately. I began to weaken with that old lust of the eye which knows no reason. And at the same time my heart was moved, as it always was when I was not angry with her, by her fragility. Age was making me stout and florid; it was dealing with her as it deals with leaves and laces, making her frail and brittle. I thought—she's fifty; with her as with me, life is passing; and her years have been emptier than mine. I remembered that I had had a husband. (And I had chosen him, making a disastrous choice, because he was the only man I knew who had something of Katharine's quality, and I was simple enough then to think that a girl must marry someone!) Yes, I had had a husband, and above all I had my love for Katharine herself, which had given much of my dull work some of the charm of a vocation; and I loved the school. Katharine had only had her books. And now the one thing that gave her pleasure was to share those books with Jassy Woodroffe. Couldn't I accept that?

After all, I thought, with my eyes still upon Katharine, the year or two of Jassy's schooling would pass and we should be left together. I must make no wound which would leave a scar to ache in those after days. I must not allow this alien influence to embitter our relationship.

I felt calmer; happier than I had done for months. I regarded Jassy impersonally, as though she were some nasty little pet animal with which Katharine was temporarily infatuated. That reduced her to her proper size. That made her bearable.

"We'll forget her," I said, rising to pour fresh hot water into the pot.

"That's noble of you," said Katharine in a voice of relief. "But she must apologize for knocking over the table." She ended the sentence rather vaguely and, looking at her, I could see that her mind had wandered. She was staring at the tea-tray.

"I'm just about to pour you another cup," I said.

"I think I'll take *her* one," said Katharine, who had had countless cups carried to her and never, in my memory, carried one to anybody. "Oh, there isn't a cup. Never mind, the basin will do."

I set down the pot suddenly. I could no longer hold it. Utter surprise and fury and a kind of hysterical mirth warred in my mind until I wondered if I were going crazy. I had just thought of Jassy as a pet dog . . . and here was Katharine carrying her tea in a basin. All the suppressed emotion of the last hour found vent upon my lips in a cackle of quavering laughter.

"What's the matter?" asked Katharine, filling the basin and lifting it carefully. "Oh this! I suppose it does look odd. But really she was in a state. This'll pull her round and prepare her for a wigging."

She smiled and moved towards the door.

After that I ignored Jassy Woodroffe as one may ignore a constant nagging pain, not acute enough to be desperate. There were moments when it called for all my resolution to do so; for in the next holiday, when it was time for our visit to Brighton, Katharine decided that she needed sea air and insisted upon her accompanying us. And after that she spent all the holidays with us. She was, I must admit, helpful and unobtrusive, always willing to run an errand, for me as well as for Katharine, polite in her manners, pleasant of speech. But she was there, and she was obnoxious to me.

However, time was passing rapidly, as it does pass when one is busy and has reached middle age. And from time to time I saw a gleam of hope. One such came on the day when Jassy changed her mode of hair-dressing. I remember the morning when I saw her first with all her long black plaits coiled and twisted and pinned across the back of her skull. Ah, I thought, you're growing up, my girl, and your days at school are numbered. You'll go away and find new people to charm and subjugate; there'll be a few letters for Katharine, and perhaps another holiday with us, and then it will end. And I shall still be here. Perhaps then Katharine will look round and see where the real friendship lay.

Most of our girls left at the age of sixteen. The majority of them looked to be married within two years, and that was not so long a time to spend in finding a husband and learning to run a house. Now and then a girl with a vain mother who resented having to produce a marriageable daughter, or a girl whose matrimonial chances were outstandingly poor, or a girl whose home life was peculiar, would stay for another year, or even two. Dilys Helmar had stayed and would soon be seventeen. I suppose it had occurred to no one to remove her. But most girls left at the end of the term following their sixteenth birthday. And Jassy's birthday fell in the Christmas term. I felt certain that I could look forward to her removal from my life at Christmas time.

Almost as soon as the term began I began to wonder what arrangements Katharine would make for her protégée's future. A post as governess in a family or as teacher in a school seemed the obvious choice for her. She had quickly made up—with Katharine's help—the arrears in her education, and had developed, as even I was bound to admit, into that rare thing, an intellectual girl with a usefully practical side to her nature. Her needlework was as good as her other lessons, and if I could have brought myself to give it she would often have had a word of praise from me.

But I did not envy the person or persons who would soon be giving her employment, for it seemed to me that she was bound to make trouble wherever she went. She was, in fact, like a highly flavoured dish which one is bound either to dote upon or to loathe. I was sure that wherever she found herself there would be, close at hand, someone who liked, and someone who hated, her. So dissension was inevitable. But I cared nothing for that so long as she was removed from our roof, under which she had done damage enough. I waited eagerly for some word which would show that Katharine was making some plans for that removal.

No such word was spoken, and September ended. The weather broke early, and it was on a night of violent wind and rain that I woke suddenly and lay for a moment thinking that the storm had wakened me. I always slept with a little lamp, dimmed by an opaque shade, burning by my bedside, for a night call to a sick child, though not of frequent occurrence, was not unknown, and it was an advantage not to be obliged to make a light when my hands and eyes were heavy with sleep. Turning my head on my pillow I looked at the table where the lamp burned and where my clock stood, its face so arranged that the light caught it.

It was twenty minutes after midnight. A bad time to wake, I thought. Just then I caught the rap of knuckles on the panel of the door, cautious but imperative.

"Hullo," I called. "Just a minute." I dragged on my dressing gown and went, barefooted, to the door, which I unlocked and opened. Jassy Woodroffe stood on the mat outside. She held a candle, and by its light I could see that her face was very pale.

"Mrs. Twysdale, it's Dilys. Could you come?"

"Certainly," I said . . . thinking, oh dear, this weather! The winter round of chills and coughs has started already. I turned back to grope for my slippers, asking, "What is the matter with her?"

"I don't know. She fainted a little while ago and I can't get her round."

"You shouldn't have tried. You should have come to me at once." I snatched up the little medicine chest which always stood on my cupboard just inside the door and stepped into the passage.

"How long ago did she faint?"

"About . . . I . . . oh, perhaps quarter of an hour."

It flashed through my mind that never in all my experience had I known anyone to faint in bed, save in cases of severe illness, but I said nothing. I thought I would soon see for myself, and lighted by Jassy's candle we passed hurriedly along the corridor towards the stairs which led to the upper dormitories. I was suddenly conscious that Jassy, who usually moved less noisily than other people, was to-night making more noise than I was, and glancing down I saw, below the hem of her dressing gown, the toes of her stout outdoor shoes.

"Why are you not wearing slippers?" I asked.

"I . . . just put on what came handiest."

"Well, try to walk quietly, we don't want to wake the whole house."

We reached the stairs, and when I put my hand on the rail I was conscious of dampness, and remember thinking how quickly humidity penetrated—or was the roof leaking again. That was all. The next moment I was inside the square room which Jassy and Dilys shared with Mamie and Celia, since they were now the four eldest girls in the school. Dilys lay perfectly still and deathly white against her pillow; the covers were neat and undisturbed. There was a strong smell of burnt feathers in the room and a mug of water, some of it spilled, stood by the bed. Mamie and Celia on the far side of the room lay apparently fast asleep. It struck me as odd that Jassy's moving about, fetching water and burning feathers, had not disturbed them, but I was, at that moment, too intent upon Dilys to have time for suspicion.

But I did say, as I opened the chest and drew out the bottle of ammoniated salts, "Where did you get the feathers?"

"From my pillow," said Jassy.

I raised Dily's head and held the salts under her nose. She sagged like a half-empty sack and seemed as impervious to ammonia as to burnt feathers. Seeing this I reached into the medicine chest again and brought out the brandy flask.

"Empty almost all that water back into the ewer," I said to Jassy, pointing to the mug on the floor, "and then hold it here."

I poured a little brandy into the teaspoonful of water she had left in the mug and, with my left arm around Dilys so that her head lolled against my shoulder, I held her and pressed the mug to her lips. After a moment which seemed like an age of anxiety she gave a little splutter, and then I could feel a difference in her body, as though the half-empty sack were slowly filling. Presently she opened her eyes and stared at me, quite blankly for a second or so, and then with terror. Trying to loosen herself from the clasp of my arm, she said sharply:

"Jassy! Wh-where are you? Jassy!"

I felt again that deadly stab of jealousy. Always in Dilys' previous little bouts of indisposition she had clung to me, and I had remembered that she was motherless, and because of that, and because of her loveliness and a kind of weakness in her, I had fussed and pampered her more than I should have done another girl. Now, bracing herself away from me, she was calling for Jassy Woodroffe.

Jassy stepped forward into the ring of candlelight and said:

"It's all right, Dilys. I'm here. Everything's quite all right."

Dilys looked at her blankly. It was as though a shutter had come down over that first expression of terror. For a second I feared she might be going to faint again. Then she looked at me and said, "Mrs. Twysdale . . . I . . . I . . ."

"It's quite all right," Jassy said again, speaking slowly and distinctly, as though addressing a person slightly deaf or stupid. "I'm here . . . and so is Mrs. Twysdale. I had to fetch her, you know, because you fainted and were such a long time coming round."

There was a note of apology in her voice. I said calmly:

"Of course you had to fetch me. I only wish you had called me before."

I was watching Dilys as I spoke, and saw her great eyes slowly filling with tears—not drawn to them by the fumes of the ammonia salts, for her chin and mouth were quivering, though she was obviously fighting for control.

"Do you feel ill?" I asked. "Have you a pain?"

"N-no, thank you, Mrs. Twysdale. I'm quite all right now. Really, I'm qu-quite all right."

"But you did feel ill, my dear, when you called Jassy. . . . What was wrong? Try to tell me, Dilys, then I shall know what to do for you. Girls don't faint in their beds for nothing. Is it . . . are you . . . is there any reason why you should feel faint just now?" The question was embarrassing to everybody, but it had to be asked. I saw Dilys' wide eyes, with their dilated pupils, seek Jassy's face, and turning my eyes to follow her glance I *thought*, thought, yet could not be sure, that I caught, as it were, the tail end of a nod. Yet when Dilys said meekly, "Yes, Mrs. Twysdale," I thought to myself—yes, it was a nod. Jassy was signing to her to be frank and admit it. And I thought—that's one thing to be said for a rougher upbringing, it makes girls less squeamish about the natural functions of their bodies. I was considerably relieved. I turned to the chest again and took out the bottle of essence of ginger, which, mixed with sugar and hot water, I always prescribed for menstrual pains.

"Jassy," I said, "you're as familiar with the kitchen as I am, and your legs are younger. Run down and make a stick fire and heat just a cupful of hot water. Let it boil and bring up the kettle and a cup with a spoonful of sugar in it."

Jassy said, quite brightly and willingly, "Certainly, Mrs. Twysdale," but Dilys, with her eyes on Jassy again, forming an eloquent appeal which I could not understand, said, "No, *truly* Mrs. Twysdale, I'm all right now. I don't want anything except to go to sleep. Tr-truly I haven't got a pain at all."

"Nonsense," I said. "A hot drink will soothe you and do you good. Is there another candle, Jassy?"

Jassy tiptoed across to the chest of drawers which stood between the beds where Mamie and Celia were still sleeping the sound sleep of the very young and brought another candlestick. The candle which Jassy had brought down with her, and which had lighted the room all this time, was standing on the similar chest between her bed and Dilys'. Being nearer to it I reached out and held it towards her so that she might light the other from it, and as I did so the snuffer loosed from its peg and rolled to the floor at my feet. While Jassy was shielding the new, frail flame with her hand, I stooped to pick it up. It had rolled past my feet, just under the edge of the bed, and now lay in a pool of water, which I saw, as I stared at it, came from a heap of clothing under the bed.

"What on earth have you here?" I asked, laying hand on the pile. Then I dragged it out—two blue cloaks, heavy and sodden, came out first, then a skirt, almost as wet, and then, piece by piece, every garment which a girl would usually wear.

As I lifted out article after article from its hiding-place I looked at the two girls. Horror, and the peculiar look which comes from guilt discovered, were written on both their faces.

· (131)

"Take off your dressing gown," I said to Jassy, when I straightened myself. She did so, and stood revealed, fully dressed; and her skirt was as wet as the one which lay on the floor.

And oh! I thought, if only, if only Dilys weren't concerned in this. And hard on the heels of that first impulsive thought came the knowledge that she was! My pretty, delicate little favourite had been involved in some nefarious adventure with Jassy Woodroffe, against whom my guardian angel had warned me, from whom my every instinct had shrunk.

"Where have you girls been?" I said.

Dilys, with a faint despairing cry, turned and buried her head in her pillow and began to cry. The small, whimpering sound, oddly like that of a trapped animal, held the whole room for a moment. Jassy stood quite silent, beside me for a moment. Then she said, in a loud, almost aggressive voice:

"I went out to see my mother, Mrs. Twysdale. And Dilys came with me to keep me company coming back."

I heard—with another ear than those with which ordinary sounds were conveyed to me—three separate sounds. One, a kind of gasp, came from Dilys on the bed, and the other two, not unlike the first and yet quite different, came from the beds on the other side of the room. Dilys' gasp expressed relief, a relaxation of tension; those of Mamie and Celia were more akin to astonishment.

"Your mother?" I cried, wheeling round to face her. "Where have you been meeting her? And why?"

"She . . ." there was the slightest possible hesitation . . . "wanted to see me. She wanted to ask me if . . . after all I wouldn't change my mind and go with her. She left me a message to meet her. I didn't know, of course, what she wanted, so I went. But I told Dilys about it, and she said she would come with me because the meeting place mother mentioned is quite a long way away, and Dilys didn't think I should go by myself."

It was like—oh, it was like hearing that a pet lamb, with a blue ribbon round its neck, had offered to accompany a wolf cub on an errand through the night.

"Is that true?" I cried, putting a hand on Dilys' shoulder and forcing her to face me.

"Y-yes," said Dilys. "Yes, that is how it was. Jassy wanted to see her mother and I went with her."

And still unconvinced, unsatisfied, I swung round to the two beds on the other side of the room.

"Mamie," I cried, "Celia! Stop pretending to be asleep. I know you've been awake all along. What do you know of this?"

They tried, pathetically, to give the effect of having just wakened from sleep, with "What, Mrs. Twysdale?" and "Oh, ma'am!" and yawns and stretching.

"Do you know anything about Dilys and Jassy creeping out after dark and coming back at midnight?" I insisted.

"Oh, no, Mrs. Twysdale. I've been asleep. I haven't heard anything," said Mamie. "Have you, Celia?"

"Nothing," said Celia, "nothing at all. We just came to bed and went to sleep."

I turned back to Jassy and Dilys.

"Why didn't your mother come here and ask for you?"

"She wouldn't have dared."

"Where did she leave the message? And who conveyed it to you?"

"She—she asked Mrs. Partridge and left the message with her. I'm sorry, Mrs. Twysdale, to have caused such a lot of bother. At the time it seemed the best way—the best thing to do. But I see now that I ought to have asked you. But I hoped you didn't . . . I mean I thought perhaps you wouldn't have liked it. I mean to you—well, the Stannary people wouldn't seem respectable."

"Jassy . . . don't," Dilys murmured.

"Well, it's true," said Jassy, giving Dilys a hard, fierce look. "And truly, Mrs. Twysdale, I didn't want Dilys to come. She only did it because she is kind. I'm sorry. But nothing need have come

(133)

of it, only the wind was so rough and it rained, and Dilys came over faint. So—so I was frightened and called you. I'm sorry."

"I should hope you are," I said heatedly. "Dilys might have died. And after all the pains I've taken to look after her and everything. Why, when I think of what might have happened to her—to you both . . . out in the darkness, so late . . . I tremble to think. Of course, I might have known. I'm not surprised at you, Jassy Woodroffe, breaking rules and . . . and . . . But to take Dilys with you, that is reprehensible indeed. Really, Dilys, I'm surprised at you. You, at any rate, must have known that no young lady goes out unescorted after dark. What came over you?"

"That was why, Mrs. Twysdale. That was why. Dilys was so shocked at the thought of my going alone that she offered to come with me. Please don't blame her. It was entirely my fault."

"So I think. And you'll hear more of this in the morning. For the present, kindly get undressed and into bed. But before you do so, tell me, how did you get out of the house?"

"By the pantry window."

"But that is barred."

"One bar is rusted and lifts away. It's been like that for a long time."

There was a curious, almost accusing note in Jassy's voice, almost as though she were implying that if I had done my duty and looked to the bars of the pantry window all this could not have happened. I experienced the same odd, futile feeling that had come over me months, years before when I tackled her upon the subject of pretending to tell fortunes. Involuntarily I looked towards the bed where the other offender was crouching with the white sheet drawn up to meet her equally white face. In the space of a minute a whole train of thought, at once furious and frightened, sped through my brain. Suppose, I thought, anything should have happened through this night's work, how on earth could I have explained it to Mr. Helmar? This was what came of taking half-gypsy kitchen girls into a school and allowing them to associate with and corrupt decent young ladies. Why, Dilys might have died of exhaustion and exposure.

"How could you?" I cried in a high shaking voice. "Dilys, you should have known better. What's happened to you? How could you suddenly become a party to such slyness, such deceit?"

"It was my fault, Mrs. Twysdale." Jassy spoke from behind me.

"You don't need to tell me that," I exclaimed, wheeling round. "I never expected anything else from you. But even *you*, you that are so clever about other things, might have known that this was no fit errand for Dilys. The dark and wild weather and bad company are nothing new to you. Had you gone by yourself I should hardly have complained. But to take Dilys with you. . . ."

"Pl-please, Mrs. Twysdale . . . I did want to go. And Jassy must have *carried* me from the end of the road. I can't remember anything after reaching the top of the hill. She was . . . she was thinking about me."

And something of justice in my mind added that Jassy had fetched me, and so run the risk of discovery.

"I can't talk about it any more," I said. "I'm far too upset. But please understand that you are both in disgrace. I'll talk to you again in the morning."

I took up the candle and, forgetting the medicine chest, came out of the room. At the foot of the stairs I thought that I should not sleep again that night unless I took two of Dr. Pillinger's Sedative Tablets. And they were in the chest which I had left upstairs. Turning, I wearily retraced my steps. As I opened the door of the bedroom I heard Jassy Woodroffe's voice, rough, forceful:

"Don't be a fool, Dilys, swallow it for God's sake. It'll make you sleep and forget everything."

She had emptied my precious brandy into the mug and was thrusting it under the nose of Dilys, who was crying as though all the sorrows of the world were hers.

The last thread of control broke in me. I slapped Jassy with all the force in my body, first on one cheek, then on the other. She reeled under the blows, then, recovering herself, dashed the mug of brandy full in my face.

In the morning, wakening to Emily's knock, I was immediately conscious that this was not merely another day. This was an occasion. I put my hand to my face and then, jumping from bed with an agility which had not been mine for many years, I went to my dressing-table. I looked a fright. My nose was swollen to twice its size, and as black as a boot, and on both my cheeks there was a curved incision where the sharp, chipped edge of the mug had broken the skin. Well, I thought, even Katharine can hardly overlook this. And I went back to bed—pulling my bell on the way—with a very light heart indeed. For not only had I now a cast-iron complaint against Jassy Woodroffe, but I felt that the worst had happened. My instinctive distrust of her, my long years of foreboding, were now ended. And I was relieved to find that my dread and hatred had culminated in nothing more serious than a bruised nose and a cut face. This is the end, I thought. And when Emily answered the bell I told her, placidly, that I had had a slight accident and should take breakfast in my room. When Miss Hamilton had breakfasted—not before, I said—I should be glad if she would put off classes and everything and come to see me.

Emily brought my breakfast and I enjoyed it as, I discovered, I had not enjoyed food for a long time. I was eating my last piece of toast when there was a knock on my door, and, thinking that Katharine had been very quick to obey my summons, I called, "Come in." But it was not Katharine; it was Amy Partridge, not in her calling attire, to which I had become accustomed, but in a cotton working dress and an uncompromising mob cap on her head.

"I hear you've had an accident, Miss Beth," she said.

"Yes . . . but it's very slight, and I feel very well, Amy. Sit down and tell me what brings you here at this hour."

"I woon't want to worry you if you feel poorly," said Amy. But she took a chair by the side of the bed and was obviously bursting with news.

"I'm quite well enough to hear anything you have to say."

"Well, thass like this here," said Amy, tucking a stray end of hair into her cap and looking at me with the excitement with which members of her class invariably betray when conveying bad news. "Mind you, thass only a suspicion I had, but I thought I ought to let you know right away."

"Yes, Amy. What is it?"

"You know, Miss Beth, that I was with you when you started the school and, in a manner of speaking, I look on it as my own. So if I'm mistook you must excuse me. . . ."

"Yes, Amy."

"Well, I'm of the opinion that one of your young ladies, Miss Beth, is sneaking out of a night to do a bit of courting, if I may put it so frank."

"Oh!"

"Well may you say 'Oh,' Miss Beth, and you know I'd be the last to worry you. But there's been a few things going on that I couldn't miss seeing."

"Just tell me," I said, thinking—but Amy was supposed to give the message, and even Amy could tell a mother from a lover, and ahah! now Jassy Woodroffe, I have you doubly damned.

"Well," said Amy again, "it's like this, Miss Beth. Back in August, in your holiday that was, there was a young officer from Colchester barracks stayed at my place to do a bit of fishing. And while he wuz there Mr. Helmar, you know, from Mortiboys on the Bywater road, dropped in for a drink and got talking and found that this young feller wuz a card player as well and arst him out to his place. And the whole of this term that young man heve been coming back, nut on his way to Mortiboys, but sort of hanging about at my place till dark, then going off somewhere and coming back late. Thass happened several times. And he don't go to Mortiboys because he don't take his horse. . . ."

"Well?" I said.

"Well," said Amy, rather shamefaced, "I daresay you know, Miss Beth, what funny ideas you get about people, and I got the notion that this young man had got in with the moonlighters—smugglers, Miss Beth. It seemed sorta mysterious to me that he come so regular and stayed out just so long and then went off so early in the morning. And I didn't want my decent house mixed up in such business. So last night I sent my man, Jess Horrocks, to foller him."

"Yes," I said. And although I knew what was coming I had the irrelevant thought that it was not fear of smuggling which had prompted Amy's spying, but sheer plain curiosity. She was always a martyr to it.

"Jess come back and reported to me. He said that our young gentleman only went to the edge of the Grove—you know, Miss Beth, that's the top end of Layer Wood. And he waited there till two young ladies come along, both wearing blue cloaks with hoods. One of them stopped and set on a gate, and the other went into the wood with our young gentleman. By that time the rain wuz coming down cats and dogs, so Jess, lazybones that he is, thought his job wuz done, and come home. But when he said two young ladies in blue cloaks with hoods, I minded to myself that that wuz what your girls wear. So I sent him back with orders to foller the young ladies this time. Which he did. The one that had been in the wood wuz crying by that time and carrying on very hysterical, Jess said. He come back behind them all the way to the corner, where one seemed to take ill. Anyway, the other had to help her along. And then Jess turned back. I give him a rare flea in the ear for nut going to help the young ladies, but he said his orders wuz to foller, not carry them. He's sharp at that kind of back-answer, for all he is so half-witted. Well, so then I thought to myself, Miss Beth, that it looked as though this might be some of your concern. So I come to tell you just what I know myself."

"I'm very grateful to you, Amy. You have done just what

you should. I'll certainly look into the matter. Of course, you must bear in mind that the girls weren't followed to this house. They may have come from somewhere else in this Square."

"I thought of that afore I come bothering you. And I been going through in my mind. Thass a funny thing, but I don't reckon there's a *young* maid, much less two, at any house round here, excepting Mrs. Shuttle's Fanny, and she walk peculiar. Jess'd have noticed that."

"Or again," I said, still conscious of the fact that Dilys was involved in this, and that her reputation must be protected, "it is possible that two of the maids, Emily and Ivy, say, might have borrowed a couple of cloaks to wear in the rain."

Amy just looked at me. And the look conveyed her opinion that we were playing some kind of game. The next move was hers.

"Ah!" she said, "that is possible, of course. But I noticed that Jess said 'young ladies.' He's a roughish fellow and would have used other names, being cross at being sent out in the rain I reckon."

"Well," I said, accepting the checkmate, "that seems to narrow it down. Tell me, Amy, did this man notice any other thing which would help in the matter of identification. I hope you asked him."

"As a matter of fact I did. But all he could say wuz that one wuz dark and one wuz fair."

"Oh! And the dark one went into the wood and the fair one sat on the gate." I had made a false move, led away by my own private assumption. Amy's stare convicted me.

"I never said that, Miss Beth. As a matter of fact, it wuz tother way about. The fair one met the young gentleman and the dark one waited for her. I reckon myself . . ."

I felt a little sick. Dilys, innocent, motherless little thing. . . . And it is really that other one's fault, I thought. Dilys would never have known about the pantry window, or faced the night walk alone.

"Yes, Amy?"

But Amy had become coy. "I don't like to name no names in

a case like this when nobody can be sure, Miss Beth. But I put two and two together and arst myself which of your girls would my young gentleman be likely to know—him having been out to Mortiboys by invitation, like I told you. D'you see?"

"Yes," I said, slowly dragging out the monosyllable. "Naturally you would think that. But Miss Helmar happened to be taken ill last evening, and I spent a good deal of time with her myself. It just shows how careful one must be before jumping to conclusions. But, Amy, speaking of Miss Helmar reminds me of your little friend, Jassy. I've been wondering, has anything ever been heard of her mother? You see, very soon she will have finished school, and we shall have to make some arrangements for her. At such a time one naturally wonders about the real parent. . . ." It was a weak excuse enough, but it served to draw from Amy the actual words which would enable me to give Jassy the lie as soon as the subject came up.

Amy's face darkened. Oh, how well I remember that sullen cold look which told of outraged dignity.

"I've never heard anything about her. Nor don't wish to," said Amy stiffly. "To tell you the truth, Miss Beth, I've bin disappointed in Jassy. Oh, I know she's a clever girl and all that, and no doubt it was kindness in Miss Hamilton to make such a pet of her. But she spoilt her. I don't care who hear me say so, she spoilt her. She oughter remember—Jassy, I mean—who set her foot on the ladder, so to speak. But she don't. And though that wuz nice of Miss Hamilton to take her away for the summer holidays along with you, the least she could of done wuz come and see me before and after."

"And didn't she?"

"Not her. I reckon I ain't good enough for a visit these days."

"I only hope then," I said, with infinite guile, "that when . . . when we've finished with her here, she won't try to foist herself on you . . . expect you to do anything more for her."

"She'd be out of fortune if she did," said Amy firmly. "I done with her after them holidays. Besides, for another thing, I don't

(140)

want any wenches round my place. Men after liquor is bad enough. No, I'd done with her. She wuz a nice little thing in her way, but as I said before, Miss Hamilton spoilt her."

"I think you're quite right, Amy," I said. And although there remained a regret in my mind that it should have been Dilys who had kept the rendezvous, my heart sang. When I did what I had planned, what I was still planning to do, there would be no Amy to side with Jassy, to speak up, to frustrate me. In fact, everything was playing into my hand.

"Well," I said. "I can't tell you, Amy, how very grateful I am for your loyalty and your shrewdness. You have been a great help, as always. I must begin to look into this matter at once. For one thing, the cloaks—if they were our girls—will still be wet. So I must get up."

"Emily said your candle blew out in the dark and you run into the edge of the door, Miss Beth. That must of hurt."

"It did. But it's better now."

I saw Amy's eye begin to measure how a door could bruise one's nose and cut both cheeks.

"It didn't happen exactly like that, Amy. One day, very soon, I'll tell *you* all about it. But not now. I must get up. So if you will excuse me. . . ."

Amy rose. Then, with the effort of her kind to extract the last, the ultimate word of gratitude she said:

"I hope you don't think I bin trying to worry you, Miss Beth."

"On the contrary, you have helped me very much, Amy, and I am more grateful than I can say."

She was gone at last. And as soon as the door had closed behind her it opened again and there was Katharine, wearing a look of concern.

"My dear, your poor face! However did it happen?" she asked. And then, just in her own way, not waiting for an answer, she went on:

"That Amy! What on earth did she want at this hour? And what a time she stayed! I came up as soon as Emily gave me your message, and I could hear her going on and on. Couldn't she *see* you were feeling poorly?"

"She came on very serious business. And in a way it was connected with my nose." I leaned back, remembering the line I was to take in this affair, and put on a plaintive, gentle air. "Katharine, I hate to tell you about it. I'm afraid it's going to hurt you a great deal."

Katharine sat down on the stool in front of my dressing-table. her back to the mirror and her face to me.

"I suppose it's about Jassy Woodroffe?" she said guardedly.

"Yes. How did you know?"

"By your face, Beth. A special kind of look comes over you when you speak about her. But go on. Don't spare my feelings. I'm all agog to know how she and Amy and your poor face are connected."

Now, I said to myself, go slowly, keep calm, and let the facts speak for themselves. And very carefully, speaking gently, without passion, I told the whole story, beginning with my midnight alarm call, and going on with Amy's story. But I did not mention the fact that Amy's man, Jess Horrocks, had noticed which of the girls had been keeping the tryst; nor did I, at first, refer to my second visit to the bedroom or Jassy's attack on me.

I watched Katharine's face as I spoke. I was at once pleased and sorry to see that its ivory pallor deepened, and that the lines on it hardened as I came to the crucial point of the story. I was glad that she was taking the thing to heart, and at the same time sorry to give her pain. But I steeled myself and thought, after all, if you will nurture a viper in your bosom it must be plucked out, harshly if necessary, and though the process may be painful, it is salutary.

When I had finished she inclined her head a little and said quietly:

"But your face, Beth. You haven't told me how that happened."

"I wish I need not. Kathy, dear, I wish I could say that I just had an accident. Look, don't ask me any more about it. It was just an accident."

"My dear Beth," she said with a grit of impatience in her voice, "don't be so transparent! I can guess what happened. At some time or another during the events you have described, Jassy hit you. Isn't that so?" I nodded, conscious of chagrin that the moment of dramatic revelation had been forestalled.

"I thought so," said Katharine. "You see I know her—knew her, quite well. She has an ungovernable temper. But I say I *knew* her because what you have just told me reveals a completely new facet to her character. I should have said that she still was a little immature for a love affair, and far too honest for such duplicity."

"Well, now you know," I said.

"Yes. Now I know."

She was wearing a little shawl over her shoulders. It was knitted in dice pattern, in two shades of lilac; and now, taking the corner of it between her fingers, she studied it with a frown of concentration, as though she were trying to sort out the pattern into so many lines of knit and purl. But I knew that her stare was blank, and that her mind was busy. After a moment or so she looked up and said:

"Beth, I think we ought to hear what the girls have to say. Could you bear to have them in here?"

"One at a time, or both together?" I asked, rather to gain time to think about her question than because I wanted an answer to my own.

"Together, I think," said Katharine. And with that she went over and pulled my bell. Emily appeared so promptly that I guessed she had not been far away, and for the hundredth time I wondered at the rapidity with which, in an establishment like ours, news of anything unusual could spread and set eyes and ears straining for further information.

While we were waiting for the girls to appear Katharine walked

to the window and stared out of it without speaking. When they
knocked on the door and I called to them to come in, she turned
and I saw that in the second between the time when she stared
from the window, looking worried and distrait, and the time
when she turned to face the room, she had put on dignity as
definitely as if it had been a garment. I had often wondered to
myself how anyone as vague and careless as Kathy, occupying to
all appearances a subordinate, if favoured place, could manage
to maintain perfect discipline in her classes. Now I saw that she
was capable of putting off vagueness and carelessness and of
assuming so stern an air that even I, guiltless and entirely in the
right, began to feel uncomfortable, and to examine my case anew,
seeking for a weak spot.

Dilys came first, looking wilted and ghastly. Even her lovely
halo of golden hair had lost some of its virtue and seemed to
cling damply to her scalp. And a sudden cold fear struck me.
Suppose, I thought, this turns out to be a question not really concerned with me and Kathy and Jassy, but with Dilys' deflowering
and ruin. For just a moment I had a crazy idea that only Dilys
mattered, only Dilys was real, and the rest of the coil was mere
silly nonsense, woven out of jealousy, my jealousy, and spite.
Then I felt again the sharp impact of the mug's rim, and the
sting of the brandy in my eyes. I straightened myself and tugged
at my pillow, thinking with satisfaction that Jassy's moment had
come. She followed Dilys into the room and shut the door softly.
She looked just as usual, perfectly neat and composed. I thought
—angrily, of course—she is composed, she thinks she will get
away with her lie: she doesn't know about Amy's visit. But
actually I believe that if she had been going to her hanging she
would have looked the same, for she was incapable of feeling anything except anger, and that only under provocation. She had no
nerves, no heart.

"Mrs. Twysdale is not feeling well, which is hardly to be
wondered at," Katharine began, "so you will kindly give me your
attention. Both of you." For Dilys, after one shuddering glance

(144)

at my face, had looked away, then back again, and was staring at me with penitent horror.

"I should be interested to hear exactly what you have to say for yourselves."

"I—I—please, Miss Hamilton," Dilys began. But Jassy, with a contemptuous movement of her hand, silenced her, and said in a low firm voice:

"It was entirely my fault, Miss Hamilton. Dilys had very little to do with it. I wanted to meet my mother, who is a very peculiar person, as I have told you, and who arranged to meet me in what you call the Grove. Dilys, being my friend, and afraid of the dark herself, insisted on coming with me. Then it rained and blew a gale, and we had been walking very quickly, and she fainted. When I couldn't bring her round myself I fetched Mrs. Twysdale, who did. Mrs. Twysdale also discovered our cloaks and the clothes I had taken off Dilys in order to put her to bed properly. And then I explained where I had been. That's all."

"That is not all," said Katharine in a voice of ice, "and you know it. Go on."

"That is all that concerns Dilys, Miss Hamilton. Mrs. Twysdale left us, implying that the whole thing would be thrashed out in the morning. Dilys began to cry and I saw the brandy flask which had been left behind. I poured what was in it—there wasn't much—into the mug and was trying to persuade Dilys to drink it when Mrs. Twysdale came back. She slapped me and I lost my temper. And I hit her with the mug." She swung suddenly towards the bed and addressed me. "I'm truly sorry about that. But very early in my life I learned to hit back in self-defence if anyone attacked me, and I just didn't think. I know that that is no excuse."

"I'm glad you realize that." Katharine's voice changed from dry rebuke to a small, almost an appealing note. "And that, Jassy, is all you have to say? It was . . . your mother whom you met?"

"Yes, Miss Hamilton. My mother."

Katharine's big brown eyes, deeply set in their hollow sockets, flashed a look at me. Then she looked back towards Jassy and said:

"Then it is my sorry duty to tell you, Jassy, that you are a liar. Your own mention of the Grove proves that beyond possible doubt. For you were followed last night. Mrs. Twysdale and I and two other people know that you went there to meet a man."

There was a moment of intense silence. It was as though every one of the four of us had been suddenly encased in ice. Then Dilys, with a little scream, flung herself towards me, fell on her knees by the side of my bed and, scrabbling at my covers with her outstretched hands, began to cry and speak at the same time, stammering incoherently.

"I-I'll tell you, I'll t-t-tell you everything. It was me. It was all m-m-my f-fault. P-please, Mrs. Twysdale, I w-wanted to all along. I'll t-tell you."

I put out a hand and gripped her shoulder.

"There's no need to do that, Dilys. I know all about it. It's all right, my dear. No one blames you. Just keep quiet and try to compose yourself."

But Dilys shrugged my hand away, gripped the bed covers and pulled herself to her feet.

"M-Miss Hamilton, please! L-listen. It was me. I was the one who m-met the young man. Jassy just came with me because I was afraid of the dark. Honestly she d-didn't do anything except c-come with me and wait."

"This is absurd," Katharine said coldly. "First Jassy lies to mislead us and protect you both. Then you lie to protect Jassy. Fortunately, we happen to know the truth. You may go, Dilys. Go to your room and stay there until you have regained your self-control. Then go where you like. This no longer concerns you."

Dilys, on the brink of a fit, began to shriek: "W-won't you believe me? It's true, I t-tell you. Jassy didn't even speak to the man. It was me. I—oh—I . . ."

"Stop it, Dilys. Do what Miss Hamilton tells you and go to your room."

But Katharine had already rung the bell, and with that same suspicious promptitude Emily had answered it.

"Miss Helmar is hysterical," Katharine said. "Take her to her room, Emily, and stay with her until she is calm."

"I w-won't go. You m-must listen to me. I've told you. It was m-me. Oh, oh!" Dilys began to shriek and threw herself backwards.

Katharine took her by the back of the neck, as one takes a puppy, and hustled her through the doorway. "Go along, you silly girl. And stop that noise."

She kicked the door with her foot and it closed with a clash. Jassy, a little paler than before, but quite calm, stood with her hands clasped in front of her. Katharine paused beside her. Her mouth moved for a second before any words came, then she said, "You get out, too. Go to my room and wait."

Katharine watched while the girl obeyed her, and then she flung herself on to the stool of my dressing-table, facing the mirror this time, and put her face in her hands. For a moment I thought that she was going to break down, and I felt a queer, long-drawn-out thrill. I tasted, in anticipation, the joy of taking Katharine in my arms, of comforting her by clasp and touch, of establishing a physical contact which could never afterwards be denied. The state of awed thraldom in which, all unconscious, she had held me these many years, was about to break and to give place to something altogether different, warm and intimate. I was pushing back the covers and pulling down my nightgown, preparing to leap from my bed, when she straightened herself and, staring into the mirror without, I am sure, seeing her own distraught reflection, said flatly:

"Well, I suppose that is the end of that. She has assaulted you and lied to us both. She must go."

"In any case," I said gently, "she would be going at the end of the term. It doesn't make much difference."

"I was planning to have her stay on—as a teacher, Beth. I hadn't had time to talk to you about it. But that was my hope. Of course, now . . ." She hesitated for a moment, beating her hands together, while I lay back, marvelling at my luck. How nearly I had escaped being saddled with Jassy for ever. Jassy as a member of the staff! Never, never again would I think that I was unlucky.

"Beth. Could there be a grain of truth in what that other child said?" Oh how cruel to be obliged to dash the hope which had sprung into her voice, into her eyes, into the very way she stood.

"I'm afraid not. Amy was very definite. You know what Amy is, curiosity personified. And with one being so dark-haired and the other so fair. Besides . . . Katharine, I don't want to make a coil about this," I put my hand very gently upon my injured nose, "but don't you think she struck me because she was so exasperated at being found out?"

"It certainly looks so. Beth, what shall I do?"

"Do? Why, Kathy, you know as well as I do that once girls begin that . . . that kind of thing, there's no holding them. Even if her time here wasn't nearly ended. . . . Surely, Kathy, there is but one thing to do. Send her away as quickly as possible."

"But where?"

"There's the man," I said, risking a little callousness in order to remind Katharine of him.

"The pity of it!" Katharine said. But I could see that my last shot had gone home. Yet still she hesitated, standing rather helplessly in the middle of my room.

"Katharine," I said, "you don't like the job of sending her off. Let me do it. I'll give her five pounds."

"Ten," Katharine said. "There's some money in the top right hand drawer of my desk, and the key is in my handkerchief box." I got out of bed and began to put on my slippers and dressing-gown. "Beth . . . are we being hasty? She's so young, and so pretty. I dread to think . . ."

"Kathy," I said, "look at my face. Can you do that and doubt that she is well able to stand up for herself? Remember the boldness, the barefaced lying."

"Yes, yes," Katharine said hastily. "You are right, Beth. I'm beginning to think that you were right all along. Go and tell her, then, please. I'll go to my class."

She hurried away, almost as though something were pursuing her. I went over to the dressing-table and began to tidy my hair. The glass reflected the faint, but unmistakable, smile of triumph which curved my lips. It's been a long war, I thought, and I bear the marks of battle. But I have won.

I went downstairs to the half-landing, crossed it and opened Katharine's sitting-room door. Jassy was sitting on the window seat, reading a book. She looked up expectantly, but her expression darkened at the sight of me. She closed the book and stood up.

"Miss Hamilton sent me to tell you what I have no doubt you already know—that it is impossible for us to keep you here any longer. You must pack your things and leave at once." I went to the door of Katharine's bedroom, opened it, crossed to her handkerchief box, and found the key. Back in the sitting-room I unlocked the top drawer of Katharine's desk and saw, muddled amongst papers and ends of sealing wax and odd lengths of string, a number of gold coins. I picked out five sovereigns, and then hesitated. We were not wealthy; the school was prosperous and we lived comfortably, but there had never been, would never be, much actual cash to spare. Besides, I thought, even to give the little wretch five pounds is a gesture of unthinking generosity. After all, she struck me. And a little cold spring of doubt began to bubble up through my mood of triumph. I should have had nothing but hatred and spite for anyone who had hurt Katharine in any way. Jassy had smashed a mug into my face, and Katharine had said, "She has a violent temper," and proposed to give her ten pounds!

Never mind, I thought, once let me get her out of the house and I shall be able to reinstate myself with Katharine. And suddenly, with almost a superstitious impulse, I snatched up a further five coins. I would save that sum somehow by self-denial. I put the money together in a little shining tower and pushed it along the desk.

"You understand," I said, "that we are not bound to give you anything, nor to concern ourselves in any way about your future. But we both feel, Miss Hamilton and I, that you are to some extent to be pitied as well as blamed. So we are giving you this so that you may be able to start honestly in the world if you choose to do so. Take care of it. Ten pounds is a large sum of money."

I gave the pile another little push. But Jassy made no move to take it. She stood quite still, with her hands hanging down, half hidden in the folds of her skirt.

"I don't want it," she said flatly. "I don't want anything except ten minutes alone with Miss Hamilton."

"That's quite impossible," I said. "For one thing, Miss Hamilton is far too much distressed to face another scene. For another, she has not the slightest wish to see you again. Surely you must realize that. Take your money and come upstairs and collect your things."

"I must see Miss Hamilton first."

I made a final desperate effort to keep my temper.

"For goodness' sake don't make yourself ridiculous," I said. "Miss Hamilton has finished with you. Do you imagine that she would even listen to what you have to say. She especially asked me to send you away because she is naturally too disgusted to have anything more to do with you."

She levelled at me the cold hard stare which I remembered and then, without speaking, sat down again on the window seat, opened her book, and bent her head over it. I had never seen such a gesture of studied insolence in my life. The blood rushed to my head so violently that the throbbing in my nose redoubled itself. And at the same time the little cold spring of fear became a great flood. I could see what would happen if Jassy came face to face with Katharine again—she would tell her the whole story, and Katharine, in a passion of repentance, and relief, would blurt out her offer of a place on the staff, and for me everything would be over. Fear and anger, both dangerous passions, filled me. I took a step forward and cried, "Shut that book, do you hear me? Shut that book and listen to what I have to say. Unless you go willingly, with what dignity is left to you I shall ring that bell and ask for Jessop to help me, and I shall throw you out and your things after you. I mean that. You've been told to go, and if you refuse I shall have you treated as I would any other intruder." She did not even look up, and I turned and marched to the bell. I was still, I thought, to all intents and purposes, mistress in this place. I rang bells and they were answered, I gave orders and they were obeyed. Jessop, the sturdy old veteran who minded the garden and kept the pump working and sawed wood and did a bit of painting, would think nothing of carrying Jassy downstairs if necessary. It is not a method I should have chosen, but then the choice was not mine. I took the bell pull in my fingers.

"You'll only make yourself look silly," said Jassy behind me. "I shall stay in this room until I am dead, whoever tries to throw me out." She spoke quietly, but with such conviction that I turned my head to look at her, still holding the bell rope in my hand. She had left the window and taken a stand behind Katharine's desk. As I looked at her she laid her hand on the heavy pewter inkpot which stood there. Almost conversationally she said, "The first person who tries to touch me will get this on the skull."

I knew that she meant it. I remembered the—the exaltation of fury with which she had dashed the mug in my face; remembered the sting of the brandy in my eyes and nostrils. Oh God, I cried to myself, what did I do on the day when I let this creature in? I glanced at the clock on the mantelpiece and saw that Katharine's class would be over in eighteen minutes' time. A kind of panic seized me; my blood seemed to run backwards and forwards in my veins, quivering with frenzied agitation. But I forced myself to calmness.

"What good will it do you to stay here and see Miss Hamilton again?" I asked reasonably. "She will only be more annoyed to find that you have disobeyed her last request, which was that you should leave the house as soon as possible. I assure you that nothing you can say to her will make her change her mind."

"I don't want to make her change her mind. I just want to explain something to her."

Her hard little face softened suddenly. I saw her lower lip tremble. She bit it fiercely before she added:

"Miss Hamilton has been so—kind to me. I don't want her to think . . . There's something I must tell her before I go."

Inspiration came to me. I glanced at the clock again and saw that the inexorable hands had measured away another two minutes. Sixteen minutes. Sixteen minutes to get her out of the house. Once she was in the street, I thought, I should be safe. Even if she wrote to Katharine it would mean nothing, for all letters came to me first. Fussed as I was, and short of time, I failed to examine my new idea thoroughly. I said rashly:

"I think I know what you have to say. You want to tell Miss Hamilton that what Dilys said just now was the truth and that you merely accompanied her. Well, I have already told Miss Hamilton that. And as you can see, it has made no difference. No difference at all. Because, you see, it is not just for stealing out at night that you are being sent away. Do you really imagine . . ." I heard my voice go suddenly high and shrill, ". . . do you really imagine that you can behave as you have done, that you can strike me, and then, with a few words about quite another subject, creep back into Miss Hamilton's favour? You overestimate yourself. By breaking rules last night you merely gave Miss Hamilton a valid excuse for ending a business which, begun in charity, has become intolerable to her. She wants to be rid of you and . . ."

I broke off. Jassy had come out from behind the desk.

"I'll go," she said, quite meekly. "I only wanted to tell her that, so that she shouldn't think I'd been—well, worse than I had. And she might have helped Dilys, too, perhaps. But if she knows there's nothing for me to say."

She moved towards the door. And after another glance at the clock I said, "I'll send Emily to help you to get your things together." Emily had often packed for girls who were called home in a hurry, or for sick ones who were fetched by over-anxious parents. She could get Jassy's few things together in ten minutes, and that left three for me to hustle her out of doors. Thank God I thought, Katharine's class this morning was in the large classroom, which was built out at the back of the house.

Jassy opened the door, and as she did so I heard the sound of hasty feet on the stairs and the swish of a silk skirt. Katharine, hatless, looking mad, looking distraught, swung round from the top of the stairs on to the half-landing and collided with Jassy, who was by this time outside the door. They fell together, and then, clutching and clinging, were carried by the impetus of Katharine's haste over the threshold and into the room.

"Oh," Katharine cried, still holding Jassy by the shoulder and speaking in a voice that hung between sobs and laughter. "Oh, thank God I got back in time. You're still here." I saw her arm slip round the girl until, from clutching her shoulder she was holding her in a close embrace. Jassy's face was turned inwards, and over the top of her head Katharine looked at me with furious accusation.

"Why didn't you tell me?" she demanded. "How could you deceive me so? If I hadn't gone to Amy. . . . Oh, Jassy, my dear, do please forgive me. How could I ever have thought . . . ?"

She put her other arm about Jassy's neck and, bending her head, began to kiss that crown of black plaits. I felt quite sick. This was Katharine, always so cool and dry and distant, Katharine to whom the slightest physical contact had always seemed repellent, Katharine who had never permitted more than the briefest brush of the lips on, say, a birthday morning, or before and after a longish separation. Katharine, positively slobbering over that little bitch. And I knew, although the hated face was hidden, that it was calm and hard and calculating, and that under those plaits the evil brain was busy, scheming how this development might be turned to its own advantage, how Katharine's thraldom might be riveted stronger and closer.

Sick fury drove out my fear. I no longer minded that Katharine knew how I had deceived her, knew to what lengths my hatred had carried me. I said boldly:

"Katharine, I should like to talk to you for a moment. Alone."

"I have something to say, too." She loosened her clasp, put a hand under Jassy's chin and tilted her face, looked at her dotingly for an instant, and then kissed her on the forehead.

"Jassy," she said, speaking normally, as though the girl had just entered the room, "I want you to do something for me." She crossed to the desk and took up a sheaf of exercises. "It's my grammar hour with the Juniors. Take it for me, will you? Here are their papers. They can correct their errors and then . . . well, you'll know what to do next. At the end of the hour come back here."

"Yes, Miss Hamilton."

The door closed behind the girl and Katharine turned to me.

"Now," she said. But I was no longer capable of feeling awe for Katharine. She had shown me her weakness. I made a direct, savage attack.

"Of all the disgusting sights I have ever seen," I began, "that was the worst. If anyone had told me that I should live to see *you* slobbering and kissing a schoolgirl I shouldn't have believed them."

"Nor would I if the same prophet had foretold that you would ever lend yourself to such spiteful duplicity. Amy told you this morning, as plainly as she dared, that Dilys Helmar was to blame. And you were willing to let me send Jassy away for that."

"It was your own jealousy that made you willing to send her away, Katharine. I see that now. Nothing else she could have done

(154)

would have made you willing to lose her. I may have kept to myself the name of the girl who went into the wood, but the fact remains that though Jassy Woodroffe only sat over a gate and waited, she is still guilty of breaking a rule and stealing out of the house at night; she is still guilty of attacking me with a mug, and of telling lies. If a man had touched her she was to be sent off with ten pounds; untouched, she is to be reinstated, hugged and kissed. There you have the truth, Katharine, and a revolting truth it is."

Katharine made an effort, a visible, painful effort to compose herself, to take refuge again in that cool dry shell under which she had hidden from the world. She walked to a chair and sat down in it, saying: "Sit down, Beth, and try to calm yourself. I want you, if you can, to explain why, knowing that Dilys was the culprit, you withheld that information and allowed me to think Jassy was to blame?"

"I've just told you—not in so many words perhaps—but the real reason is in what I have said. Katharine, you have simply lost your head on this girl. I haven't. So I was capable of seeing that her behaviour, whether she actually went to meet a lover or not, was reprehensible. Dilys Helmar is weak and silly, but alone she would never have gone out in the dark; she wouldn't have known about the loose bar in the pantry window; she would not have been able to think up an adequate excuse. Do you realize, Katharine, that if I hadn't found those wet cloaks Jassy Woodroffe would have fooled me—us—completely, and this clandestine business would still be going on? Then, when she is discovered, she has a lying tale all ready, a tale that takes every advantage of our ignorance of her family. After that, although I may have been hasty when I saw her slopping away my medicinal brandy, she attacked me violently, almost maniacally, and really hurt my face. I had merely slapped hers with my open hand. Can you blame me if, seeing that this multitude of real differences had no effect on your attitude towards her, I took advantage of the one point which I knew would move you.

(155)

I did it for your sake, Katharine. If you could only be saved through your jealousy, then you must be made jealous."

Katharine brought her open hand down on the arm of her chair in a slightly theatrical gesture:

"My God," she said, "you're the one who should talk about jealousy!"

I realized that she was looking at me with hatred. And I suddenly remembered that the jubilant thought with which I had wakened that morning, the joy and relief with which I had imagined that now, in breaking the skin of my face and bruising my nose, Jassy Woodroffe had fulfilled all my feelings of doom and foreboding about her. What a crass fool I had been. Here before my eyes, now, was the final and unmistakable sign of her work. She had made me make Katharine hate me! The anger and the disgust which had supported me seeped away all at once. Dread and self-pity took their place. My knees felt weak and I was glad to take the chair which I had ignored when Katharine had told me to sit down and be calm. I sat down, but I was not calm. The strain under which I had been living for so long combined with the emotional stress of the last few hours suddenly took a cumulative effect on me. I began to babble. I said things without previously arranging them in my mind, so that when the words were formed and audible on the air I heard them with a shock of surprise and horror. I could neither control what I said, nor stop saying it. It was as though the unconscious control which—even in passion and anger—censors and edits one's speech, had suddenly ceased action. Staring, hypnotized, into Katharine's eyes of hatred, I said:

"Yes, I am jealous too. Just now, when you clasped that little hussy in your arms and kissed her I would have killed you both if hatred would have done it. And why not? I love you, Katharine. I've never loved anyone but you. I loved you the moment I saw you, and I've gone on loving you ever since. And because of that I've worked and slaved for you; how hard you'll never know. My one aim in life has been to protect you, to please you, to make life easy for you. Never once in twenty years have you ordered a meal or mended a stocking. I've behaved to you as though you were my husband, because, in my mind, that was how I regarded you. And what have I had in return? A casual word of thanks now and then when you could look up from a book and remember to speak to me. And I bore it, thinking that you were naturally cold and unresponsive, thinking that you were dry and cool and casual. Then along comes this little nobody, this waif from the gutter, and you give her all the affection that is my due. How could I help being jealous? I, who have waited for a smile from you, gone happily all day on the memory of one kind word—I must stand by and see *her* kissed and cuddled. For twenty years I have served you and loved you, without making a single demand. And now I have to realize that I mean so little that if Jassy Woodroffe breaks my nose and lets a man handle her, she is cast off, but if she breaks my nose and keeps her caresses for you she can remain as your petted favourite. Could anything be more disgusting, more nauseating?"

I broke off, breathless with emotion. While I had been speaking Katharine had drawn herself a little straighter and stiffer in her chair as though she were trying to escape some vile contamination. A spot of dusky colour burned high up on her pale cheeks. But when she spoke her voice was calm and cool.

"God knows of what you are accusing me, Beth. You sound to be beside yourself, but I hope you're capable of believing that I never laid a finger on the girl until ten minutes ago."

"But you've wanted to," I cried, out of my own bitter knowledge. "You've wanted to. Otherwise why did you change your mind so suddenly when you knew that it was Dilys, not she, who went to meet a lover?"

"Isn't that obvious?" she asked with a kind of angry patience. "If Jassy had developed a taste for illicit adventure that kind of scene would have been repeated again and again. And a fine life you would have led me. Until I saw Amy, what defence had I against you and your talk of bad influences? Later, knowing that Jassy merely went out to accompany that little fool whose fear of the dark is greater than her lechery, I had reason on my side. With Dilys gone I think Jassy will be content to stay in her bed."

"That means, I take it, that you intend to keep her here?"

After a second's hesitation Katharine said, "Yes. I mean that." I began to laugh.

"Katharine Hamilton," I said, "I've gone all these years in the belief that you were an intelligent, honest woman. Now I know what you are. Very well then, choose your Jassy, keep her. Get her to run the house for you, and teach classes, and mend your clothes. I've borne all I intend to. I'm going."

I got up from my chair. Katharine jumped to her feet too, and stood confronting me.

"Don't be a fool, Beth. Where would you go?"

"Anywhere. What I have done here I can do in another place. I won't stay here to be tortured by the sight of that little harpy turning you into . . ."

"Don't let's bandy names," Katharine said sharply. "Look here, Beth, God knows if you feel offended with me, you've given me plenty of cause for offence too. Can't we leave it at that? Can't we settle down and make allowances for one another? We're neither of us young, and we're both working on the same job. Couldn't we come to some amicable arrangement?"

It was a placating speech, but I was not deceived. Aha, I thought, the mere threat of being left to yourself brings you to your senses.

I said deliberately, "I will stay with you, Katharine, on one condition—that Jassy Woodroffe leaves the house to-day." I felt that delicious uprush of power which visits those who makes conditions. The dusky patches on Katharine's cheeks faded, leaving her face as white as paper. She came close to me, thrusting her face before mine and speaking venomously.

"God knows I've tried to be reasonable and patient, but there is a limit to everything. Go then, if you want to go, and take your filthy mind and its vile insinuations out of my house. You profess to feel disgust with my behaviour; *you* are disgusting with your talk of love and service. I'm not blind, Beth, nor stupid. I knew, before the end of the first term, that it was a mistake for us to set up house together. If you could know the number of times that you've sickened me with your yearning eyes and little furtive touches, with your protection and understanding! And the hours and hours of boredom, either listening to your fatuous chatter or seeing you there, greasy with virtue, bursting with the effort not to talk, with 'Katharine mustn't be disturbed' written all over you. Years and years! My God, I've paid for having my stockings darned! But I bore it. I would have borne it for ever. Then, when by the merest chance I do at last find a mind that runs along with mine—a cool, eager, companionable mind, capable of staying for five minutes on a mental plane—all you can do, when you've failed to poison my mind against her, is to accuse me of some beastly perverted intercourse which is nothing but the reflection of your own warped mind. Yes, go away. It's the best thing you can do. I'll see that Lawyer Aldritch has some money for you by to-morrow."

She swung round, turning her back on me, and stood by the desk, purposely moving things about on the top of it. I looked at her, thinking that I should not see her again; that it was all over; that the years and years of service, the love and the consideration were worse than useless; they were ridiculous. And where should I go? What should I do? I, who had set out so blithely this morning to oust Jassy Woodroffe, had myself been ousted.

"Katharine," I said, "Katharine!"

She remained silent, ignoring me.

"Please," I said, "Katharine, you must listen. I'm sorry . . . I . . ."

"I'm not going to start all over again," she said in a cold, distant voice. "You have chosen to go. Please do so."

"But Katharine. . . ."

"I've nothing else to say," she said. Swinging around again she swept over to the bell and pulled it. Was she proposing to humiliate me finally by ordering my removal? I stumbled towards the door. On the half-landing was Emily, running.

"Oh, ma'am," she gabbled, "Miss Ogilvy says to come at once. Miss Helmar is off in a carriage and nobody can stop her." She broke off to stare at me. "Oh, ma'am."

"Tell Miss Hamilton, Emily. I am unwell."

"That Jassy Woodroffe's gone too, ma'am," said Emily.

"Miss Hamilton," I repeated.

With tears running down my face I went on towards my own room.

Book Three
NEUROSIS IN ARCADY

"She was, by all accounts, an admirable house-keeper. . . ."

So this story is told by DILYS HELMAR, *who brought her to Mortiboys.*

I WAS still on my bed, crying about Charles, when Jassy ran in, breathless and looking distracted, and said, "Dilys, they know all about it. I didn't say a word, but apparently we were followed and watched."

I sat up on the bed, and the ache in the back of my head, which had been growing in intensity for hours and hours, made me feel sick and dizzy.

"For God's sake, don't faint again!" Jassy said, beginning to fan me with some papers she held in her hand. "You've got to think up some excuse. Could you say it was your brother whom your father had banished from home or something? You'll have to think of something, Dilys. They're having a fearful row. They'll probably send you home."

"They won't send me home," I said. "I'm going. I shall go crazy if I have much more of this. Twizzy's reproaches would be more than I could bear just now." I swung my legs off the bed and stood up. The pain in my head made me shut my eyes and groan. "God!" I said. "My head." I thought of my valise, stowed away under my bed, and of stooping to the drawers to lift out my things. "I can't pack," I said, speaking to myself, "I'll have to go just as I am."

Jassy flung the papers she held on to my bed. "I'll pack for you," she said in rather a savage voice. "I'm supposed to be taking the Junior Grammar class, but it can't make any difference. Old Twizzy is determined to sack me. I can see that." She stooped and dragged the valise out and then jerked open my bottom drawer. She looked small and forlorn and rather desperate.

"Come home with me," I said impulsively. Jassy sat back on her heels.

"Do you mean that, Dilys? To Mortiboys?"

"Yes," I said, "to Mortiboys! It's the last place on earth anyone in their senses would want to go to. But at least we shan't be asked a lot of questions, or be slavered over, there."

"Wouldn't your father mind?"

"I don't suppose he'll notice." Jassy looked at me rather puzzled, but she said soberly:

"I'd like to come. For a little while. I've got to go somewhere. You're sure it'll be all right?"

"It'll be awful. But your being there won't make it any worse, if that's what you mean."

I rested my head against the back of the bed and shut my eyes again. Jassy kept moving about. She was very deft and rapid in all her movements, and almost before the pain ebbed enough to allow me to begin to think again, she said, in a much firmer and more confident voice:

"I've packed. Shall we go before anything else happens?"

"Did you find my purse?"

She handed it to me. I opened it and took out five shillings.

"Give that to Jessop and tell him to run to Storey's and order the carriage to be at the corner in ten minutes."

Sitting still had eased the pain in my head and I could begin to think. I thought about Charles, about all the hopes I had had, about how I had loved him. I began to cry again, hopelessly. I did not hear Jassy come back into the room, and was unaware of her presence until she put her hand, not very gently, on my shoulder.

"The carriage is ready. We can go," she said. I turned and

clutched her by the arm. "I'm glad you're coming with me," I said.

As we rolled along in the carriage I tried to force my grief out of my mind by thinking of other things. I glanced at Jassy, sitting very upright beside me, and realized again how fortunate I had been in having her for a friend. Apart from the way in which she had stood by me in the last few weeks, she was very definitely the only girl of all those I knew and had known whom I could take home to Mortiboys. I should have hated even Margaret Tucker, whose father was a corn-chandler, though a very successful one, to have entered my home in these days. Jassy was different. She came of a poor, humble family, she was not likely to be critical of Mortiboys whatever it was like. She had told me herself that she had lived in one of the cottages on the Green at Minsham St. Mary; and I knew that she had worked as a servant in the school kitchen. My home, however strange and disreputable it might appear to anyone else, would not shock her. Moreover, she was not pretty enough to cause any trouble from Old Nick—and that was a matter which must be considered nowadays. For the last three years, even since the man Sedley had written him that peculiar letter informing him of mother's death, Old Nick had been completely insane. He would go to bed with anything provided it was young and comely. The present unacknowledged mistress of Mortiboys—unless he had made a change since the beginning of term—was a swarthy, sloe-eyed creature called Melia, who had come into the house as parlour-maid. Her sudden promotion had done more than any-thing since mother's elopement to upset life inside the walls of Mortiboys, for she seemed to be related to almost all the other servants, and during the August holiday, when I had complained that our dinner was uneatable, Agnes the cook, taking advantage of the fact that she was Melia's aunt by marriage, or some such rubbish, had raised a fine scene, and Old Nick had rounded on me with several choice curses.

Remembering this, and other things, I said quietly, so that the driver should not overhear:

"Jassy, I think I ought to warn you that my home is a very peculiar place."

"Is it? It looks lovely from the outside."

"When did you see it last?"

"At Easter, three or four years ago. Miss Hamilton brought me for a drive this way."

"Oh yes, I remember. And the next term, when I gave her a wrong date she said that I ought to have imbibed history with the air I breathed. Little she knew."

"What was it you wanted to warn me about?" asked Jassy in her matter-of-fact little voice.

"Well, for one thing, it doesn't even look the same outside now. Two years ago the archway blew down in a gale, and at the same time the whole window in the Great Hall blew out, and half the tiles came off the roof. The place looks a ruin now."

"Why wasn't it mended?"

"That's what I'm trying to tell you. Old Nick—Father, that is —is quite dotty, and one form his madness takes is that he won't have anything mended, not even a window."

"Why ever not?"

"Well," I said, "sometimes I think it's just his perversity. At other times I'm certain that that is his way of taking revenge on the place. It was over the repairs to Mortiboys that Sedley and mother met. I told you about that."

Jassy nodded. "That is a romantic revenge, in a way."

"Romantic! It's horribly uncomfortable." I leaned my head on my hand, trying to steady it from the intolerable jolting, and added, "And everything is a mess, and the muddle; the servants are out of hand and father is drunk half his time. So now you know what to expect."

"Anything will be preferable to school," Jassy said comfortably.

I did not answer. Holding my head I sat with my eyes closed

until the carriage swerved sharply and the increased bumpiness of the road told me that we had left the turnpike and were in the lane. I sat up and tucked my hair under my hat. Within a few minutes we were in front of the ruined archway. Nothing had been done. It lay as it had fallen, the little house where Sharples had lived and the whole arch a mere pile of pinkish bricks with ends of dark broken beams protruding like the limbs of buried people. The other cottage, where one of the keepers lived, was still standing and still inhabited, but the fall of the main arch had torn away the outer wall of one of its bedrooms. The small empty room with its plastered walls and its door and window was somehow more unsightly and pitiable than all the rest of the ruin.

The entry to Mortiboys was blocked by the fallen bricks, but a rough track, skirting the pile of bricks, joined the lane to the drive. Storey, careful for the springs of his carriage, drove in at a funeral pace and pulled up by the porch. Ten minutes ago I should have denied that I could possibly have felt more wretched, but as we alighted my depression increased. The desolation of my ruined home matched so nearly the desolation of my broken heart. The great porch, with its black benches and beams, yawned like the mouth of a monster about to swallow us. Storey put the valises on to a bench, and as soon as he was paid drove away.

I pushed open the heavy door. Inside it was lighter, for on the left of the hall was the great window which matched the one in the Great Hall which the gale had emptied of glass. It was made of hundreds of small leaded panes, set into the stone mullions, and around the edge was a border of coloured panes, some of them bearing coats of arms. Pale, watery shafts of sunlight came in by this window, but they served only to show the untidiness and dustiness of the hall. On the right hand side the great stone fireplace was piled high with grey wood ash. There was no fire and the ashes had not been taken away for at least a week. Filmy grey flakes of it lay over everything. From a half-open door at the back of the hall came the sound of untuneful singing mingled with the indolent, intermittent sweep of a brush. I left Jassy standing, looking round with a bird-like look, in the middle of the hall and went over to the doorway. I was glad to see Janey; she was a little slut, but young and as yet unspoiled and quite civil. She scrambled to her feet and looked at me as though I were a ghost. "Miss Dilys! Whass the matter? Are you took sick?"

"Yes," I said. "I'm sick. I want my bed made and a fire lighted. And I've brought home a friend to stay with me. There must be another room got ready for her."

"I'll tell Melia."

"Tell Mrs. Capps."

"Mrs. Capps ain't here no more, Miss. There's only Melia and Cook and me. And Moult, of course."

"I see. Where's my father?"

"He's out somewhere. He's bringing three gentlemen home with him for dinner at six o'clock. Thass why I got to straighten this place."

"Well, leave it now," I said, trying to fight off the nightmare feeling of being in a strange house amongst aliens. Mrs. Capps' going was the last straw. I hadn't liked her, she was a surly, bitter old hag, but she had been a peg—unstable and rotten as everything in Mortiboys—but still a peg which had held the place together a bit. Melia was really in the saddle now.

I went back into the hall. Jassy was standing where I had left her. She looked tiny and chilled. Out of my own desolation of spirit some impulse of hospitality struggled to the surface.

"I'm sorry," I said. "It's even worse than I expected. I shouldn't have asked you here. I wouldn't have come myself, but there was nowhere else to go." I sat down on the nearest chair and began to cry.

"It's all right," Jassy said, keeping her distance. She was not one of those girls who pat and paw you and exasperate you to further tears as soon as you cry. "I like it. It's a fine place. You'll feel better when you've had a rest. Couldn't you go to bed for a little while?"

"There's nothing I'd like more. But my bed won't be fit to sleep in, and if Melia has anything to do with it, it never will be."

"We'll see about that. What's through there?"

"The library. We use it as a parlour."

"Then there'll be a sofa. Come on, Dilys. You must lie down."

"But Janey's cleaning there."

"She can clean it when you've rested. You've some right here, Dilys. It's your home."

"It isn't. It's father's. And he'll want that room cleaned by six o'clock. He's got company."

"Good Lord, how long do you think it takes to clean a room? If you'll lie down there for an hour I'll have your own room ready."

I groaned. I should have stayed at school and faced Twizzy's questions and reproaches. There was no place for me here. And certainly there was no place for Jassy, especially if she thought she was going to organize things and stand up for me. But I couldn't say or do any more. I let her lead me into the parlour and settle me on the sofa with two cushions under my head and a shawl over my feet.

As soon as I lay down the worst pain in my head seemed to be a little blunted, and a not unpleasant wave of exhaustion swept over me. I had spent the night crying and now I was hungry for sleep. But I lay for some minutes in a state of tension, momentarily expecting Melia to come bouncing in to turn me out so that Janey could go on working. At best I expected Janey to enter and go on with her brushing. But everything was still. Presently I fell asleep.

When I woke Jassy was standing by my side, arranging a tray on a table. The sofa had been rolled back a little way from the hearth, where a bright fire was blazing. The room was perfectly clean and tidy.

"What time is it?" I asked, testing my head by lifting it very carefully from the cushion. There was no pain at all.

"Just four. You've had a good sleep. Do you feel better?"

"Immensely better," I said, sitting up completely. And I did. Sleep is a wonderful thing. Five hours of it had laid a soft kind of buffer between my mind and the raw ache of last night's interview with Charles, the nerve-jangling fuss of our last hours at school, and the desolation of that wretched homecoming. I was still heartbroken, but I was physically sound again. I looked at the tray, which was properly set out, with tea and two piles of sandwiches. Then I looked at Jassy. Her face was shiny, her forehead was marked with a dusty streak, and one loop of the plaits at the back of her head had come unpinned and was hanging loose.

"You've been working like a nigger," I said remorsefully. And I thought that no one else in the world could have cleaned that awful room so thoroughly without waking a person asleep in it.

"Who is Melia?" asked Jassy, narrowing her eyes at me across the teapot.

"Father's paramour," I said flatly.

"I might have guessed that, I suppose. She seems to resent my being here." She paused and thought for a minute. "Look here, Dilys, this is going to be horribly awkward. I think I'd better go away to-morrow."

I cried out and stretched my hands towards her in a burst of desolation.

"No, Jassy, please. Don't mind what Melia says, or even father. I'll stand up to him if necessary. But you must stay with me just a little while. Till I've decided what to do, Jassy, please. It won't always be like this, I promise you. They'll leave us alone presently, and we'll go riding to get out of the house. It won't be so bad."

"Well," she said, not very willingly, "I'll stay a little. If you promise to tell me the moment you would like me to go. To tell you the truth, I've had my bellyful of living where I wasn't wanted."

"I want you," I said. "You may be certain of that. Will that do?"

We set about the tea, and as I ate and drank I worked myself into a state of rebellious self-confidence. I would have Jassy. Whatever happened she should stay as long as she liked. Neither father nor Melia was going to separate me from the only friend I had in the world. That wasn't asking much, I thought harshly; there'd never been a servant on my side, father hated the sight of me, Charles had deserted me. There was no other word to describe that cautious, chilly explanation about not being able to marry for years, and the unfairness of tying ourselves down with promises now that the regiment was ordered abroad. Jassy was the one person in the world who cared whether I lived or died, was sick or well, and I would cling to her as long as she would let me. Pull devil, pull baker! I thought.

And at that moment father walked in. He came in as he always did, just as he came from the fields or the woods, without even wiping his boots. He propped his gun in the corner, threw his game bag on the floor, dropped his hat on the first chair, and came striding towards the hearth. I got to my feet and stood still, though the long vibrations of terror and loathing and perverse affection which he roused in me coursed shudderingly along my veins.

"So you're back," he said. His voice sounded neither pleased nor angry, and not—thank God—the least bit curious.

"Yes," I said. And wondered how I could ever have been such a fool. That morning, safe in the dormitory, I had thought that I could creep back and lose myself in the careless disorder of Mortiboys. I had forgotten that this moment must come. Better by far have faced old Twizzy. And that is me all over, I thought, running away from one mess into another worse one. And I thought sickly of how I had hoped that when next I faced Old Nick I should have had Charles by my side, a man of my own, saying that he wanted to marry me. Fool, fool, fool!

"Company too," said father in that same noncommittal voice. "Wake up, my girl. Or aren't introductions fashionable any more."

"This is a friend of mine, Jassy Woodroffe. She's going to stay with me," I added, remembering my recent resolution, and thinking that I might as well strike the first blow.

"Woodroffe. Woodroffe. That sounds familiar," said Old Nick when, having acknowledged the introduction with a courtliness which he could assume very easily when it pleased him, he sank down on the end of the sofa. "Ah, I have it. That was the name of the carpenter at Minsham. As damned interfering a Radical fellow as ever walked. Funny to be reminded of him."

"That was my father," Jassy said calmly. "I don't think he would have asked a better epitaph."

Father turned and looked at Jassy. Very slowly and deliberately he looked her up and down. It was a look which he turned on me sometimes, and I could not stand it. Jassy merely stared back, her face showing nothing but placid interest.

"He was a good carpenter too," Old Nick said at last. And there was a trace of apology in his voice.

"Yes, he was that too. And many other things that you wouldn't know about. Mr. Helmar, would you like a cup of your own tea?"

"I never drink the stuff. You can give me a sandwich."

Jassy passed the plate and then refilled my cup and her own. Old Nick munched in silence, stretching his legs to the fire and watching the spirals of smoke which rose from his wet boots.

Presently Jassy said, conversationally, "I expect you wonder why we are here in the middle of term, Mr. Helmar?"

"Well, why are you?" he asked in a voice that would have discouraged me and made me stammer.

"Because we're in disgrace." Lightly, as though she were telling a funny story, she repeated exactly what she had said to Mrs. Twysdale on the night before, ending, "but Mrs. Twysdale wouldn't believe that I went to meet my mother, or that Dilys only came to keep me company. And then I lost my temper and hit her in the face with a mug. I think I ought to tell you that because you're sure to have a letter warning you against harbouring such a bad character."

"Are you a bad character?"

"I must be, to hit Mrs. Twysdale with a mug!"

"You're a damned liar, too," said Old Nick. "Little girls who hit their teachers with mugs aren't afraid of the dark; and little girls who are afraid of the dark don't hit their teachers with mugs. You can't have it both ways, young woman."

Jassy burst into one of her rollicking laughs. Nothing that Mrs. Twysdale or Miss Ogilvy had ever said could make her restrain that laugh. She threw her head back and opened her mouth and really made a noise.

"That's very clever of you, Mr. Helmar," she said, checking herself. "But you see, after that Mrs. Twysdale did make such a fuss that Dilys said she was coming home. And since I haven't got a home and jobs are hard to get in the middle of the term, she asked me here. I hope you don't mind."

"It makes no difference to me," father said. Then, as though his attention had been suddenly arrested, he asked:

"Jobs. What sort of a job could you get?"

"I could teach in a school or be a children's governess."

"How old are you then?"

"Nearly as old as Dilys. I'm sixteen."

"I shouldn't have thought it. Then it's high time you both left school." He got up and went to the cupboard and took out a bottle and a glass, poured himself a drink, and drank it at a gulp. Behind his back I signed to Jassy that we would go upstairs. I thought that we would make our escape while he was still in this amiable mood. We stood up. Old Nick, pouring another drink, stopped and looked in our direction. "You'd better both make yourselves beautiful and come down to dinner."

"Y . . . yes, father," I said, completely surprised. I had never before dined with him when he had company.

"Good God, Dilys," he said, "I thought they were going to teach you not to stammer."

"They didn't teach us anything, but we learnt a lot," said Jassy saucily. She seized my hand and pulled me towards the door.

Old Nick grunted and proceeded to fill his glass.

Going upstairs I thought that Jassy would probably say that he was a nice man. He had, I thought, been extremely amiable to her; and I knew that most girls, if a naturally surly man doesn't, for once, snap their heads off, get inflated ideas. But I was prepared to bear her comments patiently because she had got us out of an awkward hole. She had even prepared him for any letter Mrs. Twysdale might write. However, Jassy dropped my hand and, clasping both her own on her waist, turned her eyes upwards and said, "What an ordeal! I felt as though I were sitting on top of a volcano."

"You hid that feeling very well. You did marvellously, Jassy. By to-morrow he'll be used to the idea that we're here and probably won't ask another question about it. He happened to be amiable to-day. He'd probably shot well. And perhaps you wonder why I am so scared of him."

"Oh no. I'm scared of him too."

"I have a special reason to be," I said, opening the door of my own room. "You see, whenever he gets angry with me he throws mother at me. I happen to be terribly like her to look at. That sets him against me to start with. Oh, Jassy, how nice this looks. I'm sure you did it."

I looked round my bright cosy room.

"I had to choose a room for myself, since you were asleep," she said. "I hope it's all right. Just across there, the one with a sort of Chinese paper."

"That isn't a *sort* of Chinese paper," I said. "It's genuine. It's reputed to have been smuggled out of China in hollow bamboos. I remember mother talking about it. She liked it, too. Mrs. Hatton wanted to take it away with her, but it was too fragile to take down."

"It wouldn't have fitted into Green Farm very well. But I expect Barney would have liked it."

"Barney Hatton?"

Jassy nodded.

"Do you know him?"

"In a way. He was the boy who saved me from being put in the pond."

"You didn't mention his name."

"No. I was trying to make it mysterious and thrilling. But it was Barney." A gentler look than I should have thought her rather hard little face capable of assuming shone for a second and was gone. "He was . . ." she said, and then checked herself to say briskly, "We've got to make ourselves beautiful. For me that will be a long job."

The problem of clothes took possession of my mind. "What dress will you wear?"

"My best one. The red."

"That isn't suitable," I said. "Come in and shut the door. I'll find you one. Anything that fitted me two years ago will fit you now. They're all here somewhere."

I opened my cupboard and delved towards the back of it where the dresses I could no longer wear were hanging. I had plenty of dresses. The one thing Old Nick would give me was money, and during my long, lonely holidays I often spent whole days in Colchester buying clothes. It was about the only pleasure a holiday brought me. Some of the dresses I wore only once or twice, a few not at all, for I had really no use for the pretty, flimsy ones which attracted me most in the shops. They were too fussy for school wear or for dining with Old Nick, who often had not shaved for three days. And never, until this evening, had I been invited to dine with his guests.

"I'm going to be very grand," I said, with my head in the cupboard, feeling my hands come in contact with a dress of lilac satin edged with frills of white lace, "so you must, too." I knew what I was looking for, and eventually drew it out, a little dress of a colour called hyacinth blue, rather plain and made of heavy silk. The corsage, the sleeves, and the hem were finished with rouleaux of the same material. I had taken it to school, intending to wear it at the concert to which we were taken annually. But at the last minute, dressing in the chilly dormitory, my courage had failed me, and I had decided in favour of something less conspicuous. "It's just your dress, Jassy," I said, holding it out. "I've never worn it either."

She took it by the shoulders and measured it against herself, peering forward to look in my mirror. "Mercy!" she cried. "Look at me. Dilys, you might have told me. My hair!" She skipped to the door, halted on the threshold and said, "I might have said 'Thank you' first, mightn't I? Thank you, Dilys," and vanished.

I dressed slowly, taking care to conceal as far as possible my resemblance to mother. At school I was always being called stupid, and it was also one of father's epithets for me. In many ways I deserved it. My brain was slower than my feelings, and so I often did stupid things. My feelings, for instance, made me rush home to Mortiboys as a retreat, when a little cool thought would have shown me that it was nothing of the kind. That was stupid. So was my habit of stammering when nervous. Also, I found certain things very difficult to learn. Miss Hamilton accused me of not trying, but the mere effort to concentrate, especially on numbers, made my head ache until I was silly. But in other ways I was not so stupid. I could understand people in a fashion. I knew—and I don't think anyone else in school even guessed it—that Mrs. Twysdale was crazy about Miss Hamilton in a peculiar fashion, as though she were a man. That was why Mrs. Twysdale hated Jassy so much. Jassy knew she was jealous, but she didn't know *how* jealous. And in the same way I was not blind to the grudge father had against me. When I was young, in those far away days when we seemed to be a happy and united family, he had been very fond of me. Now, even if he could forget for a moment that I was mother's daughter, there was my face and my hair to remind him and jog his spite.

So to-night, because I remembered mother, dressed for the evening with a mass of little curls on her forehead, I brushed my hair upwards and backwards, leaving my brow bare; and because she had always been ivory pale I coloured my face very rosy; and because our mouths were identical in shape I reddened mine, sharpening the line of my top lip and thickening the lower.

And as I worked upon this new and undeniably pretty face I thought how odd it was that though all girls wanted to be pretty, and envied you if you were, looks were really no use at all. Charles had thought I was pretty, he had said so. But for some reason, although we hadn't quarrelled and I had been as charming to him as I could, crawling out through the pantry window to meet him, letting him know how dear to me he was, he hadn't wanted to marry me. His relief, once he had said that marriage was impossible, was like something visible and noisy. It shrieked at me. Why? What happened to men? What could happen to a man in the short interval of a week, so that at one meeting he said he loved you and kissed you until you were dizzy, and at the next said in a careful, cold way that marriage was impossible and this must be good-bye? It was nothing I had done or said, for we had not met in the interval. It was just a mystery, and the bewilderment it caused me made the grief just that little bit harder to bear.

Sitting there, staring at my reflection and noting how the pinkness of my cheeks made my eyes seem darker and brighter and my hair more yellow, I wished that Charles could see me now. He had only really *seen* me twice, once in the garden here when he had left the card party for a breath of air, and on the day when I went back to school. Our other meetings had been at night, in the dark. If he could see me now, would he kiss me? The thought sent a kind of sick longing through me, through every part of me; even my fingers ached. And at that moment, even as I was thinking of Charles and longing for him, something shifted in my brain and I was suddenly and incongruously reminded of the boy whom Jassy had mentioned some minutes before. Barney Hatton. He was the first boy I ever kissed.

Five, six years ago. The whole of that queer miserable time

came back to me, all flavoured with the taste of that autumn day.
Old Nick—only I had not then caught from the servants the
trick of calling him that—was still in the worst period of his
despair over mother. He had not yet sought any consolation from
village girls or from the doxy at "The Evening Star"; he was
merely drinking hard and gambling heavily. And he had not yet
settled down into his firm dislike for me; there were moments
then when he would treat me with maudlin tenderness and then
suddenly push me away or shout at me roughly. And I was young.
I did not understand. He had told me, quite kindly, that when
Mr. Hatton came over to play cards next time he would bring his
little boy to spend the day and be company for me, and I had
expected a child. I had the swing mended and looked out some
toys which I had discarded. I was surprised to find that the "little
boy" was a good deal older and a great deal bigger than I was, a
serious, quiet boy, whose manner was a curious blend of shyness
and aggressiveness. We were very shy of one another at first, and
I asked him nervously what he would like to do. He said, "I came
to see the house." So I showed him over. We went everywhere,
even into those parts of it where I had never ventured before, because, for as long as I could remember, I have been afraid to be
by myself far from other people's company. All morning we
explored the house. Mortiboys was not large compared with some
houses, but being told it was full of passages that turned and
twisted, full of sudden steps up and down, and of rooms that led
out of one another. Barney hardly spoke at all; he walked and
stared as though he were asleep walking, and when I tried to talk
to him he answered in a cross tone of voice. I imagined that he
was disappointed in the house and felt apologetic, wishing that
all the improvements that had been planned could have been
made before the trouble broke.

But afterwards, when we ate our meal alone together, and then
went into the grounds, he altered. He looked at me kindly and
with admiration. I was young, but not too young to know that.
And once, when he helped me over a wall and held both my hands

because I was afraid to jump, he went very red and seemed to be embarrassed for a long while. At seven o'clock Mrs. Capps, who was very strict with me, called me to come in and have supper and go to bed. Master Hatton, she said, was to wait in the hall until his father was ready. So I said, "I have to go now, Barney. Good-bye." And, going very grown-up suddenly, he took my hand and kissed it. Nobody had ever done that before and I was pleased. I looked down on his head: his hair was bright brown and very well brushed, and his neck was nice, much younger than his face. When he lifted his face I bent forward and kissed him. I never knew why, except that I thought he was nice and his neck was so young. And he kissed me back, very, very softly.

I hoped he would come again. But soon after that Old Nick and Mr. Hatton, after years and years of friendship, had a quarrel, and before it was mended I had been sent to school.

Very soon after that Mr. Hatton died. I never saw Barney again.

But in one holiday, when I was fourteen, there was a boy in the stable-yard helping Sharples. And he had the same bright brown hair and young-looking neck. And that holiday I pretended that I did not like riding alone and got the boy, Ned—that was his name, I remember—to ride with me. One day, when he was showing me a cut on his hand, I kissed him too. It wasn't the same at all. It was dreadful. For a long time it made me go hot all over to think about it.

After that I didn't kiss anyone again until I kissed Charles. And that was very different.

And yet, as I rose at last and left my dressing-table and my memories, I was thinking of Barney Hatton. Not of Charles. Charles had gone. Presently the seas would divide us, but that would mean nothing. Deeper and colder than the sea itself was the memory of that cold, careful explanation, that shrieking relief when the fatal speech had been spoken. Charles had gone. But Barney Hatton. . . . One day, when my heart had stopped aching, when I was myself again, I would think about him.

(177)

I went to see how Jassy was getting on with her dressing. The nice blue dress was spread out over her bed, and Jassy, wearing her old red one, was sitting in a chair reading a book. Her black plaits, very neat and shiny, were re-arranged in their elaborate curves and twists. Her face had its familiar privet-flower yellow pallor, and her mouth, untouched, was redder than mine.

"You didn't like it," I said regretfully, pointing to the dress.

"I loved it, Dilys. I put it on. It was lovely, but I just felt silly in it. I don't know why. I hope you don't mind. I'm just as grateful, but I feel better like this."

I looked at the red dress. It was worn and too skimpy. Too high in the neck and with meagre sleeves. But then it flashed into my mind that I had only this morning thought it a good thing that Jassy was not pretty. I realized that in offering her an attractive gown I had once again let my feelings run away with my wits. I said, with false heartiness, "I think you're very wise, Jassy. Red is your colour, blue is not. You look very nice indeed."

"But the order was to be beautiful," she said with a funny little grin. "Well, you are, Dilys. But I expect you know that."

It was the first time she had ever mentioned my appearance, and I realized that, amongst the gushing of the girls at school, her reticence had been attractive.

"My looks haven't done me much good," I said bitterly.

"There's plenty of time. They will," she said. And again I thought of Barney Hatton.

The dinner party was queer and interesting and rather exciting. Father's guests were Sir Edward Follesmark, whom everyone knew as the Mad Squire, because whenever there were rows about labourers' wages, or about men poaching, he sided with the labourers or the poachers; Sir Evelyn Fennel and his son, Stephen.

Sir Evelyn was a thin, sick-looking man with a yellow face and reddish hair receding from his temples. He was a notorious gambler. There was a legend in our part of the country that once, at the end of a mad and reckless game, he had staked his wife, and lost. The story said that Lady Fennel had laughed and insisted upon paying the winner of the game ten thousand pounds, saying that she could not value herself at less. Whether the story were true or not I could not say; it was only servants' gossip by the time I heard it. I did know that she was a rich woman, and not on good terms with Sir Evelyn. Sir Edward, who was a bachelor, was a stout, short, red-faced man with a shock of white hair. He was always untidily dressed and liked to potter about his estate working like a labourer. He was always delighted if a stranger mistook him for one of his own men. But despite his eccentricities he was the most truly nice and gentlemanly person who ever visited Mortiboys. I had known him all my life, and when I was small he used always to have a present for me in one of his bulging pockets. He was immensely rich and extremely charitable, in thought as well as deed. I think he remained on friendly terms with father after he turned queer because he was sorry for him, not because, like Sir Evelyn and, in the past, Mr. Hatton, he didn't care with whom, or where, he played so long as he could get a good game.

Stephen Fennel, who was reputed to be very clever, had just completed three years' study at Cambridge University. I had not seen him since he had been brought, a stocky, silent, critical little boy to the children's parties which mother used to give at Christmas time. He was the youngest member and the only boy in a family of girls, and I remember hearing someone say that he was very much spoiled. But now, meeting him again, I saw no evidence of that. He had improved, I thought. He seemed anxious to make himself pleasant. I should not have recognized in him the little boy who had seemed to regard all games as childish and parties a waste of time. He was not handsome, his face was already tinged with the sallow yellowness of his father's, and his hair, being black, emphasized it.

The arrival of Jassy and myself in the parlour was obviously unexpected. Old Nick had not thought it worth while to mention that his daughter was home and had been invited to dine. Perhaps he had forgotten the matter. He had drunk a good deal in the interval, though he had found time to tidy himself and to put on the best clothes he had. They were getting old-fashioned, for he had bought no new clothes since mother left him. He and Sir Edward looked quaint and old-fashioned beside the Fennels, who were both addicted to dandyism.

Sir Edward greeted me with his old bluff friendliness, and both Stephen and his father, though less familiar, and obviously masking some surprise, contrived to make me feel that I was, after all, in the right place, and young and pretty and welcome. I had been nervous on the stairs coming down, and outside in the hall, as I heard the voices in the parlour, had longed for a mother or for some older woman to take charge of the situation. But it was all right. I looked round immediately the first greetings were over, intending to introduce Jassy; but Old Nick, who had done nothing to ease the awkward moment of entry for me, his daughter, had already taken her rather clumsily by the elbow and pushed her before Sir Edward.

"I reckon you remember this young lady's father," he said off-handedly. "Woodroffe. Mixed up in that Summerfield business."

Sir Edward's kind red face went wooden for a moment, whether with his effort to pin down the name in his memory, or with surprise at Old Nick's reference to a long-ago affair, or—as might be excusable—at this introduction to the daughter of a radical carpenter on the hearth of the parlour at Mortiboys, I could not tell. But within a moment his natural benevolent expression was restored, and enhancing it was the most eager and delicate desire to give Jassy assurance and put her at her ease.

"Indeed, I remember your father, my dear. He was a friend of mine; in fact, an ally. I'm proud to meet his daughter. Fennel . . ."

Sir Edward's big booming voice interrupted Sir Evelyn in something he was saying to me, and his subsequent introduction of Jassy had just a grain of truculence in it. Again I thought, in a panic, that I had been careless and inconsiderate. I had just asked Jassy to come home with me, partly for her sake, partly for mine. I had not taken into consideration the social question. For one thing, I had not thought for a moment that Jassy and I would see anyone but Old Nick himself; for another, I should never have believed that her name would strike a chord in his memory and thus attach the tag "carpenter's daughter" to her. But I could see that Sir Evelyn was puzzled.

"Jassy and I were at school together until this morning," I said hastily, without thinking of the question which such a statement must inevitably raise.

"Until this morning, eh?" said Sir Edward. "And what . . ." But just then Moult, very stately and on his best behaviour, announced dinner; and it was Stephen, whom I felt capable of fobbing off, who, next me at table, asked why Jassy and I had come home in the middle of term.

"I'll tell you another time," I said. "It isn't entirely my story."

He smiled, and saying, "That sounds very romantic and intriguing," let the matter drop. But throughout the meal he seemed to take pains to talk to me, asking little careful questions which he could be sure I should be able to answer, and telling me about Cambridge, which I had never seen.

As soon as the meal was over the men went back into the library to play cards, and Jassy and I sat in the hall, where the ashes had been rather half-heartedly removed and a new fire lighted. We talked for some time, mainly about school, speculating upon what kind of letter Mrs. Twysdale would write to father, and following the evening routine of school with, "Now they're at supper . . ." and "Prayers has just started . . ." and "Now they're off to bed." It gave us a very emancipated feeling to be sitting there in front of the dying fire when we knew that the "Lights Out" bell had sounded.

"Miss Hamilton will miss you, Jassy," I said idly.

"I was going to leave at Christmas in any case. I think she

meant to ask me to stay on and teach. But I shouldn't have done that. I have already written to two places about posts." She gave a little sigh. "Miss Hamilton had been very good to me. She was a true friend. That's why I would have had to leave."

"Because of Twizzy?"

"Yes. Miss Hamilton is better with her without me, than she would be without her and with me. And it was going to be one or the other. I saw that a long time ago." She moved impatiently in her chair. "Don't think about them, don't talk about them. When I think of her *face*! Honestly, Dilys, I could die of shame."

"She hit you first."

"What difference does that make? It was unforgivable of me. Actually I didn't mind. I'd have done it again this morning, or this afternoon. But now, being back here, and hearing Sir Edward speak of my father. He'd have been horrified. Father, I mean." She tugged a handkerchief out of her sleeve and suddenly, to my horror, began to cry. I had never before seen her shed a tear. To make matters worse I heard the door of the salon open, a sudden sound of voices, quickly hushed by the door's closing again, and then a rather hesitant step. Stephen Fennel was coming across the hall towards us. Jassy brushed her face with the handkerchief and, falling on her knees, began to rake the fire together.

Stephen said, "I have earned a little respite, I think. May I?" He indicated the vacant place on the settle by my side. He sat down, and Jassy, quite calm now, turned from the fire and, drawing her feet under her, sat on the rug.

"Dilys," he said, "I want you to do me a favour. Ask me one day and show me all over the house, will you?"

"A poor favour," I said lightly. "But of course. Come when you like."

"I want to see the Great Hall."

"But you've seen it. Don't you remember coming to parties? We had them in there." I nodded my head to the big, heavily-nailed doorway beyond the fireplace. "It's horrid now. The window blew out you know, and it hasn't been mended. The birds fly in and out and the rain comes in. There's nothing to see."

"Nothing save one of the finest hammer roofs in England and, I believe, a genuine twelfth century minstrels' gallery. I have become interested in such things since the children's parties, Dilys. I'd hoped you had forgotten them. I was a horrid child, interested only in congruent triangles and things of that kind. Cambridge has taught me a great deal."

"If it's given you a taste for ruins," I said, "you can satisfy it easily by coming to see Mortiboys—and Jassy and me!"

"Delightful flowers often blossom amongst ruins," he said sententiously. And I thought of the stocky, silent little boy who had seemed to be so critical of everything. How queerly people developed as they grew up. What had I been myself in those distant days? So sure of myself; so delighted with my dress; so inflated because it was *my* party. Nothing of that little girl remained—except perhaps the delight in finery. I slid my hand over my satin shrouded knee. No! That was wrong. People developed, and here and there they were pruned a little by their circumstances, but the core of them altered very little. And as that thought went through my mind, with its offshoots of memories about the conditions that mould one, I heard myself asking, to my own intense surprise:

"Stephen, what happened to Barney Hatton?"

"Ah," he said, smoothing back one rebellious strand of his black hair. "Of course, there is a connection between the Hattons and this place. I was at a loss for the moment. He's still at Green Farm, for all I know. Mrs. Hatton died last winter. Mother went to the funeral. I remember. But I should think Barney is still there. By all accounts he has sunk every penny he had in the place. He's taking his farming very seriously, I believe."

"I thought of him," I said, "because once, ages ago, I showed him over the house. It wasn't such a ruin then. But he didn't seem to like it much."

(183)

"Barney worshipped Mortiboys," said Jassy in a hard, fierce little voice.

"Indeed," Stephen said, dismissing the subject. "I suppose I must go back now. But Dilys, remember you have promised to show me the house. And I'd like it too, if you—and Miss Woodroffe too, of course, if she's still here—would come over and see us. Mother would like that, I know."

"We'd like it too," I said. "Jassy and I would love to make some visits."

"I'll send word then making more definite arrangements. I'm delighted that you're home again, Dilys."

"So am I, for some reasons," I said.

"Another conquest," said Jassy, as the door closed behind him. "What it is to be pretty."

"Don't talk to me of conquests," I said bitterly. I glanced at the clock. "Just this time last night . . ."

"It seems ages ago," said Jassy, getting up and stretching like a cat. "Another life in fact." And although that glance at the clock's face had given me a momentary stab, I could not contradict her. It did seem ages ago.

Mounting the stairs with Jassy I thought that after all feelings were good guides sometimes. I had been right to come home. The day's happenings reared themselves like a barrier between me and last night's heartbreak. Even Stephen—though never, never could he raise in me a tenth of the feeling that Charles had done —but even Stephen, with his obvious admiration and his desire to see me again, contributed to that barrier.

And yet, when Jassy had said good-night, and I had hung up my dress and cleaned my face and got into bed, misery, sheer plain misery had me in its grip again. For an hour I sobbed into my pillow, wanting Charles, wanting nothing, nothing but him; living again those happy moments when he had said that he loved me, and that horrible moment when, without actually saying so in words, he had informed me that he didn't. And then, when I had cried myself into an empty hollow shell, a thought struck

(184)

me. Was my trouble merely that I wanted to be loved? Not that I myself loved too easily or too well? It was feasible. Nobody had loved me yet. Mother hadn't, or she would not have left me behind. Father didn't, or he would have gained some comfort from my presence. Charles hadn't, that was plain. And so, aware of a great lack in my life, I ran round seeking love, like a hungry puppy seeking for food, and, like a puppy, courting rebuffs and disappointments.

Under the impact of this self-revealing thought I sat up straight in bed. Had I ever loved Charles, really? Or had I just been pleased and flattered by his attentions to me? Had he actually been very wise in leaving me as he did? Had he guessed that deep down inside myself I was incapable of loving anyone except Dilys Helmar? Was that true? My head began to ache, as it always did when I tried to understand something that was beyond me. My headaches were queer. I had watched, and even questioned, other people and found that their heads ached in the front. Mine came at the back, beginning with a dull numbness at the back of the skull and growing more violent until I should not have felt worse if someone had struck me repeatedly with a heavy club. But to-night I did not, as I usually did, relinquish the problem that had started the pain. Sitting up, holding my head in my hands, I went on thinking about love and being in love, about how much of it all was an outgoing towards the other person, and how much a mere adoration of oneself as reflected in the other person's affection. I thought until the pain reached a stupefying pitch. Then I rolled over, covered my cold shoulders and fell asleep. But in the morning I knew that I had had an experience. I was not young any more. I was as old as Eve.

Within a week it felt as though Jassy and I had been at Mortiboys half a lifetime. There was a queer timelessness about the days; I had noticed it before when the holiday had seemed longer than four terms on end. Except when, as on the night of our homecoming, Old Nick had company, no one consulted the clock at all. The master's wishes, within the limits imposed by Melia's whims, ruled the house, and Old Nick's habits were as irregular as his moods. I—and Jassy with me—kept out of his way as much as possible. When we did meet, which was generally at the evening meal, he sometimes ignored us entirely, or, especially if he had been drinking, was-surly to me while extending towards Jassy a kind of savage raillery which she bore with astonishing good humour. Sometimes she succeeded in making him laugh. She had, more than anyone I ever knew, the knack of making a simple thing seem funny, or of seeing the ridiculous side of something which other people had always accepted without humour. More than once there had been trouble at school because she made girls giggle over things which had been there for years and never before occasioned a glimmer of mirth. But Jassy's quips and jokes at Mortiboys I could not wholeheartedly enjoy, because there was an element of danger even in father's mirth. Occasionally it seemed to me that he resented the amusement that Jassy afforded; anyway, he would often follow his bark of laughter with some surly, snubbing remark. And I felt happier out of his presence.

Fortunately the weather was good. And Sharples, at my request, produced an aged, steady horse called Major, which he considered a suitable mount for a beginner; so Jassy and I, with a timeless day ahead of us, could roam where we wished.

One mellow October morning we left the stable yard, skirted the great bulk of the house, wound our way past the wreck of the gateway, and halted. I know now that the same thought was in both our minds. But it was Jassy who said:

"Let's go to Minsham All Saints, Dilys. I'd like to see the place again. And the Lower Road will be all right to-day."

The Lower Road, impassable in wet weather, was indescribably lovely that morning. It was sunk between hedges that glowed with the fruit of hawthorn and the wild rose, and frothed with the feathery tangle of wild clematis. Great beeches, burning amber, stood at intervals in the hedges, and the leaves that had already fallen carpeted the ground. Now and then, through a gap in the hedge or a space between the trees, one could see the marshes, very green and flat, patterned by the silver of the creeks that wound through them.

"That's Green Farm," said Jassy at last, pointing a finger towards a crooked red chimney. "Barney Hatton's home, you know."

"I didn't know. I've never seen it," I said. My voice was cool and ordinary, but a little spurt of excitement rose in my stomach and thrust its way upwards.

The road ended, opening out to a wide green with a pond at its further end and a circle of low cottages on its outskirts.

"That's where I used to live," said Jassy, pointing to one of the cottages. "And there's the pond where Barney saved me a ducking. And here's Green Farm." I followed her pointing finger and saw a low, thatched farmhouse, set slantwise to the Green, with a narrow garden in front and a bigger one dividing it from the cottage which Jassy had indicated. It looked comfortable, but humble. Very humble after Mortiboys; and the Hattons had lived at Mortiboys!

"Shall we," said Jassy in a small, diffident voice, "shall we call on Barney? I would like to see him again. He was such a nice boy. I'd like to see what he's grown up like."

"I don't mind," I said.

"Oh, not if you don't want to. I'll go by myself if you'd rather."

"I'll come."

"This way then," and she turned Major's head towards the right and just ahead of us, set at an angle, I saw a gateway set between two low buildings of flint.

Jassy slipped out of the saddle—she was already adept at mounting and dismounting—opened the gate, led Major through, and held it open for me. Then she closed it and, with unnecessary precaution, for Major would have stood for a week, slipped his rein forward and twisted it round a post. She did it all as neatly and expertly as she did everything with her hands, and when she lifted them to settle her hat I was surprised to see that they were trembling.

"I wonder if Meggie is still here," she said. Then she skipped over the cobbles between the yard and the back door of the house and, flexing her little fist, beat on it with, I thought, unnecessary vigour. There was no answer and presently, after making a grimace to me over her shoulder, she hammered on the door again. And within a second the door was flung open and a veritable crone, wrinkled and bent and furious, thrust her head around its edge. Astonishment wiped away the fury for a second and then was replaced by an even more venomous expression.

"Jassy Woodroffe," exclaimed the crone in the high shrill voice of the very deaf. "I wondered who it wuz, beating the door fit to bring it down. What brings *you* here?"

"It's Meggie," said Jassy, and there was genuine pleasure in her voice. "And you look just the same."

"Who did you reckon I'd look like?" I saw her little bright eyes, almost lost in the mass of wrinkles, sweep Jassy from head to foot, taking in every detail of the old green habit of mine which we had spent hours in fitting and altering. "You've got very fine. Who's that with you?"

"Miss Helmar from Mortiboys."

"Mortiboys did you say?" Jassy nodded vigorously. The crone bobbed in my direction and I smiled at her. Her expression of bewildered resentment would have made anyone smile.

"We've come to see Barney. Is he at home?" Jassy shouted.

"Master Barney is ploughing the Twelve Acre."

"Twelve Acre? I know. All right, Meggie, we'll find him."

She was turning away from the door when the old woman said crossly:

"Hold your hurry. You can go traipsing about in the fields if you've a mind to, but Miss Helmar, do she want Master Barney, should come in and wait, proper fashion."

I resented this difference on Jassy's behalf and said stiffly, "Thank you, I'll stay with Jassy."

(188)

"Best both come in then," she said, and held the door wide while I dismounted and fastened Gyp, who, unlike Major, would not have waited a moment, but have been off round the yard seeking, Satan-fashion, what she might devour.

Meggie led the way through a warm and cosy kitchen which gave the impression of having been lived in always, along a dark passage and into a parlour which felt and smelt like a tomb. Everything in it shone with cleanliness, but the cold air was heavy and undisturbed. No one had sat down in that room for a long time.

The old woman pulled forward a chair and said, "Please to sit down." Then she shuffled over to an ornate corner cupboard, painted white with pretty little wreaths of gesso work picked out in natural colours. She took out, with slow deliberation, first a silver tray, which she set on the centre table, then a brown jar with a lid, then two slender fluted wine glasses and a decanter full of some pale yellow wine.

"Thass ony cowslip, but thass my own make, and good though I say it. Help yourself, Miss Helmar, and take a biscuit. Now I'll go and ring the bell and Master Barney'll be here in no time." Her wrinkled hands, the colour of earth, hovered about the tray for a second, rearranging its contents, then, with a nod, as though the ritual of hospitality had been duly observed, she shuffled away. A moment later the sound of a deep-tongued bell rang through the house.

"Surly old thing," I said.

"She wasn't surly to *you*," said Jassy composedly. "She hates me like poison. She always did. Not that I ever did her any harm. Still, she has a good heart. She once gave away all her savings. And I bet Barney is served better than . . . than most people."

"Don't spare my feelings," I said. "Always complete a sentence, Jassy Woodroffe. Barney is better served than we are at Mortiboys." It was a goodish imitation of Miss Hamilton's voice.

"Yes, ma'am," said Jassy meekly. Then in her normal voice: "But it's true. I'd like to see Meggie set about those sluts at

Mortiboys. Actually she did come from there. So did that and that and those . . ." She pointed to a little escritoire, elaborately inlaid and decorated with ormolu, to the side of the carpet, which had been cut to fit the room and bound on the raw edge with braid, and to the long curtains of faded rose-coloured velvet which dwarfed the small window. "And the whole of her life was cut down and cramped in just the same way."

"Who's? Meggie's?"

"No. My thoughts were wandering. Mrs. Hatton's. And heavens, how she would have resented my knowing that!" She gave one of her funny little sighs and turned abruptly to the table. "Shall we sample Meggie's brew? This room is like a tomb."

I heard the neck of the decanter chatter against the edge of the glass. She's nervous, I thought. And my own nerves leapt in response. There was something so formal and deliberate about sitting there in that cold, unwelcoming room, waiting for Barney to come in, interrupted from his work. This meeting, after the lapse of years, should have been casual, almost accidental. We should have looked over the gate and found him there in the yard, and the gulf between our childhoods and the present might have been bridged by the mere act of recognition. This musty room, this almost ceremonial wine, that bell tolling its summons, made the whole thing ponderous and horrible.

Almost without thinking I emptied my glass and set it down, noticing too late the sweet, light, floral quality of the wine.

"Jassy, let's go. Let's say we can't wait. I really *can't* wait. I can't breathe in this room."

"Sh," said Jassy, She stood by the table, her glass an inch from her lips, listening. She looked like a deer, disturbed in the depths of a forest. She had always a curious ability to take up graceful, almost embroidered attitudes. That was why so many people thought she was pretty, despite her big mouth and odd-shaped face. "That *is* Barney."

I remember looking towards the door of the parlour and

noticing that its white paint had worn thin and dull, and that the white china knob and finger-plates, with their little painted flowers, were cracked and chipped. And I remember hearing a heavy footstep in the long dark passage, hurried and eager at first, then faltering, until at last there was a distinct pause between the final step and the opening of the door.

Out of the blurred whirl of first impressions I gathered that the most striking thing about Barney was his size. He was enormous. His head reached to the door jamb, and his shoulders cleared the posts by an inch on either side, no more. He wore a blue shirt, faded to grey on the shoulders and outsides of the sleeves, a pair of brown breeches, heavy leggings, and thick boots to which, despite recent scraping, the sticky mud of the fields still clung in places. He had shaved that morning, and his hands and forearms had been washed within the last few minutes. They were not perfectly dry; little spirals of steam were still rising from them.

Jassy, though she may have been nervous a moment before, made one of her lightning recoveries. She ran forward like a child, stretching both hands.

"Barney. You remember us, don't you?"

"Of course." A slow smile lightened the rather harsh lines of his face. He took her hands, and then, dropping them, stretched out his right to me.

"I'm afraid we have disturbed you," I said. "Meggie told us you were busy."

"I'm always busy," he said, with another smile. His lips were thin and very flexible, curving away from sound white teeth. "And I seldom have a pleasant disturbance."

"Is this a pleasant one?" Jassy asked.

"Very pleasant. And very surprising. I often wondered what happened to you, Jassy. When Meggie said you were here I could hardly believe my ears."

"I've only been in Baildon. Sometimes I thought I'd write to you, but I was afraid you'd have forgotten me. And now I'm

(191)

staying with Dilys, so we thought we'd come over and see you."

Barney smiled again, and when his bright blue eyes with their rather bristly thick lashes looked at me, I smiled back. And Jassy smiled. But all our smiles did little to ease the queer tension that held us. Barney looked round uneasily and saw the tray.

"I'm glad Meggie remembered her manners," he said. "That's more than can be said for me, I'm afraid." He took the decanter in his big brown hand and filled the glass which I had emptied so hastily. Jassy, as though she were at home, went to the cupboard and reached down a third glass, and having set it on the tray, lifted the lid from the brown jar.

"Meggie's biscuits were famous," she said, and peeped inside. Then she leaned lower and sniffed, recoiling with a grimace of disgust.

"What's wrong?" Barney asked.

"Look." She held the jar under our noses. Inside was merely a great heap of blue and green mould. "Take a biscuit, Miss Helmar," Jassy said in Meggie's voice. We all laughed. And after that everything was better. Jassy began to chatter, saying, "Do you remember . . . ?" and "What happened to this person and that?" I sat quietly. Barney and I had only shared one experience, and whether he remembered it or had forgotten it, it was not for me to remind him. But every now and then his eyes met mine, and each time a kind of warm flood seemed to wash over me, and my whole inside quivered with excitement. I thought with resentment of Stephen Fennel and of how easily we had established a relationship. He had only to invite himself to Mortiboys and ask us to go and see his mother. And Stephen was nothing compared with Barney. It was pleasant, of course, to see Stephen's obvious admiration, and to have him treat me as a grown-up; but in a lifetime he could never raise the excitement in me that one of Barney's blue, rather furtive glances could. And when I did speak, I spoke out of peevishness, sudden and untactful.

"Barney, could you come and see us? Or were you drawn into that silly old quarrel?"

It was easy to see how, in so few years, his forehead had taken on that deep gash between the brows and his cheeks those harsh lines. They were the signs of a settled ill-humour which, banished for a moment by our presence, rushed back in answer to my question.

"If you can call that a silly . . ." he began. Then he stopped and made a visible effort to restrain himself. "I'm sorry. It probably was a silly quarrel at the beginning—most card-table disputes are silly. But it wasn't silly at the end."

"I don't know anything about it," I said.

"Then you'd better know. Perhaps you'll side with your father. I don't know how it started, I wasn't there, and my father was never any good at describing things. But he and your father quarrelled about a game, and as neither of them was strictly sober, abuse flowed pretty freely. Father swore he'd never enter Mortiboys again. That didn't matter. He couldn't afford to play anyway, and nobody minded. Even he seemed not to. But afterwards we knew differently. He began to break up and lose interest in life, as though going to Mortiboys and gambling had been the only thing that had held him together. Within nine months he was dead. I don't blame your father for that, Dilys. Nobody but a fool could do so. They'd quarrelled, and if the affair couldn't be patched over, well, one was as much to blame as the other. But . . ." he leaned forward, resting his weight on his hands, which were gripping his knees, "that wasn't the end. When he was dying, father, who could never string a couple of sentences together lucidly, suddenly began to talk. For forty-eight hours he talked. You could have called it raving if it hadn't been so sensible. And the burden of it was that he wanted to see Nick Helmar. He delved into the past, tracing the friendship from the beginning, going through and through all the things they'd done together, saying how Nick had been his only friend in the worst of his trouble, and so on, interminably. He even blamed himself for the quarrel, saying that he should have known better than to provoke Nick, who was no longer himself. And then he came back to the old request—that Nick be brought to see him. So I rode over to Mortiboys in the middle of the afternoon and asked your father, Dilys, to ride back with me and make his peace with a dying man. *And he wouldn't come!*"

"He was drunk." It was half a question, half a statement.

"He wasn't drunk. He wasn't sober, quite. But he understood. I told him that father blamed himself for the quarrel, and he dismissed that as though it meant nothing. And he wouldn't come. When I got back father cried. He cried. And I'd always thought he had no feelings at all." Barney shifted in his chair, throwing his weight back so that the chair creaked. "Oh," he said impatiently, "I know it meant nothing. He was living in the past, as the dying often do, and he was thinking, not about a crazy sot of sixty, but of a boy, a young man, who had been his friend. But I had been to Mortiboys, I had pleaded as I'd never pleaded for anything before in my life, and I can't forgive the utter callousness, the ghastly coldheartedness, that your father showed, Dilys. I'm sorry. But I shall carry that silly old quarrel, as you call it, to my grave. I wouldn't speak to him if we were the last two men left on earth."

"No," I said slowly, watching Barney as he stood up with his head almost touching the low sagging beam. "I don't blame you. I'd feel the same. And I can believe father would behave that way. There's not a scrap of kindness left in him. A crazy sot—you were right."

"And so you can't come to see us," said Jassy, breaking the silence with her prim little voice. "Well, that wouldn't matter if we could come and see you. Would it?"

Barney turned to her. "Dilys might not want to come. He's her father."

"Haven't I as good as told you that I feel as you do about it. Only I'm sorry for him sometimes. Because he was different once.

It's what happened to him made him as he is. But, of course, Barney, all this wouldn't make any difference to you and me."

"You and me," I said, and with the words the most overwhelming excitement came on me. I looked at his thick muscular neck, reddish brown, growing paler nearer the edge of his open collar; raising my eyes, but keeping my lashes lowered, I looked higher, at that thin-lipped mouth, so bitter and yet capable of such a sweet smile. You and me. You and me, Barney Hatton, one day, alone together. I thought of Charles. And the only emotion the thought roused in me was one of increased excitement. I would do better this time. I would get more out of this. I felt faint, and Jassy's voice came from a long way off.

"Does Meggie still go into the village on Thursdays?"

"She hasn't missed yet."

"Then shall we come on Thursday? And shall we bring some food? I could cook it. It would be fun."

Why hadn't I the sense and the presence of mind to suggest that? Yet it was better. Secrecy. Let no one know. Give no one cause to guess. Shelter behind Jassy's eager friendship. You and me. . . .

"I've plenty of food," Barney said.

I knew he was looking at me, and I knew in what way.

"Thursday, then," I said and stood up. "It's time we went, Jassy."

"Yes. What time shall we come, Barney?"

"I work till six. Give me half an hour to tidy myself."

"Slippers?" Jassy asked. Barney laughed.

"How I hated them! Even Meggie's devotion would quail at the idea of making me a pair now." He looked down at his enormous feet. It was curious to notice how, as soon as he spoke to Jassy, his manner became very easy and friendly. It was as though he still, at the back of his mind, regarded her as a child. I was glad.

He came with us to the yard, untethered both horses and helped me into my saddle. I thought about what his hands would be if they were not respectful. Jassy, agile as ever, scrambled up from the mounting block and, looking round, said:

"You've made great improvements, Barney." I also looked round and saw that the yard, though nothing more than a farm-yard, was far neater and in better repair than the premises at Mortiboys. The walls of all the buildings were pitched to shoulder level and whitewashed above. To the right of the house was a cartshed, and all the wagons and farm carts were drawn up level with their shafts pointing the same way. Beyond was a pigsty, and the pigs were stomach deep in clean straw. I thought of Stephen's remark that Barney was taking his farming seriously. The idea was still a trifle grotesque. But as we rode through the gate which Barney held open, I looked down to say good-bye and he looked up, and it was as though we looked clean into one another's minds. And if he had been a travelling tinker man, and Thursday's rendezvous fixed for some place under a hedge-row, I should have been there.

"We'll take the Upper Road and make the full circle, shall we?" asked Jassy. I nodded and we rode the length of the Green and past the pond without speaking again.

"Well?" Jassy said, as the horses slowed down at the slope which carried the road to higher ground.

"Well?" I said, on exactly the same note.

"He's a *lot* older, isn't he?"

"We all are."

"That's true," she said, and gave a little sigh. And for some reason neither of us mentioned Barney again until, on Thursday morning, Jassy said, "Is your father likely to miss us this evening?"

"I shouldn't think so."

"Would he mind your going to Green Farm?"

"Probably not, but it would give him an excuse to shout at me."

"Well then, if any questions are asked, we'll say that we're going to see an old aunt of mine." So she had been thinking ahead to this evening as well. But being Jassy, she had been thinking practically.

Barney and I were shy again at first. At least, shyness is not an adequate word for the state of feeling between us. It suggests a youthfulness, a gaucherie which was not actually there. It was rather the kind of deliberate constraint, mingled with nervous tension which can be seen in players before a game begins. And in my case it was combined with a feeling of unreality. Now and then, as he and I moved about the kitchen, obeying the orders of Jassy, who had instituted herself cook, with all a cook's privileges, I would look at the pots and pans, at the food we were preparing, and the great red fire in the stove, and think that this was all rubbish, a pretence that deceived nobody, a deliberate waste of time. And once again I thought that Barney and I should have rediscovered one another accidentally, preferably out of doors, and after one look into one another's eyes we should have held out our arms. There should have been none of this business of visiting and playing at cooking. Above all, there should have been no Jassy. She was so obviously enjoying herself, was so exuberant, so truly in her proper element, that it was difficult to escape her mood. She had a white apron tied round her tiny waist, and her sleeves were rolled above her elbows. Her funny little face sparkled with animation, she darted from table to stove, from stove to pantry; she chatted and laughed, and when she burnt her hand on a hot dish she swore luridly. In a way she was irresistible. Even Barney once or twice would turn, straight from giving me a look that fired my blood, to laugh like a schoolboy at some of her nonsense. And once I had the queer idea that if I could, somehow, be suddenly spirited away, all the feeling of conflict in the kitchen would be removed, the laughter would grow heartier, and together they would throw themselves into the cooking and presently would make an exceedingly merry meal. At another moment I was almost horrified to find that I was watching Jassy's performance cynically. She's showing off, I thought, giving an exhibition of what a good cook she can be, what an excellent farmer's wife she would make. And I could see that for Barney to marry her would be the most natural, most appropriate thing in the world. They matched. Barney was a farmer, but he was gently born; he was poor, but he was not likely to be happy with the kind of girl who would want to marry him. And similarly Jassy, who, orphaned, homeless, penniless, might consider herself very lucky to marry a farmer, would hardly be content with an illiterate fellow who only shaved once a week. In fact, although they had not been born for one another—for Barney was born at Mortiboys and Jassy, where? under a hedge as likely as not—they had been made, by their particular circumstances, for one another. But it was on me that Barney was turning that look which I recognized, a look compounded of admiration and hurt and sheer naked belonging. And looking at Jassy as she leaned over the stove, I thought, afterwards, my lady, afterwards. I must have him first. For I had not at that time either the desire or the intention of marrying Barney. I had wanted to marry Charles. I had been so young and so silly that I had built, upon a six weeks' acquaintanceship, a whole castle of dreams. But that was different. And I was wiser now. Charles, all unwittingly, had shown me that there was a great deal of excitement—though that is hardly the word—pleasure? —nearer, but not exact—a great deal of something, anyway, to be had on this side of marriage, and to be had without any questions as to whether the other person were eligible or not.

Barney was not eligible, but he was supremely good to look at; with every glance he gave me I could see that he was minded to play my game. We only needed to be alone. You and me. You and me. . . .

Jassy turned to the table and snatched a spoon.

"Now there's just the gravy to make and it's done. You two had better set the table."

"There's a fire in the parlour," Barney said. He looked at me.

"I tried the dining-room, but the chimney smoked too much."

"It always did," said Jassy. She pointed to the dresser. "I've put everything we need on that tray. Dilys, take the cloth."

Barney lifted the tray and I, with the cloth in one hand, opened the door into the passage, let him pass, and close it again. The long passage was dark save for the red glow of firelight which came from the parlour's open door. My heart began to gallop as I followed Barney towards the light. Neither of us spoke.

Inside the room Barney set down the tray, took a taper and lighted several candles. I spread the cloth, and then, still in silence, we set out the table. When the last spoon was in place, the last imaginary wrinkle smoothed from the cloth, we stopped and looked at one another. That silent meeting of eyes may not have lasted more than a moment, but seemed to stretch itself out until, with a kind of hysteria, I thought that we should stand there staring and dumb for ever. Which of us could move? What was the word which could break that silence? I waited. And when at last I did speak my voice was choked and low and hurried—a sick person's voice.

"Barney, do you remember that day when you came to Mortiboys?"

"I remember it. Very well. So do you."

"Yes. That's why I'm here."

"That was a long time ago. We were children." The harshness of the words showed that he was fighting. He moved his hands, seizing the top of a chair and gripping it so that the tan deserted the skin over his knuckles.

"We were children. Now we're grown up. But I never forgot you," I said. And driven, partly by impatience, partly by a desire to know whether I could move as well as speak, I took a few steps forward and laid my hand beside his. He took me by the wrist, almost roughly, and said:

"Dilys, do you know what you're doing?"

"I think so," I said, and looked at him again.

He let go my wrist and, with a little gasp, dragged me into his arms.

When at last we fell away from one another I was so dizzy that I had to clutch at the chair again, and without thinking I put my other hand to my bruised mouth. Barney said savagely:

"Now I suppose you're angry. I don't play at love-making. I'm not a fine gentleman."

"I'm not . . . not exactly playing either," I said breathlessly.

"You'd better tidy your hair," he said. And I remembered how his hand, a moment before, had cupped the back of my head, fingers tangled in the curls, pressing me closer and closer. "Lovely hair," he said. "I've dreamed of it." And then, with another change of voice, "Set it right. Jassy will be wondering."

The rest of the evening is lost in a haze in my memory, as though I had been drunk, or drugged. We were all very hilarious, and I suppose that the meal, cooked by Jassy, was good. But for me there is a gap in the evening between Barney's saying, "Jassy will be wondering," and the other moment when, tidying the kitchen, we whispered, while Jassy was in the pantry, that we would meet next evening in Saints' Spinney. And after that there is another gap, which lasted until I was in my room with the door shut. Then I sat down and looked at myself in the glass and thought, well, Dilys Helmar, what have you started now? And sanity seemed to flow back then.

I slept very little, and in the patches of wakefulness, and as soon as I woke in the morning, a part of my mind, the little practical part, was busy with the problem of what to tell Jassy. I found myself, for several reasons, none of them individually conclusive, completely unable to say to her that I was going to meet Barney alone. And this although, in the affair with Charles, which now seemed so stale and was actually so recent, she had been my confidante and accomplice. For one thing, my whole instinct veered towards secrecy; it always had; it was only my fear of the dark and my lack of knowledge of any exit from school which had driven me to confide in Jassy in the first place. For another thing, I thought that she might feel hurt by Barney's preference. I did not imagine then that she was in love with him; in fact, it was difficult for me to imagine Jassy being in love with anyone, she was so practical, so self-contained and—to my eyes —so immature; but it was plain that she liked him, and that she had regarded that evening at Green Farm as a friendly meeting, a meeting of three friends. It seemed rather hard to banish her suddenly, to say—we're not three, we're two together and you're one, alone. And there were other reasons, silly little ones, like vanity. I knew, for instance, that if I said to her that I was in love with Barney, she would think that my broken heart had healed very quickly, which was true, but not a matter I wanted commented upon, because that would make me feel silly and frivolous. And if, again, something happened and Barney, after six weeks, withdrew and left me, I didn't want Jassy to be thinking that I could never keep a man for long. Oh, there were many reasons why I did not want to take her into my confidence this time. On the other hand, not to do so made the whole thing very awkward and complicated. Ever since we came to Mortiboys we had done everything together. It was difficult to stop doing so suddenly.

In the end, after I had worried the problem until midday, I told her that I was going to visit Stephen and his mother. And even that was a little awkward because, after I had blurted out the words in an ecstasy of relief at having thought of something, I realized that by not taking her with me I might appear to be slighting her. The last thing I wanted to do was to hurt her feelings, and I turned hot and red when, after I had spoken, the full significance of the speech struck me. I cursed my slow brain.

"It'll be extremely dull, and Lady Fennel will ooze sympathy and I'll feel better if I'm by myself," I said. And then realized that excuses simply underlined things. With that a premonitory dull thud went through the back of my head and I grew angry. The devil, I thought, why should I explain and excuse? I've got my own affairs to see to. I can't muddle everything on Jassy Woodroffe's account. And of course, like most of my emotional efforts, it was all wasted. Jassy, neither concerned nor hurt nor very much interested, simply said:

"Stephen will come home with you, I suppose."

I felt a little ashamed and very much relieved. To lend an appearance of truth to my story, I left Mortiboys in the middle of the afternoon, rode in the direction of Ockley, turned off the road, and followed a path back to Saints' Spinney, and then, tethering Gyp out of sight from the road, sat down under the trees and waited until Barney came. It was dusk before he did so, and I was terrified. Unlike most girls who fear burglars, and footpads, and men-under-the-bed, I was never frightened of any human being except my father. But if I were the last person left alive on earth I should be frightened as soon as the sun had gone down. Always with the dusk there came upon me a feeling of being watched and a great dread lest I should hear or see something that should not be heard or seen. Not ghosts exactly. Stories of figures in winding sheets, or with their heads under their arms—and Mortiboys abounded in legends of such—seemed always a little too concrete and ordinary to terrify me. But I was afraid of being alone, far from other people, and I was afraid of the dark. And when Barney came, rather before time than after, he found me standing close to Gyp, almost gibbering with terror. I had moved over to the horse instinctively, and had patted her nose and held my hand on her neck because at least she was alive and warm. Then I had been taken with the fancy that my fear might infect her . . . suppose she suddenly looked at me and said, "I'm frightened too" . . . that was the kind of thought that came to me in the dark when I was alone. Mad? Perhaps that was it. Perhaps all the time what I was afraid of was being mad. When Barney came I could hardly speak. For a long time I could only cling to him and shiver. And then, all at once, I was myself again, and my frightened clutch merged imperceptibly into a resumption of the passionate embrace which had begun last evening in the parlour of Green Farm.

I was, on that night in Saints' Spinney, young, in years at least; and my experience held only the memory of a child's kiss, a stable-boy's moment of mania and a young soldier's passing fancy; now I am old, I have had three husbands and lovers innumerable. But I knew then, with the flow of my blood and the beat of my pulses, what I know now in the coldness of my mind and the mill of my thought—that only once, only once to anyone does the perfect moment, the ideal physical counterpart come. I say physical deliberately, and far, oh far, from decryingly. All my feelings for Barney were concerned with his physical being, with that bright brown hair, the size and strength of him, the thick neck, the thin mobile lips, the blue eyes, the sound of his voice. I never, at any time, wanted to share his thoughts, or cook his food, or mend his clothes. If he had been ill he would have been immediately repulsive to me, because the very charm of his strength would have been defiled by his weakness. And for the same reason I did not want him to talk to me—except very trivially. I didn't want him to think. I was a stranger to his thoughts. I hated it when he had scruples, when he tried to plan for the future, when, in fact, he tried in any way to alter and shape a thing which, to me, was perfect and whole as it was. I wanted us to go on for ever, or, since that was not possible, for as long as could be managed, two people, with no past, no future, no ties, no background, walking away from the rest of the world, away into the sanctuary of a wood, or an empty room, and there enjoying to the full the sensations that they were capable of rousing in one another.

And for a time I had my way. So short a time really. The leaves were already on the ground in Saints' Spinney the first time we met there, and when it was over the bluebells were only just coming up spikily under the new bright green of the hawthorns. Only so short a time was I able to stay his scruples, hush his talk, and shut the rest of the world away. So short a time; but those few months remain with me, a passionate, not a sentimental memory, a measuring stick against which all other relationships are revealed as poor substitutes. And if, at any moment of my after life, Barney Hatton had suddenly appeared and said, "Come to Saints' Spinney," if I could have gone in secrecy without making complications, I would have gone and blessed God for the chance. But nothing is so simple in this world.

The first complication made itself evident on that very evening as soon as I returned to Mortiboys. It was late, for Barney and I had lost all count of time, and I had imagined that Old Nick would be shut in the library and Jassy gone to her bed. But as I entered the hall, before I could see anyone, I heard a gurgle of laughter and Jassy's voice saying, "Oh, very nimble! Now I owe you five shillings. And I haven't a penny in the world."

"But debts of honour have to be paid." That was father's voice, more amiable than it had been for years.

"I know. But you shouldn't have made me bet. All the same, I never thought you'd get my Queen. Hullo, is that Dilys?" I saw her head with its coronet of plaits rear up over the back of the settle. Damnation, I thought. Now something will be said about Ockley and the Fennels. I walked round the end of the settle and saw father sprawled in a low chair close to the hearth. Between his knees and Jassy's was a small table bearing a chessboard and some of the pieces. On the other side of the hearth a similar table was drawn up, and on that stood a tray with a coffee-pot and cups, a decanter of port wine and one glass, and a plate with three biscuits left on it. Something told me that for once father had been imbibing more coffee than port wine. But as soon as I appeared round the end of the settle he reached over and filled the glass.

"Well," said Jassy, "did you enjoy yourself?"

"Pretty well," I said, and made a little face at her, trying to tell her not to pursue the subject.

"We've been playing chess," she said, instantly responsive. "It was the only game we *both* knew. But Mr. Helmar doesn't like a game that isn't a gamble, so I bet him he'd never take my Queen. He just did. And now I owe him five shillings. Wasn't it rash of me?"

"We'll call it even. You've made the only drinkable cup of coffee I've had for a long time. It's a pity you went to school. You'd have made somebody a good servant," said Old Nick with one of his unaccountable offensive changes of mood. He stood up, knocking over the chessmen as he did so.

"At that price I'll make you coffee all day long," Jassy said, without a sign of discomfiture. She stooped and picked up the pieces. And from a stooping position she looked up, smiling, "Nevertheless, when I'm rich I'll remember that I'm much in your debt, Mr. Helmar." Looking up like that and smiling she was suddenly pretty. The light of candles seemed to catch and emphasize the glossiness of her hair, the long eyelashes. I wondered if Old Nick noticed, and glanced at him. He was turned to leave us, so that his face as he looked at her was sideways. And he was looking at her with a look I didn't like.

"Good night," he said abruptly, and strode off towards the stairs. The next moment Moult, as though he had been watching and waiting, appeared and bolted the main door, and stood ready to put out the candles.

"Are you ready for bed, Dilys?" Jassy asked in an unusually clear, high voice. "Or would you like a cup of coffee? I made it, you know. Your father says nobody in this house can make coffee fit to drink. It's still hot." And she in her turn made a face at me.

"Yes, I would," I said.

I sat down and Moult vanished.

"Why shouldn't you be considered ever?" Jassy demanded, turning to me, coffee-pot in hand as soon as the door of the kitchen passage had closed. "If I were you I'd assert myself. Why should you be hurried off to bed just because your father

has chosen to retire early. The servants are above themselves."
She handed me a cup of coffee. "Actually it isn't very hot. But
they sickened me. To-night when I went to make it they all
behaved as though I were stealing their birthrights. They need
taking in hand."

"I know," I said. "But you see, if I do it there's a row and *I*
am blamed. You're different. And Jassy, there's something that
I feel I must say in that connection."

"I'm listening," she said, dropping down on the hearth and
locking her arms about her knees.

I dragged myself out of my dreams of Barney and tried to
think of what I ought to say to Jassy. I ought to tell her that
Old Nick was not to be trusted; that Melia was only one of a
whole series of creatures who had ruled him for a moment; that
he had a taste for young things; that the way she talked and
looked almost invited his attentions.

And then it occurred to my slowly-moving brain that the best
thing of all would be to get rid of her entirely. I did not want
to be obliged to make excuses to her every time I went to meet
Barney; nor did I want my return to be made in the middle of a
domestic scene like to-night's, with Old Nick sober and capable
of asking questions.

Also I felt tired. I did not want to concern myself with matters
concerning Mortiboys and Old Nick and Jassy and the servants.
Nor did I want a lukewarm cup of coffee, however cleverly
made.

"It's nothing important," I said, putting down the cup. "And
I'm tired, Jassy. Tired to death. Let's go to bed, we can talk in
the morning."

She looked at me oddly. "All right, Dilys. I'll just put these
away." She packed the board and the chessmen, saying, "They're
nice," once in a low voice as though to herself. Then she said:

"Now, for your soul's sake, ring that bell and when Moult
comes tell him that you're going to bed and he may put out the
candles."

And I did as she said, because when she looked at me with those very clear grey eyes of hers I found it easier to comply than to thwart her. It had been the same years before, when she had asked me to lend her my history book.

But when we had said good-night and she had gone to her room and the door of mine was closed, I was my own mistress again. And I decided that she must go. She must leave Mortiboys for everybody's sake. Her own, since I did not want her to follow Melia in the list of Old Nick's lights-of-love, and my own, since, with her gone, my affair with Barney would be easier, less supervised. And, curiously enough, for Old Nick's sake as well. Jassy would be less easily shuffled off than Melia and her predecessors. There was something about Jassy Woodroffe which was unfathomable. And suddenly, thinking about her . . . unwillingly, for I had willing thoughts only of Barney at that moment, I was reminded of a curious toy which I had once had years, oh years, ago. It was the shape of a woman in a bell-bottomed skirt, slightly obscene because the skirt belled out so much that the underclothes beneath it were visible. And no matter how hard you tried to stand her on her feet or lay her on her side, she always tipped over and stood on her head. That toy puzzled me for a long time, until somebody explained that there was a ball of lead inside the woman's skull. After that she ceased to fascinate me, and I had forgotten all about her until, lying wakeful, and thinking about Jassy, I was reminded of her. Jassy was like that. She had inside her an overwhelming balance. Only she always stood on her feet. You could do what you liked, you could not upset that inward, hidden balance. And it was half in mischief, half in trepidation, that I thought to myself in the darkness— what will she say, and do, when I tell her to-morrow that she had better leave Mortiboys?

The mischief had gone from the thought in the morning, and only the trepidation and a kind of pity remained. There was a sense of guilt, too. For, but for me, Jassy would have been safe and sound at school, petted by Miss Hamilton, and leisurely pursuing her own little secret schemes for moving on to a post of her own choosing after the Christmas holiday. I decided that I must make her some financial compensation, and was glad that, whatever else I lacked, I had plenty of money.

I chose my moment to speak when we were in the garden, searching amongst the autumnal wreckage for the last late-blooming flowers. The gardens at Mortiboys were in better shape than the house, for Old Nick took no interest in them, and probably never noticed that they were as trim and fertile as in the days before the tragedy. We had found, without much difficulty, a sheaf of blooms and coloured leaves, and having reached the end of a path, where a stone seat was placed near the high red wall in such a position that it caught every ray of sun and was sheltered from all but the west wind, we sat down.

I felt nervous, and I knew that directly I started to speak I should stammer badly. But at the back of my mind was the thought that to-morrow, to-morrow, only a few hours away, I was to meet Barney again; and that it would be impossible to pretend to Jassy that I was going again, so soon, to Ockley. That was my main thought; but attached to it, and in its way quite as potent, was the fear that if, making some excuse, I did get away, Jassy would again be alone with Old Nick, making quips and smiling in that damned innocent way and simply asking for trouble. I was *compelled* to speak. And finally, after a nervous clearing of the throat, I said:

"J-Jassy."

She looked at me. "Uhh?" she said, and then looked down again at the sheaf of flowers, pulling the stems into line, taking out a late rose and sniffing it. "What's worrying you, Dilys?"

"You," I said. "I— I— this is a hateful thing to say, Jassy, but h-honestly I think it would be better if you d-didn't stay here."

She laid the rose she had been sniffing carefully back on top of the sheaf.

"You needn't worry about that," she said quite calmly. "I said

(208)

that you had only to tell me when you wanted me to go. When shall I? To-morrow?"

I was quite dumb with astonishment. The least I had expected was a demand for some explanation.

"It—it isn't absolutely what *I* want, Jassy. I brought you here, and so far as I am concerned you could stay for ever. B-but there's father."

"I see. He's sick of me."

I wondered, for a reeling moment, whether I might let that stand. It would be an easy way out. But, on the other hand, I was always so unlucky that the deception was bound to be exposed. Father would show surprise at her going or something. So I said:

"No. It's not that. I'm sorry, Jassy, it's my fault. I should have known that this was no place to bring you. What I'm frightened of is that father will find you attractive and make a nuisance of himself. Actually last night . . . I saw signs of it then. I . . . I don't feel comfortable about it."

She looked at me. Her eyes were quite serious, and as clear as water, but her big mouth was curling at the ends.

"Bless your soul, Dilys! What a one you are to worry about nothing. I can handle him."

And somehow I was immediately confirmed in my conviction that for her own sake she must go. Old Nick had, for three years, shown a marked preference for kitchen-maids, village girls, all young, comely and lowly bred. And there was, despite her cleverness, something of the kitchen-maid in Jassy. It came out when she said, "I can handle him." There was a coarseness about it, and about her voice as she said it. And behind, beyond that, there was a pitiable ignorance which made me feel very old and experienced. I knew how physically inferior a woman was, and I knew how her own senses will war against and weaken her in that preliminary encounter. Jassy was thinking, innocent little thing, that her wits and her nimbleness and her will could save her . . . against Old Nick, wine-flown and amorous!

All thought of my own affair, of Barney and our tryst to-morrow, had left me by this time. I really was, wholeheartedly, anxious to protect Jassy, who seemed so young, so vulnerable in her arrogance.

"You don't understand," I said. "You have only seen father on his best behaviour. I've been watching him for years. I really think you'd better go, Jassy. And you must let me give you some money. Because it was my fault you left school and will have two months to wait before the new term . . . and the post you spoke of."

"Say *lend*," she said, still in that easy composed way. "And it needn't be much. Perhaps I could get a place before the end of the term. Then I'd only need my coach fare. Barney would give me a bed and something to eat for a little while, until I was settled."

"Barney?" I said, astounded. And despite those hours in Saints' Spinney, despite the things we had said, despite the kisses, a feeling of quivering insecurity came over me, shaking every nerve in my body. I had a vision of Jassy flitting about that kitchen, with a crisp white apron emphasizing her neat waist. Everything that I had thought about the suitability of a match between Jassy and Barney rose again and hit me, this time painfully. A kind of inner wisdom began to work in me, too, an instinctive wisdom, and I knew that the more Barney and I assuaged our hunger for one another secretly, severing our ties from the world and ordinary things, the more attractive would be the sight of Jassy, open as the air, commonplace as bread, cooking at his fire, sitting at his table, making her place in his home.

"You couldn't do that, Jassy," I said. And so rapid had my thoughts been that there seemed to have been no pause at all.

"Why not?"

"It—it wouldn't be seemly. What on earth would people say?"

"Rude things that wouldn't worry me a bit. Besides, don't you think Meggie is sufficient chaperon?"

"No. I'm sure it wouldn't do. It wouldn't do at all."

Her voice was a little harder when she said, "I've got to have a bed, haven't I? Barney is the only other person I know in the world. I'm not going back to school, if that's what you're suggesting. Nor to Mrs. Partridge. She's Twizzy's friend. So if I leave Mortiboys I shall go to Green Farm. I've no choice."

I tried to think of something. "If you had some money, Jassy, you could . . ."

"I'd rather not borrow more than I must. Don't be ridiculous, Dilys. Barney is my friend, and he has a house with seven bedrooms. I could work on the farm for my keep."

As she claimed Barney's friendship I thought, yes, there is a friendliness between them, and with that my head began to ache. The dull pain hit me with a great thud and my brain went dead. It was the old, familiar feeling of a light having gone out which I knew so well.

"You'd better stay at Mortiboys. But you'll have to be careful, Jassy. Try to keep out of Old Nick's way, especially when I'm not there. And don't be—well, perky with him. I think he likes it."

For just a second I imagined that her queer little face wore a look of triumph. It was gone instantly, and my head was aching so badly that I could not think about it much. But when she twisted on the seat, so that she was facing me fully, her face was, not kind, she was never that, but smooth with a comfortable matter-of-factness.

"Dilys, look. But for you, as you say, I should at least not be in search of a bed. It would suit me very well to stay here until Christmas. Suppose we make a bargain. You go your way and I'll go mine, with no questions and no vicarious responsibility. When you want my company you can ask for it; and if ever I

want your protection I'll let you know. We're not children."
She stood up, with the sheaf of flowers in her arms. "I'll put
these in water and then I'm going out on Major, by myself. I've
never done that yet."

She gave me a smile, a perfunctory yet sweet rearranging of
her features, nothing more, and moved with her own peculiar
grace away along the path to the house. I was amazed at the
way in which, without any categorical phrases, she had cut
to the very centre of the problem. "You go your way and I'll
go mine." What did she know? Or guess? And was it by deep
craft or by simple sincerity that she had driven me into saying,
"You'd better stay at Mortiboys"? She was, of course, very
clever at lessons; yes, and she was very guileful. But so long as
her guile was working for me I had not troubled to estimate its
depths and possibilities. One thing was certain: I had, by this
morning's work, forfeited her friendship. That smile was proof
of that. And my dead aching brain managed to remember that
Jassy did not forgive easily. Mrs. Partridge had fallen from her
favour because she had criticized Miss Hamilton. Now I had
given offence by an apparent breach of hospitality. Oh, God, what
a muddle! And how my head ached and ached!

Then I remembered that significant phrase, "No questions and
no vicarious responsibility." That meant that to-morrow night,
when I went to meet Barney, I need give no explanation. To-
morrow night, Barney. And for the first time in my memory my
brain relighted of its own accord. Usually I could only be
cured by sleep, or by a merciful interlude of unconsciousness
which people wrongly called fainting. But to-day I was healed by
a thought. The pain went. I was mended. I sat for a little while
enjoying the sunshine and thinking about Barney. And when at
last I went back to the house and saw Jassy, mounted on Major,
rounding the far corner of the house, I was able to smile and
wave, signifying that our bargain was a good one. She could
stay at Mortiboys, and we could each go her own way. And
with an uprush of physical well-being I thought, and if Old Nick

gets her it won't be my fault. I warned her; God knows anyone
so clever ought to be able to look after herself.

I gave myself up, body and mind and soul, to Barney. Each
time we parted we fixed a meeting for some time in the immediate future, and the days in between had no taste, no flavour,
no sense in them. There was a poet named Marvell whose work
we did not study at school, but Miss Hamilton once lent Jassy
a book of his poems, and in one of them, which I read, though
I don't suppose Miss Hamilton would have believed that I could
understand it, was a phrase which I remembered:

> "Always at my back I hear
> Time's winged chariot hurrying near."

That exactly described me. I knew that one day, any day,
to-day even, or to-morrow, something would happen which would
drag Barney and me back into the world. Signs and potents were
not wanting. The first time we really lay together and I gave up
the virginity which I had protected from the stable-boy with my
riding-crop, and from Charles with more subtle defences, Barney
had been miserable and penitent and talked about marriage.
And it was as though an icy hand had been laid on my breast
where lately his warm one had wandered. I didn't want to marry
Barney and have everyone talking and thinking what a bad
match I had made. I didn't want to live at Green Farm and count
pennies and learn, through sheer necessity, the business of housekeeping and butter-making and rearing calves and chickens.
I wanted just what I had. Barney, and secrecy, a world of my
own. So I said that there was no need to talk about that yet;
wait until after Christmas.

Christmas leapt at us. There seemed no time at all between
my saying "Wait until after Christmas," and the season itself.
On Boxing Day, Jassy and I were asked to the Fennels', where
there was a large, merry party, and Stephen flattered me by
singling me out by his attention. We stayed overnight, and on

the way home it began to snow. It snowed for three days and four nights; it lay to a depth of five feet in the open, and there were drifts deep enough to engulf a mounted man. We were isolated at Mortiboys, and father, who had planned a shooting party for the third day after Christmas, and who was, besides, unused to being cooped indoors, fell into such a surly temper that it was at the risk of one's life almost that one went near him. He even quarrelled with Melia. And although Jassy and I, crouched over the fire, listened to his bellowing and roaring, and then saw Melia, very red-cheeked and with her head held high, flaunting along the passage, we took little notice. They had had at least three violent rows since we had been home. It did go through my mind that Melia had lasted as long as any of his wenches, and that he was about due for a change, and I said:

"Now, I suppose, Agnes will take umbrage and we'll starve."

"And deserve to," Jassy said noncommittally. "This is where you should step in and take advantage of the rupture and straighten things out in that kitchen."

"And look a fool when they make it up again. Not me."

"But you ought to get some practice. When you're married you'll need to be able to control your servants and run a house."

"Time enough to think about that when it comes. Besides, I shall have a housekeeper. And I'd like to know what has put the idea of my marrying into your head?"

"Lady Fennel herself," Jassy said, with a peculiar smile. "Oh, not to me, of course, but I heard her talking to another woman. She seemed most enthusiastic about having you for a daughter-in-law."

Despite myself I felt warmed and comforted. That short stay at Ockley had reminded me of what I was in danger of forgetting —how pleasant and orderly life can be in a house where people are normal and kind and sane. And I was touched to think that Lady Fennel did not hold it against me that my father was a mad, drunken old reprobate who slept with his maid servants. Oh, if only Stephen had one-tenth of Barney's attractiveness!

Oh, if only Barney had been heir to Ockley Manor! I sighed and crouched nearer to the fire, thinking how ill life was arranged.

The third day of Christmas seemed interminable and dull. Yet two momentous things had happened already. For father's quarrel with Melia bore immediate results; and later on, looking back, I realized that Jassy's few careless words about Lady Fennel had fallen into my mind like a pebble falling into a pool, quietly, but starting a ripple which will widen. For on that afternoon I felt for the first time that one day, when I was older and Barney had tired of me, or I of him, it would be nice to marry Stephen. It was as though, running wild in the woods I had heard, from the open window of a house, a voice calling to me to come in, and tidy myself and behave like other people. I was not ready to do so, yet. But it was pleasant to know that I should be welcome within the circle whenever I chose to mend my ways.

The meal that evening was, as I had predicted, horrible. Old Nick, who had not been quite sober all day, began to curse as soon as the food was put before him. He cursed Moult and Agnes, the food itself, and then, looking along the table in a manner that reminded me of a bull about to charge, he shouted, "And you. Both of you. Damned parasites, like all women; sitting about on your backsides all day. One of you could have seen that there was something fit to eat." Beginning like that he worked himself into a fine fury, ending by telling me that I was just like my mother, without a thought beyond my own silly face, and then rounding on Jassy, who, he said, was a greedy harpy who made no return for her keep. Moult had retired to a little distance from the table, and stood there with an injured expression of self-righteousness on his face. And despite the feeling of sickness which attacked me, as it always did during father's rages, it was with some amusement that I saw the heavy silver dish cover suddenly hurtle through the air and strike Moult plumb in the stomach.

"Don't stand there grinning like an ape you ———" father bellowed. "Clear this muck away and bring some bread and cheese. And tell that fat ——— in the kitchen that she's sacked. They're all sacked." He lifted the whole dish, and it was about to follow its cover through the air when Jassy sprang up and snatched it.

"I'll see what can be done with it," she said, and tripped away.

Father dropped back in his chair, breathing loudly, his face a dusky red. He was never ashamed after one of his fits of temper, for shame after an outburst or a breakdown is only possible when one is conscious of criticism, either from within or without. Father did not care a sweep's curse for anything that Moult or Jassy or I might be thinking, and his faculties for self-criticism had withered long ago.

"Bring me a bottle," he said to Moult, as he was slinking out in Jassy's wake, and when it was brought he emptied three glasses in rapid succession, and then loosened his neck-cloth.

"When's that little bitch going?" he asked, no more pleasantly, but with a faint rebirth of reasonableness.

"On the t-tenth," I said, moistening my dry lips. I thought to myself that Jassy had almost too sedulously obeyed my instructions to be careful. Now he had turned against her. He had never before seemed to resent her presence, or shouted at her personally, or called her names. Probably in his dark confused mind he missed the smiles and little good-humoured retorts which Jassy had used towards him before I warned her. Though, of course, with him, you could never tell. He wasn't reasonable; and for women he seemed to have no feelings except lust and loathing, nothing in between, and even those two were very much mixed.

"She's worth a dozen of you any day."

"Yes," I said. There was some truth in the remark, and had there been none I should not have dared to contradict him.

"Don't be mealy-mouthed about it. That's your mother all over again. Sweet, sweet, and rotten. Yes and no. Mealy-mouthed. Sweet as honey and full of poison. Are you listening?"

I put both hands on the edge of the table and pulled myself out of my chair.

"I— I— must go, father."

"Sick? You look it. Go on then. Get out."

I made for the door, tore it open, slammed it behind me and leaned back against it. Once out of that odious presence I felt better. It was only my nerves that loathed him. The day was long since past when anything he said could really hurt me. There had been a time when a scene like this evening's would have made me cry for hours from misery and bewilderment. But now my mind was calloused. I was afraid of him, as one may be afraid of a mad wild animal, but as soon as there was a stout door between us the fear was gone, and so had that feeling of quivering nausea. In fact, standing there with my back pressed to the panels of the door I thought what a fool I was, now I had missed my meal. Why hadn't I had control enough to sit still and let him say what he liked, throw things at me if he had a fancy to, but not let myself be driven from the table?

As I thought this the door that led to the kitchen quarters opened, and there came through it, first, a very savoury and appetizing scent, then Moult, bearing a large tray, piled with dishes, and then Jassy, empty-handed, fastidiously wiping her fingers on her handkerchief.

She looked at me without surprise and asked gaily:

"Stood out?" "Standing out," as we called it, was a punishment at school, and the idea that Old Nick had said, "Stand out for twenty minutes," was slightly amusing. I smiled as I stood aside to let Moult enter.

"No. I was silly. I began to feel sick and just ran away. I wish now I hadn't. Something smells good. What is it? You haven't had time to cook anything."

"I didn't need to. Come and look what I've *found*."

Before I had time to protest that I couldn't go back into Old

Nick's company she had taken me by the elbow and whisked me into the room. Moult had set the tray on the side table and was standing, dubious and a little scared, looking at father, who sat where I had left him, staring down at the cloth upon which he was tracing patterns with his fork.

"I'll see to it," said Jassy, dismissing Moult with a jerk of her head towards the door. Then she laughed and, taking up the largest dish, set it under father's nose and lifted the cover.

"Does that make you feel better, Mr. Helmar? It should be good. It's your servants' supper."

"Good God!" said father, looking into the dish, where, neatly skewered and perfectly roasted, four plump partridges reposed upon a bed of bacon curls and squares of toast. He stared at the dish for a moment, and then, in a voice of ordinary anger, subtly and yet unmistakably different from the kind of perverse animal rage to which we were accustomed, he said, "This is insufferable. I'll go into that kitchen and I'll . . ." He began to raise himself on the arms of his chair.

"No, no," Jassy cried. "Eat it while it's hot. Everything else can wait."

She darted about, bringing dishes of vegetables, and gravy, serving us all with neat despatch, and at the same time relating, with comic gestures and amusing touches of mimicry, the horror of Moult and Agnes and Melia and Janey at seeing their supper snatched from under their noses. Father, with his fill of wine in him, and his fill of food going down as fast as he could shovel it, changed his mood, forgot his grievance against us and deigned to laugh at last. Finally, when Jassy removed his empty plate, he looked down at the patterns he had been drawing on the cloth and said, "That reminds me. I have a proposal to make to you, young woman."

"Are you going to make an honest cook of me at last?" Jassy said, laughing. He stared at her, astonished.

"That's just it," he said slowly. "If you'll give up this tomfool job you're going to, and undertake to run this place so that a man may have a modicum of comfort, I'll pay you whatever you ask, and give you a better home than you'd have in any school."

Jassy set her chin on her hand and looked at him, pursing her mouth. She looked astonishingly like a monkey at that moment.

"That's a nice offer, Mr. Helmar. But I'd have to make lots of conditions."

"Let's hear them."

"A completely free hand for one thing. And the sack for everybody except Janey. Then, let me see, when I leave, if you send me away that is, I want fifty pounds. You see, I have a job to go to on the tenth. But if you fall out with me it might happen to be mid-term, and I should need money in the interval. Is that fair? And the job I was going to meant my keep and six pounds a term. Is that too much?"

"No. I think I can stand that. Anything else?"

"I can't think of anything at the moment. Yes, I'd want that fifty pounds deposited with a third person. Sir Edward Folles-mark would do."

"You don't trust me?"

"I trust you so far." She put both her hands in her lap and leaned forward and said what I wouldn't have dared say for a thousand pounds: "I've got to think of myself, Mr. Helmar. At any moment you may find another Melia, and under her influence you might not be fair to me. I'm sorry, I don't want to justify your accusations about being a harpy or a parasite, and if you employ me I shall give you value for your money. But," and her eyes just flickered in my direction and returned to rest, cool and calm, on his congested face, "just recently I've been threat-ened with the prospect of having no bed for the night. That's not going to happen again if I can avoid it."

"And by God you're right!" He looked at her as though he had never seen her before. She smiled at him in a friendly ordinary fashion. It was like seeing a baby being friendly to a great savage dog. "All right, it's a bargain. And as a token, here's a term's money in advance."

He threw his great gross body back in the chair and began to fumble in his breeches' pocket. He drew out, not without difficulty, for his pocket was tight against his fat thigh and his hand was podgy, five guinea pieces, two five shillings, two florins and a shilling. He made a pile of them and pushed them across the cloth.

"That wasn't in the bond," said Jassy, "but it's very acceptable." She took up the coins and dropped them into her pocket, all save one five shilling piece. She took that between her finger and thumb and held it over his hand.

"That chess game," she said, with one of her sweetest smiles. "Debts of honour must be paid. Please forgive the delay."

Old Nick opened his hand slowly and took the coin. When it lay in his big red palm he looked at it for several seconds before putting it in his pocket.

"And now," Jassy said, jumping to her feet. "I'll go and make some coffee. New brooms, you know."

Next day the snow thawed and the wind began to blow. On New Year's Day Jassy and I rode into Minsham All Saints to visit a family called Wicks whom Jassy remembered, and which might be expected to provide fresh labour for the Mortiboys kitchen. And when the errand was completed we called at Green Farm, and in the restraining presence of a third person I met Barney again for the first time since before Christmas. There was subtle excitement in meeting a lover so. And Jassy told him all about what she called her new job, giving a vivid and very animated account of the evening when she had stolen the servants' supper.

While she was telling it I sat quite still and quiet, feasting my eyes on Barney and thinking now that the snow had gone we could renew our sweet, stolen meetings. It was like being dropped out of a warm, soft bed into a pool of icy water to hear him saying:

"Look, I don't want to offend either of you, but if it isn't too late for you to take that other job, Jassy, I think you ought to change your mind. I can't help hearing gossip, and if *half* of what I hear is true, the less you have to do with the master of Mortiboys the better. Dilys, do forgive me, but you know as well as I do, that in staying there, in any capacity, Jassy puts herself in—well, a dubious position, to say the least. There's nobody else to say it, so I must."

He threw a glance of apology at me, and then looked at her with an expression that was oddly protective, almost fraternal.

"I think Jassy knows what she has undertaken. If she doesn't it isn't for lack of warning," I said. "And I'm there, remember."

"But you won't be for long. Darling, I think we might as well tell Jassy. The first person we've told. Jassy, before you commit yourself to staying at Mortiboys you ought to know that Dilys won't be there much longer. She's going to marry me."

My first feeling was of furious anger. "Barney," I cried, "I never said—I never. You're—" I was, literally, at a loss for words. And then, as I turned my eyes from side to side, trying to fix upon something which would give me firmness and lucidity, and to frame some kind of sentence of shelter . . . for I felt as though I had been suddenly dragged into the open stark naked, I saw Jassy's face.

I can't describe it, save in a series of negatives. It hadn't turned white; it hadn't altered in any way I could specify; and yet something had happened to it. You can see the same thing if you look at a building, or a scene, in bright sunshine, and then again in say, the strange light that precedes a thunderstorm. Nothing in the scene or the building has changed . . . and yet no one could deny that there is a difference. It was like that. I knew, with a certainty beyond any shaking, that the news meant something more to her than the mere fact that it conveyed. But that stupendous self-control of hers did not desert her. She rose from her chair and came and kissed me, a mere fleeting brush of her lashes on my cheek.

(221)

She said, "I'm surprised, of course. I didn't know you knew one another well enough. But I hope you'll both be very happy."

I felt like a fool. But I had recovered enough self-possession to say, with what I hoped was dignity, "Really, Barney, you shouldn't have said that. Even if we do get married, ever, it won't be for ages." I turned to Jassy and said, "For heaven's sake don't tell anyone."

"You said leave it until after Christmas," Barney said stubbornly. "It's that now. And mewed up here for four days I've been thinking. We couldn't go on as we were, Dilys." He came over and laid his hand on my shoulder. And I knew, in that instant, how closely love and hatred lie together in the human mind. The touch of his hand, after what seemed a long absence, sent the familiar wild thrill through my body; but this time it was mingled and adulterated by the desire to hurt him. But for Jassy's presence I should have slapped him across the face.

I looked round the low, heavily-beamed parlour, where the unsuitable furniture seemed to be ducking to avoid contact with the ceiling; I thought of the kitchen and the farmyard outside. Mrs. Hatton, the farmer's wife. Absurd, grotesque!

Jassy rose from her chair and, drawing her gloves through her fingers, said, "There's a recipe I want from Meggie. I'll just go and ask her for it."

Still with a hand on my shoulder, Barney stretched his other arm and took her by the elbow as she passed us. "Jassy, after what I've told you, you will change your mind about staying at Mortiboys, won't you?"

"Why should I?" she said, looking at him with cold, clear eyes. "I wasn't counting on Dilys' company for long. Only I thought she was going to marry Stephen Fennel, not you. It's nice of you to worry about me, Barney, but it's quite wasted. Mr. Helmar and I understand one another."

She shrugged herself free of his hand and went out of the room.

"There, you see," I said, "you've done no good, and you've put us in a completely false position."

He dropped his hand—and something in my inside dropped with it.

"Why false?" he asked, rather ominously.

"Well," I said, with the feeling that I was being forced slowly and inexorably towards the edge of a precipice, "for one thing, I never said I'd marry you. You never even asked me properly. And if you had, and if I'd said I would, I wouldn't want anyone to know for a long time. It makes it all so public. It spoils it so."

"Look," he said, and putting a hand behind him he dragged up a chair and sat down so that his knees touched mine; then he took both my hands and held them, palm uppermost, in his, "I'm sorry if I annoyed you by blurting it out just now. And I'm sorry that you don't think I've asked you properly. I didn't know that you were a stickler for ceremony. But I'm asking you now. Dilys, will you marry me, just as soon as possible? I haven't a great deal to offer you, but I'm doing very well and I can give you a comfortable home. You know I love you; you've given me reason to think that you love me. There's no reason for waiting that I can see. Well, darling . . . ?"

I said, "Barney, why must it be marriage? Why can't we go on as we are? I do love you. This last week when I haven't seen you has seemed endless, I haven't really been alive. But I don't want to be *married*. It'd spoil everything. I can't explain it. I just know it would. It may be very queer of me, but I don't want my love all muddled up with a row with father, and my trying to keep house, and people talking and you seeing me in the morning before I've done my hair." I was almost crying. Barney said gently:

"You're over-romantic, darling. You can't live your whole life in Saints' Spinney, you know. And you needn't take the whole burden on yourself. I'll see your father, and Meggie will keep house, and if it's any comfort to you I'll promise not to look at you until your hair is done—though I'm sure you look lovely with it tangled. Come on, say you'll marry me, and that's all you need do."

"I can't," I said, crying outright now, for my head had started to ache.

He pushed back his chair and stood up. Going to the window he said in a curious low voice, "Tell me one thing, Dilys. Is the whole idea of marriage distasteful to you, or is it that you don't want to marry me? Is it that you love me, up to a point, but think that I am ineligible as a husband? You must forgive the bluntness of that, but I've wondered often, and it's a thing I must know."

It was so exact a summing-up of the situation that I had a crazy impulse to cry, yes, that's just it.

It would have been such a relief to say, with utter frankness, yes, that's just it, Barney; I love you, quite madly, and I know I shall never love anyone else in the same way, but I can't face living here and being a farmer's wife.

But suppose I said it, what would be the price of such relief, such frankness? Barney would be, quite rightly, disgusted, and he would refuse, justifiably, ever to have anything to do with me again. There would be no more meetings in Saints' Spinney.

So I said—and I was so conscious of my falseness that my voice seemed to ring like a base coin—"It isn't that, Barney. That's a horrid thing to suspect. It's just that having you, like this, with no one knowing or being angry or making a fuss about, is the nicest thing I've ever known. I don't want to spoil it. It's like having something precious that I don't want people pawing over with their filthy hands. I haven't had much happiness, Barney."

The last sentence, at least, rang out genuinely, with a break of self-pity in it. He turned to me, instantly responsive, with his "You poor little thing" expression on his face. But then he checked himself deliberately, and the scowl and the lines in his cheeks were darker and deeper than ever as he demanded:

"Then what did she mean by saying she thought you were going to marry Stephen Fennel?"

I saw danger in that question, and for once I was inspired, not paralysed, by it.

"Jassy has an inflated opinion of my attractiveness—probably because she isn't very pretty herself. If any man pays me the slightest attention, even picks up my handkerchief, she imagines that he is in love with me. And Stephen is very mannered nowadays. He is the same with every woman he meets."

"There wasn't any reason why she should say it then?"

"No reason at all," I said, with the confidence of half-truth. "Honestly, Barney, if Stephen came into this room at this minute and begged me on his bended knees to marry him to-morrow I'd laugh in his face."

And that was strictly true. The idea of marrying Stephen one day might be couched in my mind, dark, hidden, like a germinating seed, but I was going to have Barney again and again before that day came: Barney in Saints' Spinney, in the heart of the night, in our secret place under the trees; Barney on Thursdays sometimes in that low, dim, over-furnished bedroom just over our heads. Again and again. So that when, replete at last, I married Stephen, or anybody else, I should not expect from him what he had no power to give, that starry delight, that rounded completeness. No one but Barney had that in his gift.

I stood up and went over to him where he still stood, a little dubious, a little reluctant.

"Let's go on as we are for a while, darling. There'll be years and years to think about settling down. This only comes once."

"Easter, then?" he asked, holding me at arm's length, but with the old look coming back into his face. "You'll marry me at Easter?"

"Maybe," I said. "Only let's not talk about it any more for a long time. You've made my head ache dreadfully. There are so many things worrying me, Barney. Don't you be a worry, too."

He gave me a slight shake.

"If only you'd stop being such a little ninny and marry me right away, all your worries would be over." But I said, "Now, Barney . . ." and the shake ended in a breathless embrace. I gasped, "Thursday, Barney? Come for me on Thursday." Too far ahead, too long to wait; but the woods would still be damp from the snow.

"And now I must find Jassy," I said, pulling myself free.

She was in the kitchen, scribbling away with a frantic squeaking quill on a scrap of packing paper. Meggie, with a more contented expression on her face than I had ever seen there, leaned back in her chair, dictating in a lordly fashion, some highly complicated directions.

"Now just one more, Meggie, if you don't mind. Once—on Good Friday it was, I remember—you made a sharp sauce for the boiled fish. Tell me that one and I won't bother you any more."

"Well," said Meggie, "you take some butter. No, thass no use asking me *how* much. I told you that afore. That depends how many you're making for. Say a bit the size of a wall-nut for each pusson. And you melt it and take some best flour and you mix it . . ." The dictation rambled on. In the middle of it I looked at Barney. He was contemplating Jassy's bent head and scribbling hand with a peculiar expression in which tolerance and kindness and—yes—a kind of admiration were oddly mingled. Suddenly, as though she were conscious of it, she looked up at him, held his eyes for half a second, and then stared down at her paper as though she had seen something distasteful.

"Well, thank you very much, Meggie. I shall be everlastingly in your debt," she said brightly, jumping up and waving the paper to dry the ink.

"You're kindly welcome," said Meggie, in a voice quite unlike the one she usually used towards Jassy. "And anything else you wanta know, you only gotta ask."

(226)

We mounted and rode in silence through the village. The silence was beginning to become oppressive, and I was thinking for a word to break it when Jassy said abruptly:

"When are you being married, Dilys?"

"Not for ages."

"But it's settled?"

"You heard what Barney said?"

"Yes. I heard." There was another silence. Then she said, "I don't suppose I ought to say this, Dilys. But everybody is so eager to give me good advice, I think I'll pass a little on. If I were you I would ask Barney one question before I married him. I'd say, 'Are you in love with me or with Mortiboys?' Just that."

I said, "Please, Jassy, don't give me anything else to puzzle about. I've got a dreadful headache. Just tell me as plainly as you can, why I should ask that stupid question. What has Mortiboys to do with Barney and me?"

"Isn't it obvious? Mortiboys will be yours one day. And I happen to know that Barney is crazy about the place. I just thought that you ought to make sure. That's all."

I was furious. The idea that Barney had chosen me because of Mortiboys!

"Barney is in love with me," I said. "He knows that I hate the Mortiboys, and once I'm married nothing will ever get me back there. If I inherit it, as I suppose I shall, though I've never thought about it, I shall sell it at once. I loathe the place."

"So long as Barney knows that," she said.

"He knows," I said. "And for all that he's crazy to marry me at Easter."

"You said ages."

"Well, Easter is ages, when you're in love." But some part of me wasn't there, wasn't engaged in taunting Jassy. It was thinking—well, of course, since you don't intend to marry Barney, the question doesn't affect you much, but is there a grain of truth in that notion? Is that why Barney is so set on *marriage*?

(227)

I knew really, with my blood and my nerves I knew it, that when Barney and I were together the fact that one day Mortiboys would be mine meant nothing. Yet, at the same time, the idea sank deeply into my mind and lay there, side by side with the idea that Lady Fennel would welcome me as her daughter-in-law. Grains of mustard seed both of them compared with my passion for Barney, but both capable of bearing fruit.

"Besides," I said inconsequently, "Old Nick might easily marry again."

"Yes, of course," said Jassy. She set Major to a sharp canter which put an end to the conversation.

That night I had a nightmare. I had been prone to them as a child, and I think they accounted, in part at least, for my horror of the darkness. They had grown less and less frequent in the last few years, and I had hoped that I had outgrown them. But on this night, having gone to bed with a headache and put my head thankfully on my pillow, and counted, as I always did, the hours until I should see Barney again, I fell asleep and then seemed to wake suddenly when my door opened and let in a sharp cold draught. I was dreaming, of course, but I seemed to sit up in bed, a little frightened, and to look towards the door. A faint grey light filled the room, and by it I could see, near the door which was now shut, though the draught continued, a shapeless figure, rather tall, which was slowly approaching my bed. In a moment, during which terror mounted and I tried to call out but was—as one is in nightmares—voiceless, I could see that my visitor was a woman, muffled in grave-cloths and with a kind of scarf round her head which was nothing but a skull; yet there was a sparkle of jewels from the place where her ears should have been. That was specially horrible. She came close to the bed and said, in a low, very mournful voice, "Mrs. Hatton. Mrs. Hat-ton." I knew that she was not naming me Mrs. Hatton, but was announcing herself, Barney's mother. The sharp draught came nearer as she moved forward. It came from her in some way. She said: "I lived here, and I lived there. But you don't love him. You don't love him." She spoke the last words in a fierce, denunciatory tone and stretched out her fleshless hand very, very slowly. I knew that she was going to touch me, to shake me, as Barney had done that morning. And I knew that if she did touch me I should die. I tried to move away from her, and I tried, tried repeatedly, to scream. And at last I succeeded. Out of the soundless mouthings I heard at last the faint semblance of a word—Jassy. And I kept on screaming and screaming Jassy, Jassy, Jassy, until there was Jassy, solid and real, with a candle in one hand and her other hand on my shoulder, shaking me.

"Oh, thank you," I gasped. "I was dreaming. A dreadful, dreadful dream."

"You were making a dreadful noise," she said shakily, and I could see the candle spilling grease from the unsteadiness of her hand. "You frightened me."

"I'm sorry," I said. "I'm really sorry, Jassy. But I couldn't help it. I was having the most *terrible* dream." I pushed back my bedclothes. "Get in, Jassy, you're shuddering. Stay the rest of the night with me."

"No," she said, rather curtly. "You're all right now. Look, I'll light your candle. And you know I'm within call."

"Oh, do stay," I begged her, humble in my terror lest the dream might come again.

"Give me a blanket then, and I'll sit in a chair."

"You'd be more comfortable in bed. There's plenty of room."

Without answering, she pulled one of my blankets free, wrapped herself in it and sat down on my low chair, putting the candle beside her.

"You won't sleep," I said.

"I shall be all right," she said impatiently, and blew out the candle.

"Are you angry with me?"

"Angry? No."

"Then why won't you come in the bed?"

"Because I prefer not to. If you keep on about it I shall go away."

"I'm sorry," I said, and was silent for a few minutes until I thought of something.

"Jassy," I said quietly. "Did you know Barney's mother?"

"Of course I did."

"Did she wear ear-rings?"

"What are you talking about?"

"Did she?"

"Yes. Always. I never saw her without them. Even in the dairy. Why do you ask that?"

"She was in my dream."

"Oh! Begging you to be a good wife to her son?" There was a dreadful gibing bitterness about the question. It made me wonder. Presently, when it was too late to say anything, I realized that I had left the question unanswered.

The weather that year was kind to lovers. January was so mild that when, towards its end, there was a second brief fall of snow, the white patches, as they melted in the shrubberies, merely gave way to other whiteness, stretches of snowdrops, frail and secret under the glossy leaves of the evergreens. Winter and spring meeting and for the moment indistinguishable. After the thaw it was mild again, and very early in February the birds were mating with shrill sweet cries and sustained volleys of song in the first morning light. The evening skies had those colours of apple green and daffodil which hold, as no words can do, the whole essence of the spring

I shall remember it always. Old, old and hackneyed, that theme of love and springtime, feeling the lover's kiss in the pale sun, seeing the lover's smile in the first green tip of the lilac buds, sharing that full-throated burst of bird song, being near the heart-beats of the urgent earth. Here and now, my love, so little time, more and more.

There was a life, of course, apart from Barney, away from

Saints' Spinney. There was Mortiboys, swept and garnished, full of new servants and good fires and succulent food. There was Jassy, very busy in her quiet way, a little withdrawn and pre-occupied. There was father, rather like a surly old bull whose stall has been cleaned and hung with posies, full of an almost perverse determination that the "modicum of comfort" which he had demanded, and obtained, should not fundamentally sweeten his temper. To Jassy—as was only her due, who had made a home, as it were, in a shambles—Old Nick preserved, though at times with an obvious effort, a scrupulous politeness; but to make up for it he attacked me more frequently and more savagely than ever. And then there was Stephen, coming more and more often, driving me (alone now, for Jassy declared that she was too busy for frivolity) over to Ockley on visits which I would gladly have prolonged but for the fact that when I was there I must do without Barney, driving me down to Bywater, into Colchester for a day's shopping, and to Baildon to a concert at the Assembly Rooms. As Stephen grew more attentive I began to dread the moment when he would ask me to marry him. I was certain of its immanence, and often whiled away an idle hour wondering what I should say. And I always ended my medita-tions with the renewed certainty that I was a fool. Once more I had let my feelings get the better of my sense. There wasn't a girl in four counties who wouldn't have been glad to marry Stephen, who would, in course of time, inherit Ockley, which was beautiful, an estate in superb order, plenty of money, and a title. And yet, whenever I thought about him I ended with a hun-ger for Barney and a firm determination to play for time. If only they would both be patient all would be well. I knew, I had known from the first, that my passion for Barney was a form of madness from which, one day, I should recover. And how awful it would be if, in my madness, I committed myself irrevocably, and regained my senses only to find that I was Mrs. Hatton, chained to Green Farm, finished, done. How madly then, from amongst my chickens and calves and butter-pans, should I envy

Stephen's wife. Whereas, given time, and a little luck, I might regain my senses and find myself safe at Ockley, and although I should always be interested in Mrs. Barney Hatton of Green Farm, I should not envy her at all, for even her love would be, and I should know it, second-hand. If only both Barney and Stephen would have patience.

Stephen was not particularly menacing. He looked at me with eyes like a spaniel's, and he was as manageable as one. I was, as most girls are at that moment, master of the situation. I could have made him propose at any moment, and I could, with little more difficulty, fend him off for a time. But Barney was different. He had enjoyed a husband's rights—and after that things were never quite the same again. In the ultimate act of love a man achieves a moment of mastery which has a lasting effect. He may love the girl as much, he may treat her with careful respect, but a certain awe is gone. He is no longer so easily handled.

About six weeks before Easter—which was late that year—Barney re-opened the subject of our marriage. He did it with crafty kindness, saying that there was some alterations and improvements which must be made at Green Farm, and since the busy season was approaching, they must be begun at once.

"So, darling, though I promised not to mention the matter again until Easter, I'm driven to do so. You must say definitely now. Otherwise you might have to come into the place as it is."

"I said I'd tell you at Easter," I parried. "I might say then that I agreed to marry you, but I might not do it until next year."

We were sitting at that moment on the trunk of a fallen tree in the very heart of the Spinney, and there were masses of primroses spread out like moonlight under the trees. Barney began to uproot a nearby plant with his toe.

"Dilys," he said, after a moment or two, withdrawing his foot and twisting round so that he faced me, "something that I don't like comes over you whenever I mention the future—not just marriage, but anything ahead. You alter, you become a different person. Even your face changes."

"I know," I said. And I thought—he is truly in love with me; no one who wasn't would be so observant. And a bit of my mind ran off down the road to the future, thinking how difficult, in fact impossible, it would be to deceive Barney finally. He would always know, for instance, how much I disliked the farm.

"I am different," I went on. "When we're here, ordinarily, I'm happy and free, but as soon as you begin to talk about the future everything is spoiled. I'm unhappy and bothered."

He said, quite roughly, "To hell with this whine about everything being spoiled. You say that incessantly. What's spoiled by a decent suggestion of marriage? Surely to God you must see that we can't go on for ever slinking about this wood, or just having the house to ourselves on Thursdays. We're in love, we're both free. Isn't it the natural thing to get married as soon as we can?"

"Perhaps I'm not natural."

"What do you mean?"

"Well—I doubt whether, if you'd taken up with a nice natural girl, she'd have met you here more than once. I think most natural girls would have been shocked the first time you kissed them, Barney, and that's a fact."

"God knows that may be true," he said in rather an astonished voice. "But, Dilys, my love, don't hold that against me. I'd been in love with you since I was fifteen. I was mad for you and—let's be honest about this—you didn't mind *then*. And whatever I've done, however I've behaved, you might remember that before we went from here that night I'd spoken about marriage. Hadn't I? Hadn't I?" he repeated, as I did not answer immediately.

"Yes," I said. "And with slight pauses you've kept on about it ever since."

"Without getting a proper answer," he said. "And I'm going to have one to-night, Dilys. I've done playing. Are you going to marry me at Easter or not?"

"No," I said. "It's too soon." There, I thought, that'll teach you not to rush me into decisions.

"You're not in love with me any more." And that was true. At that moment I hated him, just as I had hated him in the parlour at the farm when he had told Jassy that we were going to be married. And I knew, quite certainly, that if, by any fantastic chance, I did marry him, I should hate him instantly and for always.

"It isn't that, Barney. That's a stupid thing to say. Weren't we just now . . . didn't you *know* then? But whenever I try to explain how I feel about things you get angry and shout. I'm just not ready to be married."

He waited for a moment and then said, deliberately and offensively:

"You're ripe for it, anyway. God knows what you'd have taken up with if I hadn't been handy. A stable-boy, I should think. You're blushing. I'm right then." He swallowed so hard that I heard the movement of his throat. "I've known it all along, really. Ever since that first night. You've been playing for time. You've used me just as fine young gentlemen use dairy maids, to ease your itch until you can find somebody fit to marry. It's a pity I'm not your friend Stephen Fennel, isn't it? By God, Dilys, I've loved you for seven years, and I'm ashamed of myself for doing it. You're nothing but a whore." And it was all so true. Every word of it was true. Yet I did love him. In a way. Love has so many ways.

"I could make you take that all back and regret having said it, couldn't I?" I asked. "If I said I'd marry you at Easter you'd be ashamed. But I'm not going to take advantage of you. I'm going home."

"Very well," he said. "And you'll go alone."

"I mean to," I said, and glanced round, estimating the quality of the darkness. "Good-bye, Barney."

He strode off without replying. And I knew that he was hurt in his most sensitive part, and that it was the same as mine. I could not bear the thought of being a farm-wife; and Barney could not bear the thought that he was socially ineligible. Oh, how clear my damned mind could be at times! But that realization forged another link. For once I was in sympathy with him.

And at the end of a fortnight, five days of which I spent at Ockley in Stephen's constant company, and the whole of which I spent in turning the matter over and over in my mind, I rode over to Green Farm and found Barney working in a field. And I said, "I'll marry you at Easter."

I meant it then. If there is, as they tell us, an All-Knowing, All-Seeing God who can assess our motives and weigh our desires, He knows that at that moment I was sincere and genuine. I had had a fortnight without Barney and five days with Stephen, and I was in a position to judge between them. And at the Day of Judgment, if it ever comes, God may remember that morning, as I rode back, leaving Barney dazed and happy in the field, I halted Gyp in the farmyard and looked round and was penitent because I had ever thought deprecatingly of it. I looked at the low house, with the windows so near the eaves; I looked at the pigsty and the cobbles and the pump and accepted them all. They were Barney's background, and they should be mine. If happiness could only come to me through humility I would be humble.

Perhaps that was the last flash of sanity I ever had.

I rode back to Mortiboys. I was determined that I would tell Jassy at once. And I would ask her to be present when I told Old Nick. Then I would write to Stephen and also to Lady Fennel, who had been very, very kind and motherly to me during my stay at Ockley. The worst would be over then.

My head began to ache as I rode home. It began a little differently, not with a sudden thud and onslaught of pain at the back of my neck, but gently, so imperceptibly in fact that I hoped, by riding slowly and breathing deeply of the fresh spring air, to avoid the full force of it. It was still aching, but not badly,

when I handed Gyp to Sharples and went into the house, inquiring
of Janey Jassy's whereabouts. I found her in a disused bedroom into which, over a period of weeks, she had been gathering
all the linen in the house. The great bed, every chair, every chest
now bore a neat pile, and there were others on the floor. In the
middle of the room stood a chair and a table. Jassy sat on the
chair and the table bore a variety of needles and threads, patches
already cut, and bolts of tape. She was mending a pillow-case.

I went and sat on the window-seat.

"Jassy," I said, "I've just seen Barney and I have promised
to marry him at Easter."

"So you have made up your mind?" she said. "Am I supposed
to be surprised?"

"Well, I am a little myself, to tell you the truth."

"Why? You're in love with him, aren't you?"

"Yes."

"And he is with you. So that's all right. As I told you on
New Year's Day, I hope you'll be very happy."

And I thought, it's a funny thing, but I can't talk to you any
more. Once I could. Look at the things I told you about Charles.
What's happened? We aren't friends any more. Why? And the
back of my skull gave a jab as I remembered that the change
had come on that very New Year's morning. No, it hadn't, I
argued with myself, it was before that; it was on the day when
I told Jassy that she should leave Mortiboys. She hadn't *liked*
me since then; but she hadn't shown it until after New Year. I
remembered that night when I dreamed of Barney's mother. Jassy
had hated me then. But I had been so entranced in my own dream
that I hadn't noticed. What else had I missed?

"I wanted you to be the first to know. And I wanted to ask you,
Jassy, whether you'd be with me when I tell father. You know
how he is with me. This will probably give him a great op-
portunity for shouting at me. I'd like you to be there."

"I'll break it to him if you like," she said, but not kindly,
scornfully.

I answered the scorn. "No. Thank you, Jassy, it was a kind offer. But I'll do it myself, if you'll just be there so that he doesn't rage too much."

"This evening?"

"Please. I think I shall lie down for a little while. My head is nagging but I may stave it off."

I lay down for over an hour, I sniffed my smelling bottle, I bathed my brow and my neck with vinegar, but my headache grew steadily worse. I got up, intending to write my letter to Stephen, but when I sat down before the paper I couldn't write at all. It was just like being faced with one of Miss Hamilton's tests. Now, as then, I knew what I wanted to write, but there was a great gap between the knowing and the setting down. I gave it up, thinking, as calmly as I could, that there was no hurry, to-morrow would do. I rang the bell and asked for a pot of tea, which, in this new Mortiboys, arrived at once, hot, fragrant. I drank several cups and swallowed two of my headache tablets in which I had once had faith, but which I had begun to doubt. Then I went and walked in the garden. But it grew worse. By the time when I had to face Jassy and Old Nick at the table I was stupid with it. There were spaces when I couldn't hear what they were saying, or see anything except little grey whirling circles.

Then we were in the library, where there were fresh chairs, more comfortable ones, fetched from somewhere, and the covers and the curtains were clean and crisp. I saw Jassy looking at me, and I made an effort and said: "F-Father, I've got something to tell you. I h-hope you won't be angry. I'm going to marry B-Barney Hatton."

"Barney Hatton," father repeated. "Is that the best you can do?" He didn't sound angry, just nasty. But it was a difficult thing to reply to, and I couldn't think of anything to say. I thought, well . . . I've said it, and that's all I need say. I wished I could have gone away then. For it was too good to be believed that Old Nick would content himself with that simple comment. And, indeed, he was already gathering himself for the assault.

"I suppose the day has gone when it was customary for the would-be suitor to ask a father's permission before making a proposal," he began. It was a mild rumble like that, we are told, which heralds a volcanic eruption. "Is that so? Am I an old fogey to resent being *told* that my son-in-law is chosen."

"N-no," I said doubtfully. "But I didn't think you'd care who I married so long as you weren't b-bothered."

"A shrewd conclusion. But isn't it a pity that you selected a lout who hasn't even the manners or the upbringing to know how these matters should be conducted?"

"Barney offered to come and tell—I mean, ask you—but I didn't think that you would want to see him. I mean, I didn't think that you would want to stand on ceremony."

"That's a pity. Because there was one thing I should have enjoyed telling that young man."

"Would you like him to come?"

"God forbid. You may take him a message. It's this . . ." and he bellowed suddenly: "Tell that little ―― that he won't get Mortiboys by marrying you. D'you hear that? I know his breed. That fool of a father of his never shuffled his cards without thinking that he'd got the place in his hand again. I could read it all over his damned silly face. And at the end . . . but we won't go into that. You'll not care to hear what kind of a low cheat your beloved's father turned out to be. But if his whelp thinks that by marrying you he's playing a trump, you may undeceive him. It may change his mind before it's too late, for what use you'd ever be to a farmer would puzzle God to explain. Jassy, get the bottle."

"I don't want Mortiboys," I said, "and I don't think Barney does." I felt impelled to say something. But as I spoke I recollected that Jassy had also warned me on the same subject, and my voice was not very certain towards the end of the sentence.

"Don't keep saying that you don't think this and you don't

think that. We know that you can't think. If you could you wouldn't think about marrying Barney Hatton. Have you ever seen the place where you'll live? Thank you. Well now, we must all drink to celebrate this momentous occasion."

He poured out three glasses of wine, slopping it as he always did, and holding his own glass for a moment as though about to propose a toast. But perhaps nothing sufficiently insulting occurred to him; he drank without speaking. Jassy lifted her glass and said, for the third time, "I hope you'll be very happy, Dilys."

"Happy!" Old Nick snarled, refilling his glass. I stood up. At the back of my dim aching mind I had a thought about how different this should have been. One's only daughter. . . . But I was used to him. I was not really hurt; in fact, I thought I had escaped lightly. Now I could go to bed, press my head into the pillow, sleep, and wake to-morrow a new woman. Blinded by the grey circles I almost felt my way out of the room. But when I reached the haven of my own bed I hardly slept at all. Even in the darkness, even with my eyes closed, I could see the sickening whirls, and my head thudded until my fingers and toes throbbed to the rhythm of the pain.

Next evening I rode to Green Farm again, planning to be there when Barney came in from work. There was no longer any need for secrecy. Need? Had there ever been need? Barney had evidently told Meggie, who was highly delighted, bobbing and smiling, and assuring me that she would serve me till she died, and see that before she did so she had someone else adequately trained. But my head was still aching. I had never known it to ache for two consecutive days before, and I was half mad with sleeplessness as well. Meggie, smiling and bobbing, seemed a long way away, and I had to make an effort to hear her. But waiting in the parlour, by the hastily-lighted fire, I thought that everything would be all right when Barney came. I remembered the time when the mere thought of him had cured my head; now, surely, the sight and the touch of him would heal me.

It didn't. Barney, too, seemed a long way away; Barney, too, seemed to be speaking from a great distance. Even when he kissed me, kissed me with a strange new tenderness as well as a renewal of old passion, I remained limp and unresponsive. I was driven to excuse myself, saying that my head ached. Quite soon, attentive and concerned, he rode home with me, and in the lane, near the broken archway, we parted, not with our usual kisses and embraces—last kisses, infinitely prolonged; last embraces, snatched, parted, returning, desperate because so long must elapse before they were renewed—instead of these there were requests upon his side that I should go straight to bed and not worry, that I would leave everything to him; and upon my side a faltering renewal of apology that I had spoilt our evening together. I was crying from exhaustion and pain and disappointment before I could get out of the stable-yard.

That night I slept in short broken snatches. And my head still ached. In the morning I was unrecognizable. My hair, usually yellow and very curly, looked lank and thin, quite straight and almost colourless. My eyes were half-closed and surrounded by brownish shadows, my nose was sharp, and my whole face sunken and doughy. Before I could face anyone I was obliged to curl my hair and paint my face, and then I looked like an old woman masquerading as a girl. And everything I did, even things so familiar as making a toilet and dressing myself, I did slowly, making an effort to remember, pausing, lost for a moment in a daze of pain and stupidity, and then going on again.

Old Nick had gone when I went down to breakfast, but Jassy was still at the table, lingering over a cup of coffee. And presently, when I had looked at her and, with incredible difficulty, thought about what I had seen, I realized that she was not looking herself either. And I thought, perhaps I *am* mad. Perhaps I am imagining things. And yet the limp, straight hair which I had just handled was real enough. I made an enormous effort and said, "Jassy, you don't look well." She straightened herself a little and said, in a more friendly and intimate voice than she had used towards me for some time:

"I've just been having one of my funny fits. You remember Hilda Besson and her mother—my seeing her getting well?"

"Yes," I said, with a faint spurt of interest, for that story had been a nine days' wonder at school.

"Well, it happened again just now. Dilys . . . it was true what he, your father, said the night before last. It sounded an idle, impetuous threat, but Mortiboys will never be yours. I saw it, quite plainly, belonging to somebody else."

"Who?"

"I can't tell you that . . . it wasn't plain enough. I was just sitting here drinking my coffee and looking at the wall, and I saw other people in it. Owning it. It's difficult to describe, but I am quite sure about it."

"Well," I said, and truthfully, "as I told Old Nick, I don't want it. There's nothing I want less. Though I suppose when I'm married to Barney I should be glad of the money I could sell it for. But I can't even bother to think about that. I've had a headache for three days now, and it's getting worse."

She looked at me without sympathy and said in a funny, thoughtful way, "Barney always wanted Mortiboys back, when he was young. He talked about it to me once. I never forgot it."

"You're hinting again that he's marrying me for the place," I said with a sudden spurt of anger that sent a sickening thud through my head. "That's the second time you've said it. I think it's mean and cruel of you. And you're utterly wrong. I saw Barney last night and told him what father had said. It didn't make the slightest difference."

"Oh, I don't suppose it would. I'm not suggesting that he isn't in love with you, Dilys. A blind baby could see that on that first evening when we had supper there. It's only . . . well, it seems a pity that he shouldn't have *both* his loves."

It occurred to me again that she was in love with him. And this time I was certain. I ought to have felt sorry for her, but mingled with my headache, and my miserable state of mind, the knowledge served only to make me furiously angry.

"Well, that's one thing you can't arrange," I said spitefully. "You seem to be omniscient, but you're not omnipotent. Barney must put up with Green Farm, and me!"

She remained quite unruffled, looking straight at me from under slightly raised eyebrows. After a little silence she asked in an ordinary voice, "Would you care to come to Colchester with me? You haven't long to shop in."

What would Mrs. Hatton need? Clogs against the farmyard mud? Oh, Barney, weren't we happy in the Spinney? Soon, very soon, there'll be a drift of wild anemones there. Lovely, lovely! But you shouldn't pick the windflowers and take them home and put them in water. They wither. They shrivel and go grey . . . shrivel like a pretty face that has to be painted. Like my face. These wild feelings that you and I have known, Barney, can't be taken indoors and chained to the kitchen table. They shrivel and are gone.

And, indeed, *all* feeling had gone from me: the warm, strong ones which had begun during my absence at Ockley, and which had sent me running to Barney in the field; and the small humble feelings with which, only three days ago, I had looked upon Green Farm and accepted it as my future home. I didn't even feel like a girl any more. I was just a vague body attached to a head which ached and ached.

But I still said and did what was expected of me. I went to Colchester and tried, as I followed Jassy from shop to shop, to think about things I needed. The effort to concentrate ended in the drapers' where Jassy was buying curtain material: the counter upon which the stuff was piled suddenly leapt up at me and hit me in the face. When I was conscious again I was in a kind of storeroom at the back of the shop, and my first thought was that now my headache would be better. But it wasn't. And after that I knew that I should have it for ever. Sleep hadn't cured it; Barney's presence hadn't cured it; and now I had been unconscious and still it was there. No feeling for me any more, except pain in the head.

(242)

Days began to pass in a mad, whirling muddle. I made no preparations for my marriage; I never even wrote the letter which would tell the Fennels about it. Sometimes I stayed in bed and Jassy, with a kind of angry solicitude, brought or sent me horrible concoctions composed largely of the loathsome red juice of raw beef. One of the new maids she had instituted was a grotesque ugly idiot girl, all but dumb, and it seemed always to be she who presented me with Jassy's doses, except when Jassy came herself.

Sometimes I got up and roamed about the house. Now and then, when the curtain of darkness which seemed to divide me from the world lifted a little, I thought that something was happening between Old Nick and Jassy. She seemed to be using all her wiles on him, and he was responding. It would end as I had told her it would; but I had warned her and could do no more, even if I had wanted to.

Of Old Nick himself I was not frightened any more. I was past feeling fear. Once when he was offensive to me I rounded on him and said everything that I had had in mind, for years, to say. I could hear my own voice, a long way off at the end of a tunnel, saying the most rage-provoking things. Jassy was present, and perhaps for that reason he merely laughed and said, "You rail like a farm-wife already." She put her hand on his arm and said:

"Don't mind her. Getting married upsets a girl's nerves."

"Does it?" he said. "Does it?"

They looked at one another and laughed a little. It was hateful to see them like that. But I couldn't mind.

Finally, out of despair I dredged up the notion that I might feel better if Barney and I could go once more to the Spinney where we had been so happy. Since I had gone into the field and told Barney I would marry him, we had been meeting openly and behaving with the restraint usual in such cases. But at last I persuaded him to come to the Spinney, instead of taking me over to Green Farm and making me wring out inadequate remarks of admiration for the improvements he was making to the house.

It was a lovely evening, mild and windless. I made my face carefully and curled my hair. I drank a cupful of the red juice and swallowed four of the useless headache tablets. I put on a muslin dress, unseasonable but pretty, and over it a warm pelisse which I could discard in the wood. For hitherto at least I had always been warm enough in Barney's arms.

The oxlips were in bud, in warm corners facing south they were already in flower, shedding a sweet, apricot-scented fragrance on the air. The bluebells, not yet broken, stood up spikily, their buds a darker blue than the flowers would be. Larches were green again and there were spatters of blackthorn, dazzlingly white, in the hedges. It was, indeed, an evening made for lovers.

But one was mad and ill and the other bewildered. I thought, I *will* escape. I *will* break through! I will get back to the joy we knew. There must be something left of the feeling that made me ride from Ockley determined to marry Barney; I must find it again.

I tried. Heaven knows I tried. I threw myself into Barney's arms. I kissed him as I had never, even in my most ecstatic moments of rapture, kissed him before. I waked such passion in him . . . but in myself nothing. There was nothing—though we lay in the old place; though Barney was as strong and ardent a lover as the wildest dream could fashion. There was nothing in me except pain and despair.

A thin-sliced moon came up over the pointed tops of the larches and I could smell the oxlips. I lay and thought: it's over, it's over, and it will always be like this. There is nothing for me in the future except this no-feeling and Green Farm. . . .

Barney put his arm under me and drew my head into the hollow of his shoulder. I could feel the wild racing of his heart growing slower and steadier. He said, "You're tired, my love. I've tired you." I began to cry softly from disappointment and hopelessness. Years and years, I thought. Even the Spinney had failed me. This was what it was to be dead . . . or very old, so that there was nothing except the brittle dry framework left. And a head that ached and ached.

Barney was puzzled by my crying; puzzled, but gentle and kind. If I had been capable of feeling then I should have been ashamed.

On my way back to Mortiboys I suddenly found myself clenching and unclenching my hands. I tried to stop it, but they moved without any connection with me. I was frightened and thought I would like to ask Jassy about them. Her behaviour to me was curious of late, but she could be kind. And she was sensible and would know if this were madness. But she was nowhere to be seen. When I had looked everywhere I thought of Old Nick's room. I wondered. I went into my own room and lay in the bed, trying to sleep, clenching and unclenching my hands.

Next morning I stayed in bed late, and about mid-morning, while I was slowly and laboriously dressing myself, Janey came up with a message to say that Mr. Fennel was waiting below.

I was dressed, but my hair was hanging like string, and my face, freshly washed, was ashen. But I went straight down, thinking that now, since I had never managed to write, I could tell Stephen my news and he would go away and that would be the end of that.

I don't think he recognized me at first, or was so shocked that he could not speak. He just stared as I went towards him, and at any other time I should have been amused at the sight of all his gallantry and mannerisms dropping away and leaving just Stephen, uncertain and unpoised.

I said weakly, "Hullo, Stephen!" And then he seemed to gulp and swallow in his throat. He said:

"Dilys! What on earth is the matter? What have they been doing to you?"

"No one's done anything to me, Stephen. I'm just not well.

My head aches and aches and I can't think. I'm glad to see you though. I've got something to tell you."

He glared round the hall.

"It's this damned place," he said blurtingly. "You shouldn't have come back here. I told mother so, but she . . . Never mind. Look, I brought the carriage. I have to go to Bywater. I hoped you'd drive with me. Do you feel well enough?"

"I can't," I said. "It takes me so long. This hair. And my face. I have to make it every day, Stephen. I have no face left."

He gave me a peculiar look and I thought, ah, here's somebody who isn't used to me. He notices. He knows I'm mad. But Stephen said very gently, as though speaking to a child:

"Is it just your head, Dilys?"

I nodded.

"They've done it between them . . . made you ill, I mean. I'm going to take you out of here. Do you feel well enough to come with me now in the carriage?"

"To Bywater?"

He gave me another peculiar look. Then he nodded.

"Yes. I think I could come to Bywater. The air might do me good, and I want to talk to you, Stephen. Can you wait?"

"Only while you get a hat. Don't bother about your face, or hair."

"But I look so . . ."

"If you go upstairs you'll be an hour. I want to get out of this place." He looked round and saw, tossed down on the wide window sill, the hat I had intended to wear the night before. Just as I was leaving I had felt its weight too oppressive and had thrown it off and forgotten it. He picked it up and offered it to me. I put it on my head, knowing, but not minding, that it must look absurd and dreadful over those limp strands of hair. As soon as my hands fell to my sides Stephen seized one of them and led me, with restrained haste, out to the waiting carriage. There was a rug lined with glossy dark fur on the seat, and when I was inside he tucked it round me. Then, telling the coachman to drive slowly and avoid bumps in the road, he sat down by my side and folded his arms.

We did not speak until the carriage bounced softly out of the lane and turned onto the high road. I sat thinking that in a moment I would tell Stephen about Barney. But the effort of trying to frame the sentence made me feel so ill that I began to doubt whether I should actually live until Easter. With a kind of amazement I began to consider the possibility that I might be going to die. Except for the amazement I felt nothing, not even self-pity. In fact, I should be better dead than married to Barney in my present state.

At the end of the lane Stephen raised himself, touched the coachman's shoulder and said, "Home."

"Not Bywater, sir?"

"Home," Stephen repeated sharply and sank back.

"I'm taking you to mother," he said. "She'll look after you."

"But, Stephen, I can't stay there. I haven't any clothes."

"We'll find some."

"But there's another thing. The thing I wanted to tell you. I've been meaning to write to you for days and days. But I couldn't. Stephen, I've promised to marry Barney at Easter."

Stephen changed colour a little, but he neither exclaimed nor protested. He twisted in his seat so that he was looking at me, and when he had run his tongue over his lips he asked, in an ordinary, conversational tone:

"Are you in love with him?"

"I have been. Now I don't know."

"Why did you promise if you weren't sure?" he asked, very reasonably.

"But I *was* sure. That is what makes it so queer and dreadful, Stephen. I was quite sure. It was the only thing to do. The only decent thing, too. I made up my mind when I stayed with you last—you remember? I was thinking about Barney all the time." Stephen's sallow face seemed to shrink a little, but I went on, not minding. Pity was another thing that I had ceased to feel. "I went straight back and told Barney I'd marry him—he'd been asking me for a long time. Then, on that same day I began to be ill, and now I don't want to marry him . . . or anybody else. And there's nothing your mother can do for me, Stephen. I think I'm going to die. I might just as well do it without bothering anyone else."

I could hear my own voice, slow, full of effort, like the voice of someone speaking in a troublesome, unfamiliar language. Then I was aware that Stephen's attention had wandered. He was staring up at the back of the coachman.

"I don't know whether he can hear or not, but it's a risk. Don't say any more for a moment. Crisp," he said, and then, rising again, tapped the man on the shoulder. "Crisp, when we reach Green Drive turn in and stop." There was silence again until, inside the Green Drive, the man halted the carriage and looked back over his shoulder, awaiting his next orders.

Stephen moved over to the seat which backed the box. "Give me the reins," he said. "Thank you. Now walk to the end of the Drive, Crisp, and sit down. I'll wave when I want you."

The man must have been blind and deaf. Blind to my appearance and deaf to what I had been saying before Stephen checked me, for he went off with a conspiratorial smile, very sly and knowing.

Stephen hooked his arm through the loop of the tight-stretched reins and settled in his seat.

"Now, Dilys, tell me all about it." The one scrap of my mind which, through all my troubles, had remained unimpaired, observed that there was something very comforting, almost feminine about him. We might have been two oldish ladies settling down for a cosy heart-to-heart chat. I suddenly realized that I had not had anyone to talk to since Jassy's withdrawal. It may have been for that reason, or because there was something almost hypnotic about Stephen, but anyway I heard my queer, distant voice telling him everything.

(248)

It was, I think, rather more than he bargained for when he said, "Tell me all about it." But I didn't care at all. I did not mind if I hurt or shocked him. That remote, detached part of my mind saw, without any emotion, the increasing sallowness of his sallow face, the pained, startled widening of his eye-pupils, the clenched discomfort of his hands. To me they counted as nothing compared to the relief I felt from the mere telling of my story.

When it was finished and I was silent again, he licked his lips and moved them, mouthing some soundless words which might have been epithets of disgust. I did not care. But he licked his lips again and this time managed to ask:

"Are you . . . do you think you're going to have a baby?"

I had never, never for one moment thought of that.

"I don't know," I said. I tried to count, but the counting part of my brain, never very active, had been dead for a long time. "I might be. It's more than likely."

I looked at him as I spoke. Why not? I did not feel ashamed. I saw a dusky red flush surge up into his sallow face and imagined that he was about to order me out of the carriage.

"You poor little thing," he said—and I did feel surprised. "You poor little lost thing!" He seemed to throw himself forward, was jerked back by the loop of the reins over his arm, freed himself impatiently and rather comically, and threw himself forward again so that he was kneeling on the floor of the carriage with his arms round me.

"Darling, you mustn't marry him. You don't love him, you just said as much, and he doesn't love you, or he wouldn't . . . wouldn't have taken advantage of your sweet innocence. You poor darling, with no one to help or advise you! Worried to death, ill with worry, and nobody even noticed. . . ." He ran on, repeating himself in this strain for several minutes. Then he said, more calmly: "Dilys, I came to Mortiboys this morning to ask you to marry me. I spoke to your father last night when he was at Ockley, but I left it too late and he was drunk, he didn't seem to understand. But I'm asking you now. Will you marry me and let me look after you?"

"You can't want to marry me *now*," I said.

"Now more than ever. I've loved you ever since that evening when you came home from Baildon—oh, before that really, but I didn't know it. I'll be so good to you, darling, and make up for all the misery you've had."

"But I promised Barney."

"To hell with him! He ought to be hanged. Taking advantage of you so."

"I was as much to blame—or more."

"Don't say that. You don't know what you're talking about. Darling, the innocence of you. . . ."

But it wasn't innocence. Not in Saints' Spinney—that was pure lust; and not now—that was just not caring what I said because it didn't matter.

"And suppose there *is* a baby?"

"No one need know. We'd be married immediately."

"You're crazy," I said.

I pushed him away from me a little and looked away down the green ride. My head was throbbing so hard that the trees seemed to be dancing, closing in and then parting again. But I realized suddenly that the quality of the pain had altered a little. It was pain, not paralysis. I could think. And I did think. I weighed, as I had so often done before, Stephen against Barney. But this time it was different. For now I could remember that last night in Saints' Spinney, when I had looked up at the moon and thought —it's over, and it will be like this for years. Barney had never meant more to me than the lust of the flesh, and that had failed. Now there was nothing to set in the scales against Ockley, and money, social security, snobbery. I cared for neither Barney nor Stephen. I was foolishly certain at that moment that even if I lived I should never thrill again to any man's touch. I was not clear enough in my mind to know then what I knew so bitterly later, that the rift in my mind would heal because it had been caused simply by the effort to accept poverty and the farm and social outlawry in order to have Barney's body. How could I guess that when the wound of that decision had healed I should be the old Dilys, burning with the old fire that only Barney could quench, going on and on, all the years of my life, seeking the forfeited pleasure, unsatisfied, insatiable, for ever pursuing and never finding, a substitute for the joy I had lost? No, thinking that all feeling was dead in me, I could not see beyond Ockley.

"Truly, Stephen, I don't know what to say. I'm in such a muddle. All my life has been a muddle."

"Say that you'll marry me and I'll put it all straight."

"I wish I could believe it."

"You must. You shall. I'll show you. May I try?"

I nodded. He raised his face and kissed me. Then he stood up and, in an excited way, waved his handkerchief to Crisp, who came running.

Book Four
LUNATIC ECLIPSE

"Sometimes, you know, I wonder whether that dumb idiot girl couldn't have told a story. . . ."

So this story is told by BELINDA WICKS, *who was subject to Visitations.*

THERE is a whole name—it is Belinda Wicks; but when people are kind they say Lindy. When they are not kind they say Latchety or Loony. Not kind are most. Loony is for people who are wrong in the head. I was right in the head once, but when I was little our father came home drunk and threw me off the bed. I fell on my head and there was pain. It was short, but afterwards I was not like the others. I can talk, and I can understand what other people talk, but when I say words they come out thick, like red flannel, or sometimes they don't come at all. So I nod my head, or shake it and make signs.

I am little, too. But I am strong. I can lift things and run very fast. And I can remember a lot. There are the things people say when I am there that they do not think I understand because I cannot talk. But I remember. I can even remember a man called Tom Woodroffe that put the fear of God into our father so he didn't get drunk or knock us down any more. But it was too late for me.

That man Tom Woodroffe gave our father a book. There were pictures in it. There was one picture with an angel in it rolling a great stone away from a hole. The angel was shiny white and there was a ring, like the outside of a plate made of light, on his head. It was lovely.

Then one day there was a wedding, and I went because it was my sister Agnes to be married. And in the church window, high up, there was the same angel. Bigger, but the same. Even the birds' wings of it were the same. I sat very still and looked at it and wondered how it could be there, big, and in the book at home, small, but the same. Then there was a sweet smell, like a rose bush, just near me, and when I looked the angel was there. It said, "I can be where I like." I said, "In two places?" And the words came out right. The people all looked at me and shushed. The angel said, "Never mind. I will talk to you another time." I said, "Where? When? Please tell me." Then it was gone, and our mum signed to my sister Jill to take me outside, Jill was angry and said I ought not to have come. I said, "I saw an angel." The words didn't come so clear as when I talked to it. But she heard and said, "Aah, you're loopy!"

After that there was the angel many times with me. It could be as big as a house or as small as a daisy. It talked to me and I could talk to it.

There was the time when I could go to work. Our mum got me places. She said I could work very well. And I was cheap. But the people never kept me long. Every time I came home our mum said, "So you're back again. Oh dear!"

Then one day She came. There was a good shape of her. There was a bad one, too, but it wasn't there then, or very often. She was kind, and when She knew my name, She said it, "Lindy," like a bird singing in a bush. She said she was looking for some help in the kitchen at the big house, Mortiboys, and our mum said about me being able to work and being cheap. And She said I could go. I was very glad.

The house is big. I lost myself sometimes. There were many servants, and they were just like the others where I had been before. They teased me and called me names. Sometimes when they do that my good shape is there and I run away or hide; but sometimes it is the bad shape, and I stamp and shout at them. One day I was crying and stamping and saying—but it was all wrong and thick—how much I hated them, when She came in and said not to tease me, people should be kind to the afflicted. She smiled at me, too.

That night the angel came, very small, and stood on my bed. It had a long white string, shiny like silver, in its hand, and it tied one end of it round my heart. It said, "Now I am going to tie the other end round her heart and you will be joined together always."

I said, "Will She know?" The angel said, "No. You are the one to know." Then it flew away and the string pulled tight. I knew that the other end was fastened. I was happy because we had been tied together, and after that there was always a pull when I was out of her sight. Sometimes it hurt. But when I was with her it was loose and did not hurt. I tried to be near her when I could. Even in the night. If it pulled hard I would get up and creep away through the dark house and sit outside the room with the pretty paper where She was asleep. And in the day I tried to be near her too. Sometimes She saw me and said, "Lindy, what are you doing there?" and sent me to my work, but kindly, smiling. So I made myself very small and quiet to be near her and She not to know.

There were some others in the house. There was the Master. He was an ugly shape all the time. It was bad temper, and he hated everybody. He was like our father before Tom Woodroffe put the fear of God in him. He was the same colour, and shouted the same way. There was the same smell, too, a bad smell. When I was in the front part of the house because to polish the floor was my work there, I knew when the Master was near because of the smell, and I would go away quickly or hide till he was past. There was a good shape to him too, like there is to everybody, but it couldn't show much. Once I saw it when She was with him.

The other person in the front of the house was Miss Dilys. She was lovely to look at. At first I thought she was a little bit like my angel, but that only the top. Her real shape wasn't settled. She was like the weeds in the pond, wavery and washed about. Once she said that the sight of me made her sick. She was a bad shape then. And sometimes when she talked to Her she was bad too. But not always.

The Master and Miss Dilys and She took their meals in the dining-room, and other times they sat in the hall or in a room called the library. There were screens near the doors to keep out the cold. I used to hide in the screens. It was easy because I am small and can move without making a noise. I was in the screen when Miss Dilys said she was going to marry young Mr. Hatton from my village. Miss Dilys was a good shape that night, but the Master was bad, and She was bad too; but whether She was good or bad the string stayed strong and tight. No matter what She did I was tied to her. And that night She cried. I knew because I was outside the room with the pretty paper and I was listening. But She only cried a little. Presently She started to swear. She used words no lady knows about, only rough men and boys. I shuddered outside the door and knew that the bad shape was inside. Mostly, when people are a bad shape, I want to run and hide, but not with her. I wanted to open the door and go in and touch her and make her better. But I didn't dare.

Then one day a little while after that the Master and She had some talking. I did not understand it, but I can remember some.

He said, "I'll put it in my will."

She said: "A will is too easily altered. It must be as I say. That is my one condition."

He said, "It shows a lamentable lack of faith."

And She said, "It also shows common sense. I may never be in a position to dictate terms again." Then he laughed and said She should have been a highway man.

Not long after that Miss Dilys got ill. When she was ill her shape was very watery and her hair wasn't like my angel's any more. There was a kind of cloud round her. I could see even when she passed me in the passage. It got thicker every day until she was just a dark cloud wandering. Then one day she went away.

There were some days and she came back. There was a man with her. He was not much himself, but when he looked at her he bloomed like a tree. I was polishing the stairs when they came and stood in the hall. I was polishing the stairs for the second time, because She was in the hall putting daffodils and pussy willow in water. I had gathered them early in the morning and put them outside the room with the pretty paper. Very early morning it was, but She wasn't in that room. I knew because when I got there the string was still tight, and when I had put the daffodils down I let it pull me where it wanted to. And it pulled me to Master's room and then loosed a little. I knew She was there. I nearly picked up the flowers and put them outside that door. But he might think they were for him, and perhaps She didn't want anybody to know. So for two reasons I left them where they were. Now She was putting them in water and I was polishing the stairs again just to be near her. When I was near her and could see her doing things I had a smooth feeling, like a cat being stroked. Or cream. Once I ate some cream when nobody was looking, and it was like that, smooth and sweet. But to be near her was better. It was better than anything.

Miss Dilys and the one they called Stephen came in and they did a little talking. Miss Dilys said, "I haven't come home for good, only for a few things I wanted. Jassy, will you give father a message for me? I've changed my mind. I'm going to marry Stephen after all."

I was looking. When Miss Dilys said that she went a very wavery shape indeed, bad and good, bad and good, and then bad, bad. The one they called Stephen just bloomed. He was lovely then, like a bush of flowers, but She went very evil. There was nothing left but her bad shape, temper and swearing. Very frightening. She said:

"You're what?" And Miss Dilys said it again. Then She said: "You're a heartless little hussy. God knows you weren't worthy to clean his boots, but he loved you. You'll break his heart." She said other things too, swearing things that only rough men and boys know.

The young man shouted too, and said he wouldn't have Dilys spoken to like that.

Then She was quiet and said, in a most serious way: "Dilys, is it because of the money? Don't mind about that. You will have Mortiboys one day, I promise you."

"But it was you who said . . ."

"I know what I *said*. But I promise you: if you marry Barney you shall have it."

Miss Dilys began to say, "It's too late . . ." and the young man was angry, and he was afraid too. Fears smell bad and I knew. He said, "You talk like a mad woman. Since when has Mortiboys been yours to promise, pray? Dilys, dear, I beg of you, come away, don't listen to her."

She put her hand on Miss Dilys' arm and held it between the wrist and the elbow and said, "But Barney loves you, Dilys. And you promised."

The young man was very frightened. And because of it he took her by the shoulder and tried to shake her hand off Miss Dilys. There was my sweeping brush there, and when he touched her I took it and ran down the stairs and beat on his head.

"Lindy! Lindy!" She said, and pulled me and shook me.

The young man put his arm round Miss Dilys and took her to the door. "This place is Bedlam, or worse," he said. "Never mind your things. You shall have everything new."

Miss Dilys said, "But there is a portrait of my mother, and the pearls she gave me."

"I will pack everything and send you," She said in a little tired voice, "because I see that possessing things is the most important thing in life with you."

Miss Dilys looked back, "At least I am going to be *married*," she said. And there was a sneer.

"Don't start anything else," the young man Stephen said, and pulled her away through the door. When it was shut She started to laugh. But it turned into crying. She sat on the settle near the hearth and cried. It was hard angry crying as well as sorrowful. The string in me pulled tighter and tighter until at last I was so close to her that I could see every hair on her head. I did not know why she was crying: I had stopped them hurting her. But I was sad too. And I put my hand on her skirt where it lay on the floor. She saw me and looked down. She put her hand on my shoulder and I nearly burst with joy. She said, "Poor Lindy. I expect you wonder what it is all about. I do myself. Nothing ever goes right for me."

She didn't say anything about hitting with brushes.

After that there was a time. And She was kind to me. She let me carry the bunch when She picked flowers in the garden, and twice I went to Colchester to carry the things She bought; and we had cakes in a shop. They were pink, and it was like eating roses.

There, and in the garden, it was good; but in the house it was bad. Though She gave me a dress and some shoes and a petticoat that was hers. The hem of it was raggy and She said could I sew, because the hem could be cut off and then it would fit me. I never cut it. I did get some scissors and start, but it was like cutting her, and my toes curled and my hands were cold. So I put it under my pillow and at night I held it. I was afraid that one day She would say, "Where is the petticoat?" But She never did. It was like hitting the young man on the head, a secret that we never said, even to ourselves.

We were all right in the house, but it was bad with her and the Master. Up to that time he didn't shout at her; but then he started. Behind the screens and in my own hiding places I watched and listened. I heard what they said, but it didn't mean anything. Only that there was temper. And a change. He called her names. He said She was a cold bitch to strip a man and cheat him. She said, "I do my best. What more can I do?" He said, "If I had another place to settle on you maybe you would do better, eh?"

Once when he was shouting She said, "Don't shout at me. I am not one of your doxies." And he said, "You're worse than any doxy. I've had better than you for a guinea."

That time She laughed and said, "You must balance your good bargains then against your bad one." And then he hit her. And I forgot that I wasn't to be behind the screen. I ran out and bit his hand. That time She was angry, and said did I ever watch or listen or spy on her again She would send me off. I fell on my knees and beat my head on her shoes and begged her not to say that. After a little She said all right, but if I spied again I must go. Then the Master said, "She must go now. Do you think I would have her here after this? The mad ——, ——" He said names that were not right. Not true. Bad, bad names he called me. He said to go away at once. I hung on her skirt and cried. And She begged him. She said, "You shan't ever see her. But please let her stay. She is fond of me, and she works hard and is cheap."

But I could feel cruelty grow in him, and he said I must go for biting him in the hand. But it was because She wanted to keep me. That was why.

It was the time of falling leaves and rain and wind. The sad time. And when he had said that I should not be there another day, he went out. He did not mind the weather. She came and said that I must stay in my little room until She had thought of a place for me. The little room was all mine, because the others said they would rather sleep three in a bed than share with me.

I sat and listened to the wind. I am sorry for it. It cries and taps on the window and says, "Let me in, please; please let me in." Sometimes I open the window and let it in and it runs round the room, quiet and happy to be indoors. That day I let it in because it cried and said, "How will you feel when you are shut out?" So I let it in, and it put its cold hands on my face.

Then She came, but not till late, nearly dark. I thought She had come to say that She had found a place and I must go. I began to howl like the wind. But She said, "I want you to help me,

Lindy. The Master is taken very ill. I must nurse him. If you do exactly what I tell you you can be a great help to me."

The doctor was there, and he gave me a bowl with rings marked inside it. I held the bowl when he made a little slit in the Master's arm, and the blood ran out up to the ring in the bowl. The Master's face was the colour of the darkest poppy, and he breathed like bellows. But some of the poppy colour and some of the breathing ran out into the bowl.

Then She said to empty it and have something to eat and come back because I was to sit up with her in the night.

I could not eat, though always I did what She said; but this time not because the string was so tight I could not swallow, because of them all She had picked me to sit in the night with her and because I was not sent to another place.

There was a happy time. In all my life that was the best time. There was a little room with a door to the Master's room and a door to the passage, and we sat there together by the fire. There was a couch, and in the night one of us lay on it and the other watched to hear and call if he made a noise. There were trays, and I carried them. I went down to eat in the kitchen sometimes and heard the talk. They talked a lot. They were afraid he would die, and what then? They said how he had taken ill and been brought home on a gate. They said how would anybody get better with her and a loony to nurse him?

I listened to it all. But it did not matter. Only there was the time when I thought about his getting better and driving me out. I hoped he would die. The dead ones do not hurt anybody, though some people will not go in the churchyard at night.

The happy time lasted. In the morning I would go down and make tea.

One morning the wind cried and I let it in, and it sat very quiet combing its hair. But when I had made the tea and was going to turn the wind out—because if I left it in there was trouble because it would touch things—it stood up and altered itself and was my angel. I was surprised. The angel kept its hand behind its back for a little time, then it said, "Look. I am going to tie you together with this now." And I looked and there was a cord like the other, but not white and shiny. Red it was, like the blood in the bowl. I went back round the table and said, "But it will hurt more. The white one is sore when I am away from her, and this will be worse because when he is better I must go away."

The angel said, "Ah, but if I tie this you will never have to go away. You will be together for always."

"But it is the colour of blood," I said.

"That is right. You love her, don't you?"

"Indeed I do. Our mum loved our father, and my sister Jill loved the young chap that was hanged for poaching. But I love her, and that is the best. But I wish there was another colour."

The angel said, "This is the colour to tie you for ever."

So I was glad, and it tied it in a knot round my heart next to the white one, but harder. Then it went away, and soon there was a great pull.

There was talking in the bedroom, and when She came out for the tea She said, "He is better. He is sensible this morning." She went to the window and pulled the curtain and looked out. She was not glad. And if he was better he would send me away. Only the angel had said together for always. Perhaps She would come too.

There were some days. He was better quickly and shouting just the same. He would not eat the food for sick people. Or drink tea and milk. He said he was poisoned and flung the food about. He said he was a man, not a baby, to suck slops. He said to bring him a bottle.

But the doctor came and said not much to eat and nothing strong to drink.

The happy times were over. There were bad ones again. She was white and thin. Once in the night when She was asleep She said, "Oh, Barney, Barney," and woke up with crying.

There was a day when he could get out of bed and sit in a chair by the fire. She said to me in the little room, "Soon he will

(261)

be about again, and I am afraid you must go then, Lindy. But I will find you a kind place and keep an eye on you."

The bedroom door was shut and I looked at it and made faces. My bad shape was there. And She looked at the door, too, and did not make faces, but there was hate in her eyes. Even our bad shapes were tied together for always like the angel said. I wanted to tell her, but I could not.

That night She said, "You can go to your bed. Lucky Lindy!" And when I got to my room there was my angel, smaller than a finger, sitting on my pillow and shining like gold. It said, "Bend down and I'll whisper to you." I bent down and there was a smell of roses. The angel said, "She doesn't want him to get better." I said, "I know. But what can I do about it?"

The angel said, "She is very sad." And then the two cords that were round my heart began to tug and pull. There was great pain, like toothache. There was so much toothache in the pain that I put my finger in the hole where our mum dug my tooth out by the root with her scissors.

I said, "It is like toothache. But the tooth is gone."

The little angel danced on the pillow and said, "Yes, toothache. Think about toothache. You must think about toothache."

I said, "Why? The tooth is gone. Our mum rooted it out with the scissors."

"But before that there was medicine."

"Yes," I said. "There was medicine."

"Think about that," said the angel and flew away.

From next door they knocked on the wall and said, "Shut up, Loony, or we'll come and make you."

I got into bed. There was a rose smell on my pillow. And there was the toothache pain in my heart. I thought about the medicine like the angel had said.

Next morning when I went up with the tea I thought I had better be sure. I practised on every stair, saying, "Don't you want him to get better?" And when I got into the little room I said it out, as clear as anybody. She gave me a frightened look and said:

"Who said that?" I tried to say, "I did. Myself." But the words came wrong, and I had to point to my chest and nod, and point downstairs and all around, shaking my head to show that nobody but me had said it. She said, "Don't say it again. Do you hear me?" But She didn't say that it wasn't true. So then I thought about the toothache medicine.

It is good for all pains. It is in a black bottle with a rag round the cork to keep the strength in. It has two smells. The top smell is sweet, like a field of hay just cut. The underneath one is sleepy, like holding a poppy too close to your face. And it has two shapes. One is good and one is bad. When people say, "Well, it's kill or cure," they mean the toothache medicine. Two drops will cure you, at least for a time, but a lot of it will kill you. Even when you have only two drops, a drop and a drop on a bit of sheep's wool in your tooth, you must spit all the time. You mustn't swallow your slaver. Because the medicine is poison.

Our mum keeps the bottle in the sag of the beam in the bedroom. There was a time when my tooth was bad first when she would give me a drop and a drop on wool to hold in it and spit hard. But afterwards, when the cure had gone out of it, she took the scissors and rooted the tooth out. There was bad pain and my face was very big on one side. But it got better, and now there was just a hole.

There were two days and the Master was better all the time and shouting, and saying he would not have slops any more, and open the window the room was stuffy, and shut it the draught was blowing his head off. All of those two days I was trying to say that I wanted to go home and see my mum. But the words came wrong and She did not understand. Though She tried.

Then the angel came again and said, "Say what you want to say to me. Yes, that is right. Now say it again. That is good. To-morrow you will be able to say it."

And next day I said, very clear, "Please may I go home?"

But it was the wrong thing to say. She looked startled and sorry.

"I thought you were happy here, Lindy. What is the matter? Have they been teasing you again?"

I shook my head hard and tried to say what I meant, but it was all thick and flannelly. Then suddenly I saw the little angel, perched on the edge of the mantelpiece and laughing. I said, "You told me wrong. I should have said I wanted to go home for one hour. One hour, for a visit."

"That's right," it said. "Now you've said it. Good-bye."

She looked round and then at me. She said, "You are a funny girl, Lindy. For a moment I thought you were speaking to somebody else. A visit. Yes, of course. You may have a whole day off if you like. You've earned it. I don't know what I should have done without you."

She put her hand on my shoulder. "Come along, we'll go and find a little present for you to take home. You'd like to take your mother something, wouldn't you?"

There was happiness in me and thankfulness, and I was proud, too, because of what She had said. She took me to the big pantry and She filled a basket and put a little cloth over it. There was half a game pie with the gravy set in a jelly, and there was a piece of pork and a plum cake.

Then I was outside the door and the cords began to drag at me. I ran very fast. I said, "Please cords be kind and let me run. I am being as quick as I can go. You need not pull at me. I am going back." A boy in a farm cart heard me and laughed and jeered. I didn't mind. The hurry pain came in my body too, but it was small beside the cord pain in my heart, and it went away when I stopped and touched my toes.

I went by the Low Road because that is the short way. But it was bad for fast running; the leaves were so thick and the rain made them slippery. When I got home I was breathing like bellows and the sweat was running down my face.

Our mum had a sick look; the old sick look when I came home other times. She said, "So you're back again. Oh dear, what shall I do with you?"

I shook my head and smiled and pointed back to show that I had just come to visit. Mum understood. So she was glad and gave me a good bun with currants, a Sunday bun. But I could not eat it then. I put it in my pocket. Then I showed her the basket and, while she was opening it and saying nice things, I went into the bedroom and reached up to the sag in the beam. The bottle was there, and there was some medicine in it. I put it in my pocket with the Sunday bun.

Mum wanted me to have pie. There was tea, too. But I could not stop. I took the basket and made mum understand that I was in a hurry and would stop another day. Then I ran back to the big house as hard as I could go.

I went to the little room and listened. She was inside the bedroom with the Master. He was growling at her and saying I shall get up to-morrow; you're in league with that —— fool of a doctor to keep me here under your thumb till I die, but I'll show you. She said not to say such things. The pain got better slowly, now I was near and could hear her talk. Then I went to my own room. I was glad that they would rather sleep three in a bed than share with me. I took out the bottle and smelt it. It was just the same with the sweet smell and the sleepy smell folded over each other.

There was my bun too. I could eat it then.

When I went in the kitchen She was there, making the Master's dinner.

Cook was angry. She didn't like it because She cooked Master's food. But She said that there were always grumbles, and She liked to know whether they were right ones or wrong ones. So She cooked.

When She saw me She was surprised and said, "I didn't expect you back yet. Did you enjoy yourself?" I nodded. The others scowled because they didn't like her talking to me friendly. Then She said, "Now you are back I think I shall take a little walk. Mr. Helmar may be able to get up to-morrow, and I may not have a chance then." I helped to carry up the dinner, and I heard her tell him that She was going out for a few minutes. He grumbled, but he didn't stop her. She shut the bedroom door and whispered to me that She would be in the garden. If he rang his bell or called, not to let anybody else get to him, but fetch her at once. I thought that because She was kind, because he had not been getting better so quickly that day and was in bed again.

I sat very quiet, listening for the bell, or a call, and ready to run, like I can run, very quickly to her. But the door opened behind me and there he was, not red any more, but white and smaller, in his bed gown and a nightcap on his head. He said fearful curses when he saw me, and called me the witch's devil, and said to get out of his sight and out of his house, and never let him see my ugly face again. I started to run, but he called after me to send somebody with a bottle of brandy. "Can you understand that much, idiot? B-r-a-n-d-y. Brandy. Quick. With a bottle inside me I can deal with that she-devil. Brandy, do you understand?"

I nodded and ran down the front stairs to get to her quickly in the garden. But at the bottom of the stairs was my angel. It said, "This is your chance. Remember the toothache medicine."

"But I don't know brandy," I said. "I hear the words he said so loud and slow, but they are in the dark for me."

"Any bottle will do," the angel said.

I knew where they were. It was nearly dark in the dining-room, but I found them. There were many, and alike to me except one not quite full to the neck. I took its cork out and filled it up with the toothache medicine.

I was afraid he would not have it when he saw me with it. I went in, very frightened. He was back in the bed, and he roared at me like Mr. Barber's bull. But I held up the bottle and then he was different. It was slyness and as if we were in a secret together.

"Good girl," he said, very pleased.

(266)

There was a jug on the table near the bed, a blue jug with a silver lid on it.

"Empty that muck in the slop jar," he said, "and fill it up from the bottle. Can you manage that?"

I nodded and poured away the good barley water She had made him.

"Now take the bottle away. That'll fox my beauty and the fool of a doctor. And mind you, not a word to anyone." That made me laugh. But he was angry again, and said, "It's come to a pretty pass that I should lie here dependent on an idiot to get me a drink to keep a little life in me! But I'll show 'em; I'll show 'em yet!"

I thought to take the bottle and hide in my room because there was a smell of toothache medicine about it. On the back stairs Cook met me. She was angry about the cooking, and because I was the one to sit up in the night. She was always looking to find a fault with me. She looked then and saw the bottle. She said nasty things about that She and I drank the poor Master's wine when he was fobbed off with pap, and them that lived longest would see most.

I put the bottle under my bed with the petticoat that I could not cut. It seemed funny to put his thing and her thing together like that.

There was the night, and I did not sleep much. On my mind there was the toothache medicine working in him, and our mum saying not to swallow what was on the wool, but spit hard and not be poisoned. Nobody knew to tell him except me, and I had done it. There would be good times always now, with us together like the angel promised.

In the morning I made the tea and went to the little room. She was asleep on the couch, very white and tired looking.

When She woke up She said, "Are you early this morning, Lindy? Or have I overslept? I was disturbed. The Master was sick."

Sick! Sick! I had not remembered the time when the poaching

chap was hanged and our Jill swallowed the medicine, and mum made her sick with the feather in her throat. So much there was to remember, I must forget some. The room in the head will not hold it all. So he was sick, and there would be a new place for me and not good times again.

She put on her robe and went carefully into the bedroom. I waited to hear roaring. But it did not happen. There was a great stillness. There was never such a stillness, not even when the wind has been howling and then I let it in.

She came back into the little room. And then there was a sound. My heart knocked like father's hammer, and so did hers. They knocked together, quick and heavy; together for always like the angel said.

She said, "Pour me a cup, Lindy, quickly. He is dead. Yesterday he was not so well, and now he is dead."

He hadn't sucked it all up. There had not been tickling of the throat with a feather. So it was all right.

She said, "I must let Miss Dilys know, and Doctor Stamper."

When the tea was drunk She went back in the room and brought out the blue jug with the lid and all the other things he had used and put them on the tray for washing.

On the stairs going down I smelt in the jug, and there were the two smells still, sweet like new hay and sleepy like poppies near the face; but there was another smell, too, sharp and strong. That was brandy. But I washed the jug and all the things with the cups.

There was too much talk. With me, when anything is done it is ended. With me it was all over with the washing of the jug. But not with the others.

I didn't hear all the talk that day, because I stayed near her, as near as I could. The cords were very tight that day. But there was bad talk when Miss Dilys came with her husband, the young man that had been like a blossoming tree. She was married now. Mrs. Fennel, they called her. And in the kitchen they said to her all about the illness, how nobody went near except us two, and how he said he was poisoned, and how She always cooked because of the complaints. I heard it all afterwards when She was in the front of the house and Mr. Fennel —he was very much busying himself all day—said, "To say the least, you seem to have taken a good deal of authority into your hands, Miss Woodroffe." He was nasty then.

She said, "Oh, of course it appears so to you. But there is something that you do not know. I may as well tell you now, since you are bound to know. Your father married me, Dilys."

Miss Dilys said, "I don't believe it. When?"

"On the seventeenth of February this year."

"A week after I . . . just when I was . . . Why on earth should he do that?"

"For the usual reason I imagine."

Mr. Fennel said, "But why this secrecy?"

"It was Mr. Helmar's wish. I think he was ashamed of it. He had had too many women, too easily. But he had lost them easily too, and the idea of marriage was his—though you will hardly believe that."

"Hardly," Mr. Fennel said. He turned to Miss Dilys and said, "Dilys, you understand what this means. She's taken Mortiboys from you."

There was some silence, and a bad cold air in the room.

Then She said, "We were free people, free to make our own bargain. Marriage was what he wanted, strange as that may sound to you. And I made my own condition, which was that he should make Mortiboys over to me then and there. It was all done in Lawyer Aldritch's office, perfectly legal and above board."

There was some more silence. Then She said, "So you see, Mr. Fennel, your attack on me is unjustified. Who should tend a sick man but his wife? Who else should assume authority? It was not even as though you and Dilys had been on good terms with him." She stood up very straight and breathed in, quite loud, through her nose. "As for this ridiculous kitchen gossip about my having starved him and neglected him, Doctor Stamper will deal with that when he arrives. Four days ago he congratulated me upon my nursing, and the way I was keeping his eating and drinking under control."

"You have sent for the doctor?"

"Does that surprise you?" she asked me in a rude voice. Then She came away and left them. I came too. I did not understand much of the talk, though I remembered it all just as they said it. But I did understand that She had been Mrs. Helmar for a long time. That was funny. I had seen them both in many shapes, but not love once. Love is easy to see. Mr. Fennel had it, especially that first time. It is enough for one to have it out of two. But two without it. That was funny.

Doctor Stamper came. There was some more talk. Everywhere in the house there was talk and guessing and people's bad shapes saying nasty things. And then there was poison. All at once everybody was saying poison, poison, poison. The frightening started in me then, because of the toothache medicine. That was poison.

At first I was frightened that they should say I did the poisoning. Because I did it. And then they would take me away and the promise the angel said would not be true. But afterwards it was worse than that, because they said She did it.

It was Doctor Stamper said it, and Miss Dilys and Mr. Fennel, and Cook and the others. It was the talk. It never stopped. Talk and talk. And then there were questions too. The world was full of men with big mouths asking questions.

And in the kitchen they said She would hang, and serve her right. Then I was mad and shouted and beat on my chest and got a bottle and tried to show what I did. Somebody held me still, and in the stillness somebody said, "She knows something. She helped, that is why she was such a favourite." There was more talk, with me in it that time.

(270)

There is a thing called accomplice. That was my name then.
I was accomplice. I do not know what it means but it was good.
They put us together.

I did not know whether to be sorry or happy. I was happy
to be with her, and for everybody to talk about us as if we were
one person; but if it was to be hanging, I was sorry. Because I
did it. And hanging is a bad thing. I know because of the young
chap that was hanged for poaching. If there was to be hanging
it must be me to hang. But I wanted us to be together until it
started.

They took us away. They put us together in a little room,
small and dark all day, with a smelly bucket in the corner.
She was very quiet, not sad. It was harder than sadness. It was
like setting a trap for a rabbit and catching a stoat in it; the
stoat is not scared like a rabbit, but is angry and still, but the
stillness is watchful; it will get away if there is a chance. Like
that it was. Except that She was sorry about me. Over and over
She said to everybody to let me go. She said She was innocent,
and that would be proved; but that against me there was not even
a shadow of a case. Nobody took any notice.

I wanted to tell her that it was me to hang. I tried and tried
to say about the toothache medicine and the bottle and the
poison that I did. But the words were worse than ever. When I
tried the words were just red flannel and a thick angry noise.
The floor was dirty and I drew on it with my finger, a brandy
bottle. I showed how it was not full and then full. I made her
look. She said:

"Oh yes, Lindy, the cook mentioned seeing you with a bottle.
Was it brandy?"

I nodded my head loose.

"But that didn't *kill* him," She said. "You mustn't think you
killed him. Brandy was bad for him, but it wouldn't be fatal.
He was poisoned."

I nodded again, and beat on my chest and tried to talk.

"But you didn't do it. Poor Lindy, to think that! No. Somebody who hated me did it. Such an obvious way to choose. But who? Who?"

She tried to keep us clean. But it was hard. The room was dirty and the smell of the bucket in the corner was everywhere. It was in the food. But there was a comb and She did our hair every day. One day when She was combing mine it stopped suddenly. I looked and her shape was there but She was gone. She stood still with the comb in her hand and her eyes were dead, staring at the bare wall. I was frightened and was still, too. It lasted a little time. Then She put the comb down and covered her face with her hands, moaning. She said, "I've never seen a false vision."

After that there was a difference. It was a rabbit now, not a stoat. The fight was gone out of her. And She was very, very kind to me. Once She said, "Lindy, you work well and understand simple orders, but I wish I knew how much you understand of all this. If we hang . . ." only in her voice I could hear that the *if* was very small, ". . . I have brought you to it." She looked at me in the face, very close and serious. "But you don't understand, poor Lindy, or you'd hate me. As I hate whoever brought me to this." She jumped up and stamped and swore and said, "May they rot in hell for ever." And that was me! I did it. I cried and knelt down and beat my head on her feet. She pulled me up and wiped my face and comforted me.

If only the angel would come and then I could tell her. I could tell her and She could tell everybody. But the angel didn't know about the little smelly room at Colchester. It was still looking for me at Minsham. It was a Minsham angel, in father's book and in the church window, and at Mortiboys. Not here.

There was a big room next, divided into parts like a stable with loose boxes. There were many people in the places. She and I were in one place together. There was one man alone with some hair made out of a horse's tail on his head. There was a bunch of flowers too. And the smell was better than in our room.

(272)

Then was the time of the talk and the questions. And the words were hard. I can remember words that I cannot say and words that I cannot understand. But not then. There were too many. People dressed up just to ask questions. And to tell things. Some things were true and some were not true. They said about the quarrels. I had been there when She and the Master quarrelled, but I had not seen the others there. They said they knew though. They said things they had heard her say. How? How could they hear those things? And they said about the food. Over and over they said about her getting the food ready herself. But that was because he had complained so. And poison. They said about when he flung the gruel away and said he was poisoned. But it was the doctor said gruel and not the steak the Master wanted. And they said about me. They said I was a lunatic, but I did everything She said. That was true. But She had never said to me about poisoning him. That was my angel.

There were days in the big room. And always when we were back together She was quiet and low and very kind to me.

Then there was a day when I could smell a rose. I looked at the horsehair man and his flowers, and there was my angel. I shouted loud. I daren't waste a minute saying to the angel why didn't it come sooner. It might go and I not have said what was important. I just shouted very loud:

"I did it. I did it. She didn't . . ." I could have told them all about it, but they shook me and stopped. A man hit me, quite hard, on the head. And She said, "You mustn't interrupt." I looked at the angel. It was looking kindly. "You tell them. You tell them it was me, and how I did it," I said. But they stopped me again. The angel said, "Hanging is nasty, but not long," and then it was gone.

It was worse after that. I had done badly again. They thought I could talk if I wanted to. And they believed I did it; but they said, and it is a hard thing to understand, that I was the hand but She was the mind. They said the word accomplice again.

After all the men talking and the questions there was the

time when She talked herself, and it was like a bird singing, but not like a bird in a flowery bush any more. It was like the last twittery songs before the sad cold weather starts. It was as though She knew that saying things wouldn't do good now. All the same She said them; She said all the things that I would have said, and more. And She spoke for me. I thought there was more heart in her when She spoke for me. But it didn't do.

Then there was a solemn time and the man with the horse-tail hair talked. It was plain that he was against us. Part of it was like Parson's talk. But it was for me really, not her. I had done it. When he said "secret deadly weapon of poison," it was me he meant. Then I must interrupt. I shouted and waved my arms, and beat on my chest. I did the taking of the bottle out and filling it; I pointed in my mouth to show about the tooth-ache medicine. I did everything I could to show that if there was hanging it was me to do it. But they didn't mind. They held me and made me be still. They were very angry.

When I was shaken and battered to be quiet there was some great silence. There was some black put on the horse-tail hair and the man said solemn words about hanging.

After that they took us away and put us back in the little room.

So it was hanging. I tried to tell her what the angel said, "Hanging is nasty, but not long." That would comfort her. But the words would not come. I cried and tried to show her on my neck—nasty, but not long. But She did not understand; She thought I cried and held my neck because I was frightened of the hanging. She was frightened, too. I could smell the fear on her, but She tried to comfort me.

Next morning—only it wasn't day and night in that dark place—but it was morning because the man threw the food at us; then She did not clean us, or comb our hair. And the food She left. I wondered and tried to ask. Then She showed me her hands. They were dead; the fingers were white like candles and the nails were blue. The white fingers were doubled in over the palms, fixed and dead. So I held the water for her to drink; I would have held the food too, but She turned her mouth away. Afterwards I did our hair and cleaned us.

The man called Lawyer Aldritch came. He was good and sorry, and spoke as though he didn't think we did it. She changed then and was eager again. They had a hard talk. She said, "You are sure that it will be in order?" He said, "Yes. As I made clear at the trial, you did not profit by the . . . death of your husband. The property was already yours. If it had been willed to you it would have been different. As it is, it is yours to do what you like with."

Then She said about leaving it all to young Mr. Hatton in our village, and Lawyer Aldritch wrote it down.

"You must sign it," he said. And She held out her hands to show him. "But I will sign it," She said, "if it is the last thing I do on this earth." She took the pen in her mouth. Lawyer Aldritch called in two men and they stood, very solemn, while She bent and twisted her head, making marks on the paper. Lawyer Aldritch sweated a lot. The men wrote their names and went away.

There was ink all round her mouth and I wiped it, but not all, there was a mark still.

She said: "Well, that's done. And I have done what I set out to do, though not this way. However, I have done it." It sounded so sad, and so ending, like when She said "the last thing I do on this earth," that I began to cry again. She tried to put her arm round me. Then She said, "Could you, would you write a letter for me?" Lawyer Aldritch said "Certainly. I will do anything I can. Will this poor creature disturb you? Shall I have her removed?" But She said, "No. Lindy never disturbs me."

He dipped his pen and She said the letter. She said She had left him Mortiboys, and hoped he would enjoy it, because did he remember a hot day when the butter wouldn't come and he said what he wanted in life. She said about the time when he and

Miss Dilys were going to be married, and the Master said no Mortiboys for them, so then She thought to get it and give it to them. She said She married him because if Mr. Hatton married Miss Dilys it didn't matter what happened to her.

It was a long letter, and sad past crying. Even I stopped crying, and Lawyer Aldritch wiped his face and moved his glasses about. She said Mr. Hatton must please believe that She didn't poison Mr. Helmar; what was wrong was to marry him when She only loved Mr. Hatton, and had done ever since he saved her from the pond. And She ended not to let the way Mortiboys came to him spoil it, but to enjoy it because if not her whole life had been wasted.

Lawyer Aldritch took his glasses off, and wiped the sweat and round his eyes as well.

She said, "I hope that is clear. This isn't quite like *writing* a letter, you know."

Lawyer Aldritch started to say that it was quite clear, but his words came out wrong and broken, too. He said something about heart-breaking.

She went back towards the wall and stood there. She said, "I hadn't thought of that. I just wanted to make it clear . . . so that he should know *why*. But I don't want to make him miserable." There was a little time. Then She said, "I'm sorry, Mr. Aldritch, after making you write it, but tear it up for me, will you, please? Yes, that is best; then he'll think I left it to him because I didn't know anybody else."

Lawyer Aldritch looked at the letter and at her, and he wiped his face some more.

"I don't like the responsibility of doing that . . ." he said.

"No. All right. Lindy, come here and tear this paper, please."

I was glad to do what she said. I tore it in little bits and they fell on the floor. She said, thank you; and She said it to Mr. Aldritch too. He mumbled some words and went away.

Then we were together, like my angel said. She sat on the board that was for sleeping and I sat on the floor with my head against her knees, like a dog. It was quiet. She was quiet, too. It was like the end of something. Presently She said, "Everything is over now, Lindy, except the hanging. Look at me." I turned my head. "I wish I knew how much you understood. We're only dying a little early, Lindy. Can you understand that? Everybody starts to die as soon as they are born. And you were afflicted, and I was always unlucky."

I tried once more to tell her what my angel said about hanging. But the words would not come and I was afraid to make a noise, trying. Then She said it. The very thing, She said. "Hanging is a nasty business, Lindy, but it doesn't last long." I nodded and smiled to show that that was what I wanted to say. "We must be quiet," She said, "and try not to make spectacles of our-selves. Can you understand that? Whatever they do to us, we must be quiet."

I nodded again, and sat very still to show that I knew about being quiet. She twisted so that one of her arms, with the poor dead hand at the end of it, lay over my shoulder. She said, "If you can understand anything, Lindy, understand this. I'm sorry from my heart that they dragged you into it. But it wasn't my fault. I'm innocent, too. I tricked him, and I hated him, and I wished him dead. But I didn't do it either."

It was no good trying to tell her again, or to beat on my chest and disturb her hand. So I sat still. I would be very quiet. I hoped they would do the hanging on me first, so She would see me quiet and be pleased with me.

DATE DUE

MR 3 '65

N026.71

GAYLORD			PRINTED IN U.S.A.